ENDORSEMENTS

This compelling and important novel confronts real issues many tiptoe around. Nonconformists and outcasts everywhere will relate to Eddie Caruthers's struggles to find himself and his place in a world that seems stacked against him. John Harrison shows us that flawed heroes can be a powerful force for good—and deserving of love, acceptance, and forgiveness.

— RUTH THOMAS-SUH
PRODUCER AND DIRECTOR OF THE AWARD-WINNING
DOCUMENTARY FILM *REJECT: THE SCIENCE OF BELONGING*

John F. Harrison's debut novel *Fighting Back* is a must-read! Within seconds of the opening, Eddie Caruthers's world turns radically upside down. The result is what seems like an innocuous journey to self-rediscovery, but this story is far deeper than whom Eddie runs into and what he learns. What I liked most is the unashamed showing by Mr. Harrison that although one can try to right one's own life, it's where and what God has to show you that matters. In Eddie's case, faith, forgiveness, and love are rediscovered against the backdrop of a hideous crime, leading the reader to conclude what in life is worth fighting for.

— ELAINE STOCK
AUTHOR OF *ALWAYS WITH YOU*

Fighting Back is not your stereotypical Christian novel where the God-fearing never sin, never raise a hand in violence, and never have to deal with the fall-out from bad choices. Instead, it insists that we as Christians face some very real issues plaguing both the world and the Church.

This book will force you to think. It will demand that you delve deeply into your own beliefs and attitudes. And it may very well call on you to make a change. *Fighting Back* is not a comfortable book, but it is a challenging one. Are you up for the challenge?

— NATHAN D. MAKI
AUTHOR OF *THE WAR WITHIN* SERIES

FIGHTING BACK

FIGHTING BACK

JOHN F. HARRISON

PRESSING WAY BOOKS

ISBN: 978-0-9980568-0-7 (print) | 978-0-9980568-1-4 (eBooks)

Cover and interior design by 1106 Design.
Edited by Arlene Prunkl of PenUltimate Editorial Services.

This is a work of fiction. Names, characters, places, and incidents are either the products of the author's imagination or are used fictitiously and not to be construed as real. Any resemblance to actual events, locales, organizations, or persons, living or dead, is coincidental.

Names: Harrison, John F. (John Frederick), 1963–

Title: Fighting back / John F. Harrison.

Description Concord, MA : Pressing Way Books, [2016]

Identifiers: ISBN: 978-0-9980568-0-7 | 0-9980568-0-4

Subjects: LCSH: Christian fiction. | Prodigal son (Parable)—Fiction. | Christianity—Psychology—Fiction. | Protestant churches—United States—Doctrines—Fiction. | Spiritual life—Christianity—Fiction. | Pacifism—Religious aspects—Christianity—Fiction. | Human trafficking—Fiction. | Violence—Moral and ethical aspects—Fiction. | Temptation—Fiction. | Christianity and justice—Fiction. | BISAC: FICTION / Christian / Suspense.

Classification: LCC: PS3608.A783474 F54 2016 | DDC: 813/.6—dc23

Dedicated to all survivors,
no matter what trauma you've outlasted.

And to Karen: not only a survivor,
but always and forever The First Reader.

TABLE OF CONTENTS

PART ONE: Transitions

PART TWO: Explorations

PART THREE: **Matters of the Heart**

PART ONE
TRANSITIONS

CHAPTER I
EIGHT SECONDS

On the spur of the moment, Eddie Caruthers decided to help a damsel in distress, and thus began his long slide into darkness. Of course, that was not apparent from where he stood. Clarity about the genesis of one's own misery comes mainly in the cold light of hindsight, too late to be of use.

The damsel was a doe-eyed young woman with a melodious voice, a sweet smile, and an astonishingly corpulent build. Rosalyn Pitts and three other women had exited the big stone church that occupied half a block on Union Avenue in downtown Framingham, Massachusetts. Hobbling with the help of a cane in each hand, Rosalyn jaywalked in the spill of the streetlights, talking cheerily and breathlessly over her shoulder to her three friends, who lingered on the sidewalk behind her as they finished their goodbyes.

Her distress arrived in a black SUV, as the driver started spewing invective at her from his open window. She was in his way, forcing him to stop and wait while she made her laborious crossing. He loudly bemoaned the size, color, and unsatisfactory forward speed of the lady's posterior, adding, "Does Old MacDonald know he's missing a cow? E-I-E-I-oh my *God!*" Rosalyn hung her head and tried to move faster.

Eddie saw and heard all this from the courtyard of Solid Rock Church, where landscaping spotlights highlighted shrubs and ornamental trees just beginning to shed their red and yellow autumn garb. Eddie was strolling under those trees in rapt conversation with his—friend, girlfriend, wife to be? He was still trying to work all that out. But whatever the lithe and lovely Shawna Bell was to him, he enjoyed her company immensely and found that her nearness made the whole wearisome world fade away.

He and Shawna had been last to leave the building after choir practice, hanging back for the few seconds it took him to set the alarm and lock the door. Eddie wasn't in the choir, but Shawna was, and he considered that reason enough to volunteer to handle building security and lockup on Thursday nights. He'd been doing that for six weeks, just for the pleasure of accompanying Shawna to her car—as slowly as possible—and listening to her small talk.

He didn't appreciate having this moment spoiled by the sudden stream of insults and profanities he was now hearing. He looked over and noted the make and model of the vehicle, an occupational habit that was now a reflex. Then he focused his attention on the driver who was intruding on his happiness. It was especially aggravating that the target of this onslaught was poor Rosalyn Pitts. Roz, who was unfailingly pleasant despite suffering perpetual discomfort from the strain on her joints; Roz, who never showed embarrassment at having to sit on a bench in the rear of Solid Rock's sanctuary, a bench placed there because she was too big to fit on the cushioned chairs used by the rest of the congregation; Roz, who doubtless had a too-short life expectancy and would probably never, ever be asked out on a date. If anybody deserved a break, it was Roz.

Eddie found himself yelling, "Hey, loudmouth, if you had any class, you'd shut up and leave the woman alone!" He fully expected an answering salvo of bluff and obscenities. People always acted tough from inside a car. Being wrapped in a four-thousand-pound steel and glass cocoon had a way of making people lose whatever inhibitions they might normally have had. Well, if listening to some thug curse at him would spare Roz further humiliation, so be it.

But the driver didn't say another word. Instead, he slammed his vehicle into reverse and whipped it into a curbside parking space. Eddie was briefly impressed with the maneuver. Not many people could fling a Range Rover around so precisely while driving backward, and fewer still would try it while sporting those oversized two-piece chrome wheels. What kind of nutcase would risk curbing rims that pricey? That fleeting question evaporated when the driver got out, slammed the door, and strode toward the courtyard.

Eddie's pulse quickened. His senses honed in on the approaching man. Still, his next words were to Shawna: "Stand clear." He glanced in her direction and made a shooing gesture with his right hand.

"Eddie!" Shawna's normally silky voice nearly squeaked, and when she spoke his name a second time she drew it out to great length. "*Eddiiieeee!* Don't get into it with him! Let's just go!"

But Eddie had already turned his attention back to the lout who had been Roz's problem and was about to become his. This man was compact, some three inches shorter than Eddie's six-foot height. "Loudmouth" had an olive complexion and dark hair slicked back. He looked to be in his late thirties, a good ten years older than Eddie. Powerfully built, his broad shoulders and muscular physique marked him a dangerous opponent. The angry stare and clenched jaw suggested he wasn't coming over to chat. He approached with head up, chest out, fingers curled but not quite clenched into fists.

Eddie figured him for a sucker puncher. The man would probably try to get up in his face, and then attempt a knockout by throwing a sneaky roundhouse punch from out of nowhere. It was an old trick, demonstrated in a thousand YouTube videos. *Not a chance he gets that close,* Eddie thought. He could see that his own reach was greater, and the guy was leading with his chin. Then, on the edge of his awareness, he saw and heard the passenger door of the stranger's Rover open and shut as a second man, much larger than the first, exited the vehicle and started toward the courtyard. *Two of them. Not good.*

6

Eddie's heart was hammering under the influence of an adrenaline surge. But this wasn't the remembered terror of all his childhood confrontations—it was just his body on autopilot, prepping itself for fight or flight. He took two calming deep breaths, as he had been trained, and positioned himself for what was coming next.

Taking two steps backward, he raised both hands slightly above his head, palms out. Most watchers would see the universal gesture of surrender, a posture that says, "I'm not a threat." Only a careful observer might notice that Eddie's hands were not held up in the classic surrender pose; instead, they were well in front of his face, ready to be instantly deployed to block, grab, or punch.

"I don't want any trouble, man." Eddie spoke loudly enough to be heard by both the advancing attacker and any bystanders who might later be asked who started it. He knew he needed to win not only the physical fight but also any legal proceedings that might ensue from it. It was never too early to lay the groundwork for that court fight.

"Well, trouble is what you got." The smaller man kept up a running commentary, declaring what part of Eddie's anatomy was about to be kicked.

They were about seven feet apart. Eddie took another step backward, and as soon as the ball of his foot hit the ground, he reversed direction and charged. *Strike while they're talking.* That was the rule, because an opponent's reaction times were slower when he was busy spouting off.

The two men closed in an instant. Eddie landed the first blows—it was not far from his already upraised hands to the aggressor's face. He missed with a straight left, but landed a right and a left in rapid succession as the other man raised his arms to block before trying to twist out of the way. None of Eddie's punches were hard enough to do serious damage, but that was not the point of the initial flurry. The point was to get the man off his plan of attack. A foe who is defending himself from you is not hitting you.

Eddie was somehow more acutely aware of the sounds of the fight than he was of the tactile sensations. He heard the impact of his fists on flesh and the stranger grunting under the rain of blows. Shawna stifled a scream somewhere to his right. The attacker recovered from his surprise, dropped into a crouch, and spread his hands. He hunched his shoulders and ducked his head to protect his face. Lunging forward, he wrapped powerful arms around Eddie and set himself to throw him to the ground. Eddie raked his thumbs across the shorter man's eyes, making him jerk his head back and loosen his grip. This gave Eddie room to insert his right arm under his opponent's armpit. By twining his arm under, behind, and back over the shoulder, he trapped the man's arm and put painful pressure on the rotator cuff, forcing his foe to bend down and twist awkwardly to the side.

The attacker's face was now at belly level. Eddie palmed the man's face with his left hand and rushed forward, pushing his overbalanced assailant, who had to scramble backward to stay on his feet. Eddie needed only three running steps. The back of the man's head met the rough granite stonework of the church with a sickening thud. Eddie might easily have followed up with a knee to the face as the logical finishing move, but he was not inclined to overkill. His trapped arm now released, the man sank to the ground, where he feebly thrashed and twitched. His eyes were open, but did not appear to see anything. From first punch to lights out had taken around eight seconds.

Eddie spun, looking for the Rover's passenger. He was standing about fifteen feet away, and not advancing. The large man looked much older than the one on the ground. His hair was mostly gray. He was paunchy, wider at the waist than at the shoulders, and inexplicably wearing sunglasses at night. He shook his head, and almost smiled. When he spoke, his voice was raspy. "I got no beef with you. I just wanna collect my hot-headed friend here and be on my way."

Eddie nodded, edging over to where Shawna and Roz's three friends were standing in a little clump. He knew better than to turn his back to the second man, but his caution proved unnecessary. The older man went straight to his fallen friend. He held him still and spoke quietly to him for a minute or two. Then he hauled him to his feet, and half dragged, half carried him back to the Rover. There was definitely some muscle under all that flab. He laid his dazed companion across the back seat before getting in the front and driving off.

Only then did any of the women in the courtyard speak, and they all began talking at once. The voice Eddie focused on was

Shawna's. "You could have *killed* that man!" She still sounded squeaky. She turned to gaze wide-eyed at the spot where the man's head had hit the wall with such an awful sound. "What were you thinking?"

Eddie considered the question. He was a little stung that she offered no congratulations for having successfully defended himself against a dangerous attacker, no words of concern for his own well-being, no thanks for having stuck up for Roz. "I was thinking . . ." He too turned and looked toward where his attacker's cranium had met the stone wall. His lip curled. "I was thinking . . . welcome to Solid Rock."

CHAPTER 2
AMBUSH

Eddie watched the big room fill with people. He wondered how much they had heard. Five church members had witnessed the fight three days ago, and he couldn't imagine that all five had stayed silent. Solid Rock's grapevine was notoriously efficient. Though no one seemed to be looking at him any differently, he was sure that word of his adventure had spread through the congregation like germs through a daycare center.

The time was 10:50 a.m. on the first Sunday in October, ten minutes before morning worship. Some two hundred people milled about the sanctuary, exchanging smiles, handshakes, and hugs. Their happy chatter echoed off the vaulted fruitwood ceiling, only to be muted by the plush carpet and thickly uphol-stered furniture. Sunlight through the tall stained-glass windows suffused the room with a warm glow. Excitement was in the air, an undercurrent of anticipation that ran from person to person. Everyone seemed caught up in it.

Almost everyone. Eddie could not bring himself to smile or exchange cheerful greetings with anyone. He sat still as a stone while the current swirled around him. He was normally part of that stream, but not today. At the end of the row, halfway between front and back, Eddie sat alone and brooded.

It had occurred to him for the first time early this morning that today might be difficult. Friday and Saturday had been mostly filled with work, leaving little time to think. When not on the job, he'd worried about the way he and Shawna had parted on Thursday. She had looked pretty freaked out after the fight. She'd hurried to her car and said, "See you Sunday," while completely avoiding eye contact with him. What, if anything, did that portend? Had her opinion of him changed? Then today at breakfast, he'd been struck by the possibility of an even bigger problem. How would the service play out? Despite his natural optimism, he was afraid of what might be coming. He could do nothing but wait and see.

Things started well enough. The organist took up a couple of hymns on the Hammond B3, a cue to the congregation to find their seats and turn their thoughts heavenward. At precisely eleven o'clock, the ministers entered the sanctuary from a side door and took their positions on the platform. The senior pastor motioned the congregation to stand for the invocation. Everyone spoke the words to the psalm that were displayed on the twin video monitors flanking the platform.

Make a joyful shout to the LORD, all you lands!
Serve the LORD with gladness;
Come before His presence with singing.
Know that the LORD, He is God;
It is He who has made us, and not we ourselves;
We are His people and the sheep of His pasture.
Enter into His gates with thanksgiving,
And into His courts with praise.
Be thankful to Him, and bless His name.
For the LORD is good;
His mercy is everlasting,
And His truth endures to all generations.

One of the ministers then led a short but impassioned prayer for God's blessing on the service, and the musicians in the praise band started the introduction to the first choir selection:

A mighty fortress is our God, a bulwark never failing;
Our helper He, amid the flood of mortal ills prevailing.

Piano, bass, guitar, and drums joined the organ to lay down a tasty blend of gospel and jazz/rock fusion. The crowd started clapping and swaying, and Eddie halfheartedly joined in.

When the selection ended, Shawna Bell stepped forward from the ranks of the choir to lead the assembled worshippers in thirty minutes of congregational songs. There were classic old hymns for the traditionalists and snappy choruses full of power chords for those whose tastes ran to more modern fare.

After each song, and sometimes right in the middle of one, the congregation broke out into spontaneous worship. People would lift their hands or wave their arms; some wept quietly while others shouted exuberantly. Eddie knew it was in response to what they were feeling because he felt it himself, even in his uneasy state of mind. A palpable sense of the Divine infused that place. It was otherworldly, as if a tiny bit of heaven had seeped into the sanctuary through the windows. The congregation remained standing through most of the song service. When that ended, it was time for the offering.

The choir sang again as a squadron of ushers passed baskets along the rows. When this was completed, Senior Pastor Greg Bowers walked to the pulpit. He was a tall, trim man with an angular, clean-shaven face and wavy blond hair that was beginning to go gray. He had a commanding presence, and his pale blue eyes radiated authority even as he opened his portion of the service with a lopsided smile and a folksy "Good morning, everybody." If he came across more like a corporate raider than a benevolent cleric, it was because he had changed careers in midlife, leaving a C-level executive position in a Fortune 1000 company to go into the ministry. Eddie was genuinely impressed that the man had walked away from that life to take on a humbler role at one-fifth the salary. He would have been even more impressed had the pastor not been so regular in reminding his listeners of all that he had sacrificed to be among them.

After welcoming visitors and making a few remarks about the weather and the day's attendance, Reverend Bowers invited everyone to follow along in their Bibles—"or for you tech-savvy folks, on your Kindles or other portable devices"—while he read a passage of scripture from the fifth chapter of the Gospel according to Matthew.

And seeing the multitudes, He went up on a mountain, and when He was seated His disciples came to Him. Then He opened His mouth and taught them, saying:

Blessed are the poor in spirit,
For theirs is the kingdom of heaven.
Blessed are those who mourn,
For they shall be comforted.
Blessed are the meek,
For they shall inherit the earth.
Blessed are those who hunger and thirst for righteousness,
For they shall be filled.
Blessed are the merciful,
For they shall obtain mercy.
Blessed are the pure in heart,
For they shall see God.
Blessed are the peacemakers,
For they shall be called sons of God.

At the end of the reading, the congregation murmured "Amen" before settling back onto their burgundy seat cushions.

The sanctuary was quiet. Pastor Bowers was known to preach two kinds of Sunday morning messages, and it was not yet apparent which one this would be. Eddie hoped it would be a faith message.

When Gregory Bowers preached faith, he was a riveting speaker. He could take a Bible narrative—David and Goliath, or Daniel in the lions' den, or any of a hundred other passages, whether famous or obscure—and slowly spin out the story so Eddie almost felt he was an eyewitness to the events from all those centuries ago. Moreover, the pastor made it seem intuitively obvious that the trials and tribulations of those ancient people were relevant today, right now. He'd methodically build the case for just how bad, how seemingly hopeless things had gotten for them. Eddie's own problems would begin to pale in comparison until they were all but forgotten as his attention was fixed on desperate people from the pages of history.

Then the message would turn a corner. Help would arrive. God would intervene. The preacher showed the myriad ways in which God had always come to the aid of the faithful just in the nick of time. Since God never changed, the preacher reminded his congregation, he would come through for them too. The faith message was always the same in essence: "Hold on. Your miracle is coming. It has happened before, and it will happen again. Whatever difficulties you are facing, you've come too far to give up now, so close to your inevitable victory." The messages would start low and slow, gradually building in intensity until the preacher was sweat-soaked and shouting, and the whole congregation was on its feet shouting right along with him. A Sunday with one of those messages was a good Sunday.

The pastor paused a few seconds. "Everyone say, 'Blessed are the meek.'" The congregation dutifully repeated the words. "Everyone say, 'Blessed are the peacemakers.'" Again, the congregation echoed the line. The repeat-after-me ritual was shopworn, but Bowers never seemed to tire of it. "Before I begin, let me clear up the semantics." This was the low and slow part. "We usually see the letters *b-l-e-s-s-e-d* and pronounce them as a one-syllable word rhyming with *best* or *crest*. We say that we are blessed with good health, or that God blessed us with a new car. Used that way, the word refers to nice things or favorable outcomes; the gifts God bestows upon us. Everybody wants to be blessed.

"But this morning we are talking about something else entirely. When we pronounce the letters *b-l-e-s-s-e-d* as a *two*-syllable word, so that it sounds like tested or nested, it describes an ideal spiritual and psychological state. To be bless-*ed*," he said, emphasizing the second syllable, "is to be happy, enviably fortunate, and spiritually prosperous. It is to feel life and joy and satisfaction in the experience of God's favor."

This all sounded good to Eddie. His inner odds maker thought it more likely than not that this was the beginning of a faith message. He felt a little of the tension leave his shoulders.

Bowers turned up the volume of his delivery a bit and spoke just a shade more rapidly. "Bless*ed*ness is the state you were designed to live in, but it is a state not enough people find.

Nearly one in ten Americans is on antidepressant drugs today. Among women in their forties and fifties, the number is one in four. It's bad enough that so many *people* are prone to feel sad, listless, lifeless, and hopeless. Today we live in the age of *pets* on Prozac! That's right; you can get antidepressants for your canine companion. Drugs for dogs! Pills for pooches! Well, I can't help your four-legged family members this morning, but I do have a message for you. *You* can be blessed. God wants you to be happy and enviably fortunate, and He is telling you how."

The preacher came out from behind the pulpit and began pacing as he spoke. "Sometimes, in order to get what God is saying, you have to be really clear about what he is *not* saying. Look at our text again. You'll note that the scripture does *not* say blessed are the tough guys, for they shall have street cred. It doesn't say blessed are the indomitable, for they shall be respected. It is not written, blessed are the brawlers, for they shall impress the girls!"

The last part was delivered in a mocking tone that made it clear today's sermon would not be a faith message. It was going to be the other kind, the kind Pastor Bowers preached when he was angry or put out with someone. And Eddie figured he must be that someone. *Here we go.*

He reviewed his actions of the other night. Had he been wrong to defend Roz? He couldn't believe fighting back against Loudmouth could have been wrong. He thought so hard that he missed hearing portions of the sermon. When his attention returned to the preacher, Reverend Bowers was saying, "We are commanded to follow peace with all men. It doesn't just mean well-mannered people or likeable people. It means all people. Jesus is the Prince of Peace, and his Word instructs us to seek peace, and to pursue it."

Then the message turned the corner, the one Eddie had been afraid was coming. "It has come to my attention," the pastor said, "that one of our own got into a fight this week on the grounds of the church." He let that sink in. "And I'm told that the church member in question went so far as to throw the first punch!" The congregation took a deep collective breath. Eddie felt sudden warmth in his cheeks. While he had no doubt that word of the fight had started spreading Thursday night, now everybody knew. And the pastor was suggesting that he had started it. Who among the witnesses told Bowers that? Yes, he had thrown the first punch, *technically*, but only after hostilities had already commenced. How could anyone have failed to see that he wasn't the aggressor?

"I don't understand how that happens!" Bowers was yelling at the top of his lungs now and pounding the pulpit. His face reddened, and he was breathing hard as he glared around the sanctuary. "According to the psalm we read this morning, we are the sheep of God's pasture. I have never seen a ferocious sheep. Have you? If you see something with fangs and claws and extreme fighting skills, you've got to ask yourself—is it really a sheep at all? Maybe it's a wolf in sheep's clothing! Why else would someone risk undermining years of outreach by this min- istry—I mean by this congregation—to the community? This is the house of God, not Fight Club! Answer me this, tough guy: are you incapable of overlooking an offense? Are you really that shallow? You must have rocks in your head! If you had an ounce of Christian character, you wouldn't feel the need to respond to every smart remark you hear on the street. You're supposed to be the salt of the earth, part of the solution to all the corruption in the world. Instead, you're part of the problem."

And so it went. Eddie had seen the pastor chew people out from the pulpit before. Reverend Bowers called these sessions "come to Jesus meetings." *Come to Jesus?* Even assuming the Lord stuck around, who could find him in an atmosphere like this? Eddie knew he was not the only person to have had that thought.

Those who had been on the receiving end of a verbal scourging like this sometimes said the pastor ventured out of bounds, that this behavior bordered on abusive. Those not directly targeted, including Eddie, had always chalked the fireworks up to tough love and straight preaching. The old folks had a saying, "It's hard, but it's right." Now Eddie wondered how all that rage in the pulpit could ever be right.

Forty minutes after reading his scripture text about the blessedness of meekness and mercy, the preacher wound down his tirade and invited the congregation to come forward to pray. The organ began to play again, a hymn of repentance called "Search Me O Lord." Scores of people spilled out of the rows of seats and headed down front. This was supposed to be Eddie's cue to do likewise. If he played his part right, he would kneel at the edge of the platform and be visibly contrite. The pastor would eventually make his way to Eddie after praying with dozens of other church members and visitors. When he laid hands on Eddie and prayed for him, today's firestorm would be over and all would be forgiven.

Though he knew what was expected of him, Eddie refused to cooperate. This was something new for him—to swim against the tide. He stood and walked to the rear of the sanctuary, stone faced. Most people who passed him going the other way avoided eye contact. From her bench in the back, Rosalyn Pitts wore a sad expression, but when he caught her eye she smiled sweetly at him and mouthed the words, "Thank you anyway." Good old Roz.

When he reached the ushers stationed by the rear doors, one of them touched his arm and asked, "Are you all right?" Eddie nodded stiffly. "I'm just *fine*. Why?" His tone was sharper than intended, and he immediately regretted repaying a kind word with a snarky one. But rather than stopping to fix it, he stepped around the ushers and out of the sanctuary. He quickly crossed the lobby and burst out of the doors into the crisp air and bright sunshine of a beautiful fall day.

He drank it in as he headed across the street to the lot where his car was parked. Eddie had been part of this congregation since he was ten years old and had always enjoyed coming to church. Not today. Today the joy was in leaving.

CHAPTER 3
SMALL WORLD

Eddie sat in his car and looked at the church through his windshield. From the outside, Solid Rock seemed a bastion of tranquility. For nearly 140 years, its massive presence had backstopped downtown Framingham, its gray walls suggesting a fortress where one could take refuge from the shifting sands and treacherous currents of the world outside its doors. A picture of the structure taken yesterday looked no different than one taken a hundred years prior. To the casual observer, the church appeared immune to the forces of change. But appearances deceive. Everything changes.

Something just had. Solid Rock had always seemed an extension of his own house and family, familiar and welcoming. Now, as he stared across the street at it, it seemed like hostile territory. The suddenness of the change was disorienting. It was like Pearl Harbor, or the fall of the Berlin Wall, or the terrorist attacks of

September 11, 2001. One moment the world was one way, and the next moment it wasn't. Today felt like the end of an era.

Whoever first said "sticks and stones will break my bones, but words will never hurt me" was in denial. The preacher's words had hurt badly. Eddie couldn't believe what had just happened. He could defend himself against a street thug, but not against a glorified motivational speaker. *I got mugged in my own church and I couldn't do a 'blessed' thing about it.*

Of all the lousy ways a guy could feel, helpless was the worst. *Helpless.* He let himself dwell on the outrage of that word, the unfairness of it. He'd been publicly ambushed, with no opportunity to tell his side of the story. Gregory Clement Bowers, a man named for two different popes and thus doubly convinced of his own infallibility, had seen to that. Why give a brother a phone call or have a meeting when you could just trash him from the pulpit in front of everyone near and dear to him? His father had been there, serving usher duty on the other side of the sanctuary. Eddie's siblings and their spouses had also been present. He hadn't told any of them about the events of Thursday, and the gossipers had likely avoided tattling to his immediate family, so this was beyond embarrassing. After the service, the pastor would surely offer a few sympathetic words to them. Only then would they realize who had been in the preacher's crosshairs.

Eddie decided to seek out some good driving roads where his frustrations could dissipate. He'd long been a proponent of "asphalt therapy," and his Mercedes Benz E350 Sport was well-suited for his intentions. While he would have preferred to still be in the Porsche he'd driven until last month, the current black sedan made him look more responsible, less flamboyant than had the bright red 911 convertible. Shawna hadn't liked that car so much. And the all-wheel-drive Benz added a margin of safety for the coming winter, though it meant sacrificing a little of the joy he got from driving a proper rear-wheel-drive sports car with a manual transmission. Every Benz was an automatic. In any case, you couldn't beat free—the dealer plate on the rear bumper meant Eddie got to drive great cars all the time without actually having to buy any of them. As he saw it, this was the primary benefit of working for the family business.

Eddie considered which way to point the car. He could drive through the northwest corner of town, where tree-lined roads wound past the stately mansions of real estate moguls and pizza magnates. A pretty area, though it wouldn't take him far afield before he encountered traffic congestion. Northeast Framingham was tract housing from the 1950s, block after block of cookie cutter ranches built to house the workers in the days when this was a factory town. South of those neighborhoods was Route 9, a commercial strip of malls, chain restaurants, and car dealerships. No point in driving there; roads like that could be tolerated but never enjoyed. There were good driving roads to the west, off Salem End Road. He'd be heading that way to go home, regardless of where he went now. The fastest way out of town was to the southwest, where storefront churches were sprinkled among barbershops and bodegas with soccer on the televisions and Brazilian flags in the windows. Getting out of town fast felt like the best option.

The church shrank in his rearview mirror. Eddie eased through the downtown rotary and followed Route 126 as it wound through Framingham and its neighbors to the southwest. In Bellingham he hopped onto I-495 north, cruising in the center lane and maintaining the posted speed limit of 65 mph. He enjoyed the sensation of floating along for a few minutes. His speed began to creep up as his thoughts returned to his present difficulties.

His father would definitely be unhappy that Eddie had gotten into a fight, and unhappier still that he hadn't mentioned it. But why would he have mentioned it? No one else in the family believed in fighting. They never had. He remembered the many times he had been picked on by bullies in grade school—he had been scrawny then, below average height, a brainy bookworm with thick glasses and little aptitude for sports. That was not a recipe for popularity in a public school. It was like being a minnow in a tank full of pint-sized piranhas. The middle school years had been especially tough. He'd been involved in only a few real fights, but he had lost them decisively. And being taunted, tripped, pushed, shoved, and threatened was practically a daily occurrence. Whatever humiliations he endured, his parents' response was always the same:

"It takes two to tangle."

And, "It takes a bigger man to walk away than it does to fight."

Eddie had tried to buy into the "bigger man" idea through-out his school years. But it was hard to feel like the bigger man while shaking in his boots. Whenever he had walked away from a potential fight it was because he feared a thrashing. No amount of philosophical spin could change how shameful that felt. His parents had wanted him to learn some sort of lesson about the nobility and dignity of principled nonviolence. What he internalized instead was that he wasn't worth much if his parents thought he wasn't worth defending. And the whole "it takes two" business seemed nonsensical. The truth was that it took two or more to have peace; it took only one to have hostilities. Responding passively to being assaulted was not peace; it was victimhood. How could being a victim make him the bigger man?

Family dynamics being what they were, he'd never had the chance to argue his convictions on the issue when he was growing up. What could be safely said to Dad was mostly "Yes, sir." Of course, Eddie was a grown man now, three months past his twenty-seventh birthday. Not that the family dynamic was likely to change much no matter how old Eddie became.

It was a fast road today. Eddie glanced at the speedometer, which now read eighty-four miles per hour as he rocketed up the interstate, weaving effortlessly through the light traffic. He had been driving as if on autopilot. He'd covered some twenty-five miles already without really noticing. The exit for Bolton was coming up fast. On impulse, he cut rather sharply across three travel lanes—*a very composed car, this Benz*—and took the big looping exit onto Route 117 West. A quick zig and a spirited zag later, he was barreling up Prospect Hill Road in Harvard, where he stopped at the scenic overlook.

Stepping out of the car, Eddie gazed down the hill at what had to be one of the most spectacular views in the region. Below him stretched the Oxbow National Wildlife Refuge, sixteen hundred acres of grassy meadows and upland forest. Far in the west loomed the hazy peaks of the Berkshires. Red and yellow maple leaves danced in the breeze. The air smelled of pine needles and dry grasses. The sun warmed his face. And no one else was there. Eddie knew from experience that the overlook would fill up with cars in a few hours when all the locals came out to watch the sunset, but for now he had the place to himself. He stood and gazed at the vista for the better part of an hour. He was in no hurry to leave. This place was an oasis, one in which his troubles could not reach him.

When his phone vibrated in his pocket, he grabbed it, saw the number of the incoming call, and sighed. Who was he kidding? In the age of instant communication, your troubles could always reach you. He answered.

"Hi, Dad."

"I was more than a little surprised to learn that the pastor was talking about my own son this morning." His voice rumbled like distant thunder.

"I was surprised too," Eddie began. "I didn't"—His father cut him off.

"I didn't raise you to get into fights."

Maybe if you had, my childhood would have been easier. Eddie was careful not to let that angry thought affect his tone of voice. "No sir, you did not," was all he said.

His father launched into a long discourse, a rhetorical theme and variations on the question "what will people think?"

Eddie didn't know what people would think. There had been no time to consider that last Thursday. He saw no reason to consider it now. All the church people he knew spent too much time and energy worrying about what the rest of the congregation thought of them. It seemed a futile exercise. There was nothing more unmanageable than other people's thoughts; nothing more fickle than public opinion.

Eddie wasn't about to raise those objections, so he listened without further comment. He longed for the peace and quiet he had been enjoying before his phone rang. At last the elder Caruthers seemed to be winding down.

"Where are you now?"

"I'm out getting a little air," Eddie answered. "I'm in Worcester County."

"Will you be here for dinner?"

"Yes, I expect to be." Eddie wasn't happy about that, but tried not to sound like it.

"Good," his father said. "We can say anything else that needs to be said in person. I'll see you shortly."

"Bye." Eddie hung up and climbed in the car, not bothering to glance back at the view as he headed down Prospect Hill Road. That sense of helplessness was returning. He wondered if he'd ever truly be rid of it. He reflected that the first thing he'd done upon reaching the age of majority had been an attempt to banish that most hated of feelings. On the morning of his eighteenth birthday, his very first adult decision had been to sign up for karate classes at a small dojo in Waltham located within walking distance of the campus of Bentley University, where he would be enrolled as a freshman just a few weeks later. He never told his parents. He admitted only to having joined a "gym" to avoid gaining the fabled freshman fifteen.

Eddie trained hard. He learned that *karate-do* means "empty-hand way," and he memorized all he could of its history and philosophy. He wore his *gi*, the traditional karate uniform with drawstring pants. Practicing the various strikes and blocks, he drilled each technique in sets of ten while counting off the repetitions in Japanese. He learned to link the moves together in choreographed mock-fight routines called *kata*. He also did freestyle sparring with his classmates, short no-contact or light-contact matches where the first combatant to reach three points was declared the winner. Eventually, he won a couple of second-place trophies for his *kata* and his sparring in regional tournaments. He enjoyed it all, progressing steadily through the ranks denoted by the different-colored belts.

Just before his junior year in college, he received a rude awakening. One of his fellow karate students, a brawny high school senior and newly minted black belt, had gotten himself bruised, bloodied, and ultimately knocked out in an after-school fight. The kid who vanquished him had no martial arts training. Still a couple of years away from a realistic shot at *shodan* rank, Eddie was surprised to learn that even a black belt was no guarantee of success in a real fight. It became evident that no assailant was going to be overcome by Eddie's hard-won ability to strike a pose and count to ten in Japanese.

Upon hearing about the misfortune of his fellow *karateka*, he had tried to grill the head instructor, the third-degree black belt who owned the school, about what had gone wrong. He wanted answers about karate's effectiveness as a self-defense method—not as a cardiac fitness regimen or as an exercise in cultural appreciation or self-esteem. But lowly purple belts were not permitted to grill the *sensei*. Eddie was advised to ask fewer questions and to train harder. Karate was not just about fighting; it was a way of life. In time, the sensei said, he would understand.

Returning to his dorm, Eddie had looked up the phone numbers of every martial arts facility in the area. He selected a dozen at random and left voicemail messages at each one describing what he wanted in a trainer. He wanted training that emphasized preparing for real fights, not sporting events. The instructor should be able to document having put his skills to effective use in a nonsporting combat situation. The training should take place both indoors and out in a variety of settings and should be done in street clothes and shoes, since that's what he'd be wearing in a real fight. And he wanted straight talk about when martial arts would not be enough to save him. He never heard back from nine of the twelve schools. Two called to tell him that what he sought was unrealistic. And then he got a call from Mike Manzanetti, the proprietor of Real Life Defensive Systems.

When Mike called, they talked for about twenty minutes before arranging for Eddie to drop by for an interview. Upon arrival, he saw that the instructor was an energetic middle-aged man about five-foot-eight with a squarish build and a rolling gait. His nose had obviously been broken, perhaps more than once. He was wearing worn jeans and a black T-shirt that bore the message "You shall know the truth, and the truth shall make you free."

"I would have expected a Taoist symbol or some martial slogan, not a text from the Gospel of John," Eddie said. "I take it you're a Christian?"

"I am, but that's not the point of the shirt," Mike answered. "It's about what we do here."

Eddie raised his eyebrows and waited for an explanation.

"You're not the first person to call me about the predicament you're in," Mike continued. "I get it from traditional martial artists all the time. They've mastered the stances, they've learned the choreography, and they've got their rainbow collection of belts and sashes. But deep down they don't know if they can really *fight*. They don't know if all their spirit yells and inside blocks and hammer fists will work against a real-life bad guy. What about that three-hundred-pound goon with the prison tattoos and no neck who corners them in a parking garage? What about the hood rat with a straight razor and a crack habit who demands their wallet and phone? Can they win the fight when their lives depend on it, on a cold winter night when the ice on the sidewalk rules out all the fancy dojo ballerina moves? Are they really a force to be reckoned with, or have they just spent four to six years of their lives getting a black belt in aerobics?" Mike shrugged. "The questions nag them, and they come to me for the truth." He said this without a hint of hyperbole or braggadocio.

"How? How do you teach them the truth?" Eddie desperately wanted to know.

"It's not so much that I *teach* them the truth. It's rather that they *seek* the truth, and I give them a way to find it. I'll do the same for you. If you train with me, you'll learn what's needed to master both stand-up and ground fighting. You'll learn what your inherent strengths and weaknesses are. You'll discover whether you freeze under pressure, or panic when you can't figure out how to escape a hold. Do you lose the will to fight when you first feel pain?" He paused, smiling, and held Eddie's gaze. "Our training methods will show you the truth about yourself."

All of this talk of "the truth" would have sounded pretentious were it not for Mike's demeanor. He had a slightly high-pitched voice, talked a bit too loudly, chuckled a lot, and seemed always about to break out into a belly laugh. He was the embodiment of jollity, a Santa Claus with lethal hands.

He continued. "Real fights are chaotic. Nothing ever goes as planned. So we don't put a lot of stock in choreographed drills. You'll learn to fight by fighting, as realistically as possible. We don't break up into age groups or weight classes. I train all kinds of people here; business owners, cops, you name it. I've got students who outweigh you by a hundred pounds, and guys with a lot more experience than you. You'll fight them all. You'll eat some punches. You'll take some falls."

Eddie wasn't so sure about this. Maybe the kind of hard contact Mike was describing was too extreme. As if perceiving his doubts, Mike said, "We'll start out low pressure. The first couple of times someone throws you to the ground and gets the mounted position or side control on you, we'll let you get up and talk you through what happened. After some time and training, we'll let him hold you down and manhandle you until you figure out how to escape. If that means you spend a half hour on your back with a huge opponent crushing the wind out of you, then so be it. You'll find out if you can improvise when necessary, and you'll find out if you have enough fire in your belly to keep fighting when nothing's working and everything hurts. You'll push yourself. In the end, you'll *know* what you're capable of. No more doubts. That's what I mean about knowing the truth and the truth making you free."

After watching Mike teach a small group of four students, Eddie had quit his karate class and never looked back. Because of Mike's mentoring, Eddie became a skilled fighter who felt prepared for any possible conflict—except the one he had just driven away from, and the one he was now driving toward.

The black ribbon of asphalt flew under his wheels. He had to make time if he was to be at Dad's house by three thirty, and he planned to stay off the interstate highway for the trip there. Back roads were more exhilarating than a highway could ever be, and a bit of a challenge only added to the pleasures of asphalt therapy. So he crisscrossed the landscape on twisty two-lane routes, going as fast as his driving skills would permit. Those skills had been honed in autocross competitions and car club track days, enabling him to go well in excess of the posted speed limits. Arriving in Framingham, he stormed down Salem End Road toward home. He was just a minute away from the house now, and it was 3:28. He congratulated himself on his great sense of timing.

On the corner a block from the house, he rolled slowly through the stop sign without quite stopping. He'd have stopped completely had he been paying enough attention to notice the police cruiser sitting off to the side. Lights and siren came on, and Eddie pulled over. Ten minutes later, he pulled into his father's driveway with a hundred-dollar ticket for the moving violation adding to his simmering anger about the morning message.

Dinner at Dad's had become a monthly appointment. It had begun in worry when Eddie's mother died. It continued year after year because the passage of time gave it the weight of tradition. It became its own reason for being.

Eddie's mother had passed away six years ago of a ruptured abdominal aortic aneurism. No one saw it coming. The ballooning artery produced no symptoms, no discomfort, until the day it burst. Death was almost immediate. One minute Donald Caruthers had been talking and joking with his wife, savoring the closeness born of thirty-six years of marriage, and the next minute she lay dead on the kitchen floor. A part of him had died with her. What remained seemed too small for the big colonial house. He tried to compensate for the emptiness and quiet by keeping multiple televisions on when he was at home, and by being at home as little as possible. Hoping to stay too busy to miss his wife much, he threw himself into his business and church. It didn't work.

The children had all rallied around their father to help him stave off loneliness. Two of them worked in the complex of businesses he had founded, so it was not as if they never saw one another. Lorna, the only sibling who didn't work in the family enterprise, had moved back to town to be close. It was she who had initially suggested these get-togethers. The idea was to make Dad's house feel like a home again by filling it with the voices of family rather than the sterile droning of the TV news. So Eddie and his two siblings, their spouses, and their children all came to Dad's house for dinner on the first Sunday of every month.

Eddie entered through the unlocked front door and headed to the dining room. He heard his father calling out a cheery hello from the kitchen, as if he hadn't just jumped down Eddie's throat less than an hour ago. The other dinner guests were settling into their accustomed spots around the dining room table, all looking like nothing was wrong.

The arrangements were always the same. Dad cooked the meat. The women brought side dishes and dessert. They sat down to Sunday dinner several hours earlier than the main meal would have been served on a weeknight. Eddie wasn't sure why. Perhaps it was a holdover from the days when church had two services on Sunday, and people had to squeeze in dinner between morning and evening worship.

Dad sat at the head of the table, closest to the kitchen. To his right sat his eldest son, Jason, doing his habitual imitation of a marble sculpture. Next to Jason sat his wife, Sarah Jane.

Across the table from Sarah Jane was Lorna, eldest of the three siblings. Beside her was her Cajun husband, William Archambeau. Eddie sat at the end of the table opposite his father. Off to the side, a card table was set up for the young children. Brent and Malinda, ages seven and five, belonged to the Archambeaus. The boy was theirs biologically; the girl had been adopted from China. Roman, age four, belonged to Jason and Sarah Jane. Like a service at Solid Rock, dinner at Dad's celebrated some of the many flavors of humanity—five chocolate, one French vanilla, and a variety pack of little kids.

Today's meal featured the usual excess of food: tossed salad, potato salad, barbecued chicken, cornbread, mixed vegetables, and pumpkin pie. Eddie was suddenly very hungry. His mouth watered through the agonizingly slow passing of the plates, and he wondered why, despite centuries of scientific advances, people hadn't learned to make this part of a meal go faster. Dad prayed a lengthy blessing over the food while stomachs growled. Finally, everyone could eat. Conversation was mercifully sparse while the six adults and three children tore into first and second helpings. Other than an occasional sentence fragment from the men about an upcoming football game or a snippet from the women about Sister so-and-so's attire at church, everyone was busily making sure there was no meat left on any chicken bones. Eventually, Dad pushed himself back from the table and asked, "So, Eddie, were you planning on telling us about the altercation in the church courtyard at some point?"

Eddie maintained a neutral tone and expression. "Probably not. It was just a minute or two out of a very long day, and didn't seem worth talking about."

"I beg to differ. You came to blows. That makes it worth talking about. How did it happen?"

Eddie recited the facts in brief while Sarah Jane passed the pie. He was careful to emphasize how he had tried to de-escalate things verbally and only attacked when his peace overture was ignored. Loudmouth had threatened him and pursued him. Eddie had been left with no choice.

"Whoever started it, it takes two to tangle."

"Yes, but it only takes one to administer a beating. I decided not to have one administered to me."

The head of the Caruthers clan closed his eyes and knitted his brow. Eddie almost felt sorry for him. His father was unaccustomed to people gainsaying his maxims in his own house, least of all one of his children.

"This pie is *delicious*." Lorna praised the dessert a little too loudly, instinctively taking on the conciliation-by-change-of-subject role that Mom would have taken had she been there. "I do believe I'll have another piece. Anyone else want more?"

Jason's wife piped up. "I'm glad you like it. I'll have another piece myself. I tinkered with the recipe a bit—a little more spice, real butter from grass-fed cows . . ." Sarah Jane was trying to assist Lorna with her diversion. She was a middle school principal who had married into the family eight years ago, and she knew the house rules well. Heated discussions and lengthy arguments were to be avoided. Any undercurrent of tension must be covered over with at least the appearance of conviviality. And rule number one: Thou shalt not contradict Dad, because that is the very definition of disrespect. As a result of these unwritten but strictly enforced house rules, disagreements never got resolved. They accumulated. They festered. Eddie had more than two decades' worth lurking just beneath the surface of every family gathering.

"I wish I could bake as well as you do," Lorna said, shaking her head.

"Here's the part I don't get." William speaking. He had retained his slow Louisiana drawl despite six years in New England. You could make yourself a sandwich in the time it took him to finish a sentence. "I don't understand why it was necessary for you to have words with this man in the first place, Eddie. You involved yourself in a quarrel that wasn't your own. I suspect that if you'd held your peace, there would have been no fight."

Somewhere around the word "involved," Lorna shot William a withering look, but he plowed on. He'd destroyed his wife's diversion and she clearly wasn't happy. Eddie, on the other hand, was only too happy to respond.

"Oh, you're right, Billy." Eddie knew that Lorna's husband preferred to be called William, tolerated Bill, and absolutely hated being called Billy. "I could have said nothing at all. That would have sent Roz the message that when someone's bullying her, no one in our blessed little community will come to her aid. We wouldn't want to risk offending the heathen. No, we only browbeat fellow believers, preferably from the pulpit. Is that your point?" Eddie was losing his grip on his previously neutral expression and tone; his delivery was becoming a bit heated.

"I'll be taking up the issue of pulpit decorum with the pastor," said his father. "Don't you worry. What happened today should have been handled differently, and I'll make sure that message is heard." His voice rumbled with the kind of *basso profundo* indignation his children had all learned to respect when they were growing up. Eddie's siblings and their spouses glanced guiltily at their little ones seated around the card table. Best to shield the youngsters from this sort of talk. But the kids seemed to take no notice of what the adults were discussing. For his part, Eddie appreciated the paternal support, but he wasn't sure how he felt about the idea of his father riding to his defense. It somehow made him feel like a kid again, even though he was now perfectly capable of defending himself. He was deciding how to broach this subject when his father continued.

"In the meantime, it concerns me that you were so quick to throw away the principle of nonviolence."

Eddie waited before replying. He wanted to frame his response just right. "I think the principle of nonviolence has been overblown.

Christian culture has embraced the nonviolence of Gandhi and Dr. King to the exclusion of any other strategy. They were both great men, but their ideas and philosophies are just that—ideas and philosophies. They're not holy writ. Being nonviolent at any cost means pinning your hopes for peace on the conscience of the other guy. What if he doesn't *have* a conscience?"

Sarah Jane leaned forward and used her teach-the-children voice. "You don't have to sink to the other guy's level. Real men don't resort to violence."

Eddie could think of few expressions he disliked as much as "real men don't." His mother had used that line on him for years, wielding it like a crowbar even when he was too young to worry about what men did or did not do. It had always felt blatantly manipulative.

When people used the phrase "real women," it was with the intent to affirm and encourage. Ads touting plus-sized clothing proclaimed that real women had curves; the message to women was to accept themselves as they were. "Those airbrushed runway models aren't real women; *you* are." By contrast, the phrase "real men" served only to censure or to shame. The message to males was, "You don't measure up. Real men don't do what you did. Change your behavior or forfeit claim to the most basic aspect of your identity." Even worse, the list of "real man" traits was endlessly variable; it set boys a moving target. Though he'd found it a noxious turn of phrase, Eddie had never protested it; the house rules meant learning to live with things. *That was then. This is now.*

Eddie locked eyes with Sarah Jane. "I'm twenty-seven years old, so kindly don't speak to me like I'm a child. And for the record, I'm all done letting people control me with that 'real men' stuff. I don't need a woman to tell me what manhood is."

Jason, who had said nothing thus far, huffed in response to this retort. The look he gave his brother seemed to promise that the two of them would discuss it later. Eddie gazed blandly back at him.

"Timothy Edward Caruthers!" He was going to get it from all sides now. Lorna was channeling their mother again, breaking out Eddie's full legal name to express her irritation. He went only by his middle name—he had never liked Timothy. His diminutive stature as a youth had made Tiny Tim references inevitable. For a while he'd tried out various monikers he thought would sound cool—TC, Tec, and even T-Car, which sounded like something a really lame rapper would call himself—before deciding he just wanted to be called Eddie. Maybe Lorna was getting back at him for addressing her husband as Billy. Whatever.

"So you take issue with a popular expression almost everybody uses. Noted. We can drop it. The real question is, what would Jesus do? You know he would turn the other cheek. Why not emulate him?"

William added, "That was my point: defusing the situation would have spoken more highly of you than winning the fight. It would have shown you to be the bigger man."

Eddie barely managed to avoid rolling his eyes. "I'd have liked to see *you* defuse that situation. It's easy to sit here and pontificate from the safety of your chair."

Dad crossed his arms in the old familiar gesture that always meant *don't make me say this twice.* "There had to be an alternative course of action. Whatever the problem," he intoned, "violence is never the answer."

"Sometimes," said Eddie, "violence *is* the answer. And I think parents acknowledge that every time they spank a child."

Sarah Jane chose that moment to take the kids out for some play in the yard. As she led them out of the dining room with promises of exciting games, Jason finally spoke.

"Incorrect."

Ooh! Three syllables! Lumpen is extra talkative today.

"Jason is right," said Dad. "Spanking is a biblical discipline. And any good parent knows it's motivated by love and concern for the one being spanked. So that's apples and oranges."

"I agree—it's biblical. And the motive may be noble. But that doesn't make it any less violent. You inflict pain on a child by striking him with your hand, or with an object like a ruler or paddle. You do it to modify the child's behavior. It hurts the kid enough that after a few applications of 'the board of education,' the mere *threat* of a spanking gets results." He leaned forward and stabbed the air with his fork, punctuating his comments. "Dad, what did you used to say to us when we were little? 'I'll give you such a spanking you won't be able to sit down for a week.' 'I brought you into this world and I can take you out.' And how about 'Stop all that crying, or I'll give you something to cry about.' Parents use violence or the threat of violence to control little kids because it works. Then when the kids get older, their parents say violence is never the answer."

Eddie didn't use the word hypocrisy, but he didn't have to; the implication was clear. *Did I go too far with that one?*

Donald Caruthers rose slowly to his feet and issued a decree. "I'll not have any more of this. This conversation is now over. We're going to talk about something else. Is that understood?"

Everyone around the table spoke in ragged unison: "Yes, sir."

After hanging out and making some small talk for the sake of appearances, Eddie said his goodbyes and went home angry. It was a short trip. Going home from his father's house just meant crossing the rear patio and traversing a few yards of lawn until he reached the detached three-car garage. Upstairs, above the garage, was Eddie's apartment.

It was a spacious one-bedroom, about nine hundred square feet, with all the fancy appliances and high-end finishes that raised the rents into the stratosphere at the luxury apartment complexes in the area. Some of his friends teased him a bit about still living at home at his age, but it wasn't as if he was freeloading in the basement. He paid rent like anybody else, albeit well below market rates. The place offered comfort, garage parking, and more privacy than any apartment complex. He'd lived here since finishing college. This space had suited him well enough through the years, and he'd been happy to call it home.

But now he was sitting in the dark, finishing his Sunday as he had started it: brooding. He relived the trauma of the morning message. He wondered how Shawna had felt about the sermon and about his abrupt departure after service. The truncated discussion at dinner seemed stuck on auto-repeat. His frustration magnified his problems. How had he so long endured a life lived on such a short leash? Considered from his couch, the world suddenly felt too small. From home to work was a journey of two miles, five minutes on a day with light traffic. From home to church was around two and a half. Except for his training sessions with Mike, Eddie's whole world was a small triangular slice of Framingham. Go to work. Go home. Go to church. Go home. Go to work. Rinse and repeat. In none of those places was he truly free to be himself, to make his own decisions, to express his own thoughts. Eddie remembered a fragment from a doxology called the "Gloria Patri," part of the liturgy in the Methodist church his family had attended when he was young:

"As it was in the beginning, is now, and ever shall be . . ."

That pretty much summed up his life and prospects. He fell asleep on the couch and dreamed he was in the fifth grade again. He was in the cafeteria. A group of eighth graders, the big fish of the middle school, were playing table hockey with a penny on a table behind Eddie. Frustrated, one of the players flung the penny at his opponent and missed. It hit Eddie in the back of the head. Ouch! Furious, Eddie turned and glared at the offender, and then pocketed the penny.

"Give it back."

"If you wanted it, you should have kept it."

"Give it back." The kid making the demand was pretty big for an eighth grader.

"Why? So you can start over and hit me again? How about you apologize?"

"I'll take that penny out of your eye, you little puke."

Eddie hastily tossed the coin back, surprised at how quickly the stab of fear made him comply. The bigger kids all laughed, and Eddie felt ashamed.

He woke up fuming. *I can't believe I still dream about that.*

Of course, it meant nothing in the grand scheme of things. It was just a forgettable childhood incident. But seventeen years later, Eddie hadn't forgotten it. There had been many such incidents. He remembered them all, and they surfaced in his dreams too often. He glanced at the wall clock. It was just after midnight. He got up, went downstairs to the empty garage bay, put on some sparring gloves, and started working the heavy bag he had hanging there. "Cardio boxing," was how he had explained the bag to his father when he first hung it. "It's the in thing at all the gyms now."

Kick low. Jab. Cross. Grab the bag. Twist it, turn it. Keep the "opponent" off balance. Apply random combinations of elbows, knees, and head butts. Push off. Create distance. Reengage. Hit it hard. He kept going until he'd worked up a good sweat. He loved his workouts. Along with his training sessions, they provided the only time Eddie could shed his tightly controlled persona and go all out.

Hitting the bag was also a great way of banishing the memory of helplessness. He was anything but helpless now. He'd learned the truth about himself. He had nothing to fear.

Anyone who threatened him now would find that out. *People have no idea.*

He felt a savage glee at that thought, quickly dampened by renewed awareness of the smothering confines of his life. *People have no idea, because I can't even tell them.* He'd mastered a skill set they'd all hate. They thought they knew who he should be, and they wouldn't accept him as he was. Why was he still here? His brooding had come full circle. But his dark mood began to dissipate as black thoughts were elbowed out of the way by a new thought making an entrance. This new idea wasn't fully formed yet. It was just a spark of potential, a grain of mustard seed. But Eddie felt a small surge of excitement as the seed began to grow.

CHAPTER 4
REASONABLE QUESTIONS

The next morning, a smiling Eddie arrived at work a half hour early. His mood and timing were both unusual given his longstanding aversion to mornings in general and Mondays in particular. Awash in enthusiasm, he was eager to engage with this particular Monday morning. Sometimes a good idea will do that. And the idea that had come to life last night was a good one indeed—he would trade his cramped little world for a much bigger one. In trading up, he'd finally gain his freedom. Sure, his family would be shocked when he told them, but only because they didn't know him as well as they thought. No one did.

Eddie stepped in through the front entrance, pocketed his keys, and locked the door behind him. The service area was already open for business, but the showroom wouldn't open until nine. He looked around at the rows of merchandise. Fast Track Automotive carried the usual assortment of accessories and routine maintenance stuff—oil, coolant, cleaning supplies. But what really drew customers to this showroom was the sporting gear. The shop carried helmets and flame-retardant suits, racing seats, five-point harnesses, fire suppression equipment, and all manner of go-fast parts. It was a speed demon's paradise.

Out back were five service bays where customers could get everything from oil changes to forced induction and full engine and drivetrain swaps. In front of the store was a line of about a dozen used cars for sale, all with aftermarket performance goodies. That was Eddie's department.

Eddie couldn't help but be proud of his father whenever he considered the success of Fast Track Automotive. He also knew how much he himself had benefited from Dad's achievement. After all, when Eddie finished college, he hadn't needed to send out résumés and sweat through interviews. His job had been waiting for him. He was well paid, had guaranteed lifetime employment, and would someday inherit ownership of half the business.

Too bad he didn't want it. He couldn't see spending decades toiling beside his dull, monosyllabic brother. FTA was not where he wanted to be at this point in his life. It was not where he'd ever wanted to be. He worked there for one reason: because it made Dad happy. He'd nodded and smiled through the years of "someday this will all be yours" speeches for the same reason. *Dad is living his dream*, he thought. *It's about time I started living mine.*

He crossed the showroom and entered his office. Firing up the desktop computer, he checked his bank balance and brokerage accounts. Calculating the totals brought a smile to his face. He could afford to take his time finding his own life path.

He thought about where he might relocate. An ideal town would be large enough to offer something to do in the evenings and far enough from Framingham to feel like a fresh start, but not so far away that he would experience some kind of culture shock upon moving there. That ruled out the Left Coast and much of the Deep South, but left all sorts of possibilities open. He looked at random town profiles and apartment ads right up until opening time. At nine o'clock sharp, he dove into his work, but since work required him to spend a lot of time online, he had numerous opportunities to wander back to the classified ads throughout the morning.

At lunch time, he called Shawna Bell and arranged to meet her for dinner that evening. This would be their third dinner date—assuming Monday night dates even counted. She was a little cool toward him on the phone, but she worked in a very busy office and sometimes didn't have time to chat. Eddie hoped it was nothing more than that. He really liked her and was determined to find out just where he stood in her hierarchy of romantic possibilities. He wondered how long a long-distance relationship could be and still work.

The next order of business was to check his personal email. To his surprise, one of the first was from Reverend Bowers requesting that the two of them meet during midweek service on Wednesday. That request meant his ordeal from yesterday wasn't over yet. Eddie typed a one-word response—"Acknowledged"—and clicked

SEND. He was not looking forward to whatever this meeting entailed. But his good mood held. Not even the man who put the bully in "bully pulpit" could dampen his spirits today.

The hours flew by. When he wasn't updating all of FTA's classified ads, posting on various car forums, or handling the half-dozen potential car buyers that came in to kick tires and bemoan the prices, Eddie thought about Shawna. A lot of guys at church would have given their eyeteeth to date her, though not necessarily for the same reasons as Eddie. All agreed she was easy on the eyes, but that was just the beginning. As a fourth-generation Pentecostal whose great-grandfather had been at Azusa Street, Shawna had what their pastor called "heritage." Her lineage was the Pentecostal equivalent of having ancestors who sailed to America on the Mayflower. She also had relatives who currently held national leadership positions in two different denominations, and more than one young minister at Solid Rock had remarked about the kind of connections a marriage to Shawna would bring. Eddie, on the other hand, did not care about such things. This was not the Old World; this was America. Here a man's potential was not tied to his family tree. Eddie wanted to make his own opportunities, not inherit them or marry them. He hoped Shawna knew this. He wanted nothing from her but her.

In addition to preachers, Shawna's family tree was sprinkled with doctors, lawyers, and politicians. The whole clan was pretty well off. She was practically "old money," while Eddie's family had come into money only in the last fifteen years or so.

Shawna's politics leaned left of center, while Eddie was a fiscal conservative who had a pronounced Libertarian streak. She was an urban sophisticate, he a child of the suburbs who longed for the country life. In fact, their differences outnumbered their similarities. He liked to imagine that her going out with him twice already was proof that opposites attract. She seemed to like him. He hoped the events of the last few days hadn't changed that. He couldn't wait to see her.

At exactly eight o'clock, he rang the doorbell at her Natick townhouse. The door opened immediately. She was ready to go, stepping out to meet him on the porch. Eddie waved over her shoulder to her two roommates, who stood smiling in the hall. Turning his high-wattage smile on Shawna, he asked, "Are you as hungry as I am?"

She looked great, as always, in a knee-length black skirt, black leather boots, a gray silk blouse and a colorful sweater. Her long black hair was done in a classic French braid—at least that was what Eddie thought the style was called—and her cinnamon complexion was flawless. She wore no jewelry except for an unobtrusive necklace with a cross pendant. Eddie had never seen her look less than perfectly put together. He could almost believe she rolled out of bed that way every morning.

At the car, Eddie opened the passenger door for Shawna, let her settle in, and closed the door for her before walking around the back of the vehicle to his own side. *Who said chivalry is dead?* Getting in, he tried not to notice the breathtaking curves that were revealed by her shoulder belt's embrace. He failed in the effort but figured he deserved spirituality points for trying. *Saved doesn't mean blind.*

He had chosen a restaurant just twenty minutes away. A former speakeasy from the Prohibition era, this eatery disguised as a farmhouse had a small dining room, a funky atmosphere, and a growing cachet. It was the kind of hidden gem Eddie loved to find, and he hoped Shawna would enjoy the discovery as much as he had when he'd first stumbled on it.

After they ordered their meals, Eddie realized that the conversation had been rather one-sided. He had been doing most of the talking, despite asking her a lot of open-ended questions about her work, her roommates, and her plans for the winter holidays. Shawna was usually engaged as well as engaging, with sparkling eyes and a ready laugh. Tonight she stuck to mostly tight-lipped smiles, and her heavy eyelids gave her an almost hooded look.

He knew that Shawna sometimes became like this when she was in an especially spiritual frame of mind. She would fixate on some noble quest, like traveling Mother Teresa style to a squalid third-world country to feed, clothe, and evangelize the poorest of the poor. At such times, she seemed barely connected to her present surroundings, only nominally interested in the mores and materials of middle-class life. Eddie respected such self-sacrificing ambitions, though he did not share them. He and his family wanted to put as much distance as possible between themselves and privation. Eddie was happy to send money to charitable causes, but he hoped Shawna wouldn't actually up and go someplace outside of his orbit.

After a few more failed attempts to engage her and draw her eyes back from whatever distant vistas they were seeing, he said, "So, how about those Red Sox? Some weather we're having, huh? And why *did* the chicken cross the road, anyway? I know you're in there—I can hear you breathing!"

At least the vaudeville act drew a genuine smile. "Sorry, Eddie. I guess I'm a little preoccupied."

"I would say so. Tell me about it?"

"It's just that recent events have made me a little . . . uncomfortable. I thought I knew you pretty well, and I've always felt safe around you. But on Thursday night, you surprised me. It was a side of you I hadn't seen. I frankly feel a little less secure knowing you are capable of such explosive . . . such explosive . . ." She was evidently trying not to say the word "violence" and failing to find an alternative.

Eddie grimaced inwardly. There would be no avoiding a discussion of the fight. He should have known. He *had* known somewhere deep down. Shawna's case of nerves from Thursday, doubtless amplified by yesterday's hatchet job of a sermon, was not just a passing thing. Eddie would have to do some damage control. He didn't want to. He only wanted to enjoy the music of her voice while they talked about happy things, to hear that tiny trace of a lisp that he found so endearing when she said words like "explosive." Oh well. They might as well get this over with.

He kept his tone gentle. "Surely you wouldn't have felt more secure if I'd run away? Left you and your friends to face whatever else that guy decided to say or do?"

"No, I wouldn't respect you if you'd run off and left us. It's just that it was all so sudden, the way you went into fight mode. It was like flipping on a light switch. One second you were chatting with me about gospel music, and the next second, *boom!* You were knocking that man out. You were so fierce, and it seemed like . . . like it wasn't the first time you'd done that. You were too good at it not to have done it before." She paused, and Eddie waited silently for her to resume. "Anyway, our pastor made it pretty clear how he feels about fighting. Are you at odds with him over this?"

"Me? I'll tell you what. I promise that if the pastor is ever attacked, I won't intervene. Okay?" This attempt at humor fell flat, as he had pretty much known it would. Come to think of it, he wasn't sure he'd been joking. He decided to try a different tack. "So what should I have done instead?"

"I don't know, Eddie," she said, sighing. "Something else. I would have wanted you to find a third way, something that was neither running nor fighting."

"I would've gladly taken a third way out, if there had been one. Sometimes life doesn't give us the choices we want."

Including tonight, he thought with a twinge of bitterness. He didn't want to argue with Shawna or defend himself to her. He wanted her to enjoy her meal while he related his grand plans to build himself a better life. He wanted her to be interested in that, and to be part of it. He wanted to drive her to his favorite scenic overlook and gaze at the moon through the sunroof while soft music played on the stereo. He wanted to hold her hand.

He wanted to kiss her. It would be their first kiss, and he had been playing the scenario all day in his head. This conversation sure wasn't moving things in that direction.

"There are almost always more choices than the ones we see." Shawna spoke those words very quietly and resumed gazing into the distance. Their entrees arrived. They ate the meal mostly in silence. At one point she brightened a bit, and asked him, "So why *did* the chicken cross the road, anyway?"

Without missing a beat, Eddie said, "To prove to the possum that it could be done." This earned him an unexpected chuckle before she withdrew into herself again.

Eddie drove her straight home. As they traveled, he put on some Sonya Robinson tunes to accompany their wordless reflections. Sonya was a jazz violinist who was equally adept at the blues, baroque, and anything else she chose to play. Her exquisite tone channeled the melancholy in the car while providing enough emotional uplift to keep Eddie from feeling truly awful.

He thought back to Thursday evening. If he could go back in time, the only thing he would change would be that quip—*welcome to Solid Rock*. He could see how it might sound callous to someone else, as if he had enjoyed the violence or found it funny. Truth was, a bit of euphoria was always associated with coming out of a life-threatening situation unscathed. And Eddie's talk could go from zero to sarcastic in a fraction of a second. Though wisecracks came naturally to him, he was neither callous nor cruel. It was a defense mechanism, a way of coping. He hoped Shawna could see that.

Too soon, the Natick townhouse came into view. Neither driver nor passenger had spoken since leaving the restaurant parking lot. There would be no hand-holding, no kissing, and no changing of Facebook profiles to "in a relationship" this night. Eddie walked her to her door, leaden hands hanging empty and forlorn at his sides.

"Thank you for dinner," Shawna said, smiling. "The meal and the music were both very good." Her voice seemed too cheerful by half. She had mastered the art of sounding warm and gracious when such niceties were called for. *Like flipping on a light switch*, Eddie thought sullenly.

As she put her key in the lock, she quickly turned and enveloped him in a hug that was startling in its ferocity. "I care about you, Eddie Caruthers. I really do. Just don't become someone I couldn't like." She released him, let herself in, and closed the door. Eddie just stood there with his mouth open. He could not have been more stunned if she'd slugged him.

The next evening, Eddie went to Real Life Defensive Systems for his regularly scheduled private lesson. He told Mike about the fight.

The instructor quizzed him for several minutes, making him repeat parts of the narrative, "Were you injured?" he asked at last.

It was a simple enough question, and a natural one to ask. Eddie frowned upon remembering that no one at home or at church had yet bothered to ask it. "No, I wasn't hurt at all," he replied.

"So, what should you have done differently?" With Mike, this was a tactical question, not an ethical one. This led them into a brief review of two-on-one tactics, and Eddie had to admit he'd erred in letting the second man out of his sight for the few seconds it took to dispatch the first guy. That could have turned out badly. Mike assured him they would review two-on-one sparring in their next small-group class.

"Final question: Where was your gun?"

"Right where it always is." Eddie patted his right hip, where a compact Glock 23 rode low in an inside-the-waistband holster. He never left home without it. Mike was one of only four people who knew Eddie carried a concealed weapon. The others were two licensed gun owners who trained alongside Eddie in the Saturday class and the Framingham police detective who had helped Eddie process his application for the carry permit. Mike had been instrumental in Eddie's decision to go armed. He'd been brutally candid in his response to Eddie's questions about the limits of empty-hand self-defense and what options remained once those limits were reached.

Mike asked Eddie to clear the gun. He did so, removing the magazine, ejecting the round in the chamber, and pulling the trigger to lock it back. Stowing the ejected cartridge in his pocket, he reinserted the magazine into the butt of the gun. This allowed him to train in safety while keeping the weight and balance of the pistol the same as it would be for real-world deployment. The Glock could not be fired until he manually cycled the slide.

After warming up on the heavy bag, Eddie spent the next forty-five minutes sparring with Mike and doing drills in both stand-up and ground-fighting scenarios. As always, he was dressed in street clothes. Like Mike, he worked out in a T-shirt customized with a saying that was meaningful to him. Whereas Mike's referenced the scripture about the truth making you free, Eddie's simply read "Recovering Pacifist."

Each of the drills included Eddie practicing his draw. He had to access his gun from every conceivable position, drawing the concealed firearm quickly and smoothly whether advancing, retreating, or even lying on the ground. The drills continued until Eddie was panting hard.

"Guns are like the fire extinguisher in your kitchen," Mike said for probably the tenth time that year. "You never need them until the day that you do. Pray that day never comes! But if it does, if you find yourself in a situation where lethal force is needed, it'll be too late to practice these drills. So do these at home until you've done them a thousand times and you can draw quickly and cleanly in any circumstance."

Eddie nodded, too winded to talk. And then they practiced some more.

CHAPTER 5
THE WRONG MAN

Eddie skirted the sanctuary and headed for the administrative wing of the church. Midweek service would be starting in a few minutes. The fact that the pastor had scheduled their meeting for church time meant another staff member would be teaching tonight's lesson. Eddie wondered who, and hoped the teaching would be good. Glancing through an open side door into the sanctuary, he saw the usual Wednesday night attendees. Though fewer in number than the "Sunday saints," there were probably eighty to one hundred people present. He could see a couple of visitors too, including a pale-skinned, bushy-haired guy in black jeans and a long, black leather coat who looked like he might have gotten lost on his way to a Goth concert. It was a little unusual to have visitors on a Wednesday night, but not unheard of. *Lord, please bless the service,* he prayed under his breath before hurrying on.

The pastor's office at Solid Rock was an imposing place. While the public face of the church was the sanctuary, and the power of God regularly fell there, this office was where a different kind of power was exercised. In this room people were promoted up the organizational chart or shunted off to the sidelines, ambitions were encouraged or nixed, rumors were birthed or squashed. Before anyone sang a solo in service or dined with the pastor at the head table during a banquet, the person was discussed in this office where approval and social acceptance were either meted out or withheld. Most church members never saw the inside of this room, and Eddie knew that was fine with them. To be summoned here was usually not a good thing.

The church's inner sanctum was a large space with polished oak floors and high ceilings. Shelves full of hardcover books lined one wall, while the opposite wall contained only a prayer bench placed under a famous painting of an elderly man praying over a simple meal. In the back of the room a massive desk was centered in front of a bay window, facing away from it. The surface of the desk was barren save for a blotter, a thick Montblanc fountain pen, an equally expensive-looking letter opener, and a copy of *Dealing with Difficult People* strategically placed near the corner. Two upholstered chairs with low seating positions faced the desk. Sitting in these chairs placed people in a position of inferiority, forcing them to look up at the pastor as he sat in his executive chair.

The contest of wills began as soon as Eddie sat down. "What I did on Sunday was one of the hardest things I've ever had to do in the pulpit." Pastor Bowers put his elbows on the desk, steepling his fingers and looking grave.

"No doubt," said Eddie with equal gravity. "It was certainly one of the hardest things I've ever had to sit through."

"You have to understand that it's not personal. We had a problem, and it's my job to put the Word on such problems."

"It's nice to know it's not personal, because it sure *feels* personal when someone publicly suggests that I'm a wolf in sheep's clothing."

"I don't think you get it," the preacher replied. "Desperate measures were called for. If the guy doing CPR on you bruises your ribs while saving your life, you shouldn't complain. You've been a valued and valuable member of this church for many years. But in recent years, I've watched you slowly withdrawing—becoming less active, less involved. I've watched you move from always sitting in the front to sitting halfway to the door, and I can't help but see the symbolism."

That much was true. Eddie had been involved in all sorts of church programs in his youth—choirs, Sunday school, tutoring, and more. He had even been a sort of goodwill ambassador for the church when the local newspaper did a human interest story on his habit of visiting area senior centers to play guitar and sing for the residents. The seniors loved the free concerts, but the pastor had been less than pleased to learn that what Eddie sang to them was mostly worldly music rather than Christian songs. He did a decent Sinatra. His Otis Redding was spot on. Under pressure to change his performances, Eddie had gradually stopped doing them. Eventually he stopped singing altogether, even in the shower, and began dropping his other church activities one by one.

The pastor continued. "And now *this* happens. This incident is alarming. I had to preach as hard as I did to drive out whatever *spirit* is moving you in this direction and making you think it's okay to court bloodshed on the grounds of a church."

Eddie had known it would come down to spirits sooner or later. It always did. He briefly thought about the old joke that asks how many Pentecostals it takes to change a light bulb. The answer is eight—one to turn the bulb, and seven to pray against the spirit of darkness. There was no point in going there, so he focused his reply on the second part of the pastor's statement.

"I didn't have a philosophical discussion with myself about the propriety of shedding blood on church property. I simply did what I had to do to keep my own blood from being shed. If bloodshed was unavoidable, then I figured better his than mine. I still believe that."

"But your viewpoint is too narrow. You're only considering yourself. I have to deal with the big picture," Bowers said, looking pained and weary. "Did you know the church was vandalized the next day? It's never happened before, but it happened after your altercation. Someone spray-painted a vulgar message on the side door. One of the deacons found it on Friday evening, and we had to spend time and money to clean it up Saturday morning."

"I didn't know about that," Eddie admitted. He felt indignant about this apparent collateral damage.

"No, I didn't think you would. But that's my point—your decisions impact more than just you. It's why we all have to live by the same rule, why we can't have people going off and doing their own thing according to their own whims and perceptions."

"So you feel that to spare the church the cost and bother of removing graffiti, I should have just let some brute assault me?"

"You wouldn't have *been* assaulted. If you had demonstrated the restraint to say nothing, do nothing, then none of this would have happened."

"The only thing necessary for the triumph of evil is that good men do nothing." Eddie wasn't sure where that quote came from. He'd heard it attributed to at least three different people over the years. But he was sure that whoever had said it was right.

"No, no, no. This is a time for serious reflection. You can't brush this off with some pithy saying you read somewhere," Bowers said, his face twisted into a sneer.

Yeah, like all that baloney sauce about CPR and bruised ribs? Eddie's lip curled, but he managed to keep his retort behind his teeth. He regretted the fact that Bowers would take his silence as a concession of the point.

"It was a mistake to yell at that guy."

"Why? I didn't yell at him nearly as much as you yelled at me. And I wasn't trying to 'impress the girls' either. I was trying to protect a friend and fellow church member from further abuse. Why was that a mistake?"

"It was a mistake because it escalated things. Then you compounded your error when he got out of his car to confront you. I'm sure he was a jerk about it. But that doesn't excuse the fact that you threw the first punch."

"Who told you I threw the first punch?"

"That's immaterial. It's what I was told, and by more than one person."

Eddie was exasperated. "Well, whoever said it didn't know what they were talking about. Didn't understand what they were seeing. And one of my least favorite features of church life is how everybody can run to the pastor and tattle on somebody anonymously. In the secular world, a man has the right to face his accusers. Why isn't it that way here?"

"First off, the right you are referring to has to do with procedure at a legal trial. You're not on trial here."

"Oh, I'm not?"

"*No.* And this attitude you're displaying is not what I expected from you. It's not good. You need to set aside your hurt feelings and come to grips with the fact that the Word of God is a sword. Sometimes it cuts. Accept the wound humbly, and that same Word will heal you. It's like I preached: we're commanded to 'follow peace with all men, and above all holiness, without which no man shall see the Lord.' It isn't easy to follow peace with some people, but there's no getting around the need to do it with everyone."

"Holiness doesn't require the cooperation of others," said Eddie. "Peace does. I can only follow peace with somebody until he breaks that peace. Scripture recognizes that. For instance, Romans 12:8 says, 'If it is possible, as much as depends on you, live peaceably with all men.' On Thursday night, peace wasn't possible. Because of him, not me."

Reverend Bowers tried a different approach. "If you don't feel that peace is entirely your responsibility, can you at least agree that it's in your best interest? The Bible says that people who live by the sword will die by it."

"Actually, I don't think it says that." The preacher's eyes widened. Before he could vocalize any objections to Eddie's audacity, the younger man pushed his point further. "If you're referring to the scene outside Gethsemane, I think people misunderstand the passage. We know that Judas led 'a great multitude' of people armed with swords and staves who came to arrest Jesus. I don't know how many people make a great multitude, but it's safe to say they vastly outnumbered the Lord's eleven disciples. When Peter tried to fight his way out, Jesus warned him that swordplay would be suicidal. If any of the disciples chose battle, they would be killed by the mob. How could such a lopsided fight end any other way? But Jesus wasn't laying out some general rule for humanity, saying that anyone who ever takes up arms is doomed to die a violent death. That's easily proven, because we all know of soldiers, cops, or armed guards who carried weapons in the line of duty, but still died peacefully of natural causes in their old age. The existence of just one exception proves that Jesus was not making a rule. Then there's the fact that in Luke's account, Jesus specifically tells his disciples to get swords, even if they have to sell a garment to buy one. Why would he say that, if he was a pacifist?"

And so it went for over an hour. Reverend Bowers reiterated part of his sermon, quoting Psalm 34:14, in which King David wrote that people should seek peace and pursue it. Eddie responded that in Psalm 144:1, the very same man had credited God with teaching his hands to war and his fingers to fight. Each time the preacher cited a verse that seemed to support his condemnation of Eddie's fighting, Eddie countered with a different verse or a different explanation of the one the pastor had used.

Pastor Bowers became visibly agitated. He picked up the pen from his desk, put it down, and picked it up again. "I can't believe you're going to sit here and argue the Bible with me. If you can't take direction from me when God said he'd give you pastors after his own heart, you have a problem. You've become your own pastor."

Eddie said nothing as Reverend Bowers continued. "Even if you discount my counsel, there are a lot of men in God's service—seasoned men, spiritual men—who understand the importance of nonviolence. It's why our entire organization decided that our members in the military should shun combat duty. Fighting is to be avoided! Thousands of Spirit-filled ministers studied the issue, prayed about it, and voted on it. Does that carry no weight with you? Or are they all wrong too, and twenty-something-year-old Eddie Caruthers is the only one with understanding?"

Eddie asked, "Was the vote unanimous?" Pastor Bowers looked momentarily confused by this question. "Because if it wasn't, I bet you the seasoned ministers who studied and prayed, and voted the *other way* felt just as Spirit-led as the majority. In any case, I think pacifism is morally bankrupt, and the way somebody else voted has no effect on that conviction."

"Morally bankrupt?" The pastor went from picking up and putting down his pen to repeatedly repositioning the book on his desk. "Oh, I want to hear this. Do enlighten us, pray tell."

Eddie wondered who "us" was. Was Bowers now using the royal "we"? Well, if "they" wanted an explanation, Eddie would give them one.

"Americans enjoy freedoms we inherited from fighters. The Bill of Rights, our Constitution—these were deeded to us by people who went to war for them. If the Founding Fathers had been pacifists, we'd have none of these things today. We'd still be British subjects."

Eddie paused for effect, but the pastor said nothing, so he continued. "Look at World War II. Hitler was taking over Europe and exterminating the Jews. It took the violence of Allied soldiers to stop him. Nobody ever liberated a concentration camp by making speeches about peace.

"Pacifists want the dirty work to be done by somebody else. They're like the Pharisees Jesus rebuked in Matthew 23: 'For they bind heavy burdens, hard to bear, and lay them on men's shoulders; but they themselves will not move them with one of their fingers.'"

Reverend Bowers slammed his book down, sputtering. "I'm not going to waste any more time arguing with you. I hoped you'd show some humility, maybe even remorse. But you've shown neither. You've got a seriously flawed worldview and a head full of arrogant illusions. You've got issues, mister, and you need to think carefully about some things. Like Shawna Bell, for instance."

Eddie stared at the preacher through narrowed eyes. "What does that mean?"

Reverend Bowers looked suddenly pleased with himself. "She likes you, you know. She thinks you'd be happier if you didn't spend so much time trying to impress her with fancy cars and fancy restaurants and such. She's not about that. But she does like you."

Eddie's whole body tensed. "Why were you two discussing me?"

"Because she's a good church member who seeks her pastor's input on important decisions. You should try it sometime. As I said, she likes you, though she thinks you try a little too hard. As for you, you could do a lot worse than Shawna Bell, and probably no better. She's got brains, beauty, talent, and heritage. She'll be quite the catch for the right man. I don't know if you're the right man."

Eddie burned inwardly. He had not taken Shawna to those nice restaurants to impress her. He enjoyed nice restaurants and had simply wanted to share some of his favorite places with her. *Why do people always try to guess your motives instead of just asking you?* He considered the irony of Shawna's background: she was fortunate enough to belong to a class of people who could sniff disdainfully at money and material things while still having an abundance of both. She'd probably do a tour of duty succoring the poor in some sinkhole of a country, and then come back to America to be a highly paid poverty expert and policy advocate. She'd write books and appear on all the cable news channels to explain why the government should raise taxes on people like his father, only to redistribute the wealth to people who'd done nothing to earn it. Even as the thought occurred to him, Eddie conceded that it was a little uncharitable; it was just the anger talking.

"Anyway," the pastor went on, "I haven't said anything either for or against you yet. I told her I'd seek the counsel of God and get back to her." He smiled.

Eddie could clearly read the message in that chilly smile. It said, "Game over. Thanks for playing."

Bowers leaned forward and stared at Eddie. "Here's what you need to do. You commit to setting a good example in your church. You promise me that nothing like what happened last Thursday is ever going to happen again. You go to the deacons and apologize for the fact that your poor judgment led to the vandalism of our facility and added to their workload. You make sure no one thinks you have a beef with me or my preaching. You re-engage with your church, and become the involved, supportive person you were at seventeen, instead of the halfway-out-the-door malcontent I think you've become. You do those things, and do them quickly, and it'll go a long way to helping me decide what guidance to offer that fine young lady."

Reverend Greg Bowers stood to his feet, signaling that the meeting was over. "And go out the side door. The front will be locked for the night by now."

So this is what it feels like to be blackmailed, Eddie thought as he strode from the church courtyard. His anger grew with every step. He was fuming when he reached his car. Bowers was just the latest in a long line of bullies stretching back to grade school. All of them used coercion to get what they wanted. Preachers liked to pretend they were different from the rest of the world, purer of heart. But they used the same tactics as everybody else.

Eddie jumped into the Benz, fired it up, and chirped the tires on the way out of the lot. He knew asphalt therapy wouldn't be treatment enough for the way he was feeling. The heavy bag was going to take a real beating tonight.

The queasy sensation had started the next morning. It took him until two to realize what was causing the flutter in his stomach and the tightness in his neck: choir rehearsal. He dreaded going back to that building, even for so enjoyable a purpose as seeing Shawna again. He called a deacon who agreed to sub for him. Eddie felt better almost immediately. He decided to take the weekend off.

Sunday morning found him on the seashore, 110 miles from Framingham. He had come down on Saturday after his class at Real Life Defensive Systems, asking his father to tell any inquisitive church folks that he was out of town for the weekend. If any place could make him feel whole again, safe again, this was it.

He was on Wellfleet's Cahoon Hollow Beach, one of the pristine beaches of the National Seashore. This being mid-October, it was free of the summer hordes of half-naked tourists. He had the place pretty much to himself. He strolled for miles, watching the gulls wheeling, the piping plovers sprinting back and forth in front of the waves, and the big gray seals popping their heads out of the surf to stare curiously at him.

He thought about Shawna for what seemed like the thousandth time since Wednesday. He was irked that she had gone to seek the pastor's opinion about dating him. Were they not all grownups here? It was clear that in at least some areas, she didn't understand him as well as she thought. She'd said that he would be happier if he stopped trying to impress her. *Actually, I'd be happier if she stopped trying to psychoanalyze me.*

She did like him, though. At least that's what Reverend Bowers had said. Her exact words to him Monday evening had been that she "cared" for him. But what precisely did that mean? After all, Shawna cared for a lot of things—the plight of the poor, the rain forest, unwanted pets. Was she romantically interested in him? Life would be awesome if she were. He felt an urge to just call her and ask, but he was hesitant to do that. He had always been the one to initiate the call. Maybe she should call him for a change.

Eddie mused his way through the afternoon, walked back to his car, and drove to The Box Lunch. He ordered a Porky Goes Hawaiian, a hot rollup with ham, melted cheese, pineapple, and some kind of sauce. Good food, cheap, and open during the off season. You couldn't ask for more than that on the Cape.

While eating, he replayed Wednesday night's showdown. If only Bowers had not come to replace the former pastor. Solid Rock's previous pastor was nothing like Greg Bowers. He had been more loved than feared, as far as a young Eddie could tell. The Caruthers family had been attending Solid Rock for four years when Pastor Bullard suddenly resigned without explanation. After a long search in which at least three different ministers insisted it was God's will for the church to hire them, Solid Rock had selected Greg Bowers. What a change that was. The old pastor hadn't used the pulpit as a platform for throwing bombs. He wasn't a hit man in a clerical collar. He had been a genuinely nice guy. Or maybe that was just the rose-colored gauze with which memory shrouded the past, forgetting the bad and turning the rest into the "good old days." Maybe all preachers were alike. Eddie wondered why Bullard had left, and what he was up to now.

Asphalt therapy would help. Eddie drove up and down the length of Old County Road from Wellfleet to Truro several times. Taking the twists and turns at speed took concentration, which was paradoxically relaxing. Toward sundown he drove west across the narrow strip of land that formed the Outer Cape, parking at First Encounter Beach. It was a fantastic place to watch the sun set over the tidal flats. Just as the sun started down, Eddie's phone lit up.

It was Shawna. *Oh, happy day!* This was progress.

He answered. "Hey, pretty lady! You'll never guess where—"

She cut him off.

"Eddie, there's been a situation, a bad situation, and you need to know." Her voice was strained, as if she was barely holding herself together.

"Go ahead," he said, suddenly feeling about ten degrees colder.

"Something happened this afternoon after we went to Cosmo's." Cosmo's was a little Greek restaurant serving pizza and subs along with slightly more substantial fare. A group of Solid Rock's twenty-somethings went there almost every Sunday. Eddie usually joined them.

"When we were leaving, these three guys jumped us in the parking lot." Shawna sounded breathless. "They had baseball bats! They beat down Big Eddie—can you imagine?—and he's hurt. Really hurt."

She was talking about Eddie Freeman. With two Eddies in the group, car guy Eddie Caruthers was "Fast Eddie" and the six-foot three-inch Eddie Freeman was "Big Eddie." He wasn't exactly a close friend, but he was as near to one as Eddie Caruthers had. He was a UPS driver; strong, boisterous, with a ready laugh. He and his parents had been members of Solid Rock almost as long as the Caruthers family had.

"How bad?" Eddie asked. "Is he in the hospital? How can I help?"

"It's really bad, but that's not the only reason I'm calling. I think it was a case of mistaken identity. They got the wrong man. I think they were looking for you."

For a few seconds, Eddie's heartbeat grew oddly erratic. "Go on," he said quietly.

"There was this new guy, a visitor. Ronnie somebody-or-other. He never told me his last name. He came to midweek service and seemed nice enough, interested in meeting people our age. When he came back again this morning, we invited him to come out to lunch with our group."

"What does Ronnie somebody-or-other look like?"

"He's white, tall, thin, kind of pale. Dresses all in black."

Eddie remembered seeing the man Wednesday. "Big hair? Like from an Eighties metal band?"

"Yeah, that's the guy."

"You think Ronnie Big Hair was one of the attackers?"

"No, he wasn't one of them."

"But you think he's connected with it?"

"Yes. Maybe. I don't know, I'm not sure. Please just let me explain at my own pace."

Eddie waited.

After a few seconds she began again.

"We went to Cosmo's. It was me, Lenny, Keiko, Amy, Carol, Brad . . . and Big Eddie. This Ron guy tagged along when we invited him. He was pretty chatty. He didn't have a lot of questions about the service, but seemed very interested in our group. Were there a lot of people our age in the church, did we always hang out together, that sort of thing. We ordered our food. He only ate a few bites of his meal before saying he had somewhere to be. Before he cut out, he shook hands again with everyone at the table and asked us our names again. I'm so bad with names myself, and I remember being kind of impressed he was taking the time to get ours right. He left right after that."

Eddie was sure Shawna would get to the attack eventually. He took a deep breath and resisted the urge to bounce up and down on his toes while he waited.

"Everyone else finished their lunch. Keiko, Brad, Big Eddie, and I were the last to leave. As we were walking across the lot, these three guys in baseball uniforms, sunglasses, and obviously fake beards came up to us. I didn't know if it was an early Halloween stunt, or one of those 'fear the beard' promotions baseball teams sometimes have. I thought it was weird, but not alarming.

"But as they were passing us, one of them looks over and says, 'Hey, are you Eddie?' Big Eddie says, 'Yeah?' You know, friendly enough, but like, 'Who are you?' Then all three of them started swinging the bats at him." Her voice quavered, becoming higher in pitch and volume. "Eddie, they hit him over and over, in the head, the arms, legs, everywhere. I swear I heard bones cracking. Blood was all over the place. I got his *teeth* on me. I mean, some of his teeth were knocked out, and *landed on me!*" She began sobbing in earnest now, reliving that moment.

Eddie wanted to console her, but she was a hundred miles away. He wanted to tell her everything would be all right—but would it? He listened in silence, because it was all he could do. He felt numb.

"Brad tried to help, but they hit him too. Keiko and I were screaming for help. People from the restaurant came running over. They were whipping out cell phones. I think some of them called 9-1-1. I think others just wanted video. This'll probably end up on YouTube, God help us. It's so sick . . . The guys in the beards all ran off down the alley. I don't know where they went after that.

"The ambulance came. We followed it to the hospital. He's in Framingham Union. We called his family. It's not looking good, Eddie. He's not conscious. He's brain injured. He's going to need reconstructive surgery on his face, and that's assuming he makes it."

"That's terrible," Eddie said. "I feel so bad for him."

Another long pause followed, punctuated by her sniffling. "I just keep seeing that Ron guy getting our names and leaving. I think it was a setup. The guy you fought must have heard us call you by name. I think he sent Ronnie to find a young black guy named Eddie at the church and then describe him to the attackers so they could jump him."

Eddie Caruthers was stunned. He paced in a circle, clenching the phone in his left hand and cradling his head with his right. He tried to untangle his thoughts. "The cell phone video might be a good thing. It could help ID the attackers." He paused. "I'm out of town right now, but I'll be back in the morning, and I'll go see him as soon as visiting hours start."

"I wouldn't just yet," Shawna said. "I just left there. His parents and sister were there. They pressed us for details about the attack. They agree that it was probably meant for you. You're not their favorite person right now. I think having to see you would just add to their stress."

"They think it's *my fault*?" Eddie dropped to his knees, closing his eyes in a futile effort to stop his head from spinning.

"They just need some space to process it all. We all do. *I* do. I need some space, Eddie. Do you know what I'm saying?"

Five achingly long seconds of silence followed. He'd spent so much time hoping they had some kind of a future together, and she was kicking him to the curb. She had put it to him gently, but it was still rejection. "Yeah. I know exactly what you're saying."

After inquiring to be sure no one else had been hurt, Eddie rang off. The air was calm and unseasonably warm. The sunset was glorious, all orange and gold splashed across a purpling sky. Eddie stood on the beach, looking without seeing, feeling his world fall apart. Feeling helpless.

CHAPTER 6
AND WHITHER THEN?

When Eddie got home Sunday evening, his father came over to give him the news about the attack. Explaining that he'd heard it from Shawna, Eddie supplied a few details his father didn't have. He stayed quiet about the mistaken identity angle, and Donald Caruthers gave no indication he was aware of it. After lamenting the senselessness of it all, they prayed together for Brother Freeman's recovery before parting.

On Monday morning Eddie was back at work. At eight thirty, he turned on his cell phone and booted up the desktop computer. Upon checking his personal email, he saw a message from Pastor Bowers. There was no subject line. Eddie guessed the man wanted to get on his case for being absent Sunday.

Eddie opened the message. No salutation. The body read:

By now you have doubtless heard about the horrible turn of events that befell Bro. Freeman. He is severely injured, and it may be only the prayers of the saints that are keeping him alive. I think we both know this attack was not random. Though you were too stubborn to admit your errors during our meeting last week, I trust you can now see how your folly has rebounded on us. During service this Wednesday, I will need to inform the church of his condition. After that announcement, I expect you to make an abject apology to the congregation for the way you failed to live up to our standards, and how your failure impacted the church in terms of last week's vandalism and this week's attack. This is not a request. This is what I require. If you do not comply, you will be stood up before the church, rebuked, and then silenced. If you do not show up for the service, you will still be silenced, and I will have to make an announcement concerning why. I strongly advise you to show up and do the right thing. But whether you do or not, this craziness must end now.

—Pastor

So it had come to this. Being silenced wasn't exactly a death sentence, but it was the closest thing the church had to one. It would make Eddie practically invisible to his fellow church members. He would be expected to show up at services, but could not participate in the life of the congregation. He couldn't testify, or sing or play an instrument, or do anything at all besides sit and listen. He was not to attend extracurricular activities like church picnics or fellowship outings. Informal get-togethers among friends, like the Sunday run to Cosmo's restaurant, would be off-limits to him. He couldn't join with other church members in praying for each other on the altar, because even his prayers would be unwelcome. As far as Eddie was concerned, the

Amish had it better. When they shunned someone, that person was forced to leave. At Solid Rock, the *persona non grata* had to stay there and feel the hostility, drink in the disapproval of the group, until such time as the sentence was lifted.

Eddie had never been subjected to this treatment, but he knew more than one person who had. He knew that everybody in the church would go along with the punishment, enforcing it whether or not they agreed with it. Obedience to leadership was one of the cardinal virtues of a good church member.

Eddie knew he was being offered a plea bargain. He could fall on his sword, admit to wrongdoing in spite of his belief that he was innocent, profess remorse, and endure the loss of face before the group. But that would also mean enduring the shame of knowing he had falsely recanted his own beliefs. Or he could refuse, and the ecclesiastical "court" would throw the book at him. Bowers was prosecutor, judge, jury, and executioner. One way or the other, Eddie was about to be convicted. The only question was what kind of sentence he would have to serve. Surrendering to the pastor's demands would be painful. Being indefinitely cut off from all fellowship would be worse. Nothing would happen before Wednesday evening, but he was beginning to feel desolate already.

Two potential customers came to the lot while Eddie thought on these things. He stumbled and mumbled through his conversations with them, and not surprisingly, came nowhere close to selling a car. He regretted having opened his email. This was no way for a salesman to go through a day.

When afternoon came, his phone started blowing up. At least half a dozen people from church wanted to be sure he knew what had happened to his friend. He assured them all that he knew, and that he was praying for Brother Freeman's recovery.

The TV news recapped the story of the attack, apparently having covered it in detail Sunday night. News anchors read teleprompters with practiced somberness and intoned about the shocking brutality of the attack that took place in broad daylight on a Sunday afternoon across from a church. As if to punish himself, Eddie listened to their accounts over and over.

One reporter interviewed the owner of Cosmo's restaurant, who expressed dismay that such a crime had happened right outside his door. He added that he was especially saddened that the victim was "one of those nice young people from the church" who were good customers and ate there all the time.

Eddie considered what a close call he'd had. Had he not been so angry about Pastor Bowers playing the Shawna card last Wednesday, he would have been in service yesterday. And he would have gone to lunch with the rest of the gang. Of course, the attack would have played out differently; he was very conscientious about maintaining his personal space, and he would not have let three armed strangers get so close to him. Because armed was what they were, and he would have seen the bats as weapons, not mere sporting equipment. *Yeah, unless I was so busy gazing dreamily into Shawna's eyes that I let my guard down.* He shuddered at the thought.

And once the attack began, what could he have done? Three-on-one was too much for empty-hand fighting, especially when you considered the bats. He would have had to draw his gun. Simply drawing the weapon might have been enough to end the threat. If it were not, he would have had to fire at moving targets . . . in a crowd . . . while unsure of his backstop. A shooter had to be aware of where a bullet would go if the shot missed. Without something solid nearby like an earthen berm to act as a backstop, bullets that missed their targets would travel a mile or more until they finally hit something or someone. That was a potential disaster. And if church folks had been shocked that he was willing and able to use his fists, the use of a gun would have them shrieking and passing out.

The steady stream of phone calls kept him informed about goings-on at the hospital. Because the patient had not regained consciousness, most visitors contented themselves with congregating in the waiting room of the ICU. Someone left a guest book in the care of his mother, who was there all the time. Each time a visitor arrived, he or she would write a note in the book. All hoped that Brother Freeman would soon wake up and take comfort in knowing how many had come to see him, say a prayer, and encourage his family.

The workday finally crept to a conclusion. Eddie went home, ate a takeout pizza for dinner, and immediately crawled into bed. His dreams were full of fighting and bloodshed and Shawna's hooded eyes. In one nightmare, Eddie found himself in a dark, brush-choked ravine, trying to climb a narrow trail up out of the shadows and onto a broad sunlit plain. His way was blocked by hordes of enemies. Some wore the armor of ancient Roman soldiers. Some wore baseball uniforms. All had angry faces and fearsome weapons. Most were strangers, but he recognized Loudmouth, his hefty passenger Raspy, and Ronnie Big Hair. Eddie fought them all, and one by one, they fell under his furious assault. A medieval knight wearing a silk tie over his chain mail shirt swung a huge broadsword, the double-edged blade arcing toward Eddie's neck. The knight's visor was open, and the face it revealed looked like Pastor Bowers. Eddie ducked the blow, and the momentum of the swing carried the knight off the trail, where, weighed down by his armor, he floundered in the mud. After each victory, Eddie looked up and saw Shawna's face hovering above him, saw her lips form the words *I care for you.* But each time, she was farther away. When he finally vanquished the last enemy and staggered into the light, she was nowhere to be seen. He groaned in his sleep, and whether it was from dreamland battle injuries or feverish longing, who could tell?

Tuesday morning came too soon, and he felt no less miserable than he had on Monday. At least Jason left him alone. It would have taken either a mighty move of God or an act of Congress to make his usually silent sibling start a conversation. But nearly everyone else Eddie knew seemed bent on talking to him about what had happened. He let his voicemail run interference.

By afternoon, some of the messages on his phone mentioned how people were beginning to notice the absence of the name

Eddie Caruthers in the guest book. They were sure it was just an oversight. Did he not know about the book? He must have stopped by to visit already, right? Especially since rumor had it that the attack had been meant for him. Surely he wouldn't want anyone to think he didn't care enough to be there for his friend, they suggested. Eddie didn't feel up to explaining that, when she'd called him on Sunday, Shawna had advised him to stay away. He gritted his teeth in frustration and concluded that this week couldn't possibly get any worse.

And then it did. Having learned from the proprietor of Cosmo's that the victim was part of a church group from Solid Rock, a TV reporter decided to interview the pastor. Reverend Bowers wore his charming-but-world-weary expression for the occasion. He was careful not to broadcast specifics about the patient's condition. But he said prayers were definitely needed. He also volunteered this: Eddie Freeman had no known enemies, so this shameful incident was most likely a case of mistaken identity. Asked to elaborate, he would say only that an altercation had occurred nearby in recent weeks, and he suspected the attackers were seeking revenge on one of the involved parties. If so, they had attacked the wrong man.

When Eddie Caruthers heard this interview on the news, he slammed both fists on his desk. *Is the preacher really out to get me killed? Or is he just dumber than a box of rocks?* If Loudmouth and his minions heard they'd gotten the wrong guy, they might come looking for the right one. Since the media had identified the victim by name, the ruffians could easily learn more about

Eddie Freeman and his friends. They might look him up on Facebook. Was Big Eddie's friend list private? Eddie sure hoped so, since he was on it. His photograph might jog Loudmouth's memory. And then they'd have his last name.

Eddie hurriedly logged onto Facebook and changed his privacy settings so that only friends could see his profile and photographs. That would keep outsiders from viewing his page, assuming they hadn't already. But it wouldn't keep them from seeing his pictures and posts on the pages of other people. Ronnie Big Hair had been careful to get the names of several of those people.

What if they obtained his last name and did a web search? They'd find the website for Fast Track Automotive. They'd find his home address, since his landline phone was in the White Pages.

He assumed they wouldn't send Ronnie to track him down. That would be too obvious. But any shoppers at FTA might be there to jump him while pretending to look at cars. The possibilities for ambush multiplied rapidly in Eddie's mind.

For the next hour, his emotional pendulum oscillated between anxiety and rage. When gripped by visions of ambush from unknown assailants, he could feel his blood pressure spiking, feel his heart twist in his chest cavity. These fearful sensations only added to the stress, threatening to send it spiraling out of control. Then the pendulum would swing to rage; rage against the animals who had hurt his friend; rage against the idea of a spiritual shepherd who flogged and blackmailed the sheep. He felt like smashing something or someone for putting him through this emotional wringer. The mood swings were exhausting. By five that afternoon, he was pacing his office and breathing hard. Suddenly he remembered that he was due at Mike's for his training session at seven. And that thought helped him regain control.

Mike had always taught that emotion was not your friend, something Eddie had forgotten this afternoon. In a fight, rage might make you feel stronger, but it actually worked against you. The stress hormones it released destroyed your fine motor skills, narrowed your field of vision, and sapped your stamina. Anger and fear were emotional luxuries a serious fighter could not afford. Eddie began breathing deeply and slowly, slowing his heart, calming his mind. He told himself that fear was a relic of childhood. He could put it down at will.

The LORD is my light and my salvation; whom shall I fear? The LORD is the strength of my life; of whom shall I be afraid?

He broke into an involuntary smile, remembering the thing that had surprised him most when he'd first seen Mike Manzanetti competing. The usually jovial man had almost no facial expressions inside the ring. "Never let an opponent see that they have hurt you," Mike always said. "At best, an enemy will derive satisfaction from your pain. At worst, they'll be inspired to greater efforts." The trainer practiced what he preached. Even in contests against larger, stronger opponents, he always looked more like a man concentrating on winning a chess match than one who was engaged in a dangerous struggle.

Eddie was grateful for the lesson and the example. He was under attack by multiple opponents. It was high time to stop wallowing in his feelings and put on his game face. He was on the defensive now, but would never win a fight by playing defense all the time. If all went well from here on out, he'd be able to turn things around and start fighting back, go from being hunted to being the hunter.

A week ago, the idea of getting out of town had been all about charting his own course, making his own decisions, and breaking out of the dull confines of his overly scripted life. Now getting away had become a tactical necessity. He'd had no real timetable for leaving before. Now he'd have to leave as soon as possible. *Tomorrow? I think I can do that.* Where exactly would he go? No idea. First things first: Get away from ground zero. Get out of range. Then come back when he could set the time, place, and tempo of the fight. Some people had a lot to answer for, and Eddie was determined to make sure they did.

Even as that thought occurred to him, he remembered that vengeance was not a Christian principle. Somewhere in the book of Romans it was written, ". . . avenge not yourselves . . . Vengeance is Mine, I will repay, says the Lord." That made him pause for a moment. Then he shook his head, denying the charge his conscience was trying to level at him. *I'm not avenging myself, I'm avenging a friend. In fact, it's not even vengeance—it's justice.* That bit of mental legerdemain wasn't enough to make him feel entirely right about his desire for payback. But he decided that it was close enough. If any gray area was involved, he could live with it.

In the meantime, he had a lot to do and little time in which to do it. He needed a clear head and a calm heart. He took another deep breath, let his face settle into an expressionless mask, and started writing lists.

That evening at Mike's, the two men sat on the mat and talked instead of training. Eddie explained the apparent connection between his fight with Loudmouth and the attack on Eddie Freeman.

"How do you feel about that?" Mike asked. "Guilty?"

"No, not guilty," Eddie said. "I feel terrible about what happened, but it wasn't my doing."

"Good. You did right, so you can hold your head up." He looked quizzically at Eddie's crestfallen expression. "So what's the problem?"

"Well, you know I spend a lot of time at church. Things are getting difficult there." Eddie told Mike about the email he'd gotten, and what silencing meant.

Mike shook his head. "Is this the place you always used to invite me to?"

Eddie nodded. He was feeling conflicted about having this conversation. He needed to be able to talk to someone, and it couldn't be a church member. Speaking critically of leadership within the church was considered sowing discord, a serious offense. But he couldn't really talk to outsiders either. The church was a family, and you weren't supposed to take family troubles to outsiders. At least that's what he'd always heard taught.

When Eddie didn't say anything, Mike got to his feet and began pacing. "Let me ask you this: suppose a man and his wife have a disagreement. He tells her that it's her wifely duty to obey him, and that if she refuses to obey, he will make her life miserable. Would you call that man abusive?"

Eddie paused a few seconds before replying. "It's not exactly like that. It's a good church most of the time. They're mostly good people. What the pastor is doing to me is horrible, but I think in his own twisted way, he thinks it's the right thing to do." He couldn't believe he was feeling the need to defend Greg Bowers and Solid Rock. He'd be a pariah there by this time tomorrow. Why offer excuses for a man about to demolish his reputation and cut him off from his friends? For that matter, why leap to the defense of friends who would become ex-friends the minute the pastor told them to? Isn't defending their abusers what many battered women did? 'My husband is a good man. He's just under a lot of pressure,' said the wife with the black eye and the broken arm. This was insane.

"I figured it must be a pretty good place most of the time," Mike said. "Otherwise, you wouldn't go there. But does that change the fact that what's happening to you now is abuse?"

Eddie grimaced. He agreed with Mike's conclusion, but didn't like hearing it from an outsider.

"I guess the practical question," Mike continued, "is what are you going to do about it? Why don't you join a different church?"

Eddie knew how hard that would be. Moving to another church in the same denomination would require a letter of transfer from his pastor. Under the circumstances, no such letter would be granted. Finding a church in another denomination that had the same faith tradition would be difficult. New England wasn't exactly a hotbed of Pentecostalism. And he'd heard most pastors weren't keen on taking in new members who were fleeing church troubles elsewhere. Eddie couldn't explain all that to Mike, so he just said, "That would be easier said than done. It's kind of a long story."

Mike was still pacing. "You're about to become an outcast in your own church, and you can't join a different one. I don't really get that, but I'll take your word for it. What about your other friends, the ones outside the church?"

Eddie was at a loss for words. He *had* no close friends outside of church. The cultural chasm between the people of Solid Rock and the rest of society was too great. Church members didn't smoke, drink, dance, or curse. They didn't tell risqué jokes, or laugh at them. They didn't approve of immodest dress or sex outside of marriage. They loathed Darwin, loved Jesus, and would rather attend a good worship service than the Super Bowl. To avoid being corrupted by the world, they had limited fellowship with people who didn't share their values. Bowers regularly quoted the Bible verse that said "Come out from among them and be separate, says the Lord. Do not touch what is unclean, and I will receive you." Mike was the only unchurched friend Eddie had, and the two of them never socialized outside of

PART ONE: TRANSITIONS

training sessions. But Eddie couldn't admit to having no other friends without seeming pathetic. This conversation needed a change of direction.

"It's a moot point," Eddie said. "I have to leave home for a while. There's a good chance the bad guys know where I live and work. I can't sit still and be a target."

"Do you need a place to stay? We have a spare room you could crash in." The offer caught Eddie by surprise. It was heartwarming and a little confusing. Mike was being more of a friend than any of the people who were supposed to love him.

"Thanks. I really appreciate the offer, but I have a road trip planned. I'll be leaving tomorrow. I'm gonna see a bit of the country, and come back when the time seems right."

"No problem, bro. Enjoy your travels. Stay safe. And come back here when you're ready. My door's always open." The two men shook hands, and Eddie departed.

By noon Wednesday, he'd checked off most of the items on his lists. He'd packed his bags. He'd secured the services of a mail drop so he could change his mailing address now and have his mail forwarded to wherever he eventually landed.

He'd also written a check for the stealthiest car on the lot, an Anthracite Gray 2004 BMW 540iT. The T was for *Touring*, BMW-speak for station wagon. He chose it because he had an immediate need for cargo space. The extensive FTA performance upgrades were an added bonus. While enduring the hour-long wait at the Registry of Motor Vehicles, he comforted himself with thoughts of the driving pleasures this car would bring.

After getting the plates on, he transferred a suitcase, duffle bag, gym bag, toolbox, and laptop case from the trunk of his demo to the new wagon. They contained everything he'd need for an extended road trip. Then he removed the demo plate from the Mercedes and headed to his father's office. He anticipated that this meeting might be the most difficult thing on today's agenda. He figured that by having it at work, the meeting would not have a chance to run long.

They talked for an hour. Dad had listened intently when Eddie shared his suspicions that the attack on his friend had been meant for him. He told him how the pastor's news interview might have jeopardized his security.

"I understand," his father said. "You need some time off?"

"I do," Eddie replied, "but there's more." He described his meeting with Bowers and the emailed ultimatum that had followed it two days ago. He watched the beginnings of a scowl forming on his father's face.

"Do you want me to intervene?"

Eddie knew the next conversation between Greg Bowers and Donald Caruthers wouldn't be fun for Bowers if Eddie said yes. Dad might cow his own children, but he wouldn't tolerate others doing it. Eddie judged him one of very few men in the congregation with the gumption to stand up to the overbearing preacher.

"No need," he said, trying to keep the disappointment out of his voice. "I'm not giving in to his demands. I'm not going back, either."

The patriarch's scowl deepened. His family had attended Solid Rock for more years than Bowers had been there. Having his whole family there most every week was one of his chief joys, and he frequently said so.

"One more thing," said Eddie. He wanted to get this part over with before his father could object to the idea of his leaving Solid Rock. "I think this is as good a time as any to make a clean break with everything. Much as I've enjoyed working here, selling cars is not really in my blood. Neither is fixing them. I'm not sure what I want to do with my life, but this isn't it. Maybe while I'm away, I'll figure out what is."

"Hold on a minute. I know things are stressful now, but don't let stress push you into a mistake. I don't think you appreciate what an opportunity you have here. How many young people do you know who are in line to inherit a business like this? Some people would give their right arm for the very thing you want to throw away."

"I do appreciate it," Eddie protested. "It just feels like an arranged marriage. I want to find my own path, not walk one someone laid out for me."

"You want to 'follow your passion' like all the self-help books are always blathering about?" He wagged a finger at Eddie. "That sounds nice, but it's not practical. If I'd followed my passion I'd probably be another history major waiting tables. But even before I was your age, I felt a responsibility to my future wife and children to spare them the kind of hardships I went through. I wasn't brought up in the kind of luxury you were."

Eddie knew all about his father's hardscrabble upbringing. The whole family had heard the stories countless times: how Dad was the youngest of six children born to an unskilled laborer and a domestic servant; how the eight of them were crammed into a drafty old house in a Dorchester slum; how they struggled to keep the heat in, the rats out, and the lights on. Donald Caruthers had been the first in his family to go to college. Though he loved art and history, he had refused to squander his financial future on such impractical degrees. He had majored in automotive service management and gotten a job in the service department of a new car dealership in Framingham.

Dad was bent on covering the highlights again. "I worked hard and saved my money. Your mother and I did without a lot. And when the time was right, I put my life savings into buying the run-down garage that used to sit on this property. I took an enormous chance so my children wouldn't have to." Eddie resisted the temptation to say that last line in unison with his father. A display of smart aleck would be neither wise nor helpful.

"I admire you for that. And I may not be half as successful as you," Eddie said, making his tone as conciliatory as possible. "But I want the chance to succeed or fail at my own dreams." He explained that he had been developing the itch to strike out on his own for a long time and how these events had made it clear that the time was now. He wished to receive the salary and vacation pay that was due him. He was sorry for the short notice, but it couldn't be helped. He handed his father the plates to the demo and the keys to the apartment over the garage. Dad could do as he saw fit with the apartment. He could rent it out as a furnished unit or put the furniture into storage for Eddie to claim later.

His father didn't resist further. His posture went slack, like a sail with the wind gone out of it. The look in his eyes was sad. Or weary. *Defeated.* Eddie urged him not to take it hard. His father said something odd in reply:

"When I was young, I had a lot of dreams. Some of them, I've achieved. Most, I haven't. At some point in my life, I stopped dreaming for myself, and started dreaming for my wife and my children. Your mother is gone. You are leaving. I don't have a lot of dreams left to me."

They had both choked up a little at that. In the end, Dad shook Eddie's hand, hugged him, and wished him well. He said, "You'll always have a home here, if you ever decide you want it. Whatever else you do, serve God and enjoy your life and I will be proud of you."

"I will," Eddie assured him. His father picked up the phone, called upstairs, and instructed the treasurer to cut Eddie a surprisingly large check. Eddie left the office and took a seat in the waiting room of the service area. Grabbing his phone, he fired off two emails. The first one was to Eddie Freeman:

Hey, bro, I'm pulling for you and praying for you to get better soon! I don't know when you will read this. It's been three days since those goons attacked you. However long it takes, I promise to do what I can to see that they are caught and punished. I'm going to be away for a while—maybe a long while—and I won't be able to come and visit. But you are not forgotten. Be strong. Get well. We'll talk again.

—Fast Eddie

The second email was to Shawna Bell:

Hi Shawna,

You asked for some space, and I'm about to give you more of it than you expected. I won't be in church tonight, or for the foreseeable future. I am relocating for an indefinite period.

I expect the Dear Leader to denounce me tonight, because I would not apologize for defending myself. Scripture teaches that we are God's property, body and soul. Surely stewardship of the body does not involve letting someone else damage or destroy it! Your pastor tried everything he could to force my hand, including threatening to end our budding relationship if I didn't do what he wanted. It turns out his machinations were unnecessary, as you decided yourself to back away from me before we had a chance to become—well, anything at all.

I would have thought you'd feel extra safe in the company of a man with both the mind-set and the means to defend you. Instead, you told me you feel less secure now that you know what I can do. I don't understand that. If you know me at all, you know I'd never hurt you.

All I did was stick up for our friend. I was protecting her. Roz has thanked me for that, but no one else seems to care. I didn't start the fight. It came to me. No one wants to talk about that either. People have leveled more criticism at me than at the man who attacked me. I'm as saddened as anyone by what happened to Big Eddie. But we're each of us liable for our own actions, and I will not be held responsible for the sins of other men.

I'm 27 years old. I've spent my life doing what other people thought I should do, and trying to be what other people thought I should be. Now I'm going to go discover who I really am. You urged me not to become someone you couldn't like. No promises on that front. But whatever I become, I will be something I have never been before—entirely true to myself.

I wish you all the best, Shawna. Take care of yourself.

Eddie hesitated, wondering whether to use "Love, Eddie" as a signoff. That didn't seem to fit the circumstances, a fact that filled him with fresh regret. So he simply typed *Eddie C* and hit the SEND button. For a moment, he imagined his words would change Shawna's mind. She'd see things his way. She'd write back and ask him to stay. She'd defy Greg Bowers and continue to date him. An intriguing fantasy, but Eddie knew that's all it was. Bowers had called Shawna a good church member who seeks her pastor's input on important decisions. She'd been raised on a steady diet of "obey them that have the rule over you," and "obedience is better than sacrifice." She would do as she was told. He would never hear from her again.

Thinking on that fact gave Eddie the impetus to take the next step in his plan. He deleted his email account from the ISP. He didn't want to have to look at a long list of old correspondence from people who wouldn't be speaking to him after tonight. If he was going to start fresh, he wanted a totally blank canvas.

He went upstairs. Jason was sitting in his office crunching numbers, and handed his younger brother an envelope containing his check. "I'm out of here," Eddie said. In reply, Jason grunted, barely looking up. Eddie almost laughed. With so many things changing so fast, Jason's reliable stoicism was strangely comforting.

Two minutes later, he was in his car, weighing his options. He could go anywhere he wanted. So where did he want to go? He had considered a lot of potential destinations over the last ten days, but hadn't settled on any. He thought of a stanza from one of Bilbo's songs in *The Fellowship of the Ring*.

> *The road goes ever on and on,*
> *Down from the door where it began*
> *Now far ahead the road has gone,*
> *And I must follow if I can*
> *Pursuing it with eager feet*
> *Until it joins some larger way*
> *Where many paths and errands meet;*
> *And whither then? I cannot say.*

PART TWO
EXPLORATIONS

CHAPTER 7
TABLE FOR ONE

Traveling with no fixed destination felt oddly liberating. Eddie knew only two things he wished to accomplish immediately: he wanted to drive through his old neighborhood one last time, and he wanted to put as much distance between himself and his troubles as possible.

Driving down Salem End Road, he supposed he had joined the tail end of the world's longest parade, a centuries-long procession of escapees. This road had been a narrow Indian path back in 1693 when several families escaping the infamous Salem Witch Trials had fled down it and founded the settlement of Salem End in what would soon be called Framingham. It was fitting that his journey should begin here, where the echoes of religious tyranny still reverberated.

There was predictable irony in the fact that the Puritans had fled persecution in England by sailing to America, where they swiftly became the persecutors. That was the way of the world. As soon as one group broke free of the control of another, it sought to impose greater control over its adherents. The oppressed became the oppressors, spawning an endless cycle of anguish and alienation. If history were a song, that would be the refrain. Bowers had merely written the latest verse.

Eddie could easily think of a dozen individuals who had fallen out with the leadership of Solid Rock over the years. Where had they gone? He had no idea about most of them. Dozens more had doubtless left on bad terms, people whose names and faces he couldn't even recall. Out of sight, out of mind; in church, the show goes on, and only the players change. Those who leave fade from the collective memory of the congregation, just as he himself now would. He'd be denounced tonight, and forgotten soon enough. Ten years from now, the majority of people at the church might be newcomers who had never heard of him.

Solid Rock's parent organization had about three thousand churches nationwide. That was small as denominations went. A big group such as the Southern Baptist Convention probably had ten or fifteen times that number. There must have been hundreds of thousands of churches of various kinds across the country. How many millions of people since the Witch Trials had been forced to upend their lives and start over as they fled one church group or another? If the ghosts of Salem End Road could testify, they'd say that heartache was the principal export of organized religion.

Stop it, he scolded himself. *You're starting a new life.* He'd never get a new outlook in his old haunts. It was time to escape the familiar.

He definitely had the right car for it. The 540i Touring put out 291 horsepower in stock form. But the raft of FTA modifications to this car included a supercharger and an appropriate engine management chip along with upgrades to wheels, tires, suspension, clutch, brakes, and exhaust. To the untrained eye, Eddie's car looked like any grandma's grocery getter, albeit with dark tinted windows and a somewhat aggressive stance. But it was really a 500 horsepower, fire-breathing dragon that could run away from most cars on the highway and out-handle even smaller, lighter cars on twisty back roads. Eddie couldn't wait to get to some of those.

He looped over to Route 9 and then picked up the Pike heading west. He pictured the whole country stretched out in front of him. Contrary to his usual habit, he left the radio off in order to listen to the music of the V8 engine and the Michelin Pilot Sport tires.

Massachusetts gave way to Connecticut, and Connecticut became New York. But interstate highways were uninspiring, no matter how cool the car. The view of tractor trailers, billboards, and rest areas never changed. Four hours after leaving Framingham, a restless and fidgety Eddie crossed the Delaware River into Pennsylvania and pulled off the highway in Matamoras. He bought a map at a Sunoco station and studied it over pancakes and eggs at a restaurant packed with senior citizens having an early dinner. It was an apt setting for Eddie, who thought of himself as an old soul in a young body. He preferred twenty-year-old cars to brand new ones, and outfitted them with period-correct wheels and audio systems. His preferred classic rock of the seventies and eighties was often supplemented with jazz and popular music from a generation earlier. And he never relied on GPS when he could find a proper map. A map let him see the whole state at once, and see how everything connected to everything else. Maps didn't track and broadcast his whereabouts. He didn't have to worry about the battery life of a map, or about someone breaking into his car to steal it. Tech was like morality; the old ways were usually better.

The restaurant was on U.S. Route 6, a road that traversed the entire state from east to west. It looked like a good route to explore. He drove until ten, and with nothing to look at in the dark, stopped at the next motel he happened to see. A sign at the entrance advised hunters to please wipe the mud off their boots before entering. Yep, he was in the country now. He was about to explore a world much larger than his little patch of Massachusetts. This trip would be a rebirth of sorts, the creation of a new life where all the decisions were his. He fell asleep dreaming of the possibilities. And the evening and the morning were the first day.

The next morning he set up a new email account and then opted for some Bible reading. He was pleased to find a Gideon's Bible in the nightstand, since his was packed somewhere in his luggage. Eddie often started his day by reading the chapter in

Proverbs that corresponded to the calendar date. Today was the sixteenth, so he turned to chapter sixteen. He read:

16:2: All the ways of a man are pure in his own eyes,
But the LORD weighs the spirits.

I guess that means the Bishop of Blowup is feeling perfectly fine about ambushing me.

16:6: In mercy and truth
Atonement is provided for iniquity;
And by the fear of the LORD one departs from evil.

You'd think church would be a good place to go to obtain mercy . . . but you'd be wrong.

16:24: Pleasant words are like a honeycomb,
Sweetness to the soul and health to the bones.

People like Bowers don't do pleasant. They'd view that as pandering. They need to be nasty to feel pure.

16:32: He who is slow to anger is better than the mighty,
And he who rules his spirit than he who takes a city.

How low on the spiritual totem pole does this verse put our fearless leader?

And so it went. In the eleven days since Reverend Bowers attacked him from the pulpit, nearly every biblical passage Eddie read somehow called all the bad memories to mind. Today was worse than usual. He was working himself into a truly foul mood. This was no way to start the day. If reading the Bible was going to do this to him, maybe he should just take a break for a while and come back to it when this episode in his life had blown over.

Putting the Bible back in the drawer, he went in search of breakfast before checking out of the motel and resuming his trip. Billboards informed him he was traveling in Potter County, and that Potter County was "God's Country." Now that he was driving in daylight, he had to admit that the landscape was glorious indeed. Surely no more potent elixir existed than blue skies, warm sunshine, and fresh air. The views were of sparsely populated back country, all fields, meadows, and rolling hills resplendent in fall hues. Autumn was a feast for the senses: the parade of colors; the whisper, rustle, and crunch of leaves; the smell of earth and drying vegetation.

Hamlet by hamlet, he crossed the state. The road in between villages was largely devoid of cars; no hint of the kind of traffic volume that was ubiquitous on the East Coast. While traversing the Allegheny National Forest—did he really have the whole road to himself now?—he grinned at a sign pointing toward State Route 666. How could he *not* check out something called The Devil's Highway? Shawna would not have approved of driving on this road, or on any road at the speeds Eddie was now going. But despite the evil name, Route 666 was an exhilarating ride—thirty-two miles of S-curves, blind corners, hairpin turns, and drastic elevation changes in the middle of nowhere. In other words, it was pure bliss. It was for roads like this that Fast Track Auto built cars. Could anything be better? He shot a look of defiance at the empty passenger seat, and spoke as if addressing the ghost of dinner dates past: "Now *those*," he said while waggling his thumb at the serpentine road behind, "*those* are some breathtaking curves!"

For three weeks, the scenery rolled past Eddie's window, through Pennsylvania, Ohio, West Virginia, Virginia, and points south. Eddie was fascinated by every mile. He reveled in the most ordinary experiences. He watched a giant amber moon rise over a cornfield, saw a family of farmers carefully hanging tobacco leaves up to dry, and gaped at a tractor dealership bigger than most car dealerships he'd ever seen. On Virginia's eastern shore, he wondered at the sight of buzzards circling in the distance, and then smelled the enormous chicken processing plant that had drawn them. Though the putrid odor was bad enough to make him hold his breath, he enjoyed even this. He could experience a million sensations, a million places, and move on without becoming trapped in any of them. This was how freedom felt.

He kept a spiral notebook full of his impressions. There he jotted down odd place names such as inspirational town monikers Freedom, Harmony, and Economy in Pennsylvania and the whimsically named Possum Trot Road in Myrtle Beach, South Carolina. Maybe he'd settle down in one of those places. Maybe not. He was in no rush to decide.

He encountered no difficulties beyond the normal challenges of traveling as an armed civilian. He had to be careful not to let the butt of his concealed firearm clunk against the bench in a restaurant booth or become caught in the slats of a chair back. As he drove farther south, the weather grew too warm for a jacket, so he wore roomy pullover shirts whose fabric was heavy enough not to allow the weapon to "print through." And then there was the problem of public restrooms—a man with a belt holster couldn't just drop his pants in a bathroom stall in which the privacy partitions didn't reach clear to the floor. These were some of the reasons many people used fanny packs to carry their weapons, but that option didn't suit Eddie. Most people considered fanny packs to be a fashion faux pas, and street-smart people knew they were gun gear. No point in giving the bad guys a heads up. And if you had to get to the weapon, drawing from a fanny pack was unacceptably slow. So Eddie stuck with a hip holster on his strong side, balancing the two-pound weight by carrying a pair of spare ten-round magazines in pouches on his left hip.

Some would consider that much firepower excessive. But Mike always said, "Two is one, and one is none." Mike had two flashlights in each of his vehicles, and two spare tires. He and his wife had twin bug-out kits with the same emergency supplies in each. His computer files were backed up on an external hard drive as well as on flash drives stored in a safe deposit box. He'd made Eddie a believer in the wisdom of redundancy. It was better to have and not need than to need and not have. Two is one, and one is none. Let the unprepared think what they want.

The hardest part of traveling armed wasn't negotiating bathrooms or booths; it was complying with the hodgepodge of state laws that governed concealed carry. His Massachusetts carry permit was honored by only nineteen states. At Mike's suggestion, Eddie had gradually acquired nonresident permits from New Hampshire, Utah, and Florida. This combination of licenses meant he was good to go in all but fourteen states.

Of course, Eddie could simply leave the hardware concealed on his hips wherever he went, but that meant taking a big risk. Unlawful carry was a felony, and would dramatically raise the stakes at any minor traffic stop. Due to the illogic of limited reciprocity, he could legally carry in Virginia and West Virginia, but not in the tiny strip of Maryland that lay between them. He could go armed in New Hope, Pennsylvania, but could not join the crowds of pedestrians crossing the bridge into neighboring Lambertville, New Jersey. He carried a color-coded map in his center console to remind him of where he was legal and where he was not.

Other than having to be keenly aware of where he was on the reciprocity map, his days on the road were carefree. He started each morning with a workout before showering and having breakfast. Back in his room, he'd dry fire his pistol, endeavoring to maintain a smooth trigger pull that didn't make the front sight jump around. After fifteen minutes of that, he'd reload the gun and hit the road by ten. Every day was asphalt therapy. On Wednesdays and Sundays, he celebrated not being subject to one of his former pastor's angry pulpit harangues. He'd have to find a new church to join at some point, but for now it was good to be unattached. Each day he drove until dark and then got a room at the first lodgings he saw. Next on the agenda was a good dinner.

That was when his normally upbeat mood would take a turn for the worse. Evenings always ended the same way, with a table for one and no one to talk to. Seeing couples paired off at tables while he ate alone every night, or hearing laughing voices pass the door of his motel room while he binge-watched *Law & Order* reruns brought on intense bouts of loneliness.

This was an unsettling experience. It wasn't that he was unfamiliar with solitude. He'd felt alone in a crowd throughout high school and college, but in those days loneliness had seemed almost noble. He had been young, zealous, and on fire for God. If his faith and his moral aversion to pot, pills, and promiscuity made him an oddball on campus, he was okay with that. In those days, an almost romantic aura surrounded his solitude, akin to that of a starving artist in a garret suffering for devotion to his art. It had been easy for Eddie to find joy in it; if the world rejected him, must not God embrace him all the more? And he'd had the support of his family and of his church through it all. But now he had no one's support, and he'd been as soundly rejected by his church as he had ever been by the world. The sense of isolation was absolute.

Worse yet, he knew the injury done him by Gregory Bowers wouldn't stop with the termination of his relationships within the congregation. No, the pastor's greatest concern had always been managing his own reputation; he had to appear to be both right and righteous, in that order. Any action of his that might be second-guessed had to be vindicated. To be sure that no one felt even a little sorry for Eddie, that no one considered his punishment too harsh, it would be necessary for the pastor to deconstruct the congregation's memory of Eddie Caruthers.

It would begin with Bowers discussing some of Eddie's perceived flaws with the church leadership—under the pretense of training his staff on how to recognize and minister to such flaws in others. Eddie fumed at that. Later, the pastor would disclose some of his heretofore confidential dealings with Eddie so the listeners could better appreciate the burdens of pastoral ministry. Eventually he would publicly blow a gasket in the name of "transparency," denouncing Eddie in the most unflattering terms possible to everyone who would listen. Before he was done, the preacher would not only ensure that no one felt sorry for Eddie, he'd make sure that they regarded Gregory Clement Bowers as a paragon among pastors for having put up with that troublemaker for so long. Any fond memories of Eddie Caruthers would vanish as completely as Eddie himself had.

Earlier conclusions needed amending. He would not merely be forgotten by those he had called friends; he would first be despised, and *then* forgotten. Eddie sighed, resigned to a parade of thoughts grown darker than the night sky. He steeled himself for yet another evening spent pushing the food around his plate at a table for one.

"What was her name?"

He looked up to see a waitress standing in front of him. "Say again?"

"What was her name, honey? I figure a handsome guy like you wearing such a sad face *must* be having girl troubles." She laughed.

She was cute and charming, and Eddie laughed with her. "You're not wrong," he said. "But now that I see you, I can't rightly remember her name."

"Good answer," she replied. "I think we're gonna get along just fine." She laughed again. "My name's Charlene. I'll be taking care of you tonight. Can I start you off with something to drink, sweetie?"

Eddie ordered a Coke. When she returned with that, he ordered an appetizer. When that came, he chose an entrée and then a dessert after that. At each stage of his meal, the server returned to make sure everything was to his liking. Everything was, especially her.

Charlene was a strawberry blond with streaks of wine red dyed into her hair. She had big blue eyes and dazzling white teeth. Eddie found her cheerful energy infectious. She was on the short side, carrying a little extra weight, but she carried it well, striking Eddie as huggable rather than heavy. What really drew his eye was the way her restaurant-issue Polo shirt was unbuttoned to reveal some impressive cleavage. He wondered what the modern terminology was for describing Charlene's build. His mother would have called her "ample" or "buxom," but Eddie was sure those were old-fashioned words. And since good church men didn't discuss such things, he had never acquired a more current vocabulary for describing that fascinating expanse of flesh that danced so beguilingly as the woman went about her serving.

The restaurant wasn't packed, so Charlene had time for conversation with Eddie. As they talked, he learned that she was pursuing a degree in architecture at the Savannah College of Art and Design. For her part, she noticed his Yankee accent and asked where he was from.

"Boston," he told her.

"Did you fly in recently?"

"No, I drove in, about an hour ago."

"That's a mighty long drive just to get away from what's-her-name," Charlene teased. "So where does your trip end?"

"I haven't decided yet," Eddie replied. "I'm staying here tonight. I could head down to Florida in the morning. Or I could stick around here, if there's something to keep my interest. Tell me, what do people do for fun in Savannah?"

"Oh, a little of this and a little of that. What sort of things are you into?"

Eddie shrugged. To talk about his love of fast cars wouldn't seem original or memorable. To say he enjoyed good preaching would likely be a nonstarter too. He settled for, "I like a little of this and a little of that."

When he had finished his dessert and his third glass of cola, Eddie figured he'd stretched the evening's conversation with the magnetic young woman just as far as he could. He sighed, asked for his bill, and paid with a credit card. When she returned with his receipt, her name and phone number were handwritten across the top. He looked up at her, eyebrows raised in surprise. "In case you need help finding something fun to do in Savannah," she said, smiling as she glided away.

Eddie smiled back and tried to look as if this sort of thing happened to him every day. Inwardly, he wanted to dance. Here was one pretty girl who wasn't guarded and mysterious about her attraction to Eddie. Here was the anti-Shawna. *Might as well see where this goes.* He carefully folded the receipt into his wallet and headed for the door. Back in his hotel room, he skipped the TV routine and found some nice music on Pandora. He went to sleep that night with a smile on his face.

Wakefulness intruded on his pleasant dreams at nine. A call had come in at seven, and Eddie was glad he kept his phone on silent. There was no one he really wanted to talk to at such an ungodly hour. He saw the call was from his father, and made a mental note to call back later.

He spent the morning researching area restaurants online and reached Charlene just before noon. The rest of the day was devoted to getting ready. He got a haircut and a new shirt, and a bottle of that body spray that, according to the commercials, made women go weak in the knees. Satisfied that he would look and smell good, he started compiling conversational ideas. When dating a church girl, he could always talk about favorite gospel groups, how great youth conference had been, or whether or not random current events had prophetic significance. None of those topics would fly tonight. He found a magazine stand and browsed *Esquire, GQ,* and *Details* looking for tips and a shot of confidence. The glossy magazines seemed more trashy than helpful, not meant for guys like him.

Of course, guys like him didn't date girls like Charlene. His former friends would be aghast if they knew, lecturing him about separation from the world, being unequally yoked, and all that. That would be easy for them. They were laughing it up at Cosmo's, not dying of loneliness far from home.

His father called again. Twice. Eddie promised himself he'd do better at keeping in touch. He and Dad would have a good long talk tomorrow. But today was all about Charlene.

That evening, they met at a restaurant in a big stone building on the waterfront. The entrance faced the brick sidewalks and cobblestones of River Street, and the windows all looked out over the Savannah River. Charlene entered wearing black platform pumps with what must have been eight-inch heels. Eddie let his eyes flit up from her feet, over her calves and a generous portion of thigh, to a little black dress that was all lace from bodice to collar. *Yow! Talk about 'fearfully and wonderfully made'!* He greeted her with a smile and a little hug and happily nodded in the affirmative when the hostess asked, "Two?" before leading them to their seats.

They shared a dimly lit booth, with Charlene seated beside him rather than across from him. The server came to take their drink order, and Eddie barely registered her presence, so intoxicated was he with the attentions of his date. When Charlene ordered something called a Tropical Dream, a mixture of rum, schnapps, vodka, and fruit juices, Eddie had a moment of panic. The magazines had said women would judge him by his taste in adult beverages. This was no time to confess that he didn't drink. The only men who didn't drink at all were either devout religionists or recovering alcoholics taking it one day at a time. Coming across as either of those was the not the way to impress someone like her. Eddie asked for a list of the restaurant's beers and settled on Corona Extra—it sounded less plebian than anything from Budweiser or Coors—and he was afraid he'd be asked to explain any unusual selections like Heady Topper or Bourbon County Brand Coffee Stout. He hoped he'd like the Corona, since it was going to be his first taste of alcohol outside of a communion service.

The beer was tolerable. The food was fine. The conversation was great, with lots of laughter and prolonged eye contact. The slow drawl that so irritated him in his brother-in-law was sexy and exotic in his date. Charlene was a touchy-feely girl, frequently reaching out to pat his arm or grab his hand. After dinner, they strolled to a nearby dive bar for another drink and a game of pool. He played terribly, not having done it before, and she beat him handily. He didn't mind at all. Then they ambled up and down several blocks of the riverfront, holding hands. Eddie felt giddy. It wasn't the beers—he'd had only two, not much for a two-hundred-pound man who'd eaten a full meal. Maybe it was because this was all happening so fast. Or maybe it was the surreal feeling of taking a romantic stroll with a ravishing white girl in the Deep South, past businesses displaying both the Stars and Stripes and the Confederate Stars and Bars side by side.

They reached his car, and he stopped to show it to her. He opened the passenger door. Instead of climbing in, she threw her arms around his neck, pressed her body up against his, and pulled him into a long, smoldering kiss. Warm and wet, her lips tasted of citrus and alcohol and the promise of good things to come.

After he settled her into her seat, Eddie got in the driver's side, leaned over and kissed her again, cupping her face in his hands. She reciprocated eagerly. When the passionate lip lock was over, both of them were a little breathless. She leaned back. "I believe you were about to show me your car."

"Indeed I was. Behold!" he said, making a sweeping gesture to encourage her to take in the view of his black leather dash with its custom maple wood trim. There wasn't much to see in the dark of night.

She giggled. "Nice car. Well, if that completes the tour . . . what's next on the agenda?"

"I think this is the point where I'm supposed to ask you if you've had an enjoyable evening," he deadpanned. It required effort to keep from grinning and whooping. He hoped she couldn't hear the ecstatic hammer of his pulse pounding in his ears. That would spoil the whole nonchalant act.

"So far, so good," she conceded with a regal nod. Then, after a brief pause, "You know, I never asked you where you're staying while you're in town."

Eddie pointed off to the left. "I'm right there at the Marriott Riverfront."

"Oh, I've heard it's very nice. Do you have a room with a view?"

"Sure do. I'm on a high floor overlooking the river. It's one of the nicest rooms I've had on this trip."

"Well, I'd love to see it—if you'd care to invite a lady up." She trailed her hand lightly over his leg and batted her eyelashes theatrically.

Boom! There it was: Eddie's deepest desire and biggest fear conveniently rolled into one. His first thought was an exultant *Yes!* That was followed an instant later by wordless dread—along with a warning tingle at the base of his neck akin to what a mouse might feel as it sniffed the cheese in the trap. Torn, he desperately wanted a way out of this dilemma, but he didn't see one.

Just then, his pocket began to vibrate. Saved by the—well, it wasn't exactly a bell, but it would buy him a few seconds to clear his head. He resisted the urge to clutch at it the way a drowning man clutches at a flotation device. Instead, he calmly pulled the phone from his pocket, sighed, and stabbed the DISMISS button on the screen.

"I'm afraid I'm going to have to give you a rain check." Eddie had found a way out. Still, the regret in his voice was unfeigned.

"Well, I didn't see *that* coming," Charlene said, her voice dejected. "Please tell me that wasn't old what's-her-name."

"No, I don't expect to be hearing from her again. That was my father." He showed her the missed calls list on his phone, with the caller ID tag "Dad" next to all of them. "He's called me, like, four times today. It's not like him to chase me, so I think it's something serious. I need to call him back. This may take a while."

"It's late. You could call him in the morning," Charlene cooed. She trailed her fingers slowly up his leg again, boldly letting her hand go where no hand had gone before.

"You're not making this easy."

"I'm not trying to." She leaned in close to whisper the next bit, so close that her lips brushed his ear. "In fact, I'm trying to make it . . . *hard*."

Eddie's willpower was floating away on a tide of sensations: the moist tickle of her breath in his ear, the light scent of her perfume in his nostrils, the warmth of her hand where it lay. He felt himself a beast long in hibernation, now suddenly awaking to the urgency of his hunger. The rational part of his brain was getting difficult to access. At any moment, some internal fuse would blow, short circuiting conscious thought and leaving him nothing but instincts and primal urges. Long seconds passed. Somehow he managed to shake his head and decline her again. "If I'm going to spend the night with Savannah's most desirable woman, I want to do it with a clear head. I'd be too worried to be any fun tonight."

Charlene accepted this explanation with a sigh. She withdrew her hand and faced forward. He drove her back to her own car, kissed the back of her hand, and promised he'd be in touch soon. It was a lie, but he could think of nothing truthful that was more appropriate. They parted pleasantly enough considering she looked as disappointed as he felt.

Two years ago, if an attractive woman had hit on Eddie, he would have been flattered but not tempted. While he had the same testosterone-fueled urges as most men his age, he had always been too intent on matters of the spirit to indulge in gratifying the flesh. Something had changed. He'd always accepted that sex outside of marriage was immoral, but morality had precious little to do with why Eddie had just punted on fourth and inches with the game on the line. Of course, it wasn't about Dad either. That phone call was just a conveniently timed excuse.

He told himself it was a tactical decision made necessary by his gun gear. If they went back to his room, clothes would start coming off. How would he explain the lethal items strapped to his belt? That was one practical issue that none of his defensive training classes had addressed. But the solution to that problem was easy enough; he could duck into the bathroom, shed the hardware, and wrap it all up in a towel. He'd put the towel on the floor with a pile of others and that would be that. They could get on with the evening's festivities without her having a clue that she was the best-protected woman in Savannah.

He tried to pretend it was because she had been drinking, and he was too much the gentleman to take advantage. That didn't ring true either. She hadn't shown the slightest sign of being intoxicated. She couldn't have been too drunk to give informed consent. Besides, she'd been the one putting the moves on, not him.

No, he had punted for only one reason: a girl with confidence like Charlene's was doubtless an experienced competitor in the bedroom Olympics, while he was not. He might talk a good game, but he would prove to be out of his league when play started. He'd studied the map, but had never made the drive, and she would probably figure that out in less than two minutes. It would be humiliating. That could not be allowed, and that was the real reason he'd sidestepped his opportunity.

Contemplating this put a scowl on his face. It galled him that a lifetime spent developing competency in so many areas had left him so deficient in this one. *I'm twenty-seven years old. Tonight was my first beer. I'm a virgin. I've never even kissed a girl before today.* Well, actually he had, but Denise Montgomery hardly counted. That had been way back in the eleventh grade, in an empty classroom after school, the result of a reckless hormonal girl deciding that what she really wanted for her sixteenth birthday was him. Denise had followed him into the room, closed the door behind them, and switched off the light. Their little encounter had lasted all of thirty seconds when they heard approaching footsteps, and the girl had bolted. No, that didn't count. He was the world's greenest twenty-seven-year-old. He had sacrificed all of youth's rites of passage to adhere to his church's standards of behavior. And what did he have to show for it? He was alienated from the church, and he couldn't cut it in the world either. The only things that clean living and principled abstinence had deeded him were a colossal ignorance about women, years of repressed desires, and the feeling that he'd stupidly wasted his youth.

The rest of the evening consisted of an excess of vending machine snacks and several hours of *Cops* reruns in his hotel room. Would he ever in his life be with a girl as sexy as Charlene? He berated himself for running from an opportunity most guys would have joyfully crawled over broken glass to get. He listened to the paired voices going up and down the hall, and his lonely frustration felt sharper for being in such proximity to the happiness of others. He was in no mood to talk now. He'd call his father in the morning, just like Charlene had suggested.

Eventually, he fell asleep fully dressed and dreamed that Charlene had come back with him after all. Their discarded clothes lay scattered around the room. Under the covers, he scaled the heights of pleasure with her, their epic passion intensified by their mutual mastery of love's arcana. Golden shafts of morning sunlight found them blissfully asleep in each other's arms with the bedclothes artistically draped over their nakedness. Dreams can be good like that.

In the real world, Eddie awoke crusty-eyed and stiff-necked, clutching a pillow to his chest and wiping drool from the corner of his mouth. He was alone on the king-sized bed. It was a gray day, and he rubbed his throbbing temples as he recalled the events of the previous evening. He rolled to his feet and shuffled to the bathroom. After washing his face and gargling, he decided that this miserable moment was as good a time as any to return his father's call and find out what the news was. With a stab of fear, he hoped that it wasn't bad news about Big Eddie.

Dad was an early riser. It was just after seven, and he picked up on the second ring. After a few seconds of hello-how-have-you-been-where-are-you-and why-haven't-I-heard-from-you, his father broke the news he had been repeatedly calling about.

"I know I said you're always welcome to come home, and you are—but you have no apartment to come home to. There was a fire two days ago. The garage burned to the ground. Everything you had in there is lost. I'm sorry, son."

Eddie's first thought was that Dad had been driving an X5 of late. BMW had recalled some thirty-two thousand vehicles from model years 2008 to 2011, including the X5, due to a fire risk caused by a circuit board that was prone to overheat. But his father would have known that, and been on top of it. "That's terrible! What caused the fire?"

"It was arson. That much seems clear. The fire started around three in the morning, at the back wall under the rear deck. The fire department found traces of accelerant. The investigation is ongoing."

"Is the house okay?"

"Yes, the house is undamaged. It was too big a space for the fire to jump."

Eddie mentally tallied the contents of his apartment. "Well, it's a good thing I like to travel light. It seems my whole life is now in my car or in my hotel room."

His father chuckled. "Thankfully, one's life does not consist in the abundance of things he possesses. Your stuff can be replaced."

"That's true. Tell me, Dad—has there been a rash of arsons in the area lately?"

"I'm not aware of any."

"Then it's probably safe to say it wasn't a random crime. Whoever set the fire knew I lived there. They did it at a time when they expected me to be home and sound asleep."

"Yes, I know, son. Be extra careful out there."

Eddie hardly heard his father. He felt his anger rising. "Thanks to that knucklehead preacher's media comments, Loudmouth and company figured out their mistake. Then they tracked me down and tried to fix it. Big Eddie was lucky he wasn't killed weeks ago. And now I'm lucky *I* wasn't killed."

"I feel your frustration," his father said. "But I do wish you wouldn't refer to our pastor as 'that knucklehead preacher,' even if his interview was not exactly Mensa material."

"He's your pastor, not mine, but I'll be nice for your sake. How is Big Eddie doing, anyway?"

"He's doing somewhat better, thank the Lord." Donald Caruthers reported that Eddie Freeman had regained consciousness. He was still in the hospital undergoing multiple surgeries. He'd need physical therapy later, but he would live. This was progress. As for the garage, insurance would rebuild that, although both the insurance company and the police had politely inquired about the elder Caruthers's personal and business finances to rule out the possibility that he had a financial motive for burning down his own garage. Investigations were ongoing, and the authorities had already been informed of the potential link between the fire and earlier events. When the call ended, Eddie took stock.

This had serious implications. A guy with such murderous associates was probably mobbed up. The news reports would have broadcast that no one died in the fire, so they were likely to keep pursuing their vendetta. They were in the driver's seat because they knew who he was, while he had no idea who his potential killers were.

If the bad guys were mobsters, maybe they were known to police. A description of Loudmouth, Ronnie Big Hair and the Range Rover might help the police catch a lucky break. It was worth a shot. He called his father back and asked him to pass along the information to the investigators.

Eddie hit the motel gym for a tougher than usual workout fueled by anger and renewed determination. Returning to his room, he showered, checked out, and found a place to have breakfast. "Just one?" asked the hostess.

"Just one," Eddie replied. In this regard at least, life was back to normal. After breakfast he found his way to US 17 and took it south to Jacksonville, Florida. Then he meandered over to the A1A, putting him almost on the beach, and drove south again.

He considered the fire. Practically speaking, he hadn't lost much. He had his laptop and his phone with him. His passport and birth certificate were in a safe deposit box. He'd lost his furniture, some clothes, his sound system, exercise equipment, and some cookware he rarely used. He could replace it all over time. He was insured, so the financial hit wouldn't be huge. The greatest harm done was psychological; someone had wanted him *dead* badly enough to make an attempt on his life. This was the second such attempt; the attack on Big Eddie Freeman had been the first. He had to find these evil people and make them stop. He needed a plan.

His thoughts drifted back to Charlene. For a moment, he felt bad that he'd never learned her last name. Then he shrugged. What difference did it make? Their paths would never cross again. His memory of the details of her face was already starting to get fuzzy. Of course, it wasn't exactly her face he'd been looking at most of the time.

Eddie laughed mirthlessly. He had dodged a bullet, and he could see that now. Things always looked different in the light of day. Had he not bailed out, he would have had to spend this morning repenting. Fornication was serious stuff, a felony sin rather than a misdemeanor. As it was, his behavior last night had not been ideal. But sipping a few beers and admiring a fine feminine physique was not the same as actually doing the bad boogie. Or was it? There was scripture to the effect that a man who looked lustfully at a woman committed adultery in his heart. No question he'd been guilty of that. What man wouldn't be, seeing a girl like Charlene?

He shook his head in wonder. Adam and Eve had had it easy. They were only prohibited from *eating* the forbidden fruit;

Eddie wasn't even supposed to appreciate how good it looked. But right was right and rules were rules, no matter how much his testosterone-addled brain struggled with compliance. He promised himself that in the future he'd avoid temptations like last night's. It felt like the right decision, even though he could not bring himself to be happy about making it. Perhaps it would be easier when he found a new home and a new church.

Two days and more than four hundred miles after leaving Savannah, he had settled to the bottom of the country. He got a room in a bed and breakfast in Boca Raton, Florida. Wikipedia told him Boca was a small city with a population about a third larger than Framingham's. Like all of Florida, the landscape was flat. Judging from the resorts and the abundance of high-end cars, there was money in Boca. The temperatures were in the eighties every day, and the beach was right across the street from Eddie's B&B. A guy could get used to this.

On his third night in town, an idea hit him so forcefully it jolted him from sleep. He had been puzzling over how to track down Loudmouth when he had so little to go on. Now an obvious solution came to him. The pugnacious punk had been driving an expensive Range Rover with ostentatious aftermarket wheels. Someone who would shell out for that sort of automotive jewelry was likely a member of a Range Rover forum. If Loudmouth could be located online, odds were good Eddie could find him in the real world. Most people had no idea how many clues they left on social media about their real identities, even while they hid behind fanciful screen names.

An additional day of brainstorming gave him two things he'd lacked when he started his trip: a plan and an itinerary. Phase one of the plan was creating the false impression that he had moved down here permanently. It took him a couple of days to locate a furnished apartment with a month-to-month lease. He planned to take a bunch of selfies so he could post "at home" photos to social media over the coming weeks. Once he had signed the lease papers, he went to a nearby UPS Store and rented a mailbox. This would let him give out a Florida mailing address when needed, but still get his mail forwarded to wherever he was really living.

For the final touches, he logged onto his Facebook account for the first time since leaving Framingham. He had briefly considered deleting it when he deleted his email, but hadn't followed through. Now he was glad he hadn't. A quick glance showed him his total number of friends had declined noticeably. No surprise there. He hoped the ones that still remained would unwittingly help with his little subterfuge.

He changed his current city to Boca Raton. After taking a selfie with some palm trees in the background, he made it his profile picture. He changed his status back to public and posted, "No more winters for me. Don't hate." Anyone searching for his page, or monitoring those of any Solid Rockers who were still connected to him, would learn of his "relocation." Maybe that would prevent any more mysterious fires or savage beatings around Framingham.

The last step in the deception was to pick up a new SIM card for his phone. That would make all his calls originate from a

Florida area code. He called his father's house, leaving a voicemail message with his new address and phone number.

He wished his Boca Raton residency wasn't an elaborate hoax. He didn't want to leave Florida's tropical breezes for cold, dark, leafless Massachusetts in November, but it had to be done. That was phase two of the plan. He got excited thinking about the fruit the next phase would bear. Even his nightly table for one couldn't dampen his mood now. There was freedom in solitude. The ghost of dinner dates past no longer haunted the car. By the end of the week he was happily cruising northbound, hugging the coastline on secondary roads and listening to classic rock on the radio. And Three Dog Night's plaintive vocals notwithstanding, he no longer felt that one was the loneliest number.

CHAPTER 8
IT TAKES A FAST CAR

Eddie took a relatively direct route from Florida to Massachusetts, arriving in mid-November. Once back, he decided to live in "America's hometown": Plymouth. He chose it primarily because it was sixty miles from Framingham, making it unlikely that he would accidentally run into anyone from his old stomping grounds. Eddie also never tired of gazing at the ocean, and Plymouth was on the shore. The nicer beaches of Cape Cod were a short drive away, and Boston was easily accessible either by car or by water taxi. Eddie scoured Craigslist and quickly found a place that looked promising.

The landlord looked askance at him when he left the "employer" section of the rental application blank. Some places, like West Palm Beach in Florida and the priciest parts of New York City, were accustomed to dealing with trust fund beneficiaries who didn't need to do anything for a living. Most other places assumed you needed a job to be able to pay the rent on an apartment. But money talks everywhere. Eddie pulled out a copy of a recent bank statement and offered to write the man a check for three months' rent up front. The landlord approved his tenancy on the spot without even doing the background check or credit check that were listed as requirements in his advertisement.

The apartment was in the heart of downtown, across the street from a diner and within walking distance to everything. It was a two-bedroom unit on the third floor of a commercial building. Eddie didn't really need two bedrooms. His old place had just one. But the spare room would be great for workout equipment. If he threw in a sleeper sofa, he'd be all set for the occasional overnight guest. Not that he'd ever been in the habit of having overnight guests, but it was always a possibility once he made some new friends. He wondered when that might be.

A week after signing the lease, he ate a traditional Thanksgiving meal at the diner and thought about the town he now called home. "America's hometown" was, in fact, an odd choice of home base for someone trying to escape the past. Far more than most places, Plymouth was defined by its past. The names of streets, parks, malls, and pubs celebrated people and events from almost four hundred years ago. About a million visitors clogged the streets each year, most of them tourists seeking to gaze at Plymouth Rock and the replica of the Mayflower. History was always front and center in Plymouth. And that reminded Eddie of church, because history in Plymouth was *religious* history.

Children nationwide were taught the story of the first Thanksgiving as soon as they were old enough to make a crayon tracing of their hand on construction paper in crude imitation of a turkey's silhouette. They learned a simplified and sanitized version of the Plymouth narrative. That version of events hid the ugly complexities of reality just like the smiling faces and sunny prose on Solid Rock's website sugarcoated the experience of membership.

In the children's version, the humble Puritans in their odd headgear sailed away from England in search of a place they could be free to worship as they wished. They made landfall at Plymouth Rock. Led by William Bradford and Myles Standish, they built a settlement and were soon befriended by the local Indians, who taught them to plant corn in hills with fish for fertilizer. That fall, Pilgrims and natives sat down for turkey dinner, inaugurating America's annual celebration of food, family, and football. And they all lived happily ever after.

Eddie had inherited his father's love of history and knew the truth was messier than the official narrative. The Pilgrims first landed at Provincetown, not Plymouth Rock. Their landing party robbed an Indian grave and stole food from a teepee. They encountered armed resistance from the Nauset tribe at First Encounter Beach, and soon sailed across the bay to Plymouth. There they met Squanto, a Patuxet Indian and former slave of the English who brokered a lasting peace between the Puritans and their immediate neighbors.

Despite peace with the natives, the Pilgrims were at war with themselves within five years. A minister was expelled in 1625 for meeting with a group of people who wished to return to the old ways of worship they had in England. One of his supporters, John Oldham, was sentenced to run a gauntlet of men who beat him with the butts of their muskets. In disgust, a Puritan named Roger Conant broke with the Plymouth leadership and founded his own settlement at Salem. Years later, the Puritans of Salem became infamous for their own brand of fanaticism. That the Salem Witch Trials were widely remembered, while the excesses of the Plymouth Puritans were not, was one of the quirks of history.

Eddie couldn't help but compare the New England Puritans to the good people of his old church. Theologically, they were polar opposites. But their attitudes were well-matched. Both saw themselves as an oasis of righteousness in a corrupt world. Both were convinced that their understanding of scripture was right and complete, and other groups with different convictions were either not the true church, or were fundamentally deficient in some way. Both were convinced they were living in the Last Days and saw portents everywhere they looked. Furthermore, the preachers Eddie knew were little better than the Pilgrims at getting along with their own kind. Puritans and Pentecostals alike could be cruel to their enemies. No creature under heaven was fiercer than the angry devout. The pious always believed they were right, and that being right justified their nastiness and hallowed their hate. The fanatic was loosed from the normal constraints of conscience that kept even the irreligious in check. That was the conceptual cord linking Plymouth Rock to Solid Rock; the zealot's conviction that his brutality was proof of his devotion to a loving God. While any hypocrite could think himself good in spite of his cruelty, it took a True Believer to think himself good *because* of his cruelty.

"More water?" The waitress almost whispered the question, as if fearful of intruding on his thoughts.

"Yes, please." She was practically tiptoeing around him. Eddie realized he'd been scowling. He trusted that actual steam wasn't issuing from his ears. This was no way to behave at Thanksgiving dinner, even if he *was* eating it alone because of Greg Bowers. Besides, he still had things for which to be thankful, though he couldn't recall them at the moment. He smiled wanly at the woman. None of this was her fault.

That was when Eddie had an epiphany. If the history of the Pilgrims meant anything, it meant that the reality of church life never changed. American clergy couldn't sentence people to run the gauntlet any more, but nearly four hundred years after the beat-down of John Oldham, church leaders of every kind still abused their own with regularity. After quitting Solid Rock, Eddie had assumed he would eventually find another church to join. Now he realized that joining a new congregation was pointless, like escaping Syria to seek refuge in North Korea. Why exchange one dictator and his thoroughly cowed flock of enablers for another? Why not just live as a free man? With that thought, Eddie felt a weight lift off his shoulders. *Scratch one more item from the to-do list.*

He began to hunt the forums in earnest the following day. This was going to be harder than it had seemed when the idea first occurred to him. Statistics on the homepage of rangerovers.net revealed 62,000 threads totaling 507,000 posts. Membership exceeded 45,000. New posts appeared daily. Eddie was looking for a needle in an enormous haystack. Finding Loudmouth this way would require a miracle, or spectacular luck, or a whole lot of time. The whole idea seemed less of a slam dunk under Plymouth's cold gray skies than it had in the Florida sunshine. He tried to stay optimistic as the hours of searching turned into days, and the days turned into weeks.

Spending Thanksgiving alone had been hard. Christmas was an order of magnitude harder. Eddie phoned season's greetings to his father after first checking the weather in Boca Raton. No point in stumbling over the answer to inevitable questions about "the weather down there." His extended family chattered and laughed in the background. A few of them got on the phone to wish him a Merry Christmas. When the call was done, the only sound was the drumbeat of his footsteps as he paced his apartment eating leftover pork fried rice and a tin of holiday cookies. He fought down the urge to pity himself and tried to think of practical things.

One big task that remained was to get a job. He'd spent somewhere in the vicinity of eight grand during his road trip. It made sense to start replacing that. Besides, nearly everyone he met was bound to ask him what he did for work. Having no answer to the question would be embarrassing. Eddie had no idea what he wanted to do for his next career. For the short term, maybe it made sense to take the path of least resistance.

The path of least resistance led to cold feet. Eddie stood in calf-deep snow and lamented the loss of feeling in his toes. He and his colleagues were brushing last night's heavy snowfall off the inventory of the big Euro-import car dealership in Kingston where Eddie had started working just after the first of the year. Clearing off cars had been part of his job at FTA too. But his family's store had only twelve to fifteen cars in inventory at a given time, and this place had over four hundred. Today was Monday, meaning both shifts were on duty. That worked out to about thirty-six cars apiece.

Once the vehicles were dug out, he and his fellow client advisors—what this dealership called its salespeople—jockeyed the cars around the lot, moving them out of their spaces so Jerry could come through with the plow, and then putting them back. Jerry had been on the sales force the longest and his seniority meant that he got to sit in a comfortable pickup truck listening to the radio and drinking hot coffee while everyone else froze. This was the fifth big storm this year, and plenty of winter remained, whether or not that famous groundhog in Pennsylvania had seen his shadow yesterday.

Three hours later, he was back in the showroom stamping his feet. He bypassed the gaggle of employees hanging around the coffee pot and headed straight for his desk. Nobody would have talked to him anyway. He hoped it was just the brutal winter weather. Bad weather meant fewer customers, and fewer customers made commissioned salespeople less welcoming of new blood. No one wanted to split an already small pie into even smaller slices. Eddie could understand that, but felt some of them took the unfriendliness too far. Grumpy old Jerry, for instance, always made a big show of not remembering Eddie's name, saying he'd trouble himself to remember it when Eddie had been on the job at least six months.

At his desk, Eddie pecked at the computer keyboard with unfeeling fingers and browsed the Range Rover forums. On slow days like this he could spend an uninterrupted hour or two looking for Loudmouth, and his efforts would seem work-related to anyone who glanced over his shoulder.

The search had progressed in fits and starts since he started his new job. As time went by, the harsh winter numbed more than just his extremities; it dulled the emotional intensity of his quest. The inferno of his October rage had been reduced to glowing embers by February, and he feared the ordinariness of daily life might smother even those. Was this how time healed all wounds?

One wound that wasn't healing was the loss of his friends. Eddie had always enjoyed solitude when alone time had been optional. Being alone was a treat then. Now it felt unfair, one more thing that had gone wrong with his life because of a loudmouthed cretin and a tyrannical cleric. His Internet searching provided some distraction, but not nearly enough. Giant snow drifts and ubiquitous black ice meant no asphalt therapy, so there was little to do but grin and bear it. The winter ground on.

On the first Saturday in March, Eddie was helping to close the showroom for the evening. Frank, another client advisor, walked over. "A bunch of us are heading out to Fridays after work. You want to come along?"

Eddie was surprised and pleased to be invited, but replied nonchalantly. "Sure, why not?"

When he arrived at TGI Fridays, six client advisors were sitting around a long table with Jerry at the head. Eddie pulled up a chair. A few of the guys nodded in his direction, but the others paid no attention. They were all listening to a salesman named Lance who said, "And when she came back to take delivery, she brought her husband!" The men around the table dissolved into laughter and high fives. Then the guy on Lance's right began telling a story, and Eddie realized everyone was taking turns describing occasions when they had either seduced a customer or been seduced by one. He cringed inwardly. *These guys are so juvenile.*

Eddie was seated beside Frank. When Frank finished his tale of conquest, he turned and looked expectantly at Eddie. "No comment," Eddie said with a slight shake of his head.

Hoots of derision went up all around the table.

"Newbie doesn't want to admit the ladies aren't interested in him," said a client advisor named Griffin.

"Or maybe it's that *he's* not interested in *them*," Lance said, smirking. "I mean, not everyone's tastes run in the same direction, if you get my drift."

Eddie fixed Lance with a warning stare. "Keep it up, and *you'll* need to run in the direction of the door, if you get my drift."

This brought more hooting from the assembled men. While Eddie viewed Lance's remark as a grave insult, it was clear that the group just saw it as normal banter. They all talked to each other this way. Eddie saw that fitting in with this bunch would require some adjustment. He forced a weak smile.

Jimmy piped up from across the table. "C'mon, dude, give us a story, then. Don't be odd man out."

While this kind of conversation was not Eddie's idea of a good time, he decided that it was probably a test of some sort, whereby the others would decide whether to let him into their social circle. Since he had no social circle of his own, anything was better than nothing. It was a break, however awkward, from his usual table for one.

"Okay, okay. The thing is, I'm on my best behavior in the showroom. I mean, customers don't necessarily disappear forever when their taillights go over the curb. If I have to deal with them again, I'd rather not have any potential drama." A few groans went up.

"Alas, newbie's still waiting for an adventure worth sharing," Griffin said with mock sympathy.

Eddie hurried on. "But *away* from the showroom is a different story. Just a few months ago, there was this gorgeous waitress at a restaurant . . ."

He proceeded to tell them the details of his time in Savannah, with enough attention paid to Charlene's appearance and manner of dress to make sure the guys would all be suitably impressed. Telling the tale made him feel like a cad, but he figured he couldn't truly sully the reputation of a young woman whose full name he didn't know and who was more than a thousand miles away. After describing their tonsil hockey match in the car, Eddie added, "Then she invited herself up to my hotel room. Fade to black." He sat back, feeling he'd made a clever exit from a story that had no climax.

"Yeah, yeah." Jerry waved his hand dismissively. "Newbie had a bodacious babe kicking the tires. She agreed to a test drive. Doesn't mean you necessarily closed the deal. So what I want to know is . . . *did you get the check?*"

All the guys were laughing heartily, and Eddie almost chuckled himself. He'd never heard "getting the check" used in that way. Still, Jerry's thrust called for both a parry and a riposte. "Hey, I could give lessons on the art of closing the deal. But why are you busting my chops, Gramps? We all know that the last time *you* got any checks, they arrived by stagecoach."

"Very funny. And the name's Jerry, not Gramps." His voice carried more than a little frost.

"And this newbie will be sure to remember that . . . just as soon as you start remembering *my* name."

The table was silent for a couple of tense seconds. Then Griffin guffawed. "Point, set, and match to the new guy, who for the record, is named Eddie Caruthers. Welcome to the team,

Eddie." From that point on, all the client advisors on his shift treated Eddie as if they'd been his friends for years. Even Jerry was reasonably cordial, and he never failed to address Eddie by name again. They went out as a group every Saturday. The talk was considerably less G-rated with this bunch than with his former church friends, but one had to make allowances for that. It was just nice to have friends.

Eddie fell into a routine that carried him through the remainder of March and into early spring. Between his long work hours, time spent browsing the forums, and workouts at a new fitness center he'd joined, he kept busy enough. The unpleasant memory of his exit from Solid Rock shrank in the rearview mirror of his memory. Things were going fine at work, and he was making decent coin. His only real frustration was the lack of progress in finding Loudmouth. After countless hours spent lurking on Range Rover forums and Facebook groups, he hadn't identified anyone who might be him.

One day he had a flash of inspiration. *I'm going about this all wrong. Instead of trying to find a needle in a haystack, I need to get the needle to come to me.* The first step was a visit to tirerack.com, trying to find the wheels he'd seen on Loudmouth's Rover back in October. He could still visualize them. It took only five minutes to locate the wheels and learn their manufacturer and model name.

Next, he created a fake profile for himself on the largest Ranger Rover forum, posing as a woman from Florida. He created his first post, the obligatory introduction.

Hi guys! I'm new to the forum and the brand, but not to cars. Got moderate wrenching skills. Am the proud owner of a just-purchased 2005 Range Rover Westminster Edition. I'm excited about my new ride, looking to make a few cosmetic updates. Could someone give me some recommendations about window tint? Also, I'm looking at aftermarket wheels. Is anyone out there running Asanti CX 188 wheels? If so, are they worth the price? And can you post pics?

The hook was baited, and the line was cast. He could do nothing now but wait.

One Saturday evening at Fridays, Frank said, "Hey, Eddie, I notice you always get cola or lemonade instead of having a real drink with the rest of us. Are you on the wagon or something?"

"No, it's nothing like that. I just don't drink—never have." That wasn't technically true since Savannah, but it was close enough.

"Why is that? Is it against your religion or something?"

"That's not exactly how I'd put it."

"Just tell us you're not a jihadist out to destroy all of us infidels," Frank said.

"No worries there, Frank. I'm a Christian."

Lance chimed in. "And that's why you don't drink? I know lots of Christians who like adult beverages. Are you like a hard-core fundamentalist or something? There's nothing in the Bible that says you can't imbibe, is there?"

Eddie hesitated. He didn't really want to be dragged into this discussion, but it seemed wrong to duck the question. He also knew no Christian consensus had been reached on the answer. As far as he could see, the Bible condemned drunkenness, but it did not expressly forbid the consumption of alcohol. Jesus had turned water to wine at a wedding feast. And Paul had counseled Timothy to drink a little wine for his stomach's sake. Though some Bible interpreters insisted that such passages referred only to unfermented grape juice, Eddie had never bought that hypothesis.

"No, there's no biblical prohibition against drinking. *Drunkenness* is prohibited. I've just always figured there's no chance I'll get drunk if I don't drink." Eddie shrugged.

"True," said Lance. "And you'll never get fat if you don't eat."

"You need food to live. That's not true of booze."

"Right. You don't need booze to live. You just need it to enjoy living!" Everybody laughed, and several of the guys raised their glasses in a toast to Lance's wit. Eddie was greatly relieved when the conversation moved on to other topics. He felt no need to hide his beliefs, but he didn't want to have to debate them with the likes of these guys either.

The next week, Griffin sprung the news that he was getting married to his longtime girlfriend. Some of the boys decided to treat him to a night on the town, and Eddie was invited. They arranged for a limo to pick them all up after work on the following Saturday. Eddie agreed to go, though no one would tell him where they were going. He thought that odd; surely Griffin was the only one who needed to be surprised?

They drove for over an hour and wound up in Providence, Rhode Island. The limo pulled up to the door of a flat, featureless slab of a building with no windows. Eddie could feel the bass thump of the music coming from inside. As they all spilled out of the back, he noticed a sea of cars in the parking lot. There had to be hundreds of them. A giant neon sign to the right of the building's entrance identified the venue as The Wolf's Den. Beneath the name, smaller lettering tagged The Wolf's Den as a "Gentlemen's Club."

"We're going to a *strip club*? Unbelievable!" Eddie rounded on the two men nearest him, Frank and Lance. "This isn't cool! I think you knew I'd never agree to come here, which is the reason you wouldn't tell me where we were going."

"Excuse *me*," said Lance, his face a picture of wide-eyed innocence. "From what you've told us in the past, I thought you were *into* sexy girls who showed a little skin. I seem to recall a very vivid description of some girl down south . . ."

"That's different," Eddie said. "That was a date. She didn't take off her clothes for a room full of dirty old men."

"We're not old!" Frank looked stricken.

"Agreed," said Lance. "We're dirty *young* men." That seemed to mollify Frank.

Eddie rolled his eyes. "Whatever. Strip clubs are trashy, and I don't go to places like this."

"If you've never gone to one, then you don't know what they're like, do you?" Lance again.

"I don't have to crawl inside a dumpster to know what it's like."

"Hey, if you're not into the dancers there are plenty of good-looking cocktail waitresses who will keep their clothes on while serving you your lemonade. I know you can appreciate a hot waitress. You made a big point of telling us so. I thought you might even pick up one or two and give us amateurs some lessons on the art of closing the deal, getting the check, and all that."

"Besides," added Frank, "we're here to show Griffin a good time. So come on in . . . or don't. Just don't spoil our evening." With that, they turned and walked toward the entrance.

Eddie felt frozen in place. What options did he have? Even the limo driver was laughing as he rolled up his window and pulled away from the entrance. *I can't stay with the car. I can't stand outside all evening, not in this chilly air.* He looked around. It didn't appear to be the kind of neighborhood in which a prudent man would go for a stroll. He could see a junkyard, a body shop, and a number of businesses with metal shutters rolled down over doors and windows. Except for the lot where he stood, the area looked deserted.

To make matters worse, he was "walking heavy" in a state where it wasn't legal for him to carry his gun. He couldn't afford to stand around looking odd or suspicious, lest he draw the attention of law enforcement. He thought of calling for a cab, but it was a long way back to Kingston. Upon pulling up a website called taxifarefinder.com on his phone, Eddie discovered it would cost him $240 to get back to his car. Why should he be forced to spend that much to undo these jokers' trickery?

Eddie's friends had disappeared inside. His consternation grew. He figured his only option was to go in and find a quiet corner. He'd do his best to ignore everything going on around him.

Inside the front doors a cashier stood in a glass booth, much like one would find at a movie theater. Eddie grudgingly paid the ten-dollar cover charge with a twenty-dollar bill, and was handed ten singles in return. He pocketed his change and stepped inside.

It was immediately evident that no quiet corners were to be found in The Wolf's Den. The place was mobbed, and Eddie couldn't see anywhere to stand where he might have a reasonable amount of personal space. He shifted his wallet to his front pants pocket and slowly forced his way to a wall near the hostess station. With his back to the wall, he took in his surroundings.

The music, which had seemed loud even outside, was almost painfully so in here. People conversed by shouting directly into each other's ears. Most of the faces in Eddie's vicinity were turned toward a large stage that occupied the center of the room. On it, two girls in formal evening wear and long white gloves were swaying to the music. Next to the stage, a line of men perched on barstools stared up at the dancers. More or less in time with the beat, the dancers began peeling off their gloves. When they started shimmying out of their gowns, Eddie looked away, eyes sweeping the other details of the room.

A number of burly guys in white jackets and bow ties were stationed around the room—near the stage, near the entrance and exit, and at the door of something called The Champagne Lounge. More stood in a section of the club furnished with round tables and big overstuffed chairs. While the floor space around him was packed, Eddie could see that the area with the furniture had some breathing room. He began edging toward that section.

As he went, he realized that the dancing girls were by no means confined to the stage. There had to be thirty or forty women circulating through the huge crowd of men. Most of them were wearing the same kind of formal attire in which the women on stage had briefly been clad. It looked like the red carpet at the Academy Awards—silk, satin, and gold lamé clinging to nubile bodies. It was much harder to ignore the women squeezing past him on every side than it was to ignore the two women on stage. Glancing up at them, he saw to his dismay that they were now wearing only a scant few square inches of clothing. He looked away again.

Each of these dancers is somebody's daughter. What a shame. An instant later, there came a competing thought. *They probably weren't dragged here at gunpoint. If they choose to make their money like this, maybe they don't need my sympathy.*

A pretty brunette in thigh-high white leather boots and a micro miniskirt blocked his path so that he almost ran into her. Before he could mumble an apology, she cupped her hand and shouted in the general direction of his ear: "Could I interest you in a private dance?" As she spoke, her eyes were scanning the crowd, as if searching for the next man to solicit if this one said no.

Though certain he didn't want anything this place had to offer, he tried to formulate an acceptable way to decline. He didn't want to sound dismissive, like he was giving her the brush-off. Maybe he should let her down easy. "Not right this minute," he said. "I want to see where my friends went. Maybe some other time." He had to address that last bit to the back of her head, as she was already melting into the crowd. He sighed.

Turning back toward the area with the comfy-looking furniture, Eddie registered the fact that every chair with a man in it had a woman in various stages of undress just in front of it. Realizing that the section wasn't a place for unattended guys to loiter, he leaned up against a pillar and marveled at the size of the crowd. He decided to just stand there and observe, mostly out of morbid curiosity. It was like rubbernecking at a car accident, albeit a very sexy car accident.

A deejay was talking over the music as it played. Mostly he was directing dancers to their stage assignments. The music varied from techno and pop tracks to heavy metal and rap, but all the songs were short, about three minutes or so. The lyrics were often filthy. Eddie was surprised to learn that many songs he knew from the radio apparently had uncensored versions for use in clubs like this.

Every three songs, the dancers on stage would rotate out. A steady procession of girls with names like Morgan, Madison, Tiffany, Diamond, and Destiny came and went from the main stage and from a second stage the deejay said was downstairs in the VIP Lounge. When he wasn't calling out assignments, his rapid-fire delivery included ads for the various programs and services the club offered. He reminded patrons to tip the waitresses who were roaming through the crowd to take drink orders. He advised men who were short of cash to get credit card cash advances at the hostess station. "And in the interest of domestic tranquility, the charge will appear on your statement as West Side Tavern, so you won't have any awkward explaining to do." He announced that The Wolf's Den would be open until two and would reopen at seven Sunday morning for the Legs & Eggs Breakfast Revue.

A ruckus just past the far end of the bar drew Eddie's attention. He'd located his friends. They were all knotted around a booth that occupied a raised platform in the corner. Its walls were of glass on the front and the near side and tiled in the back and on the far side. It looked like a huge shower stall, which is exactly what it turned out to be. Inside, wearing nothing but knee-length Wolf's Den swimming trunks, a grinning Griffin was handcuffed to a ring in the wall by two bikini-clad dancers. Above him was the shower head.

"Let's hear it for Griffin," the deejay was saying. "He's getting married May 3rd, so before he puts on the old ball and chain, we thought we'd help him feel lucky one last time! Our two beautiful attendants Roxy and Trinity are going to sponge him down in our world-famous shower scene! Now, that's what I call good, clean fun!" The deejay laughed at his pun. "And if you'll make some noise and pony up some cash for our lovely ladies, I bet we can get them to drop those tops!" The boys from the dealership were whooping it up. Dollar bills flew onto the platform.

There came the sound of a telephone ringing, its shrill burble amplified by the PA system. The deejay said, "Hello, Wolf's Den, home of the most sizzling girls in Rhode Island . . . Hey, Griffin, it's Debbie calling for you. That's your fiancée, isn't it? I'll tell her you're tied up right now!" This was followed by uproarious laughter from the crowd. Eddie wondered how many times per week the deejay repeated that little gag. *I bet he laughs at his own joke every time too.*

Water flowed from the shower head, the girls got Griffin all soapy, and somewhere along the line they decided that enough encouragement and currency had been directed their way to give the crowd what it wanted. Eddie had seen enough. He turned and shouldered his way outside, where he stood shivering in the cold spring air. The limo was nowhere in sight. He waited for what felt like an eternity until the gang came out and the stretch Cadillac pulled up.

Eddie endured the ride back to the dealership in sullen silence. His friends all reeked of alcohol and were talking much louder than necessary. They seemed to have had a great time. He got home and showered once, and then a second time, before realizing that the dirty feeling plaguing him was on the inside. His only defense was that he had been tricked. *I would never have knowingly gone to such a place.*

Over the next two weeks, he frequently relived the evening. He thought about the too-loud music, the profanity-laced lyrics, and the pervasive smell of booze. All those things were deplorable. The girls, on the other hand, were fascinating. He'd never seen so many beautiful women in one place. Even Charlene in all her glory was not arrayed like one of them. Nor had he ever seen so *much* of any woman's body before. And they came in such lovely variety: the petite and the statuesque, the willowy girls and the surgically enhanced ones, the bronze ones and the brown ones, and those whose skin was like translucent white porcelain. Yes, the girls were truly captivating. He couldn't get them out of his mind. So despite his disapproval of the place, its allure was so great that he set out for a return visit.

Driving down I-95 toward Providence, he felt a light tingling around his eyes and across his cheeks. He knew the sensation well. In a church service, this feeling would normally be accompanied with a welling of joy in his heart and an awareness of God's presence. God was present everywhere at all times. But having sensory awareness of that presence was special. Eddie knew that encounters with God were not solely intellectual in nature or even solely spiritual. Man was a composite blend of body, soul, and spirit, and what affected one of those elements often spilled over onto the other two. He'd been in church services where the physical sensations washed over him from head to toe. The old folks called it getting "under the spout where the glory comes out."

But while the tingle playing over his face was instantly familiar, no joy was associated with it now, no sense of basking in the glory of the Almighty. Instead, it felt like a warning, one conveyed gently and without words, but one that clearly meant *don't do this. Don't go there. This is wrong.*

Eddie was only a few miles from the state line. He moved into the far right travel lane and took the next exit. He intended to reverse direction and go home. But even as he was coming off the exit ramp, he had second thoughts. It was easy to argue with God. Or perhaps it was just that, because God rarely shouted or repeated himself, it was easy to doubt that he had really spoken in the first place. For a few seconds, Eddie wavered. *I got money out of the ATM, I stashed my sidearm in the trunk, and I've been driving for forty-five minutes. It would be a waste to turn and go home now. I just want to have a look around. I won't stay long.*

The sensation that had given him pause was gone. The restraining influence he had felt in his spirit, the odd sense that the Lord was giving him a reproachful look—all gone. *Just a few minutes, and I'm out of there.* His mind made up, Eddie did three turns of the cloverleaf interchange until he was once again on I-95 south. *It's not like I'm going to make a habit of it . . .*

Tuesday night at The Wolf's Den was considerably less crowded than Saturday had been. He had room to move, room to breathe. And the smaller number of men forced the girls to be more attentive than they had to be on weekends. They were competing with each other tonight, so the dancers' demeanors showed lots of honey and no vinegar. Eddie was feeling pleased with himself. He had mostly avoided ogling the nearly naked girls on stage. Though he bought drinks for several dancers, he'd confined his own drinking to soda. And he was becoming increasingly comfortable talking to beautiful women, the kind who would have made him feel intimidated in the past. Late in the evening, a leggy, platinum blond dancer named Camille took him by the hand and led him to the private dance area. He would have said no. He *meant* to say no. But she hadn't asked him anything. She just led him to a chair and sat him down in it.

She told him to give her twenty dollars and to sit with his legs apart, keeping his hands on his knees. He complied. Then, standing just in front of him so her magnificent frame filled his vision, she began to dance. Soon she was wearing no more than the dancers on stage. She turned this way and that. She put one foot up on the arm of the chair. He took in the view of her thigh from just three inches away and reminded himself to breathe.

The song ended. "Would you like me to continue?" she asked demurely. He nodded and paid her for another dance. And another. When he finally pled poverty and left the private area, his wallet was considerably lighter. He'd burned through $160 in twenty-five minutes and loved every minute of it.

After leaving the club, he found a twenty-four-hour diner and ordered a meal. When his food came, he automatically began to say grace under his breath—*thank you, Lord, for this food*—and the irony hit him. The Gospels record Jesus asking, "Why do you call me 'Lord, Lord,' and not do the things which I say?" Eddie remembered waffling in the car, how he had talked himself out of turning around while en route to the club. How could he pretend he objected to the club on Christian principles when he'd gone there of his own accord? *Eddie Caruthers, you are a hypocrite.* The realization made his meal suddenly unappetizing, as if previously good food was spoiled just by belonging to him.

He paid for his half-eaten burger, left the diner, and roared up the highway even faster than normal, trying to outrun the night's bad feelings. He turned on the radio. Music could make all things bearable. But even that most reliable of solaces failed when a track by The Cars started playing. The opening lines were:

It takes a fast car, lady
To lead a double life

Eddie turned the stereo off and vowed he'd never go anyplace like The Wolf's Den again.

CHAPTER 9
CASTING THE NET

"Dead? Are you serious?" Eddie sat down heavily and rubbed his eyes.

That was a stupid question. Of course his father was serious. "But he was doing so well . . ."

It was seven thirty in the morning. Eddie was exhausted and groggy, having gotten to bed just five hours ago after his miserable flight from The Wolf's Den. He'd gone to sleep making promises of reform, an end to the negative thinking that had clearly affected his judgment. Today was going to be the beginning of better days. And now Big Eddie was dead.

"No one saw it coming." Dad's voice sounded weary for such a morning person. "Apparently he had a blood clot break loose from somewhere, and it caused a massive stroke. They rushed him back to the hospital but couldn't save him. After all he'd been through, after all he'd overcome . . ."

They talked for thirty minutes. As with all deaths in the church, they had mixed emotions. They could rejoice that Eddie Freeman had made it from Earth to glory while they deplored the way he had to get there; at the same time, they felt sorrow for the family members who would feel the pain of his loss most keenly. Donald Caruthers promised to get back to his son with details of the funeral arrangements.

Eddie knew he wouldn't be going. Brother Freeman's family wouldn't want to see him. They blamed him for Big Eddie's injuries before, so they'd blame him for his death now. Not to mention the fact that the killers might think his funeral the perfect place to finally catch up with Eddie Caruthers. No, he couldn't take a chance on attending. Hopefully, people would understand. And if everyone believed him to be in Florida, they'd have to cut him some slack for the distance involved.

He'd send a card, of course. He just had to get it to be post-marked from Boca. He would enclose the stamped envelope with the card in it in a larger mailer to be sent to the UPS Store that served as his mail drop. When they opened the package they'd see instructions to mail the envelope from down there. Having worked that out, Eddie finished dressing and got to work fifteen minutes late. Tardiness was a big no-no at the dealership. Each morning shift started with a sales meeting at eight-thirty. Being even a minute late for that meeting brought unfavorable attention from management. Today was no exception.

The general manager called him into the office and chewed him out. He wasn't interested in any flimsy excuses about friends dying. "You look like you just rolled out of bed. Your shoes look like you shined them with a chocolate bar. You drag in here like you were up partying all night, and you're late. You better shape up, Caruthers. You've had good sales production, but that doesn't buy you an exemption from our standards. I don't put up with this sort of thing. Go home. Take an unpaid day. And starting tomorrow make sure we never need to have this conversation again." The GM turned back to his paperwork, while Eddie trudged out to his car, past suddenly busy coworkers who were pretending not to have heard anything.

Once home, Eddie crawled back into bed. Questions swirled around his head. *Did I not pray enough?* He hadn't prayed much for Big Eddie lately. It was so easy to promise to pray for people and not do it. You meant well when you said it, but life somehow got in the way.

Did the church not pray enough? He had a hard time believing that God would deprive the Freeman family of their loved one simply because those asking him *not* to hadn't asked often enough. Would more prayer have made any difference? Didn't the Bible say that God works all things according to the counsel of his will? If God's mind is made up, who are we to change it? On the other hand, scripture encouraged believers to let their requests be made known to God. God must be amenable to requests, at least sometimes, or why solicit them? Eddie had many more questions than answers.

A different question made its way to the forefront: *Now that the assault case is a murder case, will the police solve it?* The questions remained unanswered as Eddie drifted off to sleep. He didn't wake up until dinner time.

He walked to the Driftwood Publick House and Oysteria for dinner. When the food came, he didn't bother saying grace. Praying over his meal last night in Providence had filled him with guilt. He felt miserable enough already without repeating that experience. After hurriedly finishing his meal he returned home at eight.

His thoughts were on Big Eddie's killers. Confident that his Florida ruse was working, he wasn't afraid for himself. The murderers couldn't attack him if they couldn't find him. But he was extra determined to make them pay for all they had done.

He checked the Range Rover forum. Over the last week, a dozen replies to his introductory post had trickled in. A new one today had real potential. Could this be Loudmouth? The guy's screen name was The Dominator. He had a black Range Rover with the right Asanti wheels in twenty-two-inch fitment. The vehicle appeared in his signature picture. His profile summary listed his location as Massachusetts, but no city was given.

"The Dominator" seemed like the kind of screen name a musclehead like Loudmouth would choose. First thing to do was search through the history of this user's posts for more clues. He was an infrequent contributor to the forum, but he'd posted almost a hundred times since joining six years ago. Eddie read through them all. None of his posts, or those of other users responding to him, mentioned his real name or contained his photo. *Who are you, Dominator? I'm going to find out.* He made himself a cup of hot tea and settled in to work.

Eddie looked at the sig pic again. The Rover appeared in a line of three cars. The others were a Jaguar and an MG. The guy had a thing for British cars. His signature tag line read, "A good day is when they're all running." On a hunch, Eddie copied and pasted the sig pic into the search engine at images.google.com. In an instant, he was looking at links to more places where the photo appeared online. One of them was another Rover site, and one of them was a Jaguar forum. At both places, the guy went by the screen name "Alopaced."

Eddie knew most people weren't as clever as they thought they were when it came to choosing a screen name to protect their anonymity. "The Dominator" was too generic a moniker to suggest much, unless of course the man's name was Dominic. Eddie looked at the second screen name. "Alopaced" was even more obscure. He read it backward: *decapola.*

Could Decapola be this guy's last name? Eight people had that surname on Facebook. One was female, and one was a teenager. Five of the remaining six lived overseas. The one US resident was a young guy from down south, definitely not Loudmouth. Of course, not every Decapola in the world would be on Facebook.

He briefly thought of an old TV show called *Criminal Minds.* It followed a team of FBI profilers. Whenever they needed info on anyone, office IT nerd Penelope Garcia would tap out a few keystrokes and have everything they needed in an instant. If only real life worked that way.

Hoping to get lucky, he entered Dominic Decapola into the online White Pages for Massachusetts. Nothing. Neither were there listings for that name in neighboring New Hampshire or Rhode Island. Of course, that did not prove no such person existed, only that no phone number was listed in that name. But since he wasn't even sure if that was The Dominator's real surname, he was hesitant to spend too much more time in searching for it.

Maybe the screen name on the second forum was a combination of first initial and last name: D. Ecapola. But Facebook had no one at all with that surname. Two initials? D. E. Capola? Facebook had one, but he was from South America. The White Pages did list four people named D Capola in Massachusetts. Eddie still had a gut feeling he was looking for someone named Dominic.

Next, he checked out search engine aggregator kgbpeople.com. This let him search Google, You Tube, and all the major social media sites at once. It even covered blog entries. The only promising hit was a four-year-old blog post from an auto detailing company that thanked Dominic Capola for volunteering to have his car used in a new product demonstration. The car was a Jaguar. It was not a match for the car in the forum pictures. But the detailing shop was in Marlborough, just a few miles from Framingham; right car maker, right neighborhood, and maybe the right name.

Eddie moved on to the search engine at pipl.com, which could search the Deepnet, the largely invisible part of the Internet that was not indexed by standard search engines. This provided plenty of results, some of which clearly did not pertain to his target. Sifting through them, he found an alumni magazine for a Southborough private school that listed "Mr. and Mrs. Dominic Capola" as contributors. He also found an arrest record for a Dominic Capola. It was six years ago, and the charge was DUI. The report included a Southborough residential address. Since Southborough bordered Framingham and Marlborough, Eddie started feeling increasingly optimistic that he was on the right track.

He looked up the home address on Zillow. It was an impressive-looking house with a three-car garage, and the website had it valued at nearly seven hundred thousand dollars. The house was not for sale, and had last sold over ten years ago. Its owner wouldn't be a poor man. Perhaps that explained how he kept three British cars on the road. But it didn't explain much else.

This guy kept an amazingly low profile. There didn't seem to be a picture of him anywhere online. Eddie sat back and thought for a moment. Most people weren't that invisible—unless they were *trying* to be. Eddie wondered if the mystery man had family members who might be more easily located. He found the Southborough *Daily Call* and entered just the surname Capola into the newspaper's search box. Just like that, he found a feature article on a high school senior named Gabriella Capola. She was an outstanding varsity soccer player as well as an honor roll student at St. Paul's School. She was pictured receiving some sort of award. The caption read "Gabriella Capola accepts the Headmaster's Award from Doctor Kaufman as her proud parents look on." *Pay dirt*! Eddie looked at the parents in the background, and his heart sank for a moment when he saw the man wasn't Loudmouth. Then Eddie recognized Gabriella's big, paunchy father as the second guy in the SUV. This was Raspy.

But what did it mean? It meant that Loudmouth had been driving Raspy's car. Why? Maybe Raspy had been drinking and was trying to avoid another DUI. Did the reason even matter? It was Loudmouth who had belittled Roz, Loudmouth who'd started the fight and lost it, Loudmouth who had a motive for revenge. Did Raspy? He hadn't even seemed angry that night. He hadn't attacked or threatened anyone. Eddie wished he knew what Raspy's relationship to Loudmouth was, but he could think of no way to find out. This left Eddie right where he'd been when he left Framingham: nowhere. Worse yet, there didn't seem to be any way forward.

A single word sounded in his mind—hard, ugly, and whip-crack sharp. He did not permit himself to utter it. When Eddie was growing up, his father had prohibited even the most innocuous of euphemisms like *heck* or *darn*. "Cursing," Donald Caruthers maintained, "is a futile attempt by lazy or weak-minded people to lend force to their speech." In his youth, speaking the epithet he'd just thought would have gotten Eddie the mother of all beatings. Such language had never been part of his vocabulary, so he was surprised even to hear himself think it now. Maybe the gang at work was rubbing off on him. He yawned, shut down his laptop, threw away his now cold tea, and went to bed just as the night sky was giving way to the tentative gray of morning.

Under other circumstances, Eddie might have seen the coming dawn as a symbol of hope. Today it just reminded him of poor planning. He had to be at work at eight thirty.

When Eddie wasn't at work or the gym, or at home trying to think of a way to identify Loudmouth, he was trying to find Shawna's replacement. Or was it Charlene's replacement? Was he looking to fall in love, or just have fun? He wasn't sure. He'd invited a cute receptionist from the dealership out for coffee, but she had politely demurred, saying she made it a rule never to date coworkers. He'd also chatted up a few women at the local supermarket to no avail. A stunning Latina made repeated eye contact and smiled from across the room at a restaurant, but disappeared before he could make his way over to say hello.

Maybe online dating was the answer.

Thousands of women were out there looking for everything from serious relationships to casual dating at sites like plentyoffish.com. But in order to get any response, Eddie would need to make a profile with his picture. While he doubted that anyone who knew him would be browsing the site, he didn't want to take a chance. After all, he was supposed to be in Florida.

Craigslist had personal ads that he could access and respond to without having to set up a profile. Eddie read through hundreds of ads, eliminating the ones that were from too far away or that specified white males only or that wanted someone much older or younger than him. Of those that remained, most still contained deal-breakers:

"No broke men. I like being spoiled." *She's a gold digger.*

"420 friendly. Wake and bake with me!" *She's a pot smoker.*

"Not looking to change my situation, but . . ." *She's married and looking to cheat.*

Eddie ended up responding to six different ads. He got no reply from five of them. The one woman who wrote back seemed nice enough in emails; she shared his love of music and travel, wrote entertaining notes, and knew the difference between *your* and *you're, their* and *there,* and even *peak* and *pique.* They exchanged half a dozen notes over several days, and it felt as if some chemistry was developing. When the woman asked him for a photo he sent it, and never heard from her again.

Eddie knew that selling was a numbers game. Evidently, so was dating. He just wasn't up for reading a thousand ads, sending out fifty emails, and hoping that one or two of them bore fruit. Getting a date was proving to be just as hard as finding Loudmouth. *Finding someone to talk to shouldn't be so much work.*

CHAPTER 10
FALLING

Two months later

The place was called TNT, which stood for The Naked Truth. It was very large as gentlemen's clubs go, occupying two floors of a converted warehouse a few miles from The Wolf's Den. It had none of the Den's high-end pretensions—no limos in the parking lot, no staff wearing tuxedos. Patrons entering TNT were greeted by two bouncers. The first one accepted payment of the cover charge while the second one frisked the guests for weapons. The sheer size and well-practiced scowls of the bouncers were supposed to intimidate potential troublemakers into having second thoughts, but their graying ponytails and festive Hawaiian shirts softened their appearance enough to keep them from looking scary.

Eddie stood in line and waited for the bouncers to finish putting the three guys in front of him through their paces. When he reached the front of the line, bouncer number one smilingly took his ten-dollar bill, while his burly counterpart nodded in an almost friendly manner. The obligatory pat-down amounted to little more than a pat on the back. Being a regular had its perks.

The cavernous room he entered was rectangular, with a bar at both ends and a big raised stage in the middle on which three girls were dancing. One was doing acrobatic pole maneuvers, hanging upside down eight feet above the ground and looking nearly as skilled as any gymnast at the Olympics. The other two were expending much less energy, walking back and forth and talking to the various men sitting around the stage who encouraged their attentions by periodically proffering dollar bills to be stuffed into garter belts or G-strings. Behind those men, Eddie strode down the aisle toward the bar at the far end of the club. All three dancers, even the inverted one, called out in accidental unison: "Hi Eddie!" Several men twisted around on their stools to give him an envious look. Eddie waved to the girls and smiled. Yep. Being a regular had its little joys.

One of those joys beamed at him from behind the bar. Melissa Devereaux was fast becoming one of his favorite people in the world, and he always made a point of chatting with her when he could. In fact, she was his reason for stopping in tonight. The bar was crowded, and Melissa was bustling about at twice her normal pace. He knew he'd have to wait a while before getting to spend quality time with her. He didn't mind. Closing time was hours away, and plenty of distractions were available to occupy him while he awaited his chance to say what he'd come to say to her. But first, they had a ritual to perform. He edged up to the bar.

"What can I get you?" It was her usual question.

"I'll have the usual." It was his usual answer.

She served him ginger ale in a small plastic glass. Eddie frowned slightly, conveying the unspoken lament about the small serving. He paid for the soda with five ones, watching her stuff the tip into the pocket of her gaudy Hawaiian shirt. Throwing back his head, he downed the soda in two quick gulps. When he set down the empty glass, she asked if he wanted another.

"No more for me. I'm driving tonight, so one's my limit." They both chuckled at that comment as if they hadn't been through the same routine a dozen times before. "Has it been this busy all night?"

"Yeah, the place is hopping. Things should clear out a bit after eleven, and then we can talk."

"I'll try to live without you in the meantime." Eddie smiled and wandered off, circling around to the other side of the central stage in search of some diversion. Diversion bumped into him on its way out of one of the little booths that lined the back wall of the club.

"Eddie!" A short dancer with dark chocolate skin and a leonine mane of loose copper curls beamed up at him while her most recent customer squeezed out of the carrel she had just exited, edging past her and disappearing down the aisle. The woman radiating all the enthusiasm was called Chloe, although Eddie had known her long enough to dispense with her stage name.

"Justine! I haven't seen you in ages. You look great—tremendous, in fact."

The choice of adjectives was deliberate; the last time he'd seen Justine there hadn't been nearly so much of her to see.

"I took a couple of weeks off to have the procedure." She squared her shoulders and pushed out her chest. "You like? My attorney got them for me."

Eddie figured if anyone could get money to flow from attorney to client rather than the other way around, it was Justine. She'd undeniably talked *him* out of a lot of money since they'd first met. He tried not to think about how much.

"I'm massively impressed!"

She squealed and gave him a big hug. "Flattery will get you everywhere! I'm due onstage upstairs now, but when I'm done I'll come find you." Still holding the embrace, she wriggled enough to be sure her new-minted physique made a tactile impression on par with the visual one. "See you soon, baby."

He watched her prance down the aisle, straightening and making minor adjustments to the white shirt and plaid skirt of her Catholic schoolgirl outfit. Fifteen seconds later, just before reaching the corner that led to the stairs, she turned to give him another smile and a wave, apparently confident that he would still be standing there watching her go. He was.

Girls like Chloe/Justine were the primary reason Eddie had started patronizing TNT. He'd grown bored with The Wolf's Den and its carbon-copy dancers dressed as starlets or debutantes. Most of the Den's girls were drop-dead gorgeous, but getting a private dance in a club with a no-contact rule wasn't very exciting once the novelty wore off. Eddie had searched out online reviews of other area clubs and learned that TNT offered patrons a more stimulating experience. Instead of mere eye candy, this place offered lap dances that engaged the sense of touch. Dancers climbed all over the patrons in the booths, providing about as much fun as a guy could legally have with his clothes on. Unlike places with a "hands-on-knees" rule, girls here usually didn't object to wandering hands. Online rumors maintained that for the right price, some girls would provide much more than a lap dance. The presence of condom vending machines in the restrooms did nothing to dispel such rumors. Eddie had his doubts; you couldn't believe everything you read on the Internet.

He had taken to visiting TNT two or three times per week. At first, he had to deal with pesky guilt feelings. But those faded soon enough. He knew his old friends from Solid Rock would be horrified if they found out where he was spending his evenings. He'd changed in the eight months since he'd fled that church. But the distance from their world to his was not as great as they would have thought. TNT was really a church of sorts, dedicated to the cult of feminine allure. It had ushers at the door. The deejay was the song leader revving up the crowd of exuberant worshippers. And the dancers were the clergy, priestesses who ministered to the prurient instead of the penitent. Like clergy of all faiths, they constantly encouraged the men to dig deeper into their wallets and give more sacrificially. Men who gave most were loved best. This place was Solid Rock's mirror image, grounded in flesh rather than spirit. Of course, Eddie would never say anything like that to the old crowd.

He tried to imagine just what he *would* say to them if he got the chance. How could he make them understand why he kept returning here?

Imagine you grew up never having tasted chocolate. In fact, your church preached against it. Your friends told you it was fattening, and that it had no nutritional value. Your pastor, more scholarly than your friends, taught you that dark chocolate contains oxalates, a class of chemicals that can lead to the formation of kidney stones. It also contains caffeine, which can make you jittery, and tyramine, a compound linked to migraine headaches. You have no idea why anyone would deliberately ingest such stuff.

One day you accidentally wander into a high-end chocolate shop. The aroma hits you and your mouth waters despite your determination to remain uninterested. You've never smelled anything so good. Someone gives you a sample. You take it just to be polite. As it melts in your mouth, the flavor washes over your taste buds. The people who wanted to save you from chocolate never told you how wonderful it tastes! Nor did they tell you about how it makes you happier by triggering your brain to release endorphins. They neglected to mention that chocolate is rich in antioxidants and can help lower your risk of heart disease and cancer. It even lowers bad cholesterol and helps reduce blood pressure. Far from being a lot of empty calories, chocolate is rich in calcium, potassium, magnesium, and iron. Maybe the church's real problem with chocolate is simply that it's enjoyable. Isn't their motto, "If it feels good, forbid it"?

As he stood musing in the hallway where Justine had taken her leave, a pair of arms encircled Eddie from behind. A silken voice issued from lips held close to his ear. "You're not getting eyes for someone else, are you?"

His heart started to race. The girl into whose arms he was melting was Claudia. Claudia was unique. Claudia was a force of nature. He turned and inhaled an intoxicating lungful of her scent.

"There are other girls here? I hadn't noticed." He whispered the rest of his answer into the blonde waterfall that spilled past her ear. "I only have eyes for you, you know."

"That's good," she said. "You wouldn't want to disappoint me." Eddie knew Claudia's real name was Megan. Although she was Irish through and through, she looked like a figure from Nordic myth. About five-foot-ten in her stocking feet, in her five-inch stiletto heels she towered over most of the men in the club. She was big-boned and strong looking, but not a hard-body athletic type. And she was strikingly voluptuous, with stunning proportions won in the genetic lottery rather than owing to a surgeon's skill. She had electric blue eyes and wavy golden hair that hung to the small of her back. Her white corselet and kilt trimmed with gold completed the Norse goddess impression.

Taking him by the hand, she led him into one of the booths. She didn't bother asking him if he wanted a dance. Once inside, she drew the black velvet curtain across the entrance while he settled semireclined into the plush low-back chair. The current song was half over, so she sat sideways on his lap. They shared a few snippets of conversation. Mostly she just nibbled on his ear while waiting for the next song to start. He hastily unbuttoned his shirt as a precaution; he knew from experience that if he didn't, Claudia might yank the shirt open, ripping off the buttons. She could be quite enthusiastic.

The song ended. When the next one started, Claudia began her ministrations. Kneeling in the chair, she unhooked her corselet and cast it aside. Then she threw herself into and onto her work. She was very good at her job.

One song ended and another began. She kept going without asking his consent. He could not have said no in any case. The current song was unfamiliar. Some chanteuse he had never heard was singing the part of a married woman thinking about sharing an illicit kiss with some guy.

Right on cue, Claudia turned his face toward the wall and planted one on him. She had given him quick pecks before. This time the osculation was long and open-mouthed; life imitating art, or at least pop music. Eddie's eyes flew open. Satisfied that he wasn't dreaming, he settled back into the passionate kiss.

In the middle of the third song, Eddie suddenly laughed.

"What's so funny?" Claudia seemed suspicious of this unexpected outburst. Her usual carefully modulated tone had sharpened a little at the edges, hinting that something abrasive lurked under all that silk.

"It's just the song they're playing. I think it's about what happens to me when I'm with you." The song was the Robert

Palmer tune "Simply Irresistible." What had started Eddie laughing was the singer's confession that time spent with his woman made his money mysteriously vanish.

They laughed together, enjoying the joke. "How much money have you got tonight?"

Whoa, that's pretty direct. "I'm not sure. How much do I need?"

"Well, you owe me seventy-five dollars so far. Tell me you've got two hundred on you and you'll make me very happy." Her dulcet tone was back in place.

"Two hundred dollars . . . yeah, I've got it. But that's a lot of dances."

"Either it's eight regular dances or one very special one. I bet you'll like my special one."

She proceeded to test her hypothesis. He did like it. And as it turned out, those Internet rumors were true.

Minutes later, Eddie was back in the aisle wondering how he'd managed to spend so much money so fast. *Good chocolate is expensive. I really need to do something about my sweet tooth.*

Clever internal dialogue couldn't fully mask the distress Eddie felt about the line he'd just crossed. He told himself it wasn't entirely his fault. He hadn't asked for that to happen, and wasn't expecting it. *Next time, I'll know to stop things before they get that far.* That idea struck him as laughable the instant he thought it.

He slunk back to where Melissa was tending bar. Pulling up a stool, he waited for her to come over. The crowd had thinned out, though she was still serving a few guys. He watched her going about her work, hoping he didn't look as guilty as he felt.

Melissa Devereaux was cute. "Cute" was unexceptional in a club where at least a dozen girls were knockouts. Chloe was Jessica Rabbit, thanks to the cartoon fantasy physique some lawyer's money had purchased for her. Claudia was Freya, the Viking goddess of love, fertility, and sexual desire. Melissa, on the other hand, was the archetypical girl next door, a Mary Ann marooned on a tropical island full of Gingers. Of average height and average build, she was fair skinned and a little rosy cheeked, with brown eyes and straight brown hair that seemed always about to spill over her face. Her ears stuck out a bit. Yet she was more than the sum of her parts, and Eddie found that she was impressive in ways the dancers were not.

What was it about Melissa? Perhaps it was that smile. She smiled broadly and often, without an apparent agenda; it did not seem like a calculating attempt to look seductive, and no predatory gleam lurked in her eye. When she smiled, her eyes shone and her face fairly glowed. Eddie realized with a start what was so special about Melissa. *She looks happy.* All the other things he liked about her, such as her open expression, her approachability, the fact that she seemed comfortable in her own skin and not envious of the women around her—all these things stemmed from the fact that she was a basically happy person. *How long has it been since I've felt like that?*

She finally came over. "You feeling okay? You look a little out of sorts tonight."

"I suppose," Eddie said. "You got any extra sorts?" It was a lame joke, but she responded with a big smile anyway, and that was what Eddie most wanted to see. *"A merry heart does good, like medicine." Nothing in that proverb says the heart in question has to be your own.*

"Anyway," Eddie continued, "in case there's another rush on the bar, I'll get right to the point. I'm here to ask you if you'll go out to dinner with me."

"And the long face is because you're afraid I'll say no, or is it because you're afraid I'll say yes?"

"I promise I'll have a happy face if you'll say yes."

"Good. Unfortunately, I can't. I don't date customers."

"Why not?" Eddie was puzzled. "Are you saying that guys who come here aren't good enough for you?"

"Nope. Far be it from me to judge you. I just don't want to have a romantic date on a Friday night with someone who's going to spend his Saturday night with a half dozen different naked women on his lap."

Eddie frowned at the idea that the bartender here had more principles than he did. "You've got a point there. Would you go out with me if I weren't a customer?"

"You seem like an interesting guy. I'd definitely think about it. But you're here all the time. Are you really going to kick that habit for the chance to buy me dinner?"

"I'd do it in a heartbeat."

"Why? Did Chloe and Claudia turn you down?" She was still smiling, but with an edge to it now. "A lot of guys strike out with the dancers and then come running to me like I'm supposed to be grateful to be their backup plan. I always tell them to take a hike."

"I've never asked Chloe or Claudia out, or anybody else in here. I doubt they'd turn me down if I did, though."

Melissa raised an eyebrow.

"But that's only because neither of them would turn down an opportunity to have a guy spend serious money on them. They'd go out with me even if they hated me. So no, you're not my Plan B. You're the only girl in the whole state I've been planning to ask out."

He remembered hearing Lance opine that every guy wants to date a stripper but marry a church girl. As addicted as Eddie was to TNT, he had no desire to date such mercenary women, even one as beautiful and skilled as Claudia. Her ministrations reminded him of some famous female R&B vocalists; he was impressed with their technical prowess, but it somehow never touched him on a heart level. Besides, Claudia's interest in him would last until the exact moment when someone with a thicker wallet showed up.

"Like I said, Eddie, you seem like an interesting guy." She grabbed a cocktail napkin and wrote her cell phone number on it. "Let's see if you're telling the truth. Don't come here even once for three weeks. If you come in, I'll know. The girls will tell me. But if you're serious enough about going out with me to stay away from the club, then call me three weeks from tonight, and I'll say yes."

Eddie grinned. "Then I'll call you July eighteenth, mademoiselle. I'm looking forward to it." With that, he stuffed the napkin into his pocket, spun off his barstool, and strode toward the exit. He didn't even glance at the stage as he passed it.

When he was three-quarters of the way toward the door, Chloe rushed to intercept him. "Eddie! You can't be leaving already. Aren't we going to have some fun?" She pouted and held out her arms to him.

He maintained his pace. "No ma'am. Eddie has left the building." With those words, he hit the door and did not look back.

He arrived home around one. Sleep eluded him as he relived his encounter with Claudia. This wasn't how his first time was meant to be. That momentous event was supposed to be reserved for his wedding night, for a woman who loved only him, a woman who had saved herself for him as he had for her. Their union would be spiritual as well as physical, fraught with sacred import. Instead, he'd settled for an illegal commercial transaction in a sleazy club. His first-ever sexual encounter might have been Claudia's fourth of the evening. Curiosity and lust had smashed his moral compass. The shame he felt now was not just about what he had done, but about how much he had enjoyed doing it. Could he honestly repent of something he had found so thrilling? How could he avoid being tormented with the desire for more? A little past three, he drifted off to sleep with many questions and no answers.

The alarm sounded at seven, and he hit the snooze button a few extra times. As a result, he arrived at the dealership some ninety seconds after they had closed the door to the sales meeting. As soon as the meeting ended, Eddie was summarily discharged. He felt too tired to care very much.

After going home and taking a nap, he decided to take stock of his finances. He was unpleasantly surprised by what he found. He'd run through an enormous sum of money at the clubs; he figured the total must be around fifteen thousand dollars since his first return trip to The Wolf's Den. He needed to find cheaper recreation, and he needed to find a new job.

It took a week of scouring job boards and pounding the pavement, but he found a small used car lot in Weymouth that was hiring. It had no showroom. The interior was just large enough for a couple of desks up front and an office and restrooms in the back. The place was called A-1 Used Cars, a name that Eddie figured had taken some marketing genius all of three seconds to brainstorm. The building was a little weathered, and the furniture and other décor appeared not to have been updated since the 1970s. But it had an inventory of decent if uninspiring cars for sale, mostly Detroit iron, and the owner said yes when Eddie asked if he could use some help.

To his surprise, working there was much more to Eddie's liking than the dealership had been. He had no silly sales meetings to attend every morning. Casual attire was fine. Eddie was scheduled for five days a week rather than six, and the workday ended at six instead of nine. The owner, a laconic, heavyset fellow named Dave Mooney, spent more time away from the business than he spent at it. The only problem for Eddie was the lack of floor traffic. Several people each day pulled off the road to look at this or that car on the lot, but they generally didn't come in, and they couldn't be talked into a serious conversation. "Just looking," was what they always said.

One day Eddie noticed that a spider had built a web in the corner behind his desk. Rather than kill the spider and sweep away the web, Eddie decided to adopt it as a sort of mascot. The way things looked, that spider might be his only company for a while.

Eddie had lots of time to think during the day. When he wasn't thinking about how to scare up some customers, he pondered over what to do with his evenings. At first he tried to fill them with the kinds of activities he'd always enjoyed; long bouts of asphalt therapy, or going out in search of live music. He still enjoyed these things, but they weren't as satisfying as they used to be. The appetites he'd fed at TNT had only grown bigger and more demanding with time. He had to find a way to satisfy the cravings.

One night he started browsing the same online classifieds in which he'd discovered The Naked Truth. Above the section for strippers and clubs was a section labeled ESCORTS and another labeled BODY RUBS. Eddie knew what escorts did; he remembered the news stories about the escort service where "Client #9" was revealed to be the sitting governor of New York. A quick perusal of some of the ads proved the advertisers were neither subtle nor shy about what they were selling. Each ad showcased the "provider's" age, ethnicity, and measurements, along with a

variety of acronyms that Eddie supposed communicated something meaningful to regular browsers of this section.

He quickly figured out that HH referred to half-hour
sessions and QV referred to quick visits. In/Out referred to
whether the providers offered in-calls, where the customers
came to them, or out-calls, where the providers went to the
customer's home, office, or hotel. A Google search of the less
obvious acronyms clarified that FS meant "full service," GFE
meant "girlfriend experience," and PSE stood for "porn star
experience." These were straight-up prostitution ads, despite
the ubiquitous disclaimers stating that any money changing
hands was for time and companionship only. He practically
snorted in derision when he learned that No AA meant the
provider wanted no African-American clients. Even hookers
felt the need to look down on someone.

Eddie decided the whole escort scene was just too sordid. He
navigated back up to the body rubs section. Most of the advertisers
were Asian spas. The ads were splashed with photos of attractive
girls. One of the first ads Eddie saw was typical of most:

Hey Guys!
Great Place To Enjoy The RELAXATION!
PROFESSIONAL Masseuses Very Nice And Friendly!
Relax Will MELT Ur Pain And Stress Away!
We Are Always Ready To Be You WISE Choice!
Try it once and love it forever.

At the bottom of the ad was a phone number and street address. The business hours were listed as 10:00 a.m. to 11:00 p.m. Eddie was intrigued. The late hours (no appointment necessary) and the pictures hinted at an agenda that was not strictly therapeutic. Yet the ad's text held nothing salacious; "nice and friendly" could mean just that.

As he scanned the other ads, Eddie was surprised at just how ubiquitous these places were. Five of them were in and around Plymouth; seven in Framingham; and even more in Waltham. Prices were all similar, between fifty and seventy dollars per hour. He did some quick figuring: At TNT, he'd spent more than fifty dollars by the time he paid the cover charge, bought his one obligatory drink, and received five minutes' worth of private dances. Here, he could get an hour-long massage for the same money and maybe derive some health benefits. It seemed like a no-brainer. He needed to check one of these places out.

Two of them were on same street as Eddie's apartment. One was in walking distance. As it was only seven in the evening, he decided to walk over. The place was called Orange Blossom Spa, and it was upstairs over a flower shop. The sign in the window advertised reflexology, foot massage, and bodywork. Posters depicted smiling customers, mostly women, getting a relaxing massage.

Eddie pushed the door open and heard the resultant electronic chime. He was standing in a small lobby where everything was colored red or gold. A golden cat stood upright on the reception desk waving a mechanical paw in perpetual greeting. At the rear of the lobby, an arch opened into a dimly lit hallway. Eddie heard the sound of approaching footsteps, and a few seconds later watched as an old woman came into the lobby.

She grinned at him. "Hello dear! You call, make appointment?"

"No," Eddie confessed. "I just walked in. Your ad said walk-ins were okay."

"No problem, no problem." She bobbed her head, which barely reached his chest. She was still grinning. Her teeth were badly stained. To call them yellow was to be generous; they were closer to brown. Eddie hoped this grandmotherly woman, who seemed to have stepped straight off a boat from some backwater where dentistry was unheard of, was not going to be his masseuse.

"You first time here?"

Eddie nodded.

"You want one hour? Sixty dollar."

Eddie hesitated. He considered asking how many other masseuses were available, but he didn't want to be rude.

"Come, come," she said, taking his arm. "I have nice girl for you."

She led him into the hallway she had emerged from. A doorway punctuated the corridor every few feet. She opened the second from the end, and ushered him inside. The room was small, the size of a large walk-in closet, with a big massage table in the center. A padded chair occupied one corner of the room, and a little occasional table with a digital clock or timer on it sat in the other.

"Sixty dollar," she said again.

Eddie dug into his wallet, came up with three twenties, and handed them to her. The old woman gestured to a row of clothes hooks on the wall. She said, "Take off," meaning his clothes. Then, "Face down," as she pointed to the table. She backed out of the room, still smiling her earth-tone smile.

Eddie disrobed, carefully laying his trousers on the chair folded over to hide the hardware on his belt, and piling the rest of his clothes on top. Laying face-down on the table, he felt curiosity and excitement, like a kid unexpectedly given a gift-wrapped box. What surprises awaited? There came a quiet knock on the door. "Ready?"

Eddie replied, "All set," and looked up.

The woman who entered looked to be in her late twenties. She was pretty, with an oval face, full lips, and eyes as black as the thick hair that fell to the center of her back. Without a word, she draped a freshly heated towel over him. Then she walked over to the little table and set the timer. Finally, she punched a button near the light switch, and schmaltzy Chinese pop music began issuing from wall speakers. "You want media? Hard?" Her voice was pleasant enough, and she was very soft-spoken.

"Medium, please."

She set to work. She was much stronger than she looked. Eddie was glad he hadn't asked for hard.

"This okay?"

"Yes."

After a few minutes, he asked for her name.

"Janie," she said.

Eddie wondered whether the name ended in *ie* or *ey*, so he asked her to spell it. She spelled out *J-e-n-n-y*.

She'd know how to pronounce it if her mother had given her that name. Perhaps her real name was unpronounceable. He wondered if she had chosen the name Jenny herself, or if the old lady had assigned it to her when she took this job.

"It's nice to meet you, Jenny. I'm Eddie." She made no reply.

With scintillating conversation off the agenda, Eddie decided to concentrate on enjoying the massage. Ms. Not-Really-Jenny had excellent therapeutic skills. She soothed the tension out of his neck and shoulders and used her elbows to work the knots out of his back. After he'd spent forty minutes on his stomach, she had him turn over.

She held the towel while he accomplished the flip, and then reoriented it to her liking. When he squinted at the overhead light, she turned it down. It was on a rheostat, and she set it so low they were practically in the dark. Eddie wondered whether this was a prelude to an offer to indulge his sweet tooth. But Jenny was all business. She did as good a job on his scalp, ears, neck, shoulders, arms, chest, legs, and feet as she had on his other side. The timer on the little table sounded.

"Hokay, finishee!" It was the only cheerful-sounding thing she'd said for the entire hour. She turned the lights back up and exited the room. When Eddie had finished dressing, she returned with a peppermint candy and a small plastic cup of water for him. He pocketed the candy, drank the water, thanked Jenny, and handed her a twenty-dollar tip.

That was great . . . and not an ounce of funny business. I've got nothing to feel bad about for a change. He didn't let the fact that he had been at least briefly titillated by imagined possibilities put him out of his self-congratulatory mood. Everybody craved human touch, and it need not be sexual. Skin-to-skin contact had both psychological and physiological benefits for infants, senior citizens, and everyone in between. He'd read that touching and being touched lowered blood pressure and heart rate, reduced levels of the stress hormone cortisol, increased immune function, and decreased pain. And it felt wonderful.

He visited a different place the following night. It was similar to his first experience, right down to the waving cat in the lobby. Back at home, Eddie did a little more research online. He discovered review boards for massage places. These were not the kind of reviews found on Yelp or Trip Advisor; these were massage parlor reviews by and for men who visited them in search of sexual favors. These men referred to themselves as "hobbyists" or, less frequently, as "mongers." Eddie was surprised they would use the latter term; he wondered whether they were ignorant of biblical pronouncements about the eternal fate of whoremongers, or whether they knew and were being openly defiant.

He learned that Asian massage parlors, or AMPs, were located in every major metropolitan area of the country as well as in many small towns in out-of-the-way places. Most offered "extras," if the reviews were to be believed. The reviewers named names, discussed the menu of services, and rated the providers' performances from one to five stars. Just as the clubs' girls had typical stripper names, the AMPs featured a vast array of girls with the same simple, two-syllable names, probably chosen so that the foreign girls could pronounce them and the customers could remember them.

Eventually, he found some reviews of Jenny at the Orange Blossom Spa. She had apparently arrived just a few months ago; no reviews were older than that. The hobbyists who posted about Jenny claimed she offered extras, albeit somewhat reluctantly, and gave her an average rating of three stars. Eddie wasn't sure whether to believe them. He finally decided it didn't matter.

I'm not one of those creeps, Eddie told himself firmly. He liked a good massage, but wouldn't ask for extras. On the theory that spas without reviews on the hobbyist boards were strictly legit, he'd look for good places with no reviews.

He visited each such massage place he found. Sometimes he made an appointment. Other times he just showed up as a walk-in client. He sampled six more places in two weeks, meeting Amy, Susan, Lilly, two girls named Coco, and surprisingly, one named Celestina. "Differentiation is good marketing," he told her, though her command of English was too limited for her to understand him.

After eight sessions, Eddie reached some general conclusions about AMPs. The masseuses never resembled the pictures in the ads, which were all stock photos. Middle-aged women outnumbered young ones in their twenties. Few of them spoke decent English. Most gave a very good therapeutic massage. The waving golden cats were ubiquitous. And the guys on the review boards weren't lying; most of these places, even the ones without reviews, offered sexual services in addition to massage. In response to the questions or gestures the masseuses used to inquire about his wishes, Eddie always answered, "Just a massage, please." He had just a few days to go until his date with Melissa, and he wanted to be able to look her in the eye.

He picked her up at seven on Friday, July eighteenth. She looked nice.

"You look nice," he said.

She smiled, either in unpretentious acknowledgement of this truth or in modest denial of it.

First up was a round of miniature golf. They followed with dinner at a romantic restaurant. They were overdressed for the miniature golf course, and somewhat underdressed for the restaurant. When the waiter brought a wine list, Eddie asked Melissa, "Okay, Ms. Devereaux, what is the authentic pronunciation of this—Alphonse Mellot Sancerre Rouge?"

"Don't ask me . . . I don't speak a word of French."

"C'est dommage." Eddie put on his best Inspector Clouseau accent. "Are you so far removed from the old country?"

"The old country was somewhere around Warsaw. I was born Maria Dumbrowski."

Eddie laughed. "Who knew?"

"Actually, not many people know. I had my name legally changed when I was eighteen."

"Well, let's save ourselves the possibility of any linguistic mishaps with the wine list and order cranberry and seltzer."

"Good. I don't like wine anyway."

They ordered their meals. Eddie asked, "So why did you change it?"

"Would most guys find a Maria Dumbrowski as interesting as a Melissa Devereaux?"

"I'd find you just as cool if you called yourself Ann Thrax, Claire Voyant, or Brooke Trout." She continued smiling despite groaning and doing a face palm in response to the silly names. "Did you really hate your name? Or were you trying to get away from something or someone?"

"It was a little bit of each, actually."

She told him her life story with surprising frankness. Maria was born the fourth child and the only girl in a working class family in East Providence. Her father loved his sons and tolerated his daughter. When the doctors said that his wife could give him no more children, he added that item to a long list of faults and failures for which he regularly berated the woman. His wife withdrew inside herself in mute self-defense, so no one was around to pay much attention to Maria. Parental expectations of her were low, and she did her best not to exceed them.

Her poor performance in grade school was pounced on by kids who pronounced her surname with the emphasis on the first syllable: *Dumb*rowski. High school was a blur of beer, pot, and remedial classes. Ten days after her seventeenth birthday, she quit school, hopped on the back of a Harley with a local tough, and took up housekeeping with him. He possessed an exciting edginess when he was sober but a violent temper when he was drunk. He was frequently drunk. Four months later,

Maria was back on her parents' front porch with a black eye, a split lip, and not a dollar to her name. She had run away from the biker despite his slurred promise to find her and drag her back by her hair.

With nowhere else to turn, she poured out her tale of woe to her father. He shook his head and told her that since she was all grown up now, she was no longer his problem. He did reach into his pocket and give her fifty bucks for cab fare to wherever that would take her. Then he wished her good luck and shut the door. That had been eight years ago. It was the last time she had gone home. It was also the last time she had cried about anything.

She found her way to a high school girlfriend who agreed to take her in for a while. Her friend worked as a bartender at a joint called Scooter's. It was very much like TNT, but dirtier and with less atmosphere. She told Maria good money was to be made tending bar and even lent her the $395 for a thirty-two-hour course at the Boston Bartending School.

"Before I enrolled in classes, I took care of the name change. I didn't want my ex to find me again, and I convinced the judge I was afraid for my life. Besides, my father's name meant nothing to me anymore. I chose Melissa Devereaux because it sounded somehow like the person I wanted to become. Once I had the name, I got a new Social Security card, enrolled in the school, and went to work in some regular restaurants. Then when an opening came up at TNT, I jumped at it. I knew the money would be better there. And I've been trying to save some ever since. When I have enough saved, I'll be able to get some more education and do something meaningful for a living."

Eddie pondered. "So we have some things in common," he said. "We've both learned that home is where the *hurt* is. We've both seen that 'the ties that bind' are really just cobwebs; you brush them away and get on with your life. And we're both in the process of reinventing ourselves. I must say that you seem to have found a degree of happiness along the way to wherever you're going."

Melissa shrugged and brushed her hair back. "I don't believe anyone finds happiness. It's not lying around somewhere waiting to be found. We have to make our own. After a few years of anger and self-pity, I realized that being happy was more fun than being bitter. So I decided to be happy." She grinned, and then excused herself to visit the ladies' room.

Could it really be that simple? There seemed to be a lot more to this bartender than met the eye. And come to think of it, what did meet the eye was not bad at all. She was much prettier seen in normal lighting and not surrounded by TNT's silicone sisterhood.

Eddie thought about his old friends. Church people spent so much time telling one another that they alone were truly happy. Yet here was a smiling girl who had grown up with none of Eddie's advantages, who had survived an uncaring family, a subpar education, and domestic violence, and who had perhaps never been to a church service; and *she* was schooling *him* about happiness. It was entirely unexpected. After seventeen years at

Solid Rock; after all the revivals, conferences, conventions, and twice-weekly services; after at least a thousand sermons about victory, breakthrough, blessings, and joy unspeakable, the happiest-looking person Eddie knew was a high school dropout who worked slinging giggle juice at a strip joint.

They finished their meal and talked another hour while sitting in his car. Finally, he drove her back to her vehicle and walked her to its door. They both agreed they would like to go out again, and she kissed him on the cheek and said goodnight. Watching her drive away, he smiled. He kept on smiling for an hour afterward.

Eight days later, they had their second date. They spent a sunny afternoon riding rented bicycles and ended with a picnic lunch on a beach on the Massachusetts South Coast. They talked about anything and everything. The conversation came easily, and the occasional stretches of silence were not at all awkward.

When their date was over, her car would not start. Eddie listened to her crank the starter. The battery sounded good, but the engine wouldn't turn over.

"How much gas have you got?"

"It's low, but I'm not out. The low-fuel light just came on this morning. I should have something like thirty miles of range left."

"Gotcha. Hang on. I've got a hunch." Eddie went to his own car and rummaged through the back. Returning with a rubber mallet, he used it to give Melissa's gas tank a couple of good whacks. "Try it now."

The car started right up. Relief washed across Melissa's face.

"Your fuel pump is going bad," Eddie explained. "Go get some gas right away and keep it over a quarter of a tank going forward. The pump uses gasoline in the tank to keep itself cool and lubricated. Low fuel levels tempt it to seize up. Plus, there's sediment and sludge at the bottom of your tank that you don't want the pump to have to deal with. Given the age of your car, you should probably order a new pump as preventative maintenance anyway. Don't wait; deferred maintenance now means worse trouble later. I'll text you a few places online where you can order one. I'll even put it in for you if you want, to save you the repair bill."

Melissa thanked him profusely. Her farewell kiss landed half on his cheek, half on his lips.

You're very welcome. It's my pleasure, really.

Two days later, Eddie showed up for his Monday morning shift at A-1 Used Cars. When he got to his desk, he glanced at the spider in its web in the corner. It was dead; desiccated, in fact. Eddie looked closely at the web. No bug carcasses could be seen in or under it. The web had caught nothing but dust. Eddie sat down. He hadn't made a single commission in the month he'd worked here. And now even the showroom spider had starved to death. It seemed symbolic. No floor traffic for anyone; that had to be his cue.

Dave Mooney arrived at noon. Eddie printed out a letter of resignation, signed it, and handed it to Dave. The owner nodded. He didn't look surprised.

Driving home, Eddie felt suddenly depressed. He was again unemployed, and looking for work would be a grind. He imagined trying to explain to an interviewer how he'd quit his current job and been fired from the one before that. He didn't even have a résumé, and didn't know how best to approach a real job search. Nine months ago, he hadn't *needed* to know; he'd had a job for life at FTA. But he'd been forced to quit that too.

He got home and slumped in front of his computer, hoping to find something interesting to occupy his mind. No luck. Perhaps getting a massage would put him in a better mood. He pulled up the usual classifieds to check out the spa ads.

After ten minutes, he came across a misplaced Help Wanted listing. It read, "Looking for a driver to transport our ladies to outcalls in the South Shore area. Ideal candidate will be professional, reliable, punctual, and respectful. Security and/or bodyguard experience a plus. Work Thursday through Sunday. Expect three calls per night. You will be paid $50 per call." Eddie did some quick math. One hundred fifty dollars per night times four nights per week worked out to about thirty thousand a year. That was better than nothing, which was what he was earning now. It would keep him in pizza money until he found a real job.

Eddie called the number. Ninety minutes later, he was sitting in a small office in a low-rent, multi-use building in a seedy part of Quincy. Across the desk sat Spiros Alexopoulos, a disheveled fifty-something Greek with two chins and an enormous beer belly. His face was covered in razor stubble and his shirt was covered in crumbs. The fat man chain-smoked while he told Eddie the deal.

"You'll be on call Thursday through Sunday. Three calls per night is the average, but it varies. Almost all of the business comes in between 10:00 p.m. and dawn, so you need to be able to sleep in the daytime. You'll get a call; you'll pick up a girl at her place and take her to the appointment. She'll call you from inside. One code phrase means everything's fine. A different phrase means there's a problem and she's coming back out right away. If she doesn't call you, or if she gives the code that means she needs help, you'll need to go in after her and do whatever it takes to get her out safely. Think you can handle that?"

"No problem."

The potbellied man looked over his half glasses at Eddie. "No offense, but you don't look all that tough. I might want you to prove your abilities by demonstrating them on one of my other security people."

Eddie shrugged. "So who's the unlucky guy?"

Spiros laughed. The sound was like a sharp bark. "You don't scare easily, do you?"

"I don't scare at all."

The orientation resumed. "I pay you fifty bucks a trip. The girls will also tip you if you treat 'em nice, especially if you have to bail 'em out of a bad spot. But like I said, it don't happen much."

"So when do I start?"

"Not so fast. There is one golden rule you have to live by. We're in the entertainment business. Our girls provide something pretty to look at, nice conversation, and so on. All of 'em dance, as in striptease. We're licensed for that. We don't send girls out to engage in anything sexual, because that would be illegal. Understand?"

"I've seen some of the escort ads. It seems to me that a guy who agrees to pay three hundred an hour for one of your girls to show up at his door must think he's getting more than nice conversation and eye candy."

"And you'd be right—that's exactly what he thinks. But he don't get that idea from *us*. If he calls and tries to discuss sexual services, we cut him off and tell him no deal. That's because providing sex for a fee is a crime. Of course, we can't really know what goes on behind closed doors once the provider and the customer are together." The man shrugged elaborately. "But if anything illegal goes on, we don't want to hear it. And we don't want *you* to hear it, or to ever discuss it with the girls. Got it?"

"You want plausible deniability."

"Call it what you like. Whatever you call it, I insist on it. Any violation of that rule is instant termination. If you have any questions or problems, speak now or forever hold your peace."

"Just one question. Besides the security factor, why don't the girls just drive to their own appointments?"

"Most of the girls don't have a driver's license. They've lost it, and just about everything else, before they ever knock on my door. Face it, escort work at this price point is nobody's first choice of career. They're not meeting with senators, movie stars, or captains of industry." He scratched his belly and looked around the squalid little office. "There's no glamour here, hard as you may find that to believe. Our patrons are mostly Larry Lunch Bucket types, with the occasional lawyer, judge, or preacher thrown in for variety. These guys are mostly middle-aged losers who could never get the time of day from a pretty girl without paying for it. The men are desperate for a woman's attention, and the girls have hit rock bottom and are desperate for cash. I'm just an honest broker helping two down-on-their-luck groups get what they want. As long as it's not sex," he amended. "I don't supply that."

Talk about spin: the politicians can't hold a candle to this guy. Eddie disliked the man, the office, and the job description. But it would put some needed cash in his pocket. Slopping hogs would have felt cleaner, but beggars couldn't be choosers.

Eddie started driving that Thursday. The job kept him busy. Spiros owned and operated four different escort agencies from that one hole-in-the-wall office. Bookers working from home on their cell phones took the inbound calls, made the appointments, and took credit card information. Spiros kept the master schedule updated and processed the payments. He had two assistants to dispatch the drivers and keep track of who owed what to whom. Overhead was minimal, and demand for the world's oldest profession never slackened.

On Sunday evening, Eddie went to the agency to collect his wages for the week. Counting tips, he'd taken in just under eight-hundred dollars. The money felt nice in his pocket, but that didn't make up for the way the job made him feel. Driving the escorts was bad enough. Sometimes the girls stole from the clients—mostly prescription drugs, but also cash and jewelry. Being associated with such criminality darkened his mood even when he was off duty. He told himself he was just a driver, that he wasn't doing anything wrong, that the girls would do this stuff with or without him. Though he rehearsed them often, his disclaimers failed to lift his spirits.

Still hoping for a pick-me-up, he went back to the spa where he had first met Jenny. The manager showed him to the room, collected the fee, and sent in a masseuse whose name Eddie forgot right after she introduced herself. She asked all the usual coded questions.

"You first time here?" A masseuse needed to establish whether an unfamiliar customer was new to the spa or a regular customer who was "in the know" about what went on there.

"Who did you see?" This question was a test. If the customer claimed to have been there before but could not name his masseuse, extra caution was called for. Perhaps his affirmative answer to the first question had been a lie. Eddie assured the woman that Jenny would remember him.

"What kind of work you do?" That question seemed meant to smoke out law enforcement officers who were either dumb enough to answer it honestly, or who didn't have a fictitious job story already made up. Too much hesitancy answering the question would be a red flag.

"Is this okay?" Eddie knew by now that the first time that question was asked, it was merely an inquiry into whether the massage was too hard or too soft. Asked repeatedly, the question was meant to smoke out any objection to the increasingly personal nature of the contact as the massage progressed.

This girl was good. She looked younger than Jenny, and was dressed in short shorts and a tight-fitting top. She jumped up on the table and straddled him to work on his back and shoulders. Soon enough, instead of being balanced over him, she was sitting right on him. "Is this okay?"

"Very nice." Eddie smiled and let out a contented sigh.

She worked on his shoulders, and then his lower back. When she got to his glutes, she shifted the towel, pushing it up around his shoulders so she could work unhindered on his lower body. "This okay?"

"Mm-hmm."

She worked her way from his waist to his feet and hopped down. "Okay, turn over, please."

She reached under the table and produced a pillow to put under his head. He flipped over onto his back. She held the towel up and repositioned it over his midsection. Then she turned the lights down low.

"You take care of me? Tip good?"

"Always."

She affected a dramatic stage whisper. "If you take care of me, I take care of you." She put her index finger to her lips—a show of discretion, and a request for it. Then she resumed the massage, tossing the towel aside and interrupting her therapeutic routine to keep her end of their implicit bargain.

Afterward, Eddie dressed and held up his end, tipping her fifty dollars, which was ten dollars more than the review boards said was customary for the service rendered.

I wouldn't have done that if I hadn't been so depressed. As excuses go, it was plausible enough. But he found he needed a newer and better excuse the next day, and again the day after that, as his visits to AMPs quickly became a daily habit, and he no longer refused the extras.

It's not really sex.

This has health benefits.

Greg Bowers drove me to this.

He had stayed away from TNT and places like it to earn Melissa's respect so she would date him. He'd gotten rid of a bad habit and replaced it with a worse one. None of his excuses changed that. Eddie got home and considered what he had become. A year ago, he'd been a church member in at least halfway good standing. Today when he looked into the mirror, the eyes that looked back at him belonged to a monger. Furious at himself, Eddie directed blistering sarcasm at his reflection: *Mother would have been so proud.*

CHAPTER 11
SOFT HANDS AND HARD FACES

If she could be anything she chose, she would be a nurse. That was what Melissa told Eddie on their third date, when they got to talking about goals and dreams. He envied her certainty.

They were sitting in Melissa's apartment on a Tuesday evening. She had a three-room flat on the lower level of a large house. The apartment entrance was in the rear of the house, so her "front door" looked out onto the back yard. The door opened into a combination living/dining area. Off to the left was a kitchen, with a bedroom and tiny bathroom in the back. Melissa claimed it was more than adequate for her needs; she had quiet, privacy, and affordable rent. She especially liked the fact that her landlord was deaf and thus wouldn't be bothered by her late-night comings and goings.

She had invited Eddie over and cooked him a meal of pierogies, kielbasa, and cabbage. He'd never eaten such fare, but he found it surprisingly tasty. His mother had always said that hunger is the best sauce. Being smitten with the cook was a close second. He listened intently as she spoke.

"It's not just a way to get paid. It's work that *matters*. I like getting paid, mind you. I know the median annual income for an RN is somewhere around seventy grand, which is not bad for legit work. And there will never be a shortage of sick people, so I don't see the job becoming obsolete, you know? But the main thing is that it's a noble profession. It's something I could be proud of myself for doing—helping people regain their health. What's more valuable to anyone than good health?"

Eddie smiled to mask an uncomfortable thought. He knew one thing more valuable than his health, but it was something he figured he'd already lost. No need to go there.

Brushing that thought aside, he concentrated on being glad she had noble ambitions. He had no particular career ambitions, and his current work was anything but noble. The only good thing about his gig as a driver and bodyguard was that it matched her schedule well. She worked at the club Wednesday through Sunday from six until two. With only one Friday off per month, she wouldn't often be in a position to notice that he wasn't available on weekend evenings, as he would have been if he were still selling cars.

Melissa snapped him out of his musings. She poked him in the ribs before marching over to the refrigerator to retrieve dessert. "I see that look." She pointed an accusing finger. "You don't think I can pull it off. You think I'm going to be a liquid chef for the rest of my life."

"No, you misunderstand me. I've known you long enough to know you're a bright woman. You're also brave and determined. I admire you. And I have no doubt you can do anything you make up your mind to do."

She looked at him over the open refrigerator door. He tried to read her expression. She looked surprised, like no one had ever said anything remotely affirming to her. Eddie resisted the temptation to feel sorry for her. Pity was for the helpless. She wasn't that.

She peered at him for a few more seconds, as if trying to catch him out in a moment of insincerity. Then her face lit up with her trademark grin. "Thank you, sweet man! How did a nice guy like you end up at a dump like TNT?"

Eddie shrugged. "Just lucky, I guess. How else would I have met you?" *Someday I should give her an honest answer to that question. She's been an open book with me.*

After their meal, the two of them watched a movie Eddie had brought over. He delighted in her surprise at his choice of film. *Toy Story* was a family-friendly animated film, not your typical date movie. If anything, Melissa seemed relieved that he had not chosen a put-the-moves-on-your-girl kind of flick. They sat together on the couch and laughed through the show.

When it was over, she didn't rush to turn the lights back up. Instead, she looked into his eyes, and then leaned in until their lips met. They met for several minutes. This was nothing like the booze-enhanced, hormone-driven make-out session he'd had with that Savannah waitress of distant memory. That had been all lust, two people trying to devour each other to feed their own needs. This was just as fervent, but it was about sharing something rather than taking it. And this was somehow more satisfying. *Wow. It really is more blessed to give than to receive.*

Eddie was getting impatient. He'd been waiting fifteen minutes. The Orange Blossom's manager poked her head in the door and said, "Hoe down." In response to Eddie's uncomprehending look, she repeated, "Hoe down. One more minute, then girl is ready."

Oh. She means "hold on." Eddie nodded assent. A minute later, the door opened again and the masseuse came in with the *mamasan* right behind her. The girl was young. *Is she over twenty-one? Is she even over eighteen?*

"See? I bring you new girl. Her first day today. Nicole. She very pretty, yes? She give you good massage!" The old woman bobbed her head, smiled her sepia smile, and made an obscene gesture with her thumb and forefinger. "She make you very happy."

Nicole stood there wearing an expression as though she'd rather be anywhere else in the world. The boss lady barked something in Chinese, and the girl flinched before walking to the end of the massage table, where she began mechanically rubbing her thumb over about two square inches of Eddie's ankle. The old lady walked down the side of the table and began applying traditional massage strokes to Eddie's other foot and calf, all the while yammering at Nicole in a tone that belied her grandmotherly appearance. The young girl answered not a word, and kept rubbing that little patch of ankle.

Eddie propped himself on one elbow and addressed the manager. "Let her take it from here, please." Seeing the old woman's blank look, he simplified the request. "Just one girl, please. Just her. You can go now." The manager apparently understood that. She let go of his leg and headed for the door, making one last curt remark to Nicole before exiting.

Eddie heard her shuffle down the hall toward the lobby. He looked over his shoulder at the girl. She was thin, with glasses and long hair. Her slight build and Hello Kitty T-shirt made her look almost childlike. He waited a minute or two before speaking. Nicole didn't budge, didn't speak, and didn't stop rubbing his ankle.

Finally, Eddie asked, "How are you today?"

"I am fine. Thank you for asking." Her small voice matched her petite stature. She kept her eyes downcast.

"Your English is good—better than most. Have you been in this country long?" He tried to sound friendly rather than probing.

"Nine days."

"Welcome to America. Do you like it here?" She nodded in the affirmative but said nothing. Her demeanor made Eddie think of a condemned prisoner eating her ritual last meal.

Eddie lowered his voice, hoping it would not carry beyond the door. "You don't like this job, do you? You don't want to be here."

A look of fear crossed the girl's face. "Sorry. I'm sorry. I don't want to make you think that. I have to make you happy. If I don't . . . if you complain about the massage . . . big trouble for me." Her lip started to quiver.

Eddie tried to sound soothing. "You can stop rubbing my ankle. Just talk to me. Is this really your first day?"

"Yes."

"How many customers have you had?"

"You are number three."

"Did the other customers make trouble for you?"

"They want me to do the bad thing. They want me to do the sex. I don't want to do that. Then the men get angry and complain to the boss. She tell me you are a good customer—if you complain she will punish me."

"I promise I won't complain."

Silence hung in the air for a moment. Then, "Thank you." Her voice was barely audible.

"Can you quit? Just go home?"

"I cannot go home. I have nowhere to go."

Eddie was confused. "But you've been in the country over a week. You just started here today. You must have been living somewhere."

"New York."

"How did you come to be here?"

The chime in the lobby sounded. Eddie could hear muted voices as the manager greeted another customer. The walls were apparently pretty thin here. Soon he heard the scuff of the old woman's flip-flops approaching and the heavier footfalls of someone with a much longer stride behind her. They entered the adjacent room. After a few seconds, that room's door clicked shut, and the old woman shuffled back up the hallway.

Nicole finally moved away from the foot of the table and came to stand near Eddie's head. Then she asked, "What do you do for work?"

Eddie knew she likely feared the police as much as she feared her abusers. She wouldn't confide in him if she suspected he was a cop. "I sell cars." He startled himself with how quickly and easily that lie popped out. *Well, I can hardly tell her I chauffeur hookers around.* "It's nothing special. But please, finish your story of how you came here."

She looked him in the eyes. It was the first time she had directly met his gaze. Eddie figured she was evaluating him, deciding if he could be trusted. Maybe she decided he looked trustworthy. Maybe she just figured she had nothing to lose.

"I come to America to go to school. My family didn't know how to arrange it, but they know a woman who set it up. They paid her a lot of money. She help me with filling out papers and acceptance to school. She help me get a passport. She send me a plane ticket to New York, and tell me a man will meet me at the airport to take me to the college. When I get there, the man take me to a dirty little apartment. I lived with two other Chinese girls. The man tell me my parents still owe money, and I have to work to help pay it. At first I work in a restaurant. Long hours every day, washing dishes and scrub the floors. Nobody can tell me how long I have to stay there before I start school."

She spoke woodenly, her face betraying no emotion. Eddie wondered if it was the trauma of it all, or just the effect of having to translate her thoughts into English "After one week, the man came back and tell me I have a chance to make much more money. I can pay the debt faster, live in a nicer place, and go to school sooner. They will train me to do massage therapy for wealthy Americans. He say there is big demand for people who know traditional Chinese healing. It is skilled work, not so hard, and more money. Of course I say yes."

Eddie rubbed his jaw, trying to relax the muscles he'd inadvertently been clenching.

The girl continued. "Yesterday they put me and another girl in a car and drive us out of New York. We drive for more than six hours to get here. I don't even know where this place is. They bring me in and take my passport. They say they need to keep it to make sure I don't steal cash from them. The manager teach me massage for one day. I practice on the other girls who work here. Then they tell me what they want me to do . . . I don't want to do it. But I cannot leave. Where would I go?. I have no papers." Her lip started to quiver again.

"I understand," Eddie said. And he was truly beginning to understand. Nicole was a prisoner. She was helpless. He knew how

214

that felt, knew the shame and the humiliation of it. Something had to be done.

"Where do they take you when the spa closes? Where are you living now?"

"There is a room in the back. I live here."

He heard rustling sounds from across the hall. Eddie knew that was the laundry room. This place probably went through a ton of sheets and towels each day. He could hear the old woman moving around in there. He was confident she would not hear him.

"How many people work here? Do the other girls all live here too?"

"Five girls, plus the boss. Two of the girls, they come and go. They have cars. The boss trust them. Lydia lives here. She is the girl who came with me from New York. And Jenny is here. I think she live here for months."

Eddie's stomach lurched, and he tasted bile. He closed his eyes and swallowed down the horror of this revelation. Jenny was one of his favorites. The pretty girl who ended each session with her trademark "hokay, finishee," was a slave like Nicole. No wonder she had seemed so happy when their first few encounters had ended without any impropriety. As for their more recent sessions—that was too revolting to contemplate. He forced himself back to tactical considerations.

"The manager doesn't live here, right? What would keep you all from walking away after she leaves for the night?"

"It would not work. There are cameras. There are alarms."

Nicole went on to explain that pinhole cameras were installed all over the shop—some disguised as sprinkler heads, some hidden in potted plants, one inside the waving cat in the lobby. She didn't know how many there were in total, but she knew the boss could monitor them remotely. She could look in on the residents here at any time of day or night.

The shop's doors and windows were wired. Only the manager had the alarm code. While Nicole and the others were free to move about the place, exiting the spa after hours would set off the alarm.

"Turn over," Nicole said. "If the boss comes in, she expect you to be on your back by now."

Eddie complied, more than usually conscious of the need to keep the towel positioned to protect his modesty. When the maneuver was completed, Nicole continued her story, bending slightly over the massage table and leaning on her hands, a posture for conspiring.

The skin on the back of Eddie's neck prickled. The spa was too quiet. He no longer heard any activity in the laundry room, nor had he heard the sound of the old woman's flip-flops in the hall. The door suddenly swung open. Nicole stiffened. As she did, Eddie reached up and stroked her hair, smiling and emitting a throaty laugh before frowning at the old woman as she walked in. "What now?"

"So sorry. Sorry for interrupt." Her head bobbed at Eddie, and she said something gruff to Nicole in their native language. Then she backed out again. She was barefoot.

Was that coincidence or strategy? She can move quietly when she wants to. "Sorry about the unexpected touch," Eddie said.

"It's okay. I understand why you do it. Thank you."

"Do you think she heard us?"

"I am not sure. I don't think so. I am supposed to get a hot towel for your back before you turn over. She did not see me come out for the towel, so she come to scold me for forgetting."

"Okay, so you were saying: There are cameras everywhere. The old lady knows all and sees all. She's still an old lady. You're younger, faster, and probably stronger—what could she do if you walked out?"

"It's not just her! It is men like the one who drove me here. Men who come here every day to pick up the money. She would send them after me. They are not nice men."

Eddie had an enormous flash of insight. He had always naïvely assumed that AMPs were just mom-and-pop shops, the kind of businesses favored by today's Asian immigrants the way dry cleaners had been in decades past. But now it seemed this little shop was part of a sprawling network of organized crime, tricking girls into international travel and then forcing them into the sex trade. If the tentacles of such an operation reached from China to New York City to a town like Plymouth, they must reach practically everywhere. Going up against such people would be like taking on the Mafia. It would be stupid to get involved. He had enough troubles of his own.

However reasonable and logical that line of thought might be, Eddie's emotional side shouted it down. "I'll help you escape.

I don't know how yet." He spoke more deliberately than before, enunciating carefully the way people often inadvertently did when speaking to foreigners. "But I'll think of a plan and come back in a day or two. Then I'll get you out."

"I don't know if you can help me," Nicole said. "But thank you for wanting to." She made a jerky grab for his hand and squeezed for a second. "Do not say anything about the cameras. They would *kill* me for telling."

"Don't worry," Eddie said. "I won't say a word. For now, here's an idea. After I leave, put your finger down your throat." He pantomimed doing that. "Make yourself throw up. Then you can play sick for the rest of the day, and maybe tomorrow. No more customers. When I have a plan, I will come back for you."

She nodded and left the room. When he finished dressing, she was standing outside the door with the usual cup of water and a mint. Eddie drank the cup and took the candy. Out of the corner of his eye, he could see the manager watching from down the hall. He made a show of tipping Nicole fifty dollars.

As he sauntered toward the exit, the manager grinned and bobbed her head. "She is good for you? You enjoy?"

Cut the kindly grandma act, you disgusting old flesh peddler. It took an effort to keep revulsion from showing on his face. He twisted his expression into something he hoped looked lascivious. "I like her. She learns fast. I can't wait to see her again."

He heard retching sounds from the bathroom down the hall. The old woman glanced in that direction, and then back at Eddie. She looked pleased.

Eddie bounded down the stairs, seething. He hadn't felt this impassioned about anything in a long time. When he hit the street, he decided to take a brisk walk around the block to blow off steam. He turned right at the corner, heading toward the ocean. Maybe moonlight and surf sounds would help lower his blood pressure.

So many injustices crowded his thoughts as he walked. He remembered Loudmouth's cruel mockery of Roz, and how his own attempt to aid her drew a scathing denunciation from his ex-pastor. He recalled the preacher's attempt to use Shawna as a lever to force his capitulation; the fatal beating of Big Eddie; the arson fire at his old apartment; and now this. He imagined Jenny crying herself to sleep in the back room, shamed by the way she was forced to earn her living. Maybe she had nightmares in which she saw his face, one of many faces she smilingly served and secretly hated. If only he could get his hands on the architects of all this misery, he'd make them pay. But how was he supposed to get his hands on them?

At the end of the block Eddie turned right and walked up Water Street. A short distance away, a heavyset man was having trouble getting into a car. He stood next to a parked Dodge Charger, swaying a little unsteadily. Whether he was trying to select the right key or push a button on a key fob, Eddie could not be sure. Then the man dropped the keys to the street, muttered his annoyance, and looked as though he might fall over while trying to retrieve them. Farther down the street, music drifted from the open front door of a dockside tavern. *Guess I know where he just came from.*

The barroom door disgorged three men. They stepped out, looked up and down the street, and saw the inebriated man's struggles. Two started straight for him, while the third one jogged across the street and walked parallel to his companions on the other side. All moved briskly, and none of them seemed impaired. They focused intently on the guy who was still having no luck gaining entry to his car. Eddie didn't need any of the nine gifts of the Spirit to know what was about to happen.

Here at last was a problem he knew how to fix. The search for Loudmouth had run out of gas three months ago. Helping Nicole would be possible only after he figured out a plan. But the solution to this imminent mugging was not only straightforward, it was righteous. Eddie hadn't done much that could be called righteous lately, but this would qualify. Didn't the scripture say "Deliver those who are drawn toward death, and hold back those stumbling to the slaughter"? A chance to help the helpless while burning off some anger was not to be missed.

Since he was closest to the intended victim, he arrived at the man's side first. "Heads up, pal. Do you know these guys? Are they with you?"

The man looked up and saw the pair approaching. Then, without a cue from Eddie, he swung his gaze across the street and saw the third man. Recognition of his predicament showed on his face. Despite being drunk, his instincts were good.

The inebriated man balled up his fists, leaned heavily against the car, and bellowed a slurred challenge to the oncoming trio. "Whaddaya think *you* people are gonna do?"

"Just stay put," Eddie said to him. "You're in no shape to help with this."

"You a friend of his?" One of the pair of men on the near side of the street directed his question at Eddie. "You like him enough to take a beating for him? Or do you want to mind your own business and live to talk about it?"

"Tough talk from a guy who needs the help of two friends to roll a drunk."

"Wrong answer, but have it your way." The approaching men spread out, while the man on the other side of the street began to cross back over. At the same time, he pulled a wicked-looking knife from his belt. "We were just going to lighten *his* load some, but we'll gladly take two for the price of one. Now you can both hand over your wallets and phones."

Instead of his wallet, Eddie went for his gun and quickly leveled it at the knife-wielding man. All three muggers stopped in their tracks. "Never bring a knife to a gun fight," he suggested. "Now take off."

The pair on Eddie's right looked at each other, uncertainty written on their faces.

The knife wielder did not seem as daunted. "Still three of us and just one of you. I doubt you can get us all before one of us kills you."

"You may be right," Eddie replied. "But if I start shooting, I promise at least two of you won't be going home. Which of you wants to gamble on being the lucky one?"

The stand-off continued for a few tense seconds. Then, much to Eddie's surprise, the would-be victim fumbled a small revolver from a pocket and joined in his own defense: "Two. Three of you and two of us. Not one of you scumbags would live."

With a fusillade of epithets, the knife wielder started backing away. Taking their cue from their apparent leader, the other two turned and hurried off as well.

Eddie turned to the drunken man, who seemed to be rapidly regaining sobriety. Maybe scared sober wasn't a myth. Still . . . "You're in no shape to drive, dude. There's a taxi stand around the corner on the main drag. Let's put you in one. Think you can get that thing holstered again?"

Nodding, the man managed the feat. "Thanks for your help. I got myself into that mess. I hit the lottery for five grand and was in the bar celebrating. I guess I celebrated a bit too loudly."

"No problem—I was glad to help." Eddie thought for a few seconds and added, "I'd better call 9-1-1 before one of those guys does." Mike had drilled Eddie on the importance of getting his side of the story on record first whenever a weapon was involved. Better to call the police and tell them he'd defended himself and a bystander with his legally concealed weapon than to risk the other guys calling first with a story of two crazies waving guns at them for no reason. Eddie didn't want nervous cops with itchy trigger fingers rolling up on him and assuming he was the bad guy.

"No, don't do that," said the other man. "I'm on the job." At Eddie's blank look, he explained. "I'm an off-duty cop. I don't need some brother officers talking to me about public intoxication. I'll take a cab, and we'll go our separate ways. If any patrol officers show up before you're gone, I'll stand up for you." He fished in his shirt pocket and handed Eddie a business card. It identified him as James McGlaughlin, Detective, Framingham PD.

"You're a long way from home. That's going to be an expensive cab."

"No worries, buddy. I'm staying here in Plymouth for the rest of the week. It's a well-earned bit of time off."

"Good. Well it's nice to meet you, Detective. I wish it had been under better circumstances. I'm Eddie Caruthers." They shook hands. "Now, let's get you that cab."

Back home, Eddie considered his options. He could go to the Plymouth police and tell them Nicole's story. They'd probably respond forcefully to a tale of a woman held against her will and pressured to become a prostitute. Eddie wouldn't have to get directly involved with a dangerous criminal gang.

But what would happen once the cops launched an investigation? They'd have awkward questions for him, that's what. Charges might be filed against the spa. That was good. But he'd have to testify, choosing between besmirching himself with honest answers to unwelcome questions, or perjuring himself to save face. News media would cover the trial, putting an end to the well-crafted illusion that he was in Florida. Blowing his cover might put him right back in Loudmouth's sights. No, filing a police report was not an option. But he had to do *something*.

Eddie knew that his determination to rescue Nicole was partly driven by guilt. He had supplied some of the demand for the illicit and exploitive services the spas offered. Knowing that he'd been unaware of the trafficking angle helped a little. He'd assumed that women chose these jobs of their own free will. Now he knew that wasn't always true. Rescuing some victims like Nicole might help alleviate guilt for his part in their exploitation.

But guilt didn't explain it all. He'd felt guilty every time he'd fed his sweet tooth at The Wolf's Den, or TNT, or whenever he'd driven for Spiros Alexopoulos. Mere guilt over moral failings hadn't been enough to break him of the habit. Even his desire to be worthy of Melissa's affection hadn't kept him from having a secret life. Now he wanted nothing to do with those places beyond shutting them down. He briefly pondered what could be driving this new sense of mission. "Enough navel gazing," he admonished himself out loud. No amount of introspection would save Nicole. He needed information and he needed a plan.

An Internet search provided the necessary facts. He learned that trafficking was a huge business worldwide, with more illicit profits than the drug and weapons trades combined. Some traffickers supplied slaves to be migrant farm workers or to work on fishing boats. Some Chinese restaurants used slave labor, as did some of those Asian nail salons that had recently popped up all over. And many trafficked persons worked in the sex trades as truck-stop prostitutes, hookers based in strip clubs, and "therapists" at massage parlors. Eddie flashed back to the look on Nicole's face, saw her quivering lip as she stood forlornly rubbing his ankle in that little room. He had to save her.

Eddie forced his attention back to his research. The trafficking industry stood on four pillars: recruiters who lured the victims; transporters who took the slaves to worksites in the destination countries; exploiters who managed the worksites; and enforcers who kept the slaves in line. Arrayed against these criminal organizations were government agencies and nonprofits devoted to educating the public about the evils of the trade.

Eddie found several nonprofits that helped those who had been liberated from slavery, but didn't find any dedicated to actually doing the liberating. That seemed to depend on law enforcement agencies. When it came to massage parlors, most police departments had a record of arresting the captive workers because they were caught soliciting money for sex acts, while those who owned the businesses claimed ignorance and were not charged. Sometimes an AMP would be shut down, only to reopen in a few weeks "under new management." They were like cockroaches: for every spa that got whacked, usually for licensing violations, three more would pop up.

Eddie wondered how a little old lady like the one at Orange Blossom Spa decided to get into the slave trade. He tried to picture her at home reading *Pandering for Dummies*, or perhaps a magazine called *Modern Madam*. Maybe the old woman cuddled her grandchildren and sent them off to bed with a piece of candy before soaking her tired feet and recovering from a long day spent pimping out other people's granddaughters. How did she sleep at night?

Eddie pulled up the "Therapeutic" ads section on Craigslist. He found the most recent ad for the Orange Blossom. As he read it, he realized the language was nearly identical to ads he'd seen for AMPs in other towns. Maybe that was because the same people wrote the ads? A criminal outfit with branches in China, New York City, and Plymouth wouldn't have just one outlet in Massachusetts. On the assumption that ads with identical wording had identical ownership, Eddie started a list of phrases found in multiple ads:

1. *No games unless you want them.*
2. *You will not be disappointed.*
3. *Try it once and love it forever.*
4. *We have new girls every two weeks.*

And Eddy's personal favorite:

5. *Enjoy your happy comfort life with your skillful kindly.*

That bit of gobbledygook would have been hilarious under other circumstances. And the "new girls every two weeks" line sounded downright scary in light of Nicole's allegations. What kind of business could afford that kind of turnover? It must be one that needed to keep its employees from settling in, getting their bearings, and making any friends in a community.

After several hours, Eddie had built five AMP "chains" of spas he believed to be under common ownership, based on the identical wording and stock photos in their ads. Orange Blossom Spa, where Nicole and Jenny worked, seemed connected to spas in Quincy, Randolph, Somerville, Newton, and Framingham. He took special note of the Framingham location. It was on Union Avenue, just one block from Solid Rock Church. *Say it isn't so.* Innocent women might be held in bondage a stone's throw from where two hundred people met weekly to sing and shout about deliverance and freedom. He had to do something, and do it fast.

First, he'd need some corroboration of Nicole's claims. The next evening was Tuesday, one of his nights off. He had an early dinner with Mel, and then visited what he believed was the Orange Blossom affiliate in Randolph. It was located in an interior suite on the second floor of a small office building. They closed at ten, so he arrived at nine-fifteen and asked for a one-hour massage. The idea was to be there past closing time.

The woman who met him at the door told him he'd have to wait a few minutes while another customer was getting ready to leave. Eddie knew that mongers preferred to avoid the potential embarrassment of running into someone they might know, and they appreciated it when the AMPs helped them come and go without being seen. She led him to a small room and closed the door. The room had a bed and a bureau with a clock and several bottles of perfume on it. Two coats and several items of women's clothing lay piled on the bed. In the back of the room a little nook had been transformed into a closet by means of a makeshift curtain. The curtain didn't reach the floor, and Eddie could see a pair of suitcases, an umbrella, and some cardboard boxes. This room was clearly someone's living quarters.

She returned for him in a few minutes and led him back to a massage room. He was an unknown at this spa, and the masseuse was well-behaved. She did ask him all the requisite questions, to which he gave vague replies. She didn't drop hints about extras, for which Eddie was glad, though some of what she did—accidentally?—with her hands could be interpreted as suggestive. When the session was finished, he took his time getting dressed. Walking out through the lobby, he saw another woman lying on a leather couch on the far end of the room. She was partially wrapped in a blanket and wearing a bra but no blouse. She waved and told him to come back soon. *She's gone to bed for the night. They both live here.*

Nicole was telling the truth about employees living in the spas. And his online research had indicated that such living arrangements could be evidence of trafficked persons. Another tip-off was the presence of people who spoke very little English but had a working knowledge of sexually explicit words and phrases.

Wednesday morning he tried the presumed Somerville affiliate. Two girls were sitting in the lobby. One greeted him pleasantly. She did not have much of an accent. The other girl smiled slightly but averted her gaze and said nothing.

"One hour . . . with her?" Eddie pointed to the silent girl.

He paid the dollar-a-minute fee that seemed to be the standard for the Chinese places. Thai places charged seventy or eighty dollars for an hour, but he had never gone to one of those. From what he'd read, you could not be sure that even the prettiest "girls" at the Thai places had been born with two X chromosomes. So Eddie had stuck to Chinese parlors to avoid accidental encounters with so-called lady boys.

Once things were underway, he tried to engage the girl in conversation. He started by asking for her name.

"Ahh-leez," she said. He asked her to repeat it. She seemed unable to decide whether to put the emphasis on the first syllable or the second one. After struggling a minute to decipher it, he decided she meant "Alice."

"What do you think of Somerville?"

She shrugged and shook her head.

"Is there good public transportation here? Is that how you get to work?" She shook her head again, but gave no answer.

"How do you like this weather?"

"Sorry. English bad. Sorry."

He let her work in silence until a few minutes after the flip. Hating what he was about to do, he gritted his teeth and took the plunge. Putting an interrogative in his vocal inflection, he uttered a common vulgarity that described a sexual act.

Her expression clouded over. "Forty dollar," she said without hesitation.

She doesn't know enough English to discuss the weather, but she knows sex talk. Let's try another. He voiced another obscene turn of phrase, and she again responded as if she were a waitress reciting the dinner specials at a restaurant.

"Eighty. Okay?" The expression on her face spoke of weary resignation.

"Not today. It's too much money." Eddie thought that was a lame thing to say. But if he just said no, she'd wonder why. Maybe she'd worry she just spilled the beans to a cop.

"This?" She made a gesture pantomiming the cheaper of the two services she'd offered.

Eddie shook his head no. "Just massage."

On the way home, he thought about how to rescue Nicole. Simple was best. He could go in wearing a hat, get a massage, and pretend to forget the hat in the room. Just after he stepped outside the spa, Nicole could run out to bring it to him. The old lady wouldn't move to prevent that. Once Nicole was out the door, they could just keep going to his car. *And then I take her . . . where?*

The more he thought about it, the more problems he found with that plan.

Nicole's great escape would be video recorded. The manager would know exactly who she had followed out the door. So he'd only be able to pull that off once. But Nicole wasn't the only captive. Shouldn't he be equally concerned about rescuing Jenny and any other girls there who wanted out? And what about those in the other spas he'd visited—girls like poor "Ahh-leez"?

That afternoon he went back to the Orange Blossom and asked for Nicole.

"She not here," said the old madam with the hazelnut dentition. "She go 'nother store."

That news hurt. Eddie maintained an indifferent expression—*don't show emotion!*—but he feared that their conversation the other evening had been overhead after all, and Nicole had been punished. Where had she been sent? Was she somewhere local, or back in New York? Had she been hurt? He had to find her. He'd made her a promise.

Wednesday night he went to the escort service's office and told the owner he'd changed his mind about the job. He was done, effective immediately. Alexopoulos berated him for the short notice, and demanded to know the reason for it. "I want to be able to sleep at night," Eddie said.

Over the next week, he revisited most of the AMPs he thought were in Orange Blossom's "chain." He found no sign of Nicole in Quincy, Randolph, Somerville, or Newton. None of the girls he queried knew anything about her. He didn't bother getting a massage; he simply left once he determined Nicole wasn't there. The only store in the chain he hadn't visited was Framingham. He decided to go, though the prospect of returning to his old stomping grounds felt risky. He didn't want to run into anyone who might recognize him. Still, he had to take the chance. It was Thursday night, eight days after he'd learned Nicole was gone. He shook the tension out of his shoulders and set out.

Traffic on Route 3 was slow due to an earlier accident. He arrived in Framingham an hour later than intended, pounding on the steering wheel in frustration. At 8:55 p.m. he hit the downtown rotary and drove past the church. The lights were on in the sanctuary, meaning choir practice was winding down and would be letting out any minute. He didn't want to drive past a crowd of former friends, even in the dark. Thankfully, no one was in the courtyard yet. Good.

He eased the car a block up the street, and turned left into the parking lot with the neon bodywork sign overlooking it from a second-floor window. How was it that he had never noticed it before? A quartet of lamp posts shed cones of light onto the otherwise dark parking lot. Eddie slalomed around the bright spots and parked in a dark corner from which he could see both the front of the building and Solid Rock down the street. His was the only car in the lot. Eddie exited the car, quietly closed and locked the door, and jogged to the front door of the building.

Ducking inside, he found himself in a rectangular two-story lobby with a staircase that wrapped around the perimeter so that climbers faced four different directions before arriving on the second-floor landing. From the landing you could look down at the front door or straight out a large central window that overlooked the parking lot. An archway opened from the landing into a long, poorly lit hallway with doors on both sides. A sign on the first door on the left identified Ace Massage. The door was locked. Eddie was about to ring the bell when some motion outside caught his attention.

A vehicle was entering the lot at a good clip. Rather than sliding into one of the marked parking spaces, it zoomed right up to the sidewalk in front of the glass doors and stopped so hard that the front end dove. *Cops or robbers? Probably someone who really needs a restroom right this minute.*

Eddie stepped back to the landing. He heard three vehicle doors open and shut. *Okay, it's not a guy who couldn't wait.* The front door of the building opened, and a group of people spilled in—two Asian women closely followed by two men. Neither girl was Nicole. The women started across the lobby, but the taller of the two men grabbed their arms. "This way," he growled, herding them roughly toward the stairs.

Bully boy was vampire pale, dressed all in black and wearing a white man's afro. Behind him trailed a suntanned body builder type with an ugly mug. Something was familiar—

Loudmouth! That physique and the hard lines of that face couldn't be mistaken. And the other guy was probably Ronnie Big Hair. His appearance matched Eddie's memory of the visitor he had glimpsed in Solid Rock's sanctuary the night of the big meeting with Bowers. Seeing Loudmouth and RBH together proved the sinister purpose of Ronnie's visit to the church last year. Shawna had been right. *These people tried to kill me.*

Eddie ducked into the hallway before they turned the first corner on the stairs. This was not a good place for a confrontation—there wasn't much room to maneuver. And they'd use the girls as shields or hostages. *Think! They'll be here any second.*

He hurried past Ace Massage and took a ninety-degree right into an even narrower passage just as he heard the first footsteps come through the archway behind him. They stopped in front of the door to the massage parlor. After a few seconds the door opened and a woman's voice said something Eddie couldn't quite make out. He heard the foursome trooping in. Then a voice he knew all too well said, "Wait a minute. Give me the key to the bathroom."

A door to Eddie's left had a sign identifying it as a restroom. Five seconds later, footsteps were coming down the hall toward him. The only other door off this hallway was to a janitor's closet at the end. A yellow bucket with wheels and a mop leaned against that door. Heart pounding, Eddie grabbed the mop and used it to wheel the bucket out into the main hallway just as Loudmouth was turning the corner. The little ruffian had to turn sideways to avoid a collision.

"Oh—excuse me, sir." Eddie mumbled the words mostly to the floor, barely looking up at the man as he passed. He hoped that Loudmouth would not really register his presence, that the mop and bucket would grant him a menial laborer's standard cloak of invisibility. He kept his shoulders slumped, his walk that of a tired man who was resigned to a joyless job. He turned right at the corner and headed to the back of the building. He felt rather than saw Loudmouth's eyes on him.

Will he recognize me after almost a year?

"Hey," Loudmouth said to his back. "What happened to the regular janitor I always see in here?"

"Couldn't tell you. Don't know him. I'm just a temp." Eddie spoke over his shoulder, without changing his pace. He briefly wondered if lying to evil people for a good cause was a bad thing. He could still feel Loudmouth watching him as he went through the exit door at the far end of the hall.

Once on the back landing, Eddie set the mop and bucket aside. Just as he started down the stairs, he heard footfalls coming up. Halfway down, he met a man dressed like a real janitor; black leather work shoes with rubber soles; blue twill work pants held up by a well-worn leather belt, from which hung a key ring with a lot of keys on it; a collared beige shirt with a company logo over the breast pocket. He nodded as he passed, and Eddie nodded back. Eddie reached the bottom of the stairs just as the other man reached the top.

"For cryin' out loud! Who put this here?"

That had to be the regular janitor, and he didn't sound happy about his bucket. Eddie heard the squeak of the bucket's wheels as the man began pushing it back down the hall. At the bottom of the stairs, Eddie left through an exit door that led outside. As he eased the door quietly shut behind him, he heard the crash of someone hitting the panic bar on the door upstairs. "Hey!" The voice belonged to Loudmouth.

Eddie sprinted around the corner of the building. Adrenaline made him almost giddy. *That was close!* Upon reaching the front lot, he saw that the vehicle waiting by the door was the black Rover with the fancy wheels. He moved close enough to read and memorize the registration plate and then cut over to his own car.

All the puzzle pieces fell together as he drove away. Tonight was Thursday. His first encounter with Loudmouth had been on a Thursday night, just a block from here in Solid Rock's

Courtyard. Ace Massage ads touted new girls every two weeks. Loudmouth worked for the traffickers as a transporter, and maybe an enforcer too. The muscle-bound gangster had been coming from Ace Massage on his regular route when he accosted Roz ten months ago.

What should I do now? For months Eddie had been so intent on identifying and finding Loudmouth that he'd given little thought to what he would do once he found him. Put a beating on him, for sure. But even a thorough beat-down wouldn't be retribution enough for what Loudmouth and RBH had done.

Eddie had a better option now. He could tie these criminals to the enslavement of women like Nicole. He imagined the two men in shackles and orange jumpsuits, looking at long federal sentences for human trafficking, each trying to get a better deal by pointing the finger at the other for arson and murder. It was a heartwarming thought. All that was needed was to figure out how to make it happen.

The devil, of course, was in the details.

CHAPTER 12
EXIT WOUNDS

The basic plan was simple. Eddie would buy a dashboard camera, park near an AMP, and wait for the black Rover to show up. He'd get video of the criminals and their human cargo. He'd send it along with a detailed letter to every law enforcement agency that might be interested. It would be easy. The only problem was figuring out which AMP to stake out. Loudmouth had twice visited the Framingham place at night. So he must be starting his rounds earlier in the day at some other link in the AMP chain. Eddie needed video shot in daylight. All he had to do was figure out where to wait. Getting the goods on these guys would be a thrill.

Deciding to start with the Somerville AMP where he'd met Alice, he set up the dash cam, brought a handheld camera along for good measure, and arrived thirty minutes before opening time. He selected a parking space in the square that offered a view of the front door and fed the parking meter. He spread a map out in his lap and placed a sightseer's tour book on his dash to suggest to any observers that he had a reasonable explanation for hanging around. Then he settled in to wait.

When the two hours on the parking meter expired, he moved to a different space. No sense spooking some store employee by sitting in front of the same window all day. After four hours, he moved again and went to a nearby pizza parlor to use the restroom and buy a couple of slices. After two more hours of waiting, there was no sign of the black SUV. The thrill of the chase had long since evaporated, replaced by stiff joints and second guessing. *What if this AMP isn't even on Loudmouth's route? Should I sit here all week to rule the place out?*

After three fruitless days, he decided to try his luck at the Randolph location. He had no luck there either. Maybe his "spa chains" weren't right or complete. He'd looked in the classifieds for Boston, but maybe the AMPs Loudmouth covered didn't advertise there. On a whim, he pulled up the Worcester edition of the same classifieds on his phone. Scrolling down, he quickly found spas with similar ads in Westborough, Milford, and Worcester. Assuming they were all related and not just stealing each other's ad copy, that made for over a dozen links in the chain. How was he going to keep an eye on all of that? He needed some help, but from whom? Should he hire a private investigator? Could he afford one?

Frustrated, he started driving and turned on his radio. Ten minutes later, the Allman Brothers sang him a possible solution to his problem. The name of the song was "Melissa."

"I'm all ears."

Resist. Must resist. Eddie just smiled. She might be sensitive to being teased about her slightly protuberant ears.

They were sitting in Eddie's living room. Mel and her adorable ears were the first guests to grace his apartment with their presence since he'd moved in nine months ago. She was breaking in his couch—not even he had ever sat on it—and he was thinking how much nicer his abode seemed with her in it. He had told her that he needed a favor. He knew he had to proceed carefully here, because he wanted to give her all the facts she needed without revealing too much about himself.

"The short version is that I need some information. It shouldn't be terribly hard to get, but it'll likely be time consuming, and about as exciting as watching moss grow. But it would mean an awful lot to me."

"So what is this dull information that means so much to you, but that you need my help to get?"

"It's something I promised a friend."

In response to Melissa's inquiring look, Eddie leaned forward in his chair.

"About a year ago, I was living in Metro West. One night I was walking with a friend when some guy in an SUV started talking smack to a woman who was crossing the street. The woman was very overweight, and the guy was yelling some of the meanest and rudest things imaginable at her. I told him to get some manners and leave the poor woman alone. He didn't like that, so he got out and came after me."

Melissa's eyes widened. "No way! So what happened?"

"I tried to de-escalate things, told him to cool down. But he was one of these muscle-bound tough guys with something to prove. He was determined to beat me up." Melissa shook her head in disgust and listened as he continued.

"Fortunately, I'm not very easy to beat up." Eddie grinned. "I have some self-defense skills, and I used them. I knocked his behind right out." Eddie couldn't decide if she looked impressed or merely surprised at that turn of events. He hoped it wasn't just surprise; that would be rather insulting. He continued. "The lady went on her way, I went on my way, and I thought that was the end of it."

"But Loudmouth—that's how I've always thought of him— wanted revenge. He had people combing the neighborhood for me, and they eventually found a friend of mine who they mistook for me, because he also happened to be named Eddie."

"Wait, they knew your name?"

"Yeah, the friend I was talking to at the time of the fight yelled out my name when the action started. Anyway, three guys jumped the other Eddie just over a week later and put him in the hospital. He eventually died of his injuries."

"I'm so sorry." Melissa reached for his hand. "I take it that none of them got caught?"

"You take it correctly. While Big Eddie was still alive, I promised him I'd see these people brought to justice. I had no idea how I was going to do that. I didn't even know who they were. I just felt like I owed him that."

"Do they know they got the wrong guy? If they know, then they're probably still looking for you, right?"

This was true. The arson at his apartment proved they'd realized their mistake with Big Eddie. And if Loudmouth had recognized him at Ace Spa, he knew his target was no longer in Florida. Still, he saw no point in worrying Melissa unduly. "They have no idea where to find me now that I no longer live there." Eddie was glad to be able to tell his story to a sympathetic listener. It was nice to know someone cared. And her hand in his felt pretty good. *I'm losing my train of thought. Where was I?*

"Let me ask you a question," he said. "Do you know anything about human trafficking?"

She said she didn't, so Eddie gave her the highlights of what he'd learned in his online research.

She interrupted him to ask, "Did we just change the subject, or does this somehow relate to the promise you made your friend?"

"Oh, it relates all right. See, I moved out of Metro West shortly after the fight, and as I said, I had no idea how to find

Loudmouth. Well, I happened to be in the old neighborhood the other day, and I saw Loudmouth and another guy hustling two young women into a building where the only open business was a massage parlor. I figured they were traffickers."

Eddie continued. "Lots of massage parlors are just glorified brothels. If this guy is transporting women to force them into prostitution, he's an even bigger lowlife than I thought. And if I can prove it, if I can show the authorities what he's been doing, he'll be sent away for a long time. That would feel like justice for my friend."

"And you want me to get this proof for you. How?"

"No, I'll get the proof. I just want help narrowing down where to search. I know the car he's been driving. Based on my online research, I think he supplies multiple massage parlors with girls. I've been staking out some of those places using a dashboard camera, but there are too many parlors for me to cover them all. I need you to park near a few of the places and watch for his car. If it shows up, you call me with where and when, tell me what direction he came from, and what direction he goes when he leaves. If you see him doing something that looks criminal, let me know. But I don't want you to get close to the guy. I don't want you to tail him. Just call me, and I'll do the rest."

"Well . . . okay. But by the time you get there, he'll be long gone."

"Yes, but every bit of info I get will help me put together the pattern of his movements. Then I should be able to find him and film him myself."

"Maybe I should follow him at least until you show up. He might go someplace unexpected or even lead us right to his headquarters or something."

"Have you been listening, Mel? That's too dangerous. This guy or his minions *killed* my friend. You have to promise me you won't do anything except report in. I want it so that even if he happens to notice you sitting in your car, he won't think anything of it. You *have* to stay safe."

"You're cute when you're being protective. But are you always this bossy with your women?"

"So you're officially my woman now?"

"Don't get ahead of yourself." She poked him in the ribs. "I'm just trying to understand how you think."

"Well, official woman or no, I'd like to keep you around."

"So would I. How much time do you think this would take? I still have to work, you know."

"I know. But it will be strictly daytime work, a few hours starting just before nine. You'll have plenty of time to eat and make it to the club for your shift."

"I work until two most nights. Getting up and out before nine o'clock means I won't get much beauty sleep."

"You don't *need* much beauty sleep."

Melissa looked dubious. Eddie pressed on. "You told me you lived with a real brute years back, and how you managed to get away. He's probably treating some other unlucky lady as badly as he treated you. I took a road trip to get away from my enemies, then resettled in Plymouth, so I know what escape is like. What if instead of merely escaping people like that, we could make them pay for the things they did? What if we could keep them from abusing someone else? You could help me avenge my friend and save a lot of women in the process."

Melissa waited a few seconds before answering. "I like the sound of that. I'd be helping you out by doing something boring and time consuming, but also heroic. And while I'm making the world a better place, what will you be doing?" Her smile was back.

"I'll be doing the same thing. And I'll also be helping to make your dreams come true."

"And how's that?"

"As payment, how about I pay the tuition for your first semester of nursing school? You've said nursing is what you want to do with your life, but saving the money for the education has been a challenge. It's the only thing I can think to do that would mean as much to you as your help is going to mean to me. Just get yourself admitted somewhere."

She looked incredulous. "Do you know how much money you're talking about? You could probably hire a private investigator for much less than that."

"Yes, I could. But if I'm going to bolster somebody's bottom line, I'd rather it be yours."

"You don't have other friends who would do this for you, friends who cared about Big Eddie as much as you did?"

"I'm running a little low on friends these days. Most of my former friends blame me for his death. You know, 'if you hadn't opened your mouth, none of this would have happened.'"

"Sheesh! With friends like that . . ."

This was getting uncomfortably close to talking about the whole I'm-a-wretched-outcast-from-my-church thing. Eddie tried to move the conversation along.

"I agree. You're the only person I know who might help me."

Then she said, "About this nursing school business—you don't need to offer me money to help you. I'd do it just because you need it. When something feels right to me, that's all the reason I need."

"I didn't mean it as some kind of a bribe. I just don't want to take and not give. I want to help you too."

She gave him that searching look she used when she wasn't quite sure if he was serious. "Do you really have that kind of money? Would you really do that for me?"

Eddie wasn't flat broke yet, but he had run through a lot of his money. Writing a big tuition check might exhaust the last of it. He needed to find another job quick. But he was determined to put a brave face on things. He grinned and looked around the apartment. "Just because a guy is renting doesn't mean he's broke. And as for the second question, just look into my eyes . . . if you need convincing."

"I don't get it. I mean, it sounds wonderful, but . . . we've been dating for like six weeks. I think dinner and movies are pretty normal, maybe flowers. But this . . . why would you do such a big thing for me?"

Eddie's heart was suddenly full to overflowing with everything he loved about Melissa. He found impassioned words rushing from his heart to his mouth without pausing to get clearance from his brain. "I'd do *anything* for you!"

If he'd had time, he would have asked himself how that slipped out. And he would have wondered if he'd just made himself less attractive to her by being so up front with his feelings—didn't women lose interest in guys they could catch, preferring to pine after the uninterested ones? But he had no time for such thoughts, because no sooner had he spoken than his arms were full of Melissa, and she was holding him tightly while his spirit soared.

After a moment she had another question. "So when do we start?"

They agreed to start the next day. Eddie gave her a list of all the spas in his suspected "chain," and she arbitrarily chose to begin her stakeout at the one in Milford.

"Okay, I'll be at the one in Westborough, which is closest to where you are. Call me if you see anything, and I'll be there. And promise me you won't take any chances."

"You worry too much. I'll be sitting in a parked car looking out the window. What could go wrong?"

Eddie tried not to think about the answer to that question.

Yawning enormously, Eddie sat outside Moonflower Bodywork near the center of Westborough and fought to stay alert. Sleep had eluded him the night before, and the warm humid air on this last morning of August just added to his drowsiness. Slapping his legs and humming tunelessly, he kept an eye on the body-work place for four hours without seeing anything of note. He assumed that Melissa was having an equally unproductive day, since his phone had not sounded.

Just after one, it finally rang. The noise startled him. He glanced at the phone, saw the missed call indicator—*how did that happen?*—and saw that the incoming call was Melissa. He hit the answer button.

"Hi Mel. Are you as bored as I am?"

"I've been too busy to be bored. I've got the goods on your guy. I'm on my way home now. Come meet me, and I'll fill you in and make your day."

"What do you mean, you got the goods?"

"All will be revealed! I'm on I-495 now. How fast can you get to my place?"

"I'll be there in a flash. Bye."

Thirty minutes later, Eddie was pacing around Melissa's living room listening to her explain what she had learned and how she had learned it. He was trying not to sound too upset. "Why didn't you just call me when you first saw them?"

"I *did*," she protested. "You didn't answer. You look wiped—maybe you fell asleep? Anyway, I decided to follow them myself. You should be glad I did. You might have been spinning your wheels for weeks without me."

Melissa had watched the distinctive black Rover pull up to the Milford spa. One man had gotten out of the driver's seat.

From Mel's description of him, it was neither Loudmouth nor Ronnie Big Hair. This had been a young man, maybe in his early twenties, tough looking but not overly muscular. He had gone into the massage parlor and come out two or three minutes later carrying a small pouch. Melissa thought it looked like the bags some businesses drop into the night depository at banks. He jumped back into the Rover and drove off.

"I called you while he was inside. When he came out, I decided to follow him for just a bit before calling you back. And it's a good thing I did. His next stop was someplace not on your list. He stopped at a place on Route 126 in Framingham. This time the passenger got out, and I'm pretty sure it was your Loudmouth. I got cell phone video of the car parked in front of the massage parlor and of Loudmouth coming out with one of those pouches."

Eddie tried not to betray too much emotion as she paused to gauge his reaction. He was elated that she had observed something useful, but dismayed at the crazy risk she had taken in following the Rover. "I told you not to do that" seemed the wrong thing to say, so he said nothing.

She continued. "They went from there to another place in Framingham. This one is on your list. I had to park on the street, though, and couldn't get any video. But then they went to another spa just a couple of blocks away on the same street. That place wasn't on your list either. I parked in a sub shop across the street and managed to get good video of that one."

Eddie wanted to congratulate her, but was too worried. "Are you sure you weren't spotted?"

"Pretty sure," she said. "I had one scary moment at the last place I followed them to. It's in Waltham. The driver, the one who isn't Loudmouth, went in and stayed a long time. He was in there like twenty-five minutes instead of the usual two or three. I'd almost decided to leave when he came back out carrying a pouch and talking on his cell. I was parked about three car lengths away from the door. I swear he looked right at me. I must have gotten ten gray hairs right then and there! He's one cold-looking dude." She shuddered at the memory.

"Anyway, after a couple of seconds, he put the phone away, climbed in the car, and drove off. But that little scare kind of killed my enthusiasm, so I decided not to follow any more. He drove off east down Main Street in Waltham, and I did a U-turn and drove home."

Melissa pulled a folded piece of paper out of the pocket of her plaid shirt. "These are the names and locations of every spa I saw them visit, along with the time they stopped at each. They definitely picked up an envelope or a pouch at each spa, although I didn't get to film it every time. I didn't see any evidence of human trafficking. But if those places are really brothels, these guys are the bag men." She pulled out her phone and tapped at the screen. "Now," she said as she typed, "I just emailed you the video I took. Can you make good use of all this?"

"I sure can. Between what I've seen and what you've documented, I could put together a pretty compelling letter to the police departments in all those towns. And that's just for starters." He paused in his pacing. "I should be mad at you for taking such big chances. But I'm not. You just made my day, my month, and maybe my whole year. You're pretty awesome."

"I know." She grinned, and her laughter made her whole face light up. "Well, seeing as how I've done so much for you, there's something I'd like you to do for me."

"Name it." Eddie was feeling exultant.

She stood and began unbuttoning her shirt. "Give me a good back rub. All those hours in the car have made me stiff." She was dressed in layers, wearing a black top with spaghetti straps under the plaid shirt. After peeling off the shirt, she tossed it toward a basket in the corner as she sat on the couch. She sighed and started to stretch out on her stomach.

As she did, her front door exploded inward with a thunderous crack and a shower of splinters. Melissa screamed. A man Eddie had never seen before lunged into the apartment gripping the heavy sledge hammer he'd used to take down the door.

The man bellowed at Melissa. "Who are you, and why were you following us?" By way of answer, she screamed again, shorter this time. Scrambling to her feet, she began backing toward the bedroom. Not that it offered any escape—the front door was the only way out.

Eddie, still in the corner where he had been standing when the door was breached, moved to get between the intruder and Mel. "Get out, *right now!*" The man looked startled, as if noticing Eddie for the first time. But he was holding the big sledge, and Eddie's hands were empty.

Sneering and pointing at Melissa, the man said, "I asked you a question. Answer it."

"Drop dead," Melissa retorted.

Baby's got guts, Eddie thought. There were so many reasons to be proud of her. "I told you to leave," Eddie added. "Get out, or be carried out."

"Whoa, hold on, what have we *here*?" The new voice belonged to Loudmouth, who was walking through the shattered doorway. "I don't recognize the babe, but this dude and I go way back. He and I have some unfinished business. Isn't that right, Eddie?"

"That's your fault," Eddie snapped. "You picked a fight with me and lost. If you'd left well enough alone, we'd have both forgotten about each other by now." As he spoke, he quickly estimated distances and angles of attack. The guy with the sledge was about ten feet away, and Loudmouth was just inside the doorway, some twenty feet distant. "Why didn't you just leave things be?"

"Because! Because you freakin' busted my skull!" Loudmouth was suddenly screaming at the top of his lungs. Eddie hadn't seen such a feral expression since the last time he saw Reverend Bowers preach. "Because they had to put a steel plate in my head! Because I had multiple seizures. Because of the dizzy spells and the headaches and them taking away my driver's license. That's why I can't leave it be. You're going to pay for my pain!"

Eddie's voice, by contrast, evinced a deadly calm. "Innocent people have already paid for your pain—and one of them's dead. Who's going to pay for that?"

"I don't give a rip! That other guy was not my fault, and not my problem. You're my problem, and I'm finally gonna deal with you." Loudmouth paused and seemed to regain a measure of composure. He reached into his pocket and withdrew a folding combat knife before continuing to talk at lower volume.

"This is the deal: Zeke here is going to break your legs. Then we'll prop you up where you can watch us get to know your nosey friend here." He eyed Melissa and licked his lips suggestively. "And when I say 'know,' I mean that in the old biblical sense. You can appreciate that, eh, choir boy?" He thumbed open the knife and looked back at Eddie. "When we're done with her, I'm going to *gut* you both and go get lunch." He looked at Melissa again. "Sorry, sweet cakes, but you know what curiosity did to the cat. So if there are no questions . . . do it, Zeke. Break his legs."

Time slowed to a crawl for Eddie. He saw Zeke shift his weight back and toward his right foot in preparation for a right-handed swing of the hammer. Facing him, Eddie lunged to his right, while Loudmouth moved to block the way out. But Eddie wasn't planning to flee. As if on autopilot, he did what he'd rehearsed thousands of times. With his left hand he pulled his shirt up, exposing the gun on his hip. With his right hand he drew it from the holster. He brought the gun up to eye level, front sight sharply in focus in the foreground, Zeke's blurry torso in the background. Zeke's body was rotating toward Eddie as he stepped forward to swing the hammer. Eddie squeezed the trigger twice.

Boom! Boom! Zeke let go of the hammer and seemed to fly backward, his body still rotating under the force of the aborted swing. He collapsed in a heap.

Eddie turned toward Loudmouth. The thug was charging, left hand extended, the knife held close to his body in his right hand. Eddie avoided being stabbed only because his gun was already deployed. As it was, he had no time to align his sights for aimed fire. Pointing the gun in Loudmouth's general direction, he fired as rapidly as he could.

Loudmouth's body jerked and twitched with the impacts, but he kept coming. Instinctively, Eddie wanted to circle right, away from the knife hand, but he was trapped against a wall on that side. Circling left would bring him closer to the path of the onrushing blade. He had no room to back up. As Loudmouth charged him, Eddie lashed out with his left foot, aiming for the groin. Loudmouth pulled up short and brought his hands down to defend, a reflex no man could override. Eddie kept the gun up, and his next shot hit his enemy's open mouth, blew out the back of his neck, and embedded itself in the shattered door frame. Loudmouth fell to the ground, so close that his blood spattered Eddie's shoes. The knife was still in his hand.

Eddie stepped clear of the bodies and the pooling blood, stunned at the carnage. He forced himself to remain calm as he depressed the magazine release on his gun, pocketed the partially spent magazine, and replaced it with a fresh one from the carrier on his left hip. There might be more bad guys out there. Best to be fully loaded when he met them. Only then did he look back to where Mel was standing. She looked badly shaken, but she was still holding it together. He extended a hand to her, and she took it. He walked her outside.

There seemed to be no more bad guys lurking anywhere, but this wasn't over yet. Eddie knew the next phase of this horror show was "the race for the phone." Maybe a neighbor or passerby had heard the gunfire and called 9-1-1. If the cops arrived on scene before he called in with his own version of events, they would treat the first armed man they encountered as the bad guy. Eddie fumbled for his wallet, pulling out a card with printing on both sides. Then he called 9-1-1.

This marked the end of the physical fight and the beginning of the legal one. Mike had often warned him that the immense stress of a shooting made people talk too much. They called the police and babbled uncontrollably. They didn't consider that their every word was being recorded. Sometimes they talked themselves right into a holding cell by saying how much they despised the person they'd just shot. The solution was to use a card like the one Eddie had gotten from the U.S. Concealed Carry Association. It was designed to idiot-proof this most crucial of phone calls.

When dispatch answered, he gave the address and read from the back of the card: "'I was afraid for my life and was forced to defend myself with a gun. Please send police officers and an ambulance, right away.'" In answer to the dispatcher's questions, which he could barely hear over the ringing in his ears, he repeated the address and clarified that the scene was in the rear apartment. "I'm with a friend. This is her place. There were two armed intruders. I was afraid for our lives. We need police and an ambulance right away." Then he broke the connection.

Eddie knew that a heavy-caliber handgun discharged indoors produced a percussive report in excess of 140 decibels, more than loud enough to cause instant and permanent hearing loss. That was why people at shooting ranges wore ear protection. Eddie's ears would ring for days to come, and his aural acuity would never return to normal. Neither would Melissa's.

He talked loudly to Melissa while they waited. He wasn't sure whether she was listening, but it made him feel better to talk. He was still feeling shaky from the adrenaline dump. "Real gunfights are nothing like TV or the movies," he said. "James Bond whips out his little Walther PPK handgun and drops a bad guy with a single offhand shot from thirty paces without aiming. The sound doesn't hurt his ears. And killing doesn't bother him. He just makes a corny pun and goes back to chatting up the girl. He doesn't even have to wait around for someone to come clean up the mess, because there is no mess. The dead guy never bleeds. It's nothing at all like . . . like this."

Melissa sank to her knees with a case of the dry heaves. Eddie closed his eyes, swallowed hard, and willed himself not to do the same.

"Listen, Mel. When the police get here, try to follow my lead. Don't say too much. You don't want to blurt out things you'll regret later—things that suggest malice or guilt. The cops will ask stuff we can't remember accurately, like how many shots were fired. If we guess and they later prove we were wrong, they'll think we lied. Better to say nothing until we've cleared our heads and gotten a lawyer."

Sirens screamed, and half a dozen police officers arrived to find Eddie and Melissa seated at the patio table. Eddie had placed the gun on the ground several feet away. It was unloaded, the magazine out, slide locked back to show that it was rendered harmless. His state concealed-carry permit was sitting beside the gun. Eddie pointed to the shattered door. "Two people are down inside. They attacked us with weapons." Then he added, "I'll point out all the evidence I can. I'll sign a complaint. I'll cooperate fully, but I'd prefer not to make any other statements until I've consulted my attorney and calmed down."

Uniformed officers and detectives swarmed over the apartment. Emergency medical technicians brought Zeke out on a stretcher and an ambulance carried him away, siren blaring. Various members of officialdom came and went, including a police photographer, a medical examiner, and an assistant district attorney. Other paramedics carried Loudmouth out in a body bag. That ambulance drove away in silence. Neighbors peered out their windows, and others milled around on the sidewalk outside the perimeter marked off by yellow police tape. A scrum of media types gathered, talking to whatever bystanders they could get to comment about an event they hadn't seen.

Detectives bagged Eddie's gun for evidence. He had expected that, and didn't really mind—he had others that would suffice in the interim. Two detectives walked Melissa over to one of their cars so they could question her outside of Eddie's earshot. He did mind that, wondering what she would say.

He reached his attorney, an NRA member and staunch defender of the Second Amendment Eddie had retained shortly after getting his first carry permit. The lawyer arranged to meet him at the police station in an hour. The police were good to Eddie, much to his surprise. They didn't arrest him or in any way treat him like a suspect. They'd read the scene and seemed as if they knew the score.

After the interviews at the station ended, they were free to go. Eddie instinctively drove Melissa in the direction of her apartment. "Don't take me there," she said. "It's not like I'm going to be able to lay down my head and actually sleep there tonight. I may never be able to sleep there again."

"Yeah, I can understand that. My spare bedroom is yours for the night. Do you want to stop at your place to pick up some clothes and toiletries, maybe your purse?"

"No, not really. I don't want to see the place. If you'll stop at a drugstore, we can get what I need for tonight. I'll figure out what to do about clothes in the morning."

They got on I-95 and headed in the direction of Plymouth. They rode in silence for ten or fifteen minutes. Then Melissa said, "I would never have figured you for a gunslinger. Is there anything else about you that I ought to know?"

She spent the entire next day in bed. She arose Tuesday evening, showered, and informed Eddie that she'd gotten an email from her landlord. Her tenancy was being terminated, and she had until the end of next month to move out. "We survived, Eddie. Somehow it feels like I'm being punished for that fact."

"Well, none of this has worked out quite like we wanted." He hoped his gift for humorous understatement would inject some lightness into the heavy atmosphere. "I'm glad I was there for you. I'm sorry you had to go through that. I shouldn't have involved you"

"I'm a big girl," she countered, "and I made my own choices. I knew what kind of people they were when I agreed to help you. You told me not to follow them, and it's not your fault I did. It's just that my life was complicated enough, and now it's gonna get a whole lot worse."

Eddie nodded in commiseration. "That's a shame about your landlord. People are funny. Most folks are incapable of defending themselves. They think they'll never need to, because *laws* will keep them safe, or the police will keep them safe, or God won't let anything bad happen to them. They conveniently forget that criminals ignore laws, and police arrive after the crime has already been committed. And God sometimes lets bad things happen. But people cling to their illusions and mistrust anyone who takes responsibility for their own safety. And they never met a gun they didn't hate."

He sighed and looked into Melissa's eyes. "Are you *sure* you"—

"I'm not like your other friends," she interrupted, poking him in the ribs. "I blame those animals that attacked us. Not you. Clear?" He nodded, grateful for her clear thinking. With that settled, she changed the subject. "So what are you reading?"

Eddie spun his laptop so that she could better see what he had been looking at. The online version of Framingham's newspaper carried an article about the shooting. It identified Eddie as the shooter and the dead man as Paul Cimino. Also shot was a seventeen-year-old male, unnamed because he was a minor. His family said he would never walk again, assuming he lived. Melissa's name was also not disclosed, as the paper followed a longstanding policy of protecting women's identities when allegations of attempted sexual assault were involved.

A link to a sidebar piece contained the usual hand wringing about the "easy availability of guns." It mentioned that Paul Cimino had a record that included several drug arrests. Without saying it outright, it hinted that the shooting at Mel's place might have been drug-related. Police had offered "no comment" on that possibility, and while no arrests had been made, the DA's office refused to rule out the possibility of charges down the road.

"They're trying to make the shooting look dirty." Eddie was disgusted.

Worst of all was the fact the sidebar article had a link to the decade-old human interest story on Eddie, the one where he had been lauded for visiting seniors' centers and singing for the residents. The writer lamented how a "once promising young man" from a local church ended up at the home of "an employee of a Rhode Island gentlemen's club," where he had shot and killed one man and gravely wounded a child—*child* was hardly the word Eddie would have used—neither of whom appeared to have had a firearm. The reader comments were as predictable as they were maddening:

"Why couldn't he have fired a warning shot?" Fired it where? Should he have fired into the ceiling and maybe killed somebody upstairs? Should he have fired at the floor and risked a ricochet hitting him or Melissa? Was he supposed to have time for a warning shot after Zeke started to swing that sledge hammer at him?

"Why couldn't he have shot the guys in the legs instead of shooting to kill?" There was no such thing as "shoot to kill." You shot to stop, and a shot to the body had a much better chance of stopping the threat than did a shot to a limb. Besides, actually hitting a moving limb was near impossible except for dumb luck. And if a major blood vessel got severed, a leg shot could be fatal anyway.

By far the most upsetting comment Eddie saw was one that read: "My cousin is one of the EMTs who was on the scene. He said the kid was shot through the arm, like his hands were up. Clint Eastwood Dirty Harry wannabe shot a kid who was trying to surrender. Throw away the key." *And here I thought God alone was omniscient.* Eddie was seeing red.

Melissa had been watching Eddie's face as he read. "Stop," she said. "You're only tormenting yourself."

"No question about that. I just don't know how to stop."

"Yes you do."

Eddie sighed and forced a smile. "Then by all means, refresh my memory. I seem to have forgotten."

She took him by the hand and led him to the couch. She lay down on it, and commanded him to lie beside her. When he complied, she said, "Now wrap your arms around me nice and tight, and I bet some nontormenting thoughts will come to you."

This time his smile wasn't forced. "Somehow I think this evening is about to get a lot better."

His shirt pocket suddenly sounded as if it contained an angry bee. "Don't answer it," Melissa implored.

"I just want to see who it is." He looked at the incoming number and held up one finger to Melissa. "This won't take a minute." She shook her head like one trying and failing to teach a simple concept to a slow child.

"Hi Dad," he answered.

"It's Jason."

Eddie frowned and struggled to a sitting position.

"Well, this is a surprise. Why are you calling me from Dad's house?"

"Because Dad can't call you himself. He's in the cardiac care unit at Leonard Morse Hospital. He had a heart attack after seeing the news about you. I thought you ought to know what you've done. He wants to see you. You might want to show up and make your peace with him." Jason hung up. Eddie stared blankly at the phone.

Melissa had heard both sides of the conversation. She didn't say a word, as if she knew no words could help. She slid off the couch, kneeled in front of Eddie, and enfolded him in her embrace. If compassion were light, her face would have shone like the sun. It wasn't enough. Eddie felt himself lost in coldest, deepest space, seeing the sun's light from a distance far beyond reach of any warmth.

Jason intercepted him as Eddie marched down the hall of the cardiac care unit. "It was a massive heart attack. He was talking to me about you. He read the news. I was trying to console him. Then his eyes got big and he fell on his face. Hit his head real hard. I called 9-1-1, and the paramedics worked a long time to get his heart restarted. He's conscious, but in bad shape." Here Jason gripped Eddie's arm. "He dies, it's on you. You put him here. You'll have to live with that."

Eddie was already painfully aware of that. He'd been berating himself since Jason's phone call, and this was just salt rubbed into a fresh wound. Still, he forced a placid expression. "Did you rehearse that speech long? Not bad. Try it once more, with feeling this time." He yanked his arm free and stepped around his brother. He could feel the angry eyes boring into the back of his head.

Mike had been right: "Never let an opponent see that they have hurt you. At best, an enemy will derive satisfaction from your pain. At worst, they'll be inspired to greater efforts." That was the truth, even if the enemy happened to be family.

The hospital bed made his dad look shriveled and ancient. He lay there semireclined in a standard-issue hospital gown, that dignity-robbing backless garment done up in little-boy print patterns on a baby-blue background. Seeing his proud father in that emasculating thing was somehow more upsetting than the terrible bruising on his face, the oxygen mask, or the IV fluid drip hooked up to his arm. On Dad's left, a phalanx of machines monitored his vitals, dispensed medications, and periodically checked his blood pressure. They produced a muted cacophony of beeps, buzzes, and compressed air sounds. On his right were huddled the other members of his family. They produced a muted chorus of promises and prayers: "He'll recover quickly, you'll see. He's always been strong." And, "Heal him, Lord, in the name of Jesus!"

Eddie stood in the doorway and took all of it in for a full minute before he could will himself to walk into the room. His sister and the in-laws either didn't see him or studiously ignored him. He made his way to the foot of the bed. Jason trailed in behind him and sat in the corner. Eddie looked down at what had become of his once robust father. He thought him asleep or unconscious, but just then Donald Caruthers opened his eyes.

Seeing Eddie, he motioned him closer. Eddie squeezed past the in-laws, who were slow to yield to his advance. When he reached his father's side, the elder Caruthers reached up and squeezed his hand, then gestured at a bedside table that had been rolled against the wall. Thinking he wanted the table, Lorna started to roll it toward him. He shook his head no and pointed again. His well-worn Bible was on top of the table. He wanted that. She handed it to him.

Donald Caruthers leafed feebly through the pages until he found the Gospel of Luke. He turned to the fifteenth chapter and, fastening his eyes on Eddie, pointed to a spot on the page. Eddie looked down to see which verse was being pointed out. It was verse eleven. His dad handed the Bible to Eddie.

Lorna spoke up. "We've been reading him his favorite passages off and on all evening. He must want you to read that one to him."

Eddie began reading where Dad had indicated:

Jesus continued: "There was a man who had two sons."

Eddie sighed. He knew this story well, and it was not the kind of comforting passage normally read at the bedsides of the sick. This was going to be awkward. He paused and swallowed, then continued reading. He wasn't going to refuse his father on an occasion like this.

"The younger one said to his father, 'Father, give me my share of the estate.' So he divided his property between them.

"Not long after that, the younger son got together all he had, set off for a distant country and there squandered his wealth in wild living. After he had spent everything, there was a severe famine in that whole

country, and he began to be in need. So he went and hired himself out to a citizen of that country, who sent him to his fields to feed pigs. He longed to fill his stomach with the pods that the pigs were eating, but no one gave him anything.

"When he came to his senses, he said, 'How many of my father's hired servants have food to spare, and here I am starving to death! I will set out and go back to my father and say to him: "Father, I have sinned against heaven and against you. I am no longer worthy to be called your son; make me like one of your hired servants."' So he got up and went to his father."

Suddenly, that old familiar sensation suffused the room. Eddie felt the unmistakable touch of God's Spirit. This time it conveyed neither joy nor rebuke—only awe. He got the distinct impression that God was there *with* him, but not *for* him, that it was Donald Caruthers who had heaven's attention, and the rest of the family was just privileged to be in the right place at the right time. Lorna began weeping freely, and Jason sat with a stunned look on his face. Eddie continued reading with some difficulty.

"But while he was still a long way off, his father saw him and was filled with compassion for him; he ran to his son, threw his arms around him and kissed him."

Eddie recited the next verse from memory, looking squarely into his dad's eyes.

"The son said to him, 'Father, I have sinned against heaven and against you. I am no longer worthy to be called your son.'"

The moment stretched out. Eddie blinked quickly a couple of times, and then continued reading.

"But the father said to his servants, 'Quick! Bring the best robe and put it on him. Put a ring on his finger and sandals on his feet. Bring the fattened calf and kill it. Let's have a feast and celebrate. For this son of mine was dead and is alive again; he was lost and is found.' So they began to celebrate."

With an effort, Donald Caruthers again grasped Eddie's free hand. He lifted his head and looked intently across the room at Jason, holding his gaze. Finally, Jason grated out a single word: "Understood."

Then the family patriarch turned to look at Lorna, and she nodded her assent. "If he has truly come to his senses . . . yes, we'll do as you wish."

Dad Caruthers released Eddie and lay back on his pillow with a long sigh. Then he closed his eyes. A nurse stepped into the room right then. "Maybe you all should let him rest for a while. This is taking a lot out of him." As everyone filed out of the room, the nurse added to no one in particular, "He's a fighter. He's fighting for his life, and we're doing everything we can to help him."

Eddie smiled his thanks at her encouragement, but he knew she was wrong. *He's not fighting for his life. He was fighting for my soul, and the soul of his family. Win or lose, his fight is now over.*

The siblings all spent the night at the hospital. Eddie was in the cafeteria with Lorna and William when Jason and Sarah Jane brought the news: Donald Caruthers had exited this life at one minute after sunrise. They'd watched him take his last breath. Lorna burst into tears. Jason stood stoically. Sarah Jane took his hand and patted it anyway, blinking back tears in her own eyes. William stood and moved behind his wife, putting his hands on her shoulders. He murmured "I'm sorry" to her over and over. Eddie stood to his feet without a word and trudged back to his car for the hour-long drive back to Plymouth, thinking how badly he needed Melissa's embrace.

When he reached his apartment, he found it empty. A note from Mel read, "Got a ride to a girlfriend's place. I didn't want to spend the night alone. Thanks for letting me crash yesterday. I'm afraid I devoured half the contents of your fridge. Stress eating, I guess. Didn't even enjoy it. I have so much to say, but not in a note. We'll talk soon."

He shouldn't have just run off without giving her any idea of when he'd be back. He should have called her from the hospital. Now he had no idea what it was she wanted to say to him. Probably, "Thanks for saving me, but you scare me now. I'm gone."

That idea cut him to the quick. Neither the estrangement from Shawna, nor the falling out with Solid Rock, nor the arson at his apartment, nor even the death of Eddie Freeman had hurt like this. But the events of this day were unbearable. *I caused my dad to die of shock and heartache. Jason was right—I have to live with that.* And Mel had decided to exit stage left, maybe never to reappear.

Eddie felt like crying, but he couldn't. He groaned, and his shoulders briefly shook, but his eyes remained dry. This was what it felt like to be truly alone; no one to talk to, no one to turn to, denied even the company of his own tears.

PART THREE
MATTERS OF THE HEART

CHAPTER 13
HOME AT LAST

You're gonna be okay. The thought came as if from a great distance. It was reminiscent of the way a corner man encourages his fighter when the man has been stunned in the ring. Eddie concentrated on focusing through the fog of his emotions, straining to hear the needed encouragement. *Don't just stand there—keep moving. Counterpunch!*

Loudmouth was dead. Nothing further could be done to him.

Big Eddie was no longer around to hear the news. Nothing could be done about that either.

And Dad . . . *Snap out of it!*

Ronnie Big Hair was still out there somewhere. And somewhere, Nicole was a captive, living in fear and shame. It wasn't much, but it gave him a place to start focusing. The fog began to lift; more thinking, less feeling. It was early evening. He'd slept most of the day and was eager to shake off his depression and do something. He grabbed a paper and pen and stood at the kitchen counter, making a list of things to do.

He started by finding the mailing address for the police department in each town where Melissa had taken video for him. To these he added the district attorneys for the two counties involved, along with the state representatives for each district. He planned to compose one letter for all the law enforcement officials, a different one for the state reps, and a third letter to be sent to area newspapers and the investigative reporters at local TV stations.

Father, I have sinned against heaven and against you. That line came to mind apropos of nothing. It was the verse from the parable of the prodigal son, the one he'd read to his dad on his deathbed. This was no time to let the pain back in. He needed to concentrate on the list. There'd be time for wallowing at the funeral, assuming he couldn't figure out a way to tamp down his grief by then.

Next on the list was college research. He sat at the kitchen table and perused the websites of a half dozen area schools that offered nursing degrees. After studying their tuition and fees, he sent Melissa two thousand dollars via PayPal. Eddie was pretty close to broke now. He owed his attorney for meeting him at the police station. He had enough left for maybe one more month's bills, and then he'd be in trouble. Still, he was happy about the payment to Melissa. He wished he could see the look on her face when she opened her email. In fact, he just wanted to see her face again, period.

Father, I have sinned against heaven and against you. This was getting frustrating. Eddie could usually concentrate on a given task for long periods without his thoughts wandering off on tangents. What was it Mike Manzanetti always said about focus?

Mike can't help you with this. That thought sounded like Eddie's normal mental "speech," but it carried an unaccustomed weight of authority and somehow didn't feel as though it came from within. It was almost as if someone else had spoken using Eddie's voice. His heart thudded in his chest as he realized Someone Else had indeed spoken.

The tears that would not put in an appearance earlier came like a flood now. He spoke the confession out loud: "Father, I have sinned against heaven."

What followed wasn't exactly prayer, and it wasn't meditation. Later, looking back, Eddie was never able to find words to describe what the next few hours were like. It was just as well; most people reacted skeptically to any narrative that included the words "God said." Eddie sat silently at his kitchen table, conscious of heaven's scrutiny. He was before the judge, unable to mount a defense. After all, what could he say? He had no reasons to set in order, no excuses that would hold water.

Bits and pieces of his life flashed through his mind. It was akin to looking down a telescope from the wrong end. From a distance, he saw himself as a child eagerly reading his Bible late into the night; being baptized and filled with the Holy Spirit at the age of thirteen; singing to the residents of an assisted living center and rejoicing in their smiles; testifying in church about his unswerving commitment to God. The view shifted to show him the last time he'd seen his father on his feet, that day when Dad had sent him into the world with well wishes and money, telling him to serve God. A heartbeat later, Eddie saw himself kissing Charlene in his car and lusting after her body. He traded his hard-earned money for lap dances. He heard the loud music and heavy breathing as he lost his virginity to that high-mileage blonde at The Naked Truth. He watched himself slinking away from the AMPs, where he'd been pleasured by women whose names he never knew and whose faces he could barely recall.

Through it all, he heard his own words and thoughts testifying against him: "I will," he had promised his father about serving God. "We are God's property, body and soul," he had emailed Shawna. "I'll never go anyplace like that again," he had lied to himself after leaving The Wolf's Den. Eddie Caruthers, child of God, had made himself irrefutably, inescapably vile. *I'm so sorry for everything.*

What an underachieving little word "sorry" was. If you dialed a wrong number, you told the answering party you were sorry. If you were five minutes late for a lunch meeting, you told those present you were sorry. You said it whether you meant it or not, just because it was polite. And if your dearest friend were to lose a parent, a spouse, or a child, all you could really say to them was that you were so very sorry. It was supposed to be a one-size-fits-all word, but it failed utterly. *I'm sorry I lied about my whereabouts. I'm sorry I squandered my money. I'm sorry for being a whoremonger. I'm . . . sorry.* He wanted to have something less pathetic to say, a word weighty enough for all of this. He couldn't think of one.

"But I'm changing," he said weakly to the empty air. "I've already stopped going to the spas." *Why?* The question was felt rather than heard. The answer was instantly self-evident. Hatred, not love, had been the driving force behind his change in attitude, his desire to save Nicole. He hated helplessness more than he loved God.

He desperately wanted to become the fervent Christian he once was, but was loathe to make promises. Promises were easy. Keeping them was not. He knew he lacked the necessary strength of will. What hope was there for him?

It's not all about you. That thought-voice spoke in his mind again, the one that sounded like his own but wasn't. Eddie's awareness shifted from his sins and shortcomings to God, from *self* to God. And what he felt from God was . . . anything but rage. He felt no revulsion, no contempt. Stern disapproval, to be sure, too heavy for Eddie to bear alone. He was astonished to realize that God must be helping him bear it, keeping the full weight of it from crushing his spirit. And shining through it all was compassion, and patience, and love. God was not like people. People would despise him if they knew half of what he'd done. God knew all, and loved him anyway. With that understanding, shame gave way to immense gratitude. Yes, he'd steered himself off course. Badly off course. But he knew the way back. The same God that loved him and forgave him would help him on the journey.

The next hour—or was it hours, plural?—passed in blissful fellowship, a communion with God such as he hadn't experienced since his early teens, in the days before the complexities of church life obscured the simplicity of the gospel. When he got up from the table, his step was light and his heart was buoyant. The night was spent. The sun was rising. And a scripture came to his mind, the fifth verse of Psalm 30:

> *For His anger is but for a moment,*
> *His favor is for life;*
> *Weeping may endure for a night,*
> *But joy comes in the morning.*

He waited until nine o'clock before calling Melissa. "Hi, Mel. Are you doing okay?" He wondered if she'd seen her email yet.

"I'm alive. How is your father doing?"

"He's . . . not alive. It's been just over twenty-four hours now."

"Oh Eddie, I'm so sorry. Is there anything I can do?"

"Thanks. I'm okay, really. I got your note. Sorry I wasn't in touch sooner."

"You had more urgent things to deal with than getting in touch with me. I understand. And I've made good use of the time."

"What do you mean?"

She paused before she answered. "I'm evaluating things— where I am, and where I'm going. When you're faced with the real possibility of your own death, you start to take stock. And last night . . ."

"What? What happened last night?"

"It's hard to explain. It was a weird and disturbing night, but it wasn't all bad. Like I said, it's hard to explain. But the main thing is that I have to make some changes, get my life together. I need a little time to get it sorted out."

Eddie had heard this tune before. "I'd very much like to walk beside you while you do that."

"I'm glad you feel that way. You're a sweet man. But I need to do this alone."

He was tempted to plead with her not to shut him out of her life. Instead, he just said, "I understand."

"I'm sure we'll talk again, Eddie. If we're meant to be, we will."

"You have my number, Mel. Use it any time."

When their conversation was over, Eddie didn't feel nearly as bad as he'd expected to feel. True, Mel's backpedaling was disappointing, though not entirely unexpected. He'd lost a lot in a very short time. But the joy that had flooded his heart these last few hours was not so easily erased. He squared his shoulders and reached for yesterday's list. When in doubt, do the next thing.

By the end of the day, he'd written letters to everyone on his list: police chiefs, politicians, journalists. Where appropriate, he included copies of Mel's video. Feeling the need for caution, he wore gloves while handling the paper, envelopes, stamps, and flash drives. His fingerprints were on file with the state—that had been required for him to get his concealed-carry permit.

While he doubted that anyone would go to great lengths to determine who had sent his unsigned letters, he was taking no chances. He mailed everything from an out-of-town post office.

He hoped his effort was not too late for Jenny and Alice and especially Nicole. One way or another, this would surely help somebody. And if it got Ronnie Big Hair busted, then justice would be served as completely as it could be, at least in this life.

He went from the post office straight to Mike Manzanetti's house. He wasn't sure why that felt like the next thing he should do, but it did. When he arrived, he found the basement door to the gym locked. Mike had always kept it open so his students could come in and spar or work out on the equipment whenever the mood hit them. He walked around to the front of the house and stepped onto the screened-in porch. Mike was stretched out on a cot a few feet away. A blanket was draped over him and a blindfold covered his eyes.

"Hey there, can I help you?"

Mike hadn't moved, but his voice held the same loud cheeriness Eddie remembered.

"Hey Mike, it's me, Eddie Caruthers."

Mike sat up and turned slowly sideways, putting his feet on the ground. "How you doin', bro? Long time no see."

"I'm doing great, though that's a recent change. How about you?"

"I've been better," Mike conceded, turning his head toward the sound of Eddie's voice.

"I knew something was wrong. This is the longest I've ever seen you go without jumping up to pace. And what's with the blindfold?"

"I was in a pretty bad car accident a while back. I broke an ankle and both arms. Worse yet, I ended up with two detached retinas. The bones healed up pretty quickly. The eyes are taking a lot longer. I have to wear this to keep from being distracted by anything visual. The doctor says I'm supposed to lie here and not move my eyeballs at all, so they can heal. It's a lot harder than it sounds."

"Dude, that's awful. How long have you been like this?"

"It's been three months and counting. But what's up with you? A couple of guys I know called up and said you were involved in a shooting. Is that true?"

"Yeah, it's true. It was self-defense, a clean shooting—my gun against a sledgehammer and a knife. The bad guys were going to rape the woman I was visiting and then kill us both. My training saved us. I guess she and I both owe you for that."

"Think nothing of it, my man. That's what I'm here for. You feel different?"

"I don't feel like a superhero, if that's what you mean. I would've chosen another way out if I could have. I know what you meant when you used to tell me to pray I'd never need the gun. I'd shoot again in a heartbeat, and hate the experience just as much."

"Good. You lose any friends over this yet?"

"I didn't have many to start. I'm not sure if I've lost any." *Of course, there's Melissa. Let's not go there.*

"You will. It goes with the territory. By killing in self-defense, you just joined a very small club, and most people won't understand. Don't let it depress you."

Eddie thought that sounded like the voice of experience talking. "If my losses thus far haven't depressed me," he said, "I don't think anything will. But what are *you* going to do? You obviously can't teach in your condition."

"That's true. No training, no students. I lie here day after day, trying to figure out what I'm going to do after we lose the house. I can't support my family like this." His usually jovial demeanor was a grimace.

"Things are really that bad?"

"Dude, it's hard to get disability insurance in my line of work. When I got laid up, the income stopped. The bills didn't."

"So how much time do you have?"

"Another thirty days, give or take."

Eddie considered for a moment. The spark of a plan came to him almost immediately. "Who are your three most advanced students?"

"Well, let me think. Assuming you haven't let yourself go entirely to pot, then that would be Andrei, Dmitri, and you. Why?"

"I have an idea."

They talked for the next two hours, fleshing out a plan to save Mike's home and business. Eddie would take over Mike's classes, backed up by Andrei and Dmitri if they agreed, and as far as their schedules would allow. Mike had always taught adults only. But to bulk up the student roster, they'd do a short-term marketing blitz around ideas like "bully-proof your child," and "assault-proof your daughter." They'd split the revenue sixty-forty, with 40 percent of the revenue from each class going to whoever taught it, and 60 percent going to help Mike keep his home.

Other details had to be worked out. For instance, Eddie would need to find a place to stay that was much closer than Plymouth. When they finished talking, he was brimming with satisfaction. It felt good to do something good for someone else, and he was getting a job out of the deal as a bonus.

"Thanks again," Mike was saying as Eddie prepared to leave. "Hey, why don't you drop by around dinner time on Friday? Lisa and I would both enjoy the company."

"Actually, I can't," Eddie said. "I have to go to a wake."

"Your father was a great man."

The elderly woman who was clasping his hand was at least the tenth person to utter those exact words to Eddie at the wake. While he appreciated the sentiment, he didn't know quite how to respond. "Thank you" didn't seem quite right for acknowledging a compliment paid to a third party. And "I know" felt wrong too, though Eddie was more aware than ever that his father had been a great man. In the end he settled for nodding and smiling and patting her hand, saying nothing.

Eddie had never met this woman before. So many strangers had attended this wake, and it made him extra vigilant. Loudmouth was no longer able to make trouble for anyone. But the same could not be said for Ronnie Big Hair and whatever other criminal associates Loudmouth might have had. He had no way to know whether someone in the sanctuary was there seeking revenge. Eddie glanced around frequently and chafed at the close quarters.

The crowd was enormous. Solid Rock's sanctuary was full, and the line spilled out the door, down the steps, and around to the courtyard. And when those people reached the front row and greeted the family of the deceased, almost all of them had a story about the kindness of Donald Caruthers.

There were old women whose cars he had maintained and repaired, either for free, or in the case of major repairs, for whatever amount they could afford. There were former neighbors whose driveways he'd plowed, also for free, even after he had moved out of the old neighborhood into the big house in Framingham. There was the widower he had counseled through the first difficult months of bereavement, less than two years after losing his own wife.

"He visited my son in jail."

"He filled our fridge when my husband hurt his back and couldn't work."

"I know he was a busy man, but he always made time to talk."

And so it went, on and on. Two young women with tear-stained faces who came in together stuck out among the hundreds of mourners. They were baristas at a coffee shop his father had frequented. Apparently Dad had provided a listening ear at various times when they both needed it. One explained, "He gave great advice. He didn't come across as a Bible thumper, really"—she paused, looking briefly fearful that her choice of words might have given offense—"but when you talked with him, you came away knowing right from wrong." Her fellow barista was more succinct. "He was just the nicest man I ever met."

Eddie had a few tense moments. Shaking the hands of all those church members would have been awkward even if he had done nothing more newsworthy than leave the church on bad terms with the pastor. This was much worse. He was grateful that most members kept their private thoughts behind their eyes, conveyed their condolences, and moved on without saying anything more.

The funeral was the next day. Reverend Bowers officiated. The clergy formed a processional down the center aisle, chanting the words of John 11:25-26:

> *Jesus said to her, "I am the resurrection and the life. He who believes in Me, though he may die, he shall live. And whoever lives and believes in Me shall never die."*

After scripture readings, choir selections, and congregational songs, Pastor Bowers got up to deliver the message. He lauded Donald Caruthers's many contributions to the church. He talked of his generosity, his faithfulness as an usher, how he rarely missed a service. Eddie suspected that none of those things meant as much to God as all the fixed cars and plowed driveways and donated food he'd heard about yesterday. Surely being the nicest man someone had ever met carried more weight in the heavenly halls of justice than a perfect attendance record at Sunday school. Still, it was heartwarming to hear that Solid Rock appreciated his dad.

And the congregation of Solid Rock turned out for the funeral, although not in the numbers Eddie expected. He was surprised at the absence of certain people he assumed would be there, including Shawna Bell. For his part, Gregory Bowers outdid himself. He spoke for twenty-five minutes, and his remarks were eloquent and edifying. The preacher bore little resemblance to the red-faced demagogue screaming into the microphone last October. Today reminded Eddie of what was good about belonging to a church.

The processional to the cemetery and the graveside service went by in a blur. Afterward, everyone returned to the church for food in the fellowship hall. Eddie was not in the mood, but he had long ago learned the truth; namely, that there was no occasion either in life or in death that church folks didn't regard as a reason to eat. Hours later, Eddie drove back home exhausted and laden down with chicken, casseroles, cakes, and pies.

Home was no longer Plymouth. He was staying at his father's house. Jason and Lorna each owned homes of their own. Staying at Dad's, Eddie could live rent-free and keep the place up while the estate was being settled. This arrangement also made it easy for him to get to Mike's place to carry his share of the teaching schedule. He terminated his Plymouth tenancy and rented a truck to move all his furniture into the apartment above the rebuilt garage. Eddie moved into a guest bedroom in the main house. This place that had once felt like a cage he couldn't wait to escape was now a repository of cherished memories. He knew his stay would not be permanent, but for now, it was good to be home.

A few days after the funeral, the Caruthers siblings met at the office of their father's attorney. After expressing his sympathies, the lawyer walked them through the provisions of Dad's estate plan. It was complex, with multiple trusts and life insurance policies. While Eddie didn't fully understand things like Revocable Living Trusts and Irrevocable Life Insurance Trusts, he understood a couple of main points. First, Dad had left them all very well off. And second, they would not have to wait long for most of it because the trust assets didn't need to go through the slow process of probate that applied to assets controlled by Dad's last will and testament. Fast Track Automotive went entirely to Jason, as expected. Eddie and Lorna received equivalent inheritances in cash, thanks to the life insurance policies. The house was to be sold and split three ways, unless one of the children wanted to buy out the other two. Eddie did the math in his head and realized that his share of the inheritance would probably approach $1.5 million.

That information was staggering. He'd been so foolish with his money over the past year. He'd run through all of it. He'd come to this meeting unsure if he was going to receive anything.

Now, if he played his cards right, he was pretty much set for life. While he would gladly have traded the money for a chance to have his father back, he was enormously grateful for this turn of events.

Later that afternoon he was back in Waltham discussing marketing plans with Mike, Andrei, and Dmitri. They were all confident they could save the school Mike had built and save Mike's home from the bank.

When all the talking was done, Eddie took turns sparring with the two brothers. Andrei and Dmitri were in their early thirties and looked like ambulatory mountains. Both of the brothers from Belarus stood over six-four, and each weighed well over three hundred pounds. They had been training for more years than Eddie, and each helped the other stay sharp even after Mike's injury sidelined him. Eddie, on the other hand, had developed a noticeable case of "ring rust." He ended up eating a few punches he would have slipped in the old days and was caught by some takedowns he would have stuffed before.

Mike, whose eyes were still covered per his doctor's orders, couldn't see the action but could readily understand what he heard.

"Eddie, what's all this huffing and puffing I hear? You're standing in place too long—either retreat or close the distance! Don't stay in punching range with an opponent that big and strong! Don't let him cut off the ring and corner you like that! See the environment, not just the opponent!" Mike had pretty salient observations for a sightless man.

It would take a couple of weeks, but Eddie knew his ring skills would return. Today's bruises would make him a better fighter, and a better trainer of fighters. In the meantime, he didn't mind the minor injuries and muscular soreness. In fact, he was enjoying himself immensely. It was good to be home.

On Sunday, Eddie went to service at his old church. Yes, a man can read the Bible at home, and Eddie had been doing just that since that long night in his Plymouth kitchen. And yes, a man could pray at home. He'd been doing that too. But it felt as though his turnaround, his *homecoming*, would not be complete without going back to church.

Arriving just before the top of the hour, he was surprised to see only about eighty or ninety people in the sanctuary. There had been closer to two hundred the last time he'd attended service here. Sure, some people would be out of town, or maybe home sick; but half the congregation? Jason, Lorna, and the in-laws were there, all sitting in a row. Eddie was happy to be there, albeit a bit nervous. He decided to sit by himself, where he'd sat the last time he was here. Rosalyn Pitts beamed at him as he passed her bench. One of the ushers nodded and smiled at him, and Eddie grinned back. He took his seat just as the ministers filed onto the platform.

Everyone stood for the invocation, the reading of Psalm 100. The last three lines really resonated:

> For the LORD is good;
> His mercy is everlasting,
> And His truth endures to all generations.

Eddie added his joyful shout to the others that went up around the sanctuary. He was awash in pure happiness. The good feeling lasted through the end of the song service.

When Pastor Bowers came to the pulpit, the last murmurs of praise were rippling through the congregation. The first words out of the preacher's mouth were, "Come on, you can do better than that. You need to make some noise in here!"

There was a smattering of applause and a handful of people shouting "hallelujah," but it didn't seem as heartfelt as the earlier worship. Rather than a spontaneous outburst, it felt like mere submission, obedience to the demands of the preacher. Bowers was just getting started.

"You know I can't stand anything dead," he shouted. "We serve the living God. You won't encounter God in a dead church. Don't worship him by opening a stale can of lukewarm praise. Let's turn up the heat! I know there are a lot of empty seats in here, but don't let it stifle your praise. You ought to make some extra noise for yourself and the person who should be sitting in the empty chair beside you."

He continued in that vein, pacing back and forth, eyes closed, tendons bulging in his neck. "Come on, make some noise in here! Praise him for his mighty acts. Praise him according to his excellent greatness. Church, you know the drill: when the praises go up, the blessings come down!"

The church band launched into an impromptu performance of an uptempo praise song. After the choir had sung the short chorus half a dozen times, the pastor resumed exhorting.

"You create the environment for miracles. You want blessings? You want deliverance? You want to kick the devil out of your life? You determine what can happen in this service. You create the climate in which God can move. Did you come here wanting church as usual, or do you want breakthrough? If you want breakthrough, then give God some *praise!*"

Eddie observed that many people seemed ready to give God praise at that moment, but appeared torn between doing so and giving polite attention to the pastor as he continued his remarks without pause. "I told you back in January that this would be a year of revival. And it will be! So what if a lot of seats are vacant now. The people who left lacked vision. They lacked faith. That's okay—it happens. God just weeded out the unbelief from the congregation."

This was the angry, frustrated Pastor Bowers that Eddie remembered so well from his last service. So the empty chairs weren't a fluke. The congregation had shrunken substantially, and the preacher was ranting to the remainder. "You stay faithful! You stay in your place of blessing. Revival is coming. You who stay will see his blessings poured out *and the quitters won't.*" He did not add the taunt sung by elementary school children everywhere—"naa-na-na-naa-naa!"—but it would have fit right in with the tone of his remarks.

Bowers continued shouting for another ten minutes. At long last, he said the words Eddie was waiting for: "You may be seated." The crowd sat down with a collective exhalation.

Reverend Bowers announced that he had been working on a particular message all week, but now felt compelled to preach a different one. "Sometimes you have to throw away your notes." He took his text from the fifteenth chapter of Luke. This passage was very familiar to Eddie; it was the parable of the prodigal son. He'd given it plenty of thought since that night in the hospital. The pastor read the passage, concluding with verse eighteen:

> *"I will arise and go to my father, and will say to him, "Father, I have sinned against heaven and before you, and I am no longer worthy to be called your son. Make me like one of your hired servants."*

Bowers said, "The story goes on, but we'll stop reading there for the sake of time." Then he announced the title of the message: Real Repentance. In his habitual style, he began his remarks with calm and measured delivery. "We have here a very sad and disturbing story. It tells of a young man who, despite being raised in a godly house, so disrespects and dishonors his father that he basically tells the man he wishes he were dead. That's the upshot of demanding his cut of the inheritance while the father still lived. But that's the kind of guy this son was."

Guard your heart with all diligence. Eddie sensed that voice again, the one that sounded like his own but wasn't. It was very still, very small within him, but the warning was clear. Inwardly, Eddie took up a defensive posture, determined not to leave his spirit wide open for attack. *If it's wrong, let it roll off me*, he prayed.

"The word *prodigal* means wasteful," the pastor continued. "So after terribly insulting his father, the prodigal son takes off for parts unknown, somewhere very far away. There he wasted all his money on riotous living. And the news made it all the way back home. You may think your sins are secret, but the truth always gets out."

Bowers went on like this for fifteen minutes or so, pointing out how the prodigal son's job feeding pigs represented hitting rock bottom. After all, it would have been one of the most disgusting jobs imaginable to someone raised on the Law of Moses. Eddie thought about his job as a driver for Spiros Alexopoulos. *I can't disagree with you there, preacher: rock bottom.*

Then came the part where the preacher downshifted and put the pedal down. "But the big difference between the prodigal son and people today is that the biblical prodigal repented. He went home and humbled himself. Today's prodigal doesn't humble himself and ask for a servant's role. No, after walking out on God and living like the devil, he strolls back into God's house laughing and grinning and showing not a hint of remorse." Bowers was in high dudgeon now, repeatedly banging the pulpit with his fist.

"The son in the biblical story was living *la vida loca*, getting into whatever passed for sex, drugs, and rock and roll in that era. Today's prodigal is not just a party-hearty kind of guy. No, today's prodigal leaves a trail of death and destruction in his wake, and then saunters into church like he's doing God a favor by coming back!

"Here's a word of warning for the modern prodigal: we've had a lot of funerals around here of late, but I would hate to have to preach at yours. Do you really think you're ready to meet your maker? I don't think so. If you can't humble yourself like the original prodigal did, there's no room for you in the congregation of the righteous."

Eddie heard little of the rest of the sermon. It was if a heavy curtain were drawn around his mind and heart, muffling the sound, giving him a measure of peace behind its protective shield. He glanced around the sanctuary and caught several people glaring at him. While his relationship with God had done a 180-degree course correction, getting back in the good graces of these people would be much harder, if not impossible. He was a pariah here. Perhaps that was all they would ever allow him to be. He'd repented before God, but they didn't know that. Perhaps they expected him to do penance for all the awful things that had happened. *If I had crawled in wearing sackcloth and ashes, would that have appeased them? Do they want me to kowtow and bang my head on the floor?*

One thing was obvious: the pastor's rage had not diminished during Eddie's absence. It had simply waited for him, taking up where it left off. If anything, it had gotten worse; a year ago, no one had died yet. Now three people had, maybe four. And if the pastor was going to be perpetually angry, the church would too.

Service ended, and he walked toward the exits as the crowd was being urged to come to the altar. He was not especially hurt or upset, and neither was he shocked. The day was too beautiful to be ruined by one angry person, or even by a building full of them. If God had forgiven him, why should he rend his garments over some preacher who never would? And if no one here was prepared to spread a little love his way, he still had love enough to spare for someone else. On his way to the exit, he stopped and sat beside Roz on her bench. She looked smaller than he remembered.

"Hey Roz," he said, softly enough that his voice wouldn't carry beyond her. "What's your favorite restaurant?"

"I don't know." She looked at him quizzically. "I guess I'd say The Cheesecake Factory. Why?"

"Well, if you have no objections and no other plans, I'd like to take you there for dinner tonight."

Her face registered surprise. "You want to take me out to dinner?"

"Well, only if you're willing. I don't want to get you in trouble with the powers that be. But I've got my life turned around now. I'm going to celebrate that, and I'd like it if you'd join me."

Rosalyn Pitts smiled sweetly. "In that case, can you pick me up at seven?"

"It's a date. See you then."

CHAPTER 14
PARABLES AND PIZZA

Eddie spent two hours that afternoon washing and detailing his car. He vacuumed the carpets and dusted the air vents. He polished the wood trim and cleaned control surfaces like seat adjustors. He polished the glass. Everything was spotless, inside and out. When he was done, he showered and dressed, spending about half as much time on himself as he had on the car.

He rang Roz's doorbell at seven o'clock sharp. As they were walking toward the car, he realized she didn't have her cane with her. She seemed to be walking well enough without it. "You look great," he said sincerely.

"Thank you," she effused. "You can go ahead and say what you mean; I don't mind. I've indeed been losing weight. I'm down 110 pounds so far."

"Congratulations! That's awesome. How have you been doing it?"

"No magic involved. The biggest change I made was a change of heart. I decided that I could go to my grave as the sad object of everyone's pity, or I could take it upon myself to become the person I wanted to be."

She reminded him of Mel and her simple decision to be happy rather than wallow in self-pity. Both were clearly strong-minded women. "You—" Eddie was tempted to say "You go, girl" but decided that sounded silly. "You're an inspiration. Tell me more."

"There's really not much to tell. I started making small changes. For instance, I confined my snacking to nothing but fresh fruit, baby carrots, nuts, that sort of thing. No candy, sweets, or chips. Then I replaced soda with unsweetened tea. Then I started walking. At first, it was just from my door to the corner and back. Lord have mercy, that was hard! But I did it every day, rain or shine. One day I managed to walk around the whole block. I walked really early in the morning, before most people were up. I didn't want to make a spectacle of myself hobbling around. But it got a little easier every day. Now I walk a full mile at a time. A year from now I plan to *run* that mile."

Her voice was brimming with pride and determination. She was still not a small woman, and Eddie guessed she yet weighed over three hundred pounds. But she had made remarkable progress. And as Eddie took in her shining eyes, her smile, and her glowing complexion, he realized that she was very pretty indeed, as well as being an inspiration to everyone with a seemingly insurmountable goal.

"I'm happy for you, Roz. And I'm proud of you for your perseverance."

At the restaurant, she ordered a small salad with no dressing, along with the petite grilled salmon. As they ate, she caught him up on all the news. "A lot happened while you were gone. Where should I start? Okay, you may have noticed the attendance was much smaller than before. We've had a bit of an exodus. Pastor preached a long string of angry messages after you left. Some families felt it was too much and stopped coming. The more people left, the angrier the preaching got. I'm hoping the vicious cycle ends soon, and not just because I like upbeat preaching. Church offerings are way down, and that puts pressure on the rest of us to give more and more."

Eddie nodded, but said nothing.

Roz sighed and continued, "You also may have noticed you didn't see Shawna Bell."

Eddie smiled. "Yes, I briefly took note of that fact."

"She left about three months ago. She pined after you for quite a while, you know. She brought you up in conversation a lot. I think she felt bad about the way you two left things. At one point, she went to Pastor Bowers to ask what sort of outreach was being done to bring you back. He told her the ball was entirely in your court, and she wasn't at all happy about that. She gave him an earful about leaving the ninety-nine and going after the one lost sheep. He sat her down from the choir right after that."

"Confronting Bowers took guts." Eddie knew church members were more likely to defy a judge in his own courtroom than challenge a pastor in his own church. "I'm flattered to know she cared enough to do that. I feel bad at how it worked out for her."

"Well, it gets stranger," Roz continued. "All of a sudden she started dating a minister from some Reformed Baptist church in Burlington. It was a whirlwind romance. They up and got married, and I don't think any of us have heard from her since."

Eddie flashed back to a nightmare he'd had shortly after learning of the attack on Brother Freeman. He had dreamed he was trying to climb a narrow trail out of a dark ravine—*the valley of the shadow of death?* He had to fight a succession of enemies to win free, including soldiers, baseball players, and even Pastor Bowers. After each victory, he looked up and saw Shawna's face, farther away each time. When he finally vanquished the last enemy and came into the sunlight, she had vanished.

"I'm not surprised to hear Shawna's gone," he said. "I kind of figured that was coming." Come to think of it, the detail of Bowers floundering in the mud after trying to decapitate him seemed prophetic too. No need to mention that. "But I'm having a hard time picturing her as a Calvinist. I mean, that's quite a change in both style and substance."

"Yes, I imagine she's had to walk back a lot of beliefs that she'd spent her whole saved life affirming. But you know how it is when you feel you've met your soul mate."

"No, I can't say that I do," Eddie confessed. "What exactly is a soul mate, anyway?"

"Well, Aristotle said love is a single soul inhabiting two bodies."

"In that case, I'm inclined to agree with Plato, who said that love is a serious mental disease." Eddie smiled just a little, despite trying not to.

Roz countered with, "Love is of all passions the strongest, for it attacks simultaneously the head, the heart, and the senses. That was Lao Tzu."

"Attacks, huh? Then Pat Benatar was right when she sang 'Love is a Battlefield'."

"'Love is Like Oxygen!' And I don't know who sang that."

"That was 'The Sweet'. It's like oxygen because 'Love is in the Air'," Eddie explained.

"And yet, 'Love is Thicker than Water'. Go figure." She began to giggle.

"Well, that little paradox just proves that 'Love is a Many-Splendored Thing'."

They kept the string going, naming every song they could think of with the word *love* in the title. Soon Eddie was singing "The Things We Do for Love" into a pretend microphone, as Roz laughed until tears rolled down her face. Eddie realized it was the first time in years that he'd sung anything outside of a church service. After a rough start, today was getting better and better. "I guess I should thank you for helping me throw away my dignity," Eddie teased.

"No problem," Roz said. "I'm happy to help. But I didn't mean to gossip about Shawna. Why don't you tell me about you?"

"Well," Eddie said, pausing. Obviously, he'd have to skip some of the sordid details. "You've doubtless heard the highlights, or shall

I say lowlights of my recent past. If I had to summarize for you, I'd say this: you're more tied in to my story than you know. The guy who accosted you after choir practice that night last year—I call him Loudmouth—was no ordinary bully. You probably know he wanted revenge on me, and that led to the attack on Eddie Freeman. Reverend Bowers blamed me for that. That's why he silenced me. The silencing is not why I left town, though. That was for my own safety. I intended to figure out who the attackers were and come back to see justice done. My problem was that when I left, I wandered into some dark places. Everything Christian reminded me of church, and I couldn't think about church without getting angry. So I stopped thinking about God altogether."

Roz listened with a mixture of sympathy and understanding written on her face. Eddie paused just long enough to wonder if a few more years under the ministry of Reverend Bowers would turn her sweet nature sour. He went on with his story. "I'll spare you the details. Suffice it to say that I was pretty thoroughly backslidden at that point.

"Long story short, I accidentally ran across Loudmouth and discovered he was involved in human trafficking. A new friend of mine was helping me gather evidence against him. He and one of his pals saw her and followed her home. I'm still not sure how they did that, but they did. I was visiting her when they broke in. They were going to kill us both, so I did what I had to do. That's when I made the news."

"How do you feel now? You know, about having shot someone?"

"Grateful to be alive," Eddie said. "I'm not all shell-shocked and traumatized, if that's what you mean. I made my peace with the idea of self-defense when I was still a teenager. I've thought about situations that might require me to use lethal force. I've trained for them for years. That training saved two lives. I have no regrets about that."

He paused again, remembering. Roz waited patiently until he resumed. "Anyway, the shock of hearing about me on the news is why my dad had a heart attack. I saw him in the hospital just before he died. The last thing he did in this life was urge me to get right with God again. He forgave me. But I don't think that's something Solid Rock is ever going to do."

They talked at length of Eddie's dad, and then of Eddie's plans for the future. "I don't have a lot of concrete plans yet. I'll get the future figured out little by little. But in the meantime, I'm okay, Roz. I want you to know that your old friend Eddie is once again the same guy you used to know, no matter who else refuses to believe that."

"I believe it," Roz said simply. "And I'm very, very glad to hear it." They smiled at each other for a moment. "Now offer me dessert, so I can practice saying no."

On Monday afternoon, Eddie got a voicemail from Roz thanking him for a lovely dinner. She also gave him a heads up. "Somebody from church saw us at the restaurant, and Pastor Bowers has already heard about it. He called to remind me that you were still silenced. He said he no longer has your contact information, or he would have gotten hold of you too. If you return to service, he's going to demand that you not have fellowship with anyone. In fact, he's going to ask you to leave the church and make a fresh start somewhere else. I'm sorry, Eddie, but I thought you'd want to know." After a second or two of silence, she spoke again, softly and with uncharacteristic melancholy. "For the record, I'm glad we got together. You're a great guy. In a better world, we'd be able to stay in touch. But you know how it is. Take care."

Did Roz ever envy regular people, people who lived in blissful ignorance of how smothering and controlling a church could be? Regular people inhabited a world where adults were free to choose their own friends and dinner companions. Eddie shook his head. He was determined to live as a Christian, but not in a cage, and not at the end of a leash and choke chain. His life, his decision. She had made a different choice, as was her right. *Be well, Roz.*

Monday night found him sitting at a downtown Framingham pizza shop. He sat along the side wall, facing the door. Munching a bag of chips and the crusts of the two slices he had just eaten, he thought about what ifs. What if he hadn't responded to Loudmouth abusing Roz? What if Loudmouth had never said anything in the first place? What if Roz had reached her ideal weight two years ago? *What if I'd hit Bowers with a good right cross yesterday just for the fun of it?* He was still tempted to put that on his bucket list.

"The only thing we can say for sure is that if things were different, they wouldn't be the same."

Eddie started. "Excuse me?" The speaker was a solidly built black man with gray hair, sideburns, and a bushy moustache. Eddie hadn't noticed him come in, which irked him. He had seated himself at this table precisely so he could keep an eye on people's comings and goings. Situational awareness was the lion's share of self-defense. Now this guy had materialized out of thin air and read his mind.

The man said, "You are Eddie Caruthers, I presume."

Is my mug really that famous around here? Does everyone recognize me? "That's a fair presumption. And who might you be? And why did you say what you said, as if you knew what I was thinking?" Eddie braced himself for action in case the man had hostile intentions.

"Ah, I said it because you had that look on your face, the one people get when they sit and ponder how they came to be where they are. Call it an educated guess on my part, if you like." The man grinned. "As for my name . . . how quickly they forget! I'm Byron Bullard, and you knew me when you were a lot younger and had less on your mind."

Eddie stared blankly for a long second, and then his face lit up. "Reverend Bullard! I can't believe it's you."

The former pastor of Solid Rock had changed quite a bit in the fourteen years since Eddie had last seen him. His hair had been all black back then, and there'd been more of it on his head and less on his face. He seemed thicker now, and not quite so tall. Although that latter recollection could be because fourteen-year-old Eddie had been shorter himself, making the pastor look taller by comparison.

Eddie gestured at a chair. "Please, sit down. It'd be nice to get caught up."

"Just let me get myself a slice and a Coke, and I'll be right back."

When his former pastor returned, Eddie had lots of questions. "So where did you go all those years ago? Why did you leave? What are you doing now?"

"One at a time," Bullard said, chuckling. "To start with, I didn't go anywhere, really. I stayed in Framingham and I still live here. I'm still a pastor, though I did take a few years off from that."

"Where is your church? And why did you leave ours? I was pretty young, but I remember lots of rumors flying around. You'd become frustrated with a lack of political advancement in the organization, you'd converted to another faith, you'd run off with some woman—all kinds of crazy stuff."

"Is that right?" Bullard shook his head, but his twinkling eyes spoke of amusement rather than shock or anger. "I knew people would talk, though I had no idea what they'd say. Gossip is a disease spread by mouth, you know. It's easy to catch, and hard to cure. Lord knows I spent years trying to inoculate Solid Rock against it."

"Well, I didn't gossip about you. At least, I don't think I did. But I'd like to know what happened. It seemed to everyone that you just disappeared."

The older man sighed and folded his hands. "It wasn't about organizational politics. It wasn't about me falling into sin. And in no way did I change my doctrinal beliefs. The simple truth is that jobs can change people. I knew a young idealist who ran for statewide office to make the world a better place. He was going to be an advocate for the poor, a voice for the voiceless, all of that. But he didn't change the world. The world changed him. He ended up getting busted in a bribery scandal. You see what I'm saying?"

"I can see how certain jobs could change people for the worse," Eddie said. "Take police officers. A rookie cop right out of the academy is probably full of idealism. He wants to protect and serve. Fast forward twenty years, and he's become a bully with a badge, working on his second divorce. I get that. But it's hard to believe that the ministry does that to people."

"Then you don't know many ministers, or you haven't been paying attention," Bullard countered. "The ministry was changing me, and I didn't like the man I was becoming. I ran for the exit before things could get worse. I intended to change careers, but I couldn't shed the calling. I'm still a pastor, but things are very different for me now. I'll tell you more about it later, if you're interested. But first, I want to know a little about you."

Eddie snorted. "I think everything about me has been in the papers."

"The papers can tell me everything except for what I care about most. How are you bearing up after the funeral?"

"I'm doing okay. I expected to be much worse. Dad basically died of shock after hearing about me. I thought I'd be wracked with guilt over it, but I'm not. I think the fact that he forgave me is a big part of that."

"Well, I'm sorry for your loss, but very glad to hear how that part of things turned out. Have you been back to church since all this happened?"

"Yes, I have," Eddie said, pausing and staring at his half-eaten crusts. "It wasn't pretty. I've repented, and I know God's forgiven me, but Pastor Bowers hasn't. He wants a big display of self-abasement first."

Bullard nodded. "I can't say that I'm surprised. Tell me, do you know the meaning of the parable of the prodigal son?"

Eddie let out a harsh laugh. "I know that one pretty well. Dad had me read it to him on his deathbed. He wanted to encourage me to come back to God and make sure my siblings received me graciously when I did. God used some of those same verses to speak to me the day after Dad died, showing me how far I'd fallen and helping me find my way back. If things had stopped there, it would probably be my favorite Bible reading of all time. But yesterday, Reverend Bowers attacked me with that parable. He made me look like a monster, and half the congregation was giving me the evil eye before he was done. So yes, I'm quite familiar with the contents of that story."

Reverend Bullard shook his head again. "Ah, but the question you answered was not the one I asked. You've spent enough years in church that I assumed you were familiar with the *contents* of the parable. What I asked you was whether you know what it *means*."

Eddie pondered that for a moment. "Maybe you should tell me what it means, and I'll tell you if I knew."

The reverend smiled. "That's fair enough." He reached into his jacket and pulled out a pocket New Testament. "Not as good as a whole Bible, but it's more convenient to carry around. Now let's see."

He settled back in his chair and inhaled deeply as he thumbed through the well-worn pages. "First, you must understand that the story of the prodigal son is not a stand-alone parable. It's the third installment of a trilogy, relating to the first two kind of like *The Return of the King* relates to the earlier installments of *The Lord of the Rings*. It's the capstone of the series. You know what I'm saying?" He didn't wait for an answer.

"The reason the story was told is found in the first verse of Luke 15, where a bunch of publicans and sinners gather around Jesus to hear his teaching. They are Christ's natural audience, since he came to seek and save that which was lost. But the Pharisees and scribes took exception to this, as would many a religious conservative today. So they complained about Jesus, saying, 'This man receives sinners and *eats* with them.'"

Eddie thought about his get-together with Roz. "Funny how so many folks feel a need to comment on your dinner companions. But I see your point here. The Pharisees assume that the real Messiah wouldn't condescend to keep company with such undeserving people."

"You've got it so far. Now in response to their grumbling, Jesus gives the Pharisees a parable: the parable of the lost sheep.

PART THREE: MATTERS OF THE HEART

In it, a man with a hundred sheep loses one, and he leaves the ninety-nine to go in search of the missing one. He rejoices upon finding it, because sheep have value. He even invites friends and neighbors to rejoice with him. Notice that the first to rejoice is the owner of the sheep, not the friends and neighbors. Yes?"

Eddie wasn't quite sure where Bullard was going with that point, but he nodded. The preacher continued his exposition.

"Jesus says that *in the same manner*, there is joy in heaven over one sinner who repents, more joy than is felt over ninety-nine just persons who need no repentance." Eddie could sense an overlooked truth hiding at the fringes of his understanding. He just couldn't identify it yet.

"Then Jesus doubles down on the lesson by adding the parable of the lost coin," Bullard explained. "It's the second installment of the trilogy. In this story, a woman loses a coin and searches the house for it. She's apparently poor enough that the loss of a coin is a big deal. So when she finds it, she is happy, and calls her friends and neighbors to rejoice with her. Again, I point out that the rejoicing starts with the coin's owner, not the friends and neighbors. And Jesus tells the audience that it works the same way in heaven."

"And why is that an important point?"

"I'll come back to that. For now, let's go to verse eleven, where Jesus breaks out the third parable of the trilogy. We've misnamed it, by the way. It's not the parable of the *prodigal* son, as if the point of the story was Junior's wastefulness. It's the parable of the *lost* son. Lost sheep, lost coin, lost son—that's consistent."

Bullard hadn't touched his pizza. At the rate he was going, it would soon be cold. He was obviously more interested in the lesson than in the food. He kept his voice to a conversational level, but his animated delivery drew more than one curious look from people at nearby tables.

He continued. "You've got three main characters in this one: the father, who symbolizes God; the prodigal, who stands for publicans and sinners; and the elder brother, who represents the scribes and Pharisees. So baby brother moves away and falls into sin. But then he comes to his senses and goes home. He figures he no longer deserves to be called his father's son, but hopes he could be accepted as a dishwasher or a gardener or something. And while he is yet a long way off from the house, the father sees him coming and *runs* to meet him. That's just like God. Isn't that what happened to you? Or did you have to get all the way back to the local church before God took notice of you?"

Eddie answered softly, "God met me at my kitchen table. I was a long way from visiting Solid Rock, both geographically and metaphorically."

"That's what I thought. So the father receives the lost son back and will have none of this 'make me a servant' stuff. Instead, he blesses him. He has the staff dress him up nicely. He tells them to prepare a feast. His exact words are 'Let *us* rejoice.' Most church people miss this entirely. They'll tell you, 'the angels rejoice over one sinner who repents.' That's not what the book says. Yes, the angels rejoice, but we need to keep things in perspective. They're staff. They're the help. It's the head of the house whose attitude matters most to Junior. That's why Jesus said there is rejoicing *in the presence* of the angels when one sinner repents, and not simply 'the angels rejoice when one sinner repents.' *God* gets happy, and he's not ashamed to celebrate in front of the servants, and to call them to rejoice with him. This is so important that Jesus illustrated it three times; the owner of the sheep, the owner of the coin, the father of the son. Chew on that for a moment. Remembering that God himself rejoices at your return will take the sting off the fact that some *people* can't bring themselves to be happy about it."

"That's awesome stuff! I never thought of it that way." Eddie grinned, enjoying the warm feeling this new understanding gave him.

"It never occurs to most people. They can envision God as stern and wrathful, but they can't envision him rejoicing. If we can't imagine that, we don't know God as well as we think."

"So the meaning of the parable is . . ."

"We're not quite there yet. But I'm getting close to it." Bullard looked back down at his Bible. "So at this point in the story the older brother has heard music and dancing, and he comes back from the fields to see what all the fuss is about. When he learns that his lost brother has returned and Father is throwing a party over it, he gets angry."

"Reverend Bowers didn't preach this part of the story."

"I'm not surprised. This part of the story is about him. The elder brother resents the father's kindness to the prodigal. That's because big brother mistakenly believes that God's gifts reflect the goodness of the recipient, rather than the goodness of the giver. He understands merit, not grace. And by the standards of merit, big brother feels shortchanged. 'I've served you all these years, and what do I have to show for it?'

"We've all heard preachers lament the financial hardships faced by their congregations. Some of them go on to gripe about *other* churches—churches that aren't as doctrinally sound, that aren't working as hard, yet *those* churches are rolling in cash. They're getting big crowds. The implication is that it's not fair. The elder brother feels God owes him for his faithful service, and the sight of Junior getting undeserved favor makes him angry at God. How foolish is that?"

"Ouch! That's hard preaching." Eddie chuckled.

"It's hard, but it's right. Isn't that what they say?" The two men shared a laugh before Bullard launched back into his exposition of the parable.

"Notice something else here. God is not primarily interested in apologies for sins; he's interested in repentance. To repent is to turn around. God wants to see you change your ways and live right. In the parable, the father doesn't make Junior prostrate himself before big brother and the servants.

"Pharisees, on the other hand, wish to be appeased. They demand abject apologies. They want you to grovel. They want you to wear your shame like a scarlet letter for as long as it takes for their anger to dissipate, because they believe your abasement would somehow affirm their righteousness and show that God is still in the business of dispensing justice. They don't think

Calvary was justice enough for *your* sin. They think a long season of penance should be part of the deal. You must have looked joyful when you returned to Solid Rock, having already gotten right with God. In the parable, the elder brother took offense at joy. He thought a public flogging was more appropriate than music and dancing."

Eddie nodded.

"It gets worse. The elder brother in the parable is actually delusional. He has the gall to say he's never transgressed the father's commandment at any time. Come on, now—who among us can say that to God with a straight face? 'If we say we have no sin, we deceive ourselves, and the truth is not in us.'

"Now, few modern Pharisees are that brazen. Instead, they humbly acknowledge that they're not perfect. They say this like it's a great admission, a revelation to the world, like no one would have known about their imperfections if they hadn't confessed. Watch out when a deeply religious person says 'I'm not perfect.' It often means he thinks he's pretty close. Ask him about his failings, and he'll mumble something about all the times he put his trust in the wrong people, or some such self-serving hooey. That's all the imperfection he'll own up to."

Eddie was floored. It all made so much sense. The words crystallized vague thoughts he'd had for years but could never quite articulate.

"Let's go back to our story. Big brother feels Junior's sins need fleshing out. Does the father appreciate how *bad* his younger son was? He's spent his inheritance on prostitutes! Today's Pharisee knows that forgiveness is a necessary Christian virtue, but he believes he can safely defer that duty if the sin to be forgiven is bad enough. And he thinks a just God wouldn't forgive serious sins very quickly. Since he can't bring himself to be like God, he'll settle for imagining that God is like him.

"There's another reason he brings up prostitutes: he is disgusted with the particular sins of the prodigal, and he's proud to know that *he* would never do those things. If I had to guess, I'd say that a lot of elder brother types pray like the Pharisee in Luke 18: 'God, I thank you that I am not like other men: extortioners, unjust, adulterers—'"

"—or Eddie Caruthers, the worst of the worst," Eddie added, his lip set to maximum torque.

"Now don't you go and make the opposite mistake!" The preacher wagged his finger. "Because for every modern Pharisee congratulating himself that he's not a fornicator, a whoremonger, or worse, there's a sinner saying, 'I thank you God that I am not like this Pharisee: self-righteous, mean, unforgiving, abusive toward the flock, and resentful of God's grace.' See, each brother thinks that his own faults aren't nearly as bad as that *other* hypocrite's."

Ouch again. That hit a little too close to home.

"Uh-huh, that's hard preaching too." Bullard smiled a knowing smile, but it was sympathetic. Eddie could detect no venom, no "gotcha" in the preacher's words or in his facial expression. This man could wield the sword, but he took no obvious pleasure in it.

The lesson went on. "One more thing before I wrap it up. This parable doesn't have a definite ending like the other two. I mean, the sheep is found and everyone is happy. The coin is found and everyone is happy. In this one, the son is returned, and the story ends with the father entreating the elder brother to join the festivities. But it doesn't say how big brother responded. That's still being decided on a case-by-case basis."

The preacher leaned back in his chair and shook his head at his untouched pizza. "So this is what you must know about the parable of the lost son: Its main purpose was to rebuke the Pharisees for their attitude toward the fallen. It's not primarily about the prodigal; it's about the elder brother. The scribes and Pharisees could understand rejoicing over recovered livestock and recovered coin, but they couldn't be happy about a recovered brother. Now, having given you that background, I can summarize the whole parable in two sentences. Ready?"

"Go," said Eddie.

"A certain father had two sons, *neither of whom was very much like him*. And he loved them both."

Eddie was too astounded to say much else. At the end of their conversation, they exchanged phone numbers and promised to talk again soon. Bullard dumped his cold slab of pizza in the trash as they exited. "I don't even like pizza," he laughed.

"Then why on Earth did you come into a pizza shop?"

Byron shrugged. "I felt led. I was driving by, and felt a sudden urge to park and go in. I always pay attention to things like that. Not all of a man's work can be planned. Sometimes

I'm at my most useful when I'm sensitive enough to just be in the right place at the right time. I knew going into a pizza joint wasn't *my* idea. So I went in, and there you were."

"Well, I'm glad you did. If it's okay with you, I'll call you in a couple of days to arrange another sit-down. I think we have more to talk about."

As it turned out, Eddie got busy between teaching at Real Life Defensive Systems and all the things that needed doing at his father's house. A few days turned into a week, and then two.

Nearly three weeks later, he was sitting at the dining room table in the family manse, skimming the local paper, when he saw an article describing how Framingham PD had raided several massage parlors in town. His heart leaped. *Did my letters pay off?*

Three AMPs had been hit, all places where Mel had shadowed Loudmouth and Zeke. In each case, an undercover officer had gone into the establishment, been solicited for a sex act, and arrested the offending masseuse. The article listed the names of those arrested. All of them were in their twenties or early thirties. None were identified as owners or managers of the establishments.

Eddie thought of the girls he had seen being hustled into Ace Massage. He wondered if they were among the people who had been charged. Something was very wrong when human trafficking victims got arrested and their traffickers did not. *I wanted to help these people, and it seems like I only made their predicament worse.* Since the article used real names rather than spa aliases, he had no way to tell if Nicole or any of the girls he'd met at other spas were among the detained.

That's when Eddie thought of Byron Bullard. There was a man of wisdom. Maybe he'd be able to help. Eddie had no idea what to do. But he knew he had to do something.

That thought was still uppermost in his mind when he went to sleep that evening. He had to do *something.*

CHAPTER 15
THE ELASTIC LIMIT

With a loud crack, the door splintered. An unknown man lunged into the bedroom, his face twisted into a savage expression of rage. Eddie rolled off the mattress, the fingers of his right hand closing on the grip of the pistol under the bed before his knees hit the floor. As he brought the gun up to firing position and struggled to focus on the luminous dot of the front sight, he realized he'd been dreaming. The door was intact. No one was there.

Both relieved and disgusted, he knew there was no point getting back in bed until his heart stopped pounding. He'd had this dream three times in as many weeks. Turning on the bedroom light, he took the pistol with him to check all the doors and windows on the lower levels of the house. All was secure. Eddie went back to the bedroom, grabbed a Bible off the nightstand, and read a few Psalms. He willed his thoughts to face the future rather than the past. He'd be meeting Reverend Bullard around lunchtime, and was eager to hear whatever advice was forthcoming.

As it turned out, Bullard offered no guidance. He met Eddie at a local deli and listened carefully, but smilingly declined to give advice. "I don't know enough to advise you," he said.

"What do you want to know?"

"Well, for starters, how did this issue get on your radar?"

Eddie was tempted to weave a carefully constructed narrative that would cover what he knew about trafficking without revealing how his awareness of the issue had been acquired. He was pretty certain he could talk about what he'd learned online without mentioning that he'd actually visited AMPs himself. He wasn't sure how he was going to explain where he'd been heading when he saw Loudmouth with RBH and the captive women.

After a few minutes of beating around the bush, he decided to start from the very beginning and just tell it all. It was a risk. Bowers had gone ballistic on the basis of much less information than this guy was about to get. But Eddie was done with all the lies and omissions. He wasn't going to tiptoe around his past. *The past doesn't define me. Either people will get that, or they won't.*

Bullard listened while Eddie covered everything from the first fight with Loudmouth to the home invasion at Melissa's apartment. Eddie made no attempt at spin control, sticking to unadorned facts no matter how they made him look.

"I appreciate your honesty," Bullard said. "That was coura-geous. It shouldn't take any special courage to be honest with people, but it does. That's doubly true in church. Most church folks learn early on that confessing your faults one to another is biblical, but not really safe. Everything you say to people can and will be used against you later."

He paused and looked Eddie in the eye. "Well, in the *right kind* of church, it's safe. I can promise you I won't be saving this information up. In fact, I'm blessed with a forgetful spirit. I'll remember these details as long as I need them to minister to you, and then, with the help of God, I'll forget them. A man can only carry around so much unpleasantness in his head before it starts to affect him."

Eddie wasn't sure what to say, so he just nodded. He hoped Bullard would take the nod as a combination of appreciation and understanding and anything else appropriate.

Bullard asked, "Any emotional issues around having killed someone?"

Feeling the heat rise in his cheeks, Eddie said, "No one's ever going to ask me the right question, are they?" In response to the preacher's uncomprehending expression, he continued, "People won't ask me how it felt to be the victim of a home invasion, to be threatened with death by people holding sledgehammers and knives. No one will ask how I felt knowing I prevented the rape of my friend and saved both our lives. All I will be endlessly asked is whether I feel bad about shooting the would-be rapists and murderers."

Eddie leaned forward and lowered his voice so that it would not carry. "Here's where I am emotionally: I'm thrilled to be alive and uninjured. I'm happy my weapons-handling was better than theirs. That's it. Roz wanted me to be in shock. Bowers wanted me to be filled with remorse. Shock is for the unprepared. Remorse is for the guilty. I am neither of those things. I did what I needed to do to live. Do I have emotional issues around the shooting? Just one: I'm dismayed that anyone expects me to feel guilt or regret about *surviving*."

Byron Bullard was silent for half a minute while Eddie did a little deep breathing and willed himself back to equilibrium. "You're right," the older man said. "That wasn't the most empathetic question I've ever asked. I'm sorry. I wouldn't want to be in your shoes, but no one should expect you to feel shame about wearing them. Please, go on."

Eddie tried to hide his surprise. He'd just heard a preacher admit to being wrong. Reverend Bullard had apologized without ostentation, equivocation, or apparent embarrassment. He tried to imagine Bowers doing that, and couldn't. Bullard instantly climbed several notches in his estimation.

"There's not much else to tell. Dad died. Melissa took off. Bowers hates me, and his biggest priority seems to be making sure I have no saved friends. In the meantime, I can't forget what I promised Nicole. *Now* will you give me some advice?"

Reverend Bullard smiled again, a mix of affection and sympathy. "No," he said. "But I'm confident you'll figure things out on your own."

Eddie groaned, so Bullard added, "I know what you're thinking. But this conversation was not a waste. I can't give you the advice you sought, but I can give you something of value. I'm talking about answers to questions you haven't asked, but desperately need to. Are you interested?"

"How could I not be?"

They agreed to meet again at the deli in two days.

Eddie lay on the couch at sunset that evening and listened for a sound. Any sound at all. He had lived alone since graduating college and was accustomed to quiet surroundings. But his father's house seemed extra quiet, *deathly* quiet, and the silence was hard to take. It felt like living in a mausoleum. Everything was exactly as his father had left it. The shaving kit in the bathroom, the medicines on the kitchen counter, the family photos on the mantel, were all reminiscent of a shrine.

Trying to inject a little life into the atmosphere, he dialed up some Latin jazz on the radio and turned it up loud before sprawling back on the couch. This was more like it. He was accompanying a particularly energetic track by playing air bass when his brother Jason let himself in—all the siblings had keys to the place—and slammed the front door before stomping up to Eddie. "The preacher was right. You don't seem to be in mourning like the rest of us. Maybe you forget that you're the reason we buried the owner of that couch."

"When, where, and how I mourn is my business," Eddie snapped. "Not some preacher's. Not yours."

"*Do* you mourn? Have you? Dad's been dead a month and it sounds like a party in here."

"Get a clue, Jason. You want me to cry for Dad? He's in heaven. I don't mourn that; I envy it. You want to see me cry over my own losses? Why? Would it make you feel better about yours? Or maybe you're like Bowers, and would just enjoy seeing me suffer?"

"Maybe a little suffering would make a better person out of you."

"Oh, I see you've been *thinking* again. And so soon after the last time—your head must hurt."

"Stop with the wisecracks, or I'll make more than your head hurt." Jason balled his fists.

"So now you're an ex-pacifist too? Good! I always thought it was a stupid philosophy. You can fight me if you want. But is this how you plan to honor Dad's last request?"

Jason positively bellowed. "Don't you *dare* talk to me about honoring Dad. You've dishonored him and everything he stood for."

Eddie turned off the stereo and then spoke very softly. "All right, buddy, forget your empty promise at the hospital. You want to hurt me. Fine, I'll give you your chance. Come on."

Walking backward, Eddie led the way through the house and out into the backyard. When the two brothers reached the grass, he said, "So bring it, bro. Take your best shot."

He half expected Jason to decline. The absurdity of the proposal seemed self-evident to him. He didn't expect the big lummox to actually take a swing at him, but that's what happened. And it was a haymaker too. Had it connected, it would have knocked Eddie into next week.

Jason was big and strong, but he was not quick, and he telegraphed the punch. Eddie slipped it easily, dancing backward with a laugh of surprise. The laughter infuriated Jason, who lunged forward and threw a succession of wild punches. Five, six, seven . . . each of his punches could have ended the encounter had they struck something more than empty air. Eddie continued bobbing and weaving, but he was no longer laughing. When Jason got close enough to try a right hook, Eddie moved diagonally and slipped behind him, slapping him on the back of the head before dancing out of range again.

With a roar, Jason turned and charged. He wasn't adequately protecting his face, and Eddie instinctively lined up a right cross, his strongest punch. At the last second, he changed his mind. *He's family.* Eddie stood his ground and took the impact, unresisting. Jason hit him like a runaway train, and his momentum carried Eddie back toward the wall of the house. Eddie pivoted on his rear foot like a dancer twirling his partner so that he and Jason reversed positions. Caught by surprise, Jason slammed backward into the wall with all the force of their combined weight. He grunted in pain.

In an instant, Eddie grabbed Jason's head and twisted hard, pulling it down so his brother's ears were parallel with the ground. At the same time, he brought his knee up. Then somehow he stopped it. *Family!* That one-word thought intruded and overrode

Eddie's nearly autonomic fighting moves. Instead of delivering a smashing knee to the head, he stepped out to the side and twisted his body, swinging his hands—and Jason's head—in a wide arc. It had the effect of stretching his brother out horizontally and bringing him to the ground.

Eddie wasn't about to let him back up. Jason struggled and yelled and swung his arms and legs valiantly. But Eddie had spent seven years working his ground game with the likes of Dmitri and Andrei, and he knew how to use gravity and body mechanics to keep even a large man pinned with a minimum of effort. After several minutes, Jason was panting heavily, and Eddie was smiling again.

"Well, dear brother, you might want to rethink your strategy." He shifted his position so that he was seated beside his prone brother, leaning on his chest and holding the big man's elbows so that Jason could neither roll over nor sit up. "I've only played defense so far, and look where you are. You don't want me to go on offense. I suggest we talk rather than fight. Whaddaya say?"

Jason glared for a few seconds, his huffing and puffing the only sound. Finally he said, "All right, you win. I'm done. We just talk."

And talk they did, sitting right there on the ground in their grass-stained clothes. They cleared the air about misunderstandings, hurts, and accumulated hard feelings from half a lifetime.

"You were the most spoiled growing up. You got more stuff than Lorna or me, and you got much less discipline than either of us."

"You would always lord it over us, like being born eldest son actually made you something special."

"You had such a smart mouth. Do you think I didn't know about all those awful nicknames you had for me?"

"You were Mom's favorite. All I ever heard was 'why can't you be more like your brother!' Can you imagine how it feels for your own mother to wish you were someone else?"

They went on like that for two hours. As it turned out, none of those things were the real reason Jason had been angry enough to fight. The real issue was Fast Track Automotive.

"I'm not ready to run it. The employees loved Dad. The vendors loved Dad. The customers loved Dad. They don't love me. Maybe nothing I do will change that. If I run FTA into the ground, I'll have let Dad down. We were supposed to deal with this together, years from now. I'm only in this mess today because of you."

"You can't know that," Eddie said, suddenly feeling old and tired. "Maybe I was the straw that broke the camel's back. But if it was Dad's time, it was his time. If I'd done nothing wrong, he still might have died of some other cause, and it wouldn't have been any easier or more convenient for you. Don't try to make me carry that weight. I've owned up to my sins. But I'm not responsible for *anyone's* reaction to them. That includes Bowers, you, and even Dad. I have done some awful things. But I didn't make him die."

Jason looked at the ground and said nothing.

"I'll tell you what else," Eddie said. "You're not the only one worried about the future. I shot two people. I know I did what I had to do. But the DA hasn't ruled yet. That means I could get hit with an indictment any day. I could end up on trial because we have a district attorney who hates guns."

"I hadn't thought of that."

"I think about it every day. So maybe instead of brawling, we should both pray for each other, huh? That seems a lot more brotherly to me."

"Affirmative. Fighting isn't my thing. But before we do anything else, you should ask me why I came here tonight."

"Okay, why did you come here tonight?"

"To tell you that Lorna has decided she wants to live here. She plans to buy the house from the trust. You need to find yourself another place."

"She can have it. She's got a husband and kids. This is way too much house for me."

"I'll let her know. One question: When did you start carrying a gun?"

"I started the year I turned twenty-one."

"Wow. None of us had any idea." He paused a few seconds. "Well, if it saved your life, I'm glad you had it when you needed it. How often do you carry it?"

"Only when I'm awake."

"So you're carrying a gun right now?"

"I'm awake right now, so, yes."

The big man took in this news. Eddie could almost see the gears turning. After several seconds, Jason asked, "Was I in danger of being shot?"

Eddie smiled. "Relax. Not the way *you* fight."

Reverend Bullard arrived at the deli for their third meeting holding a notebook and an empty soda can. He sat down across from Eddie without ordering any food. He began speaking without preamble as Eddie was polishing off a sub.

"You've had a rough way to go. And there are still challenges facing you. I see them as all rooted in the same fundamental problem—the elastic limit."

Eddie talked around his last mouthful of sandwich. "What's the elastic limit?"

Bullard reached for his empty soda can. "See how perfectly shaped this is? It's a cylinder with totally smooth sides. Now if I apply a little pressure to it, it deforms." By way of demonstration, he squeezed lightly with his fingers until the can made the telltale metallic popping sound. "Even though I've bent it out of shape, it's not really damaged. Because it has elasticity, when I remove the pressure, it pops right back into shape." A second pop confirmed that the can did indeed return to its original shape when Bullard let go of it.

"Now, I can do that all day, at least until the sound becomes too annoying." He laughed. "As long as the can is only pushed so far, it can always recover itself. But I could squeeze it so hard it gets crushed. That would ruin it. Beyond a certain point, it can't recover itself. And you can't straighten it back out, regardless of how hard you try. The can has to be melted down and recast. Otherwise it will never be right again."

Eddie nodded to show his comprehension. "And that point, the point where it can't snap back—"

"—is the elastic limit," Bowers finished. "Some materials are more elastic than others. A rubber band is far more elastic than this can. But you can still stretch a rubber band until it snaps. Everything has an elastic limit. Every *person* has an elastic limit. Push people beyond that limit, and they'll become permanently deformed. So far, so good?"

"It seems reasonable enough. Does this have to do with the questions I haven't asked, but desperately need to?"

"Yes. Imagine this can is you. It's your psyche, your soul, your spirit, everything you are. You are subject to pressure from all kinds of forces. For example, your personal relationships come with responsibilities that put pressure on you." Bullard flexed the can and made the popping sound again. "Fortunately, God has designed counter-forces to create push-back and keep the pressure from bending you out of shape."

Eddie was intrigued, but couldn't yet connect the dots. "Can you be more specific?"

"Take children and parents, for instance. The Bible says 'children, obey your parents in all things, for this is well pleasing to the Lord.' That open-ended responsibility to obey creates pressure on the child. It could be an onerous requirement if the parents are arbitrary or unfair. But the obligations run both ways. It's not all on the child. That's why the Bible also says 'fathers, do not provoke your children, lest they become discouraged.' If all parties to the relationship act right, it keeps things in balance."

"Okay, I can see that," Eddie said.

"God has designed all relationships that way," Reverend Bullard explained. "A wife's duty to reverence her husband might be burdensome if not balanced by the husband's duty to love his wife as profoundly as Christ loved the church, to honor her, cherish her, and to give himself for her in Christ-like meekness. The force of responsibility is never applied in just one direction, so nobody's spirit gets crushed.

"It's the same at church. Did Pastor Bowers ever preach the verse that says to obey them that have the rule over you?

"Only about a hundred times," Eddie said, confident the preacher already knew that.

Bullard asked, "What is the reciprocal responsibility, the countering force that keeps that requirement from being onerous to church members?"

Eddie shrugged. "I have no idea."

"You'll find it in the twentieth chapter of Matthew. It's the fact that church leaders aren't supposed to seek to exercise authority over people. They are to regard themselves as servants, not rulers. Your duty to obey leadership isn't onerous as long as leadership isn't itching to be obeyed. Power is one of the main temptations of ministry. Preachers get fixated on the importance of submission the minute we get put in charge of something. It's a one-sided application of force, and it regularly pushes church members beyond their elastic limit."

"I like the idea of balanced responsibilities," Eddie said. "That's way different than what is usually taught. Pastor Bowers once told me, 'If I'm right, I'm right, and if I'm wrong, I'm right—I'm the pastor, and you have to do what I say either way.'"

Bullard laughed. "Imagine a husband using that line on his wife and thinking he's going to have a healthy marriage."

"Where did you say your church was again?" Eddie was suddenly curious about how a service there would compare to one at Solid Rock.

"I didn't, "Bullard said. "We're a distributed congregation, meaning we don't meet in a single dedicated building. We have small groups of people that meet in homes all over the area."

"And you like that better than having a traditional congregation?"

"I do. Here, take a look at this." Bullard grabbed his notebook, opened it to a particular page, and handed it to Eddie. "How much of this resonates with you?"

At the top of the page was written the title *Byron Bullard's Ninety-Five Theses*. Eddie grinned. "Oh, like Martin Luther nailing his list of grievances to the door of Wittenberg Cathedral five centuries ago? Most historians think that's a myth, you know."

"So I've read," Bullard said. "And I don't plan to nail these to any church doors. It's just that I had to call it *something*."

Eddie rapidly read down the list, which occupied several pages. There really were ninety-five of them, all spelled out in Bullard's careful penmanship. Some of the numbered points jumped out at him.

- The single biggest source of stress in the lives of many Christians is the church they attend.

- The way most churches operate is hard on everyone, pastors not least of all.

- Sheep are not draft animals.

- Pastors are the only shepherds who, upon losing half the flock, conclude that the problem is poor quality sheep.

- Pastors are the only shepherds who, upon losing half the sheep, conclude that God is culling the flock.

- The modern church is a business enterprise. It is in the business of event production. We call the events "services."

- The enterprise church makes a CEO of the pastor. But the two roles are very different. A pastor *ministers* to people for their benefit; a CEO *manages* people for the benefit of the enterprise. Pastor and CEO have different priorities: the minister easily justifies leaving the ninety-nine to seek the one lost sheep. The manager can never justify this.

- Nothing affects the tone and content of the preaching as much as high church overhead.

- Statistics prove the most dangerous place to have a heart attack is inside a hospital. Likewise, the most dangerous place to backslide is inside a church, and for the same reasons.

- The preeminent characteristic of despotic regimes, whether churches or states, is that they brook no criticism.

- The nature of church groups is such that new converts focus on pursuing God, while established members focus on eluding criticism.

- Good church members outnumber good Christians.
- There is no hurt like church hurt.

Eddie read the entire list and then looked at Bullard with astonishment. "This is definitely not what I expected from a pastor! Pardon my bluntness, but I'm guessing you don't have many friends in the ministry."

Bullard shrugged. "You'd be right, but it's not because of this list. I've shared this list with very few people. I have a reason for sharing it with you. But list or no list, the fact is most pastors don't have many friends."

"Why is that?"

"Well, as you just read, I think the way we do church is very broken. And it takes a toll on everybody. I've compiled some statistics on pastors that will blow your mind." Bullard took his notebook back and flipped forward several pages past the ninety-five theses. "Check this out."

He skimmed his finger down the page he was looking at and read excerpts to Eddie. "Every year in America, four thousand new churches are started, but seven thousand churches close. So the total number of churches is shrinking each year. Around fifteen hundred pastors leave the ministry each month. Of people who go into the ministry after graduating seminary or Bible college, 80 percent leave the ministry within five years. Nearly 50 percent of pastors' marriages end in divorce. And 70 percent of pastors have no close personal friends. I could go on, but you get the idea. As a group, pastors are stressed, burned out, and failing left and right."

"Wow! That's depressing. I never knew how bad things were."

"Now pretend those stats were about bank presidents or McDonald's franchise owners rather than pastors. Any business or industry looking at statistics like that would conclude something was seriously wrong with their business model. And they would look to change that model. But church people don't do that. We respond to the statistics with Facebook posts reminding people to pray for their pastor. And we keep doing church exactly the way we've always done it. You can see how well that's working. I walked away from that business model because I think pastors and the institutions they lead have largely been pushed beyond their elastic limits. As a result, churches don't function like they're meant to. This hurts the people in the pulpits, and I believe it hurts the people in the pews even more. My ninety-five theses are just an attempt to catalog the results of the forces that are crushing so many cans."

Not wanting to be impolite, Eddie hesitated a second before asking his next question. "Are the ninety-five theses autobiographical? You said before that you didn't like the person you were becoming when you were leading Solid Rock."

Bullard answered without hesitation or apparent defensiveness. "Not all of them describe who I was or how I did things then, but a number of them do."

"And your way of doing church now gets better results?" Eddie asked.

The preacher's look of calm assurance was nicely counterbalanced by modest words. "Don't misunderstand me," he cautioned.

"I'm criticizing a particular church model, but I'm not saying my way is flawless. And I'm not trying to dismantle the enterprise church. I'm trying to offer an alternative to it, so that people have choices. I think my church more resembles the original model. We have issues too. But I think the problems we encounter are fewer and less severe than those of an enterprise church."

"I'm intrigued. What's your way of doing church like?"

"I'll invite you to check us out if you like," Bullard said. "But before we get entirely away from the subject of the elastic limit, let me make a few more important points.

"Relationships aren't the only sources of pressure on you," the preacher continued. "Sometimes the forces that deform us are self-generated. For example, our sins exert pressure on us, mind, soul, and spirit."

Bullard tore a blank piece of paper from the notebook and began writing scripture references on it as he talked. "As you might expect, God has provided a countering force. We all sin." He grabbed the can with his left hand and squeezed it until the sound indicated it had been deformed. "But God has given us the gift of repentance. It's the path back to a clean heart and a right spirit." He allowed the can to pop back out as he wrote Psalm 51 on the paper.

"The problem," he continued, "is that we might substitute other things for repentance. We choose excuses, explanations, rationalizations. We lie to ourselves about what we've done and why we've done it. If you lie to yourself today, it becomes harder to be honest with yourself tomorrow. You stop recognizing your sin for what it is. You don't repent, and without the countering force of repentance, sin warps you." He squeezed the can hard and mangled it.

"You got off the path and got lost in the high weeds for a while. I'm glad you made your way back. Recognize that some of the places you went and things you did may have hooks in you. They'll pull on you from time to time. Don't dabble, and don't lie to yourself if you fall. Repent, and get back up again." He held up the crushed can. "Don't risk getting yourself damaged beyond repair."

"Hold on," Eddie protested. "God's mercy is everlasting. That says to me that recovery for the fallen should *always* be possible. How can there be any level of damage God can't repair?"

"The issue here is not what God can do. It's what *you* can do. As long as people can sincerely repent, there is hope. But where does repentance come from? Scripture says that godly sorrow produces repentance leading to salvation. The modern way to say 'godly sorrow' is contrition. We feel remorse for our sins, causing us to turn away from them. But when we sin knowingly and repeatedly, we run the risk of becoming so acclimated to it that we lose the ability to feel contrition.

"Some people persist in doing things they know are wrong, figuring they can always repent later. They plan to live like the devil now, and turn to God after they've had their fun. After all, 'his mercies are new every morning.'"

Eddie nodded, remembering his first drive to The Wolf's Den. He'd known he shouldn't go but talked himself into going anyway.

Bullard said, "What these people fail to realize is that although God's capacity for forgiveness is infinite, human capacity for feeling contrition is not. Without contrition there is no true repentance. This means people, not God, are the limiting factor when it comes to recovering right standing with God."

Eddie pondered this. The preacher hadn't shouted or pounded the table or lapsed into the singsong cadences popular in some pulpits. There was no organ music, no choir, and no altar call. Yet Eddie felt as much spiritual power in this moment as he could recall from any service at Solid Rock. "That was really profound. I've been in church most of my life," he said. "Why have I never heard this taught?"

Reverend Bullard shrugged and tore off the sheet from his notebook. It now contained a long list of scripture references. "Do your homework on this. Search the scriptures and see for yourself if the things I've told you are correct."

"Thank you. I will," Eddie promised. He went home thinking of aluminum cans. He was thankful that his relationship with God had "popped" back into place; he had not been permanently damaged, at least in that regard. But did the elastic limit perhaps apply to other areas? Had all his fight training and experiences fundamentally warped him in some way?

He considered King David. David had been a fighter, a warrior king. While he was still a teen, he made his name by killing Goliath. First he brained the Philistine with a stone launched from a slingshot. Then he used the giant's own sword to cut his head off. *How do you stand over another human being, slice his head off his body, hold the gory trophy up for all to see, and not be changed by that?*

As king, David was surrounded by his "mighty men," some of whom had slain hundreds of people in hand-to-hand combat. Was it all in a day's work for them? Did they retire to their farms and live happily ever after? Or did they have post-traumatic stress disorder, suffering sleepless nights, jumping at shadows, and having lifelong anger management issues? Did they think about all the widows and orphans they had created? Were they all just a little bent out of shape, like Byron Bullard's soda can?

Eddie thought, too, about how times had changed since Bible days. Western society was gentler now, more civilized. At least it liked to think of itself that way. David had slain men by the tens of thousands, and people sang and danced in celebration of his exploits. Eddie had knocked out one man in Solid Rock's courtyard and had been shunned for that act of self-defense. Was he too hard? Or was church culture too soft? If he deliberately took on the traffickers and added to his body count, no one would celebrate. *I'm okay with that. But will I push myself beyond my elastic limit in the process?*

He prayed for answers to these questions. He longed to hear that still small voice but was met with profound silence. Eddie knew and appreciated the fact that God was not a genie in a bottle to be summoned at need. So many people got mad at God, even refused to acknowledge his existence, because he hadn't granted some request of theirs or because he allowed something to happen that they would have preferred him to prevent. That was stupid. God could do whatever he wanted, when and how he wanted: God was sovereign. God was *God*. So he would answer Eddie's questions in his own time, in accordance with his own purposes. Or maybe he wouldn't answer at all. *Who am I not to be okay with that?* Even so, the silence was hard to take.

CHAPTER 16
DEFERRED MAINTENANCE

On the second Sunday in October, Eddie drove to Natick for service at one of Reverend Bullard's house churches. He was keen with anticipation. Just over a year before, Greg Bowers had ambushed him from the pulpit at Solid Rock. Eddie had gone to church only one time since then, and that service hadn't gone any better. As if that weren't enough, Roz had informed him the next day that Bowers didn't want him coming back. The feeling was mutual, but that didn't make Eddie feel any better about being thrown out. He hoped this new place might provide a fresh start.

The service took place in a raised ranch not far from Shawna Bell's old address. A dozen people attended. The pastor introduced Eddie to everyone, and they all sat around the living room chatting until the clock struck eleven.

They stood as Bullard led them in a brief opening prayer. For the next twenty minutes or so, they sang worship songs as one person after another made suggestions. The accompaniment consisted of a single acoustic guitar. At first, Eddie was sure he'd miss the scale and scope of services in a big church. But singing God's praises in this small group of cheerful people felt just as good as doing it in a massive crowd. God didn't need a critical mass of people to make his presence felt.

After the singing, Bullard asked if there were any prayer requests. One man asked for prayer for his sister, who he said had recently been diagnosed with cancer. Several other people made requests—this man needed a job, that woman's young child was plagued with nightmares; someone else wanted prayer for the salvation of her unbelieving spouse. When the requests were finished, the people stood in a rough circle and joined hands. Though Bullard led, the people all prayed out loud simultaneously, just as the congregation did at Solid Rock.

After the prayer requests, Bullard then solicited what he called care requests. He explained, "We pray to ask God to do the things we need that we cannot do for ourselves. Care requests are how we ask *each other* to help with things we are capable of doing, even if not by ourselves." One woman who looked as if she was in her seventies mentioned that her gutters were clogged and she couldn't afford to hire someone to clean them. One man had to replace his car's exhaust system in order to pass inspection. While he had the tools and the parts, he needed a second pair of hands to help with the heavy lifting.

People talked among themselves for a few minutes. A pair of brothers asked the old woman if she had ladders. Assured that she did, they agreed to stop by her house after service, as soon as they could change clothes, and take care of her gutters. Bullard offered to lend his help to the man who needed some borrowed muscle for his auto repair.

"By this will all know that you are my disciples if you have love for one another." The preacher spoke the words of John 13:35 like a formal benediction, bringing that portion of the service to a close. Then he opened his Bible, saying he was going to teach on forgiveness. Rather than choosing a text and announcing a title as was typical of preaching at Solid Rock, he simply read out large portions of what the New Testament had to say on the subject. Then he began to deliver his own remarks.

Eddie didn't retain everything that was said, but a few things stuck out. "Some people fail to forgive," said the preacher, "not necessarily because they are mean or evil, but because they don't know how. Anyone can *tell* you to forgive, but if he doesn't know how, he can't *teach* you to forgive, can't train you, can't model or demonstrate it for you. This happens because people are not clear on what forgiveness is."

He went on. "Forgiveness is not what's automatically left over in your emotions when your outrage wears off. Forgiveness isn't trying to forget or pretending you have no memory of the wrong you've suffered. Forgiveness is *reframing* the offense. Here's what I mean by that. You might want to write this down."

Eddie noticed that most of the people had notebooks.

"Forgiveness is taking a *positive view of the offense*, rather than a negative view of the offender, because you view the offense as an opportunity for you to demonstrate Christ-like character." Bullard paused, and the only sound was of pens scribbling on paper. "you can also view the offense as an opportunity to discover the particular spiritual needs of the offender, so you may minister to that person's needs in love."

"That's really deep," someone commented.

"It is indeed," Bullard replied. "But I can't take credit for it. A preacher friend of mine came up with this particular illumination. But it's the best teaching on the subject that I've heard, so I'm sharing it. Biblical forgiveness is possible only when your love for God and your love for others exceed your love of self. When self dominates, you'll respond to every offense by building walls of self-protection. When love prevails, you can reframe the offense as I've described. Love provides the sole motive for forgiveness among brethren; namely, the uncaused desire to restore the fellowship that was broken by the offense.

"The problem isn't always ignorance. Remember the parable of the lost son. Some elder brothers refuse to forgive because they're spiteful or hypocritical. That's as true of many religious leaders today as it was of the Pharisees in Bible days. Still, the restored prodigal must forgive the churlishness of all the elder brothers in his life, wherever they may be."

Bullard taught for about an hour. When he was finished, he apologized for going a little longer than usual. "We forgive you," someone piped up.

"Good," Bullard replied. "Now maybe you can view this as an opportunity to minister to my need for something to eat."

Everyone laughed, and the people stood up for a prayer of dismissal. When it was finished, they filed into the dining room. Several people carried in platters of food from the kitchen, a spread of sandwiches and finger foods with coffee, tea, and lemonade to drink. The crowd broke into little groups and talked and laughed for another thirty minutes.

Eddie thanked Reverend Bullard for inviting him. "It was a great service. At first, it felt odd not having a sanctuary with a platform and a pulpit. But after a few minutes, it didn't matter."

"I don't need a pulpit on a platform," Bullard replied, his eyes twinkling. "I stand before the people to lead them. I stand among the people to help them. I've no reason to stand above them."

The words surprised Eddie, and he could think of nothing to say.

Bullard continued as if not noticing Eddie's sudden speechlessness. "These people are a real faith community, even when they are outside these walls," he explained. "They are friends and neighbors in real life. Everyone here is from the local area. In enterprise churches, people often come from such great distances that they never see their fellow church members except at services. I'd rather have ten small house churches in ten different towns than have people from ten towns converging on one distant location."

"So how many of these house churches do you have?"

"We have three houses at the moment. I teach here on Sunday mornings, in Framingham Sunday evening, and Thursday nights in Sudbury. I'd love to make that a Sunday service, but I can't be in two places at once. I've been asking the Lord for some help."

"I'll pray that you get some."

Bullard smiled, a knowing look in his eye. Eddie got the feeling he understood the meaning of that expression. It meant, "Be careful what you pray for."

The next day, Eddie was again thinking about the problem of the AMPs and their captive workers. Though he had prayed about it multiple times, he still hadn't heard or felt anything like divine direction on how to proceed. So he decided to stop waiting and devise his own plan. That was when he heard the voice-that-was-not-quite-his speaking in his thoughts, repeating something he had said to himself almost a year ago at the start of his road trip: *This is how freedom feels.*

In that thought was the merest suggestion of ironic humor. Eddie almost laughed out loud. It was so simple, and so obvious. He had wanted to live as a free man. A free man wouldn't sit paralyzed, waiting for someone to tell him what to do next. As a Christian, Eddie needed to submit to the will of God as it was revealed to him. But absent specific instruction, he was free to do what seemed best to him. Taking on the traffickers or not was Eddie's call. *This* is *what freedom feels like. And it feels pretty good.*

He turned on some background music on his dad's stereo system and began pacing. After an hour lost in thought, he grabbed a pen and paper and sat down at the kitchen table. Across the top of the paper he wrote headings for four columns: personnel, equipment, cost, and steps. Then he began writing lists.

While he pored over his lists, two hours vanished. Then his phone buzzed in his pocket. He looked at the number of the incoming call and a big smile spread over his face.

"Mel! I'm so glad you called. How are you?"

"I'm fine," she answered. "A little embarrassed, maybe—I've been meaning to call you for a while now."

"No worries," Eddie said. It had only been a few weeks. Six weeks, to be precise. Not that he was counting.

"I'm calling for two reasons," Melissa said. "First is to offer you a belated thank-you for sending me that money. I am putting it to good use. I'm going to start school in January."

"Excellent! I'm happy for you, and glad I could help." It was wonderful to hear Melissa's voice again, but Eddie felt ill at ease. If she had avoided calling him for six weeks, this was probably not an easy call for her to make. That probably meant it wouldn't be an easy conversation for him. "What's the second reason?"

"Why did that guy call you 'choir boy'?"

Oh boy. She was asking about the night of the home invasion. Loudmouth had called him "choir boy" because he knew him to be affiliated with Solid Rock. In discussions with Melissa, Eddie had carefully avoided mentioning the church or too much about his past.

She continued, "I've always felt you were so mysterious. You seemed out of place at TNT, and I could never put my finger on why. That's probably why I agreed to go out with you in the first place, to figure you out. You told me you grew up in Metro-West, but never said what town. Who does that? I only learned it was Framingham when we both saw your name in the paper. You told me you sold cars at that little place in Weymouth. I decided to surprise you and drop by with lunch one day in August, and the guy there told me you'd quit two weeks earlier. You talked to me nearly every day on the phone and never mentioned it. And when you asked me to help case those massage joints, I got the impression you knew about them from more than just Internet research. I was just about to ask you about it when those animals attacked us. The one guy called you a choir boy. Then you pulled out a gun I didn't know you had and shot them both. I know that's what saved my life, and I'll be forever grateful for that. But when you put it all together, I was dating a guy I didn't even know. I've been down that road once, and it was a disaster."

Eddie realized he needed to be totally candid with her. She deserved that. There was no honor in trying to finesse his way through the story to save himself embarrassment. Besides, he was living for God now, and that meant telling the unvarnished truth.

A second later, another realization hit: this conversation would mark the official end of their relationship. She had not been raised in a religious home. Either she'd think his revived religious devotion a turn-off, or she'd lose all respect for him when she learned about his many failings. Maybe both. He steeled himself and plowed ahead.

"I'll tell you everything there is to know," he said. "You got some time?"

"Take all the time you need," she said.

"He called me 'choir boy' because we first met outside the church I used to go to." Eddie sighed, debating where to start. "I found God when I was thirteen. My parents raised me in a Christian home, but you don't inherit your faith the way you inherit your genes or something. Real faith comes from personally encountering God, and that happened to me fifteen years ago."

Melissa didn't say anything, so after a brief pause, Eddie kept talking. "At first, it was awesome. I'd never been so happy, so full of joy. I used to break out in song for no reason. I devoured the Bible as if I had personally discovered the world's only copy of the Good Book. I loved learning about God, worshipping God, serving God any way I could. Everything was all about God . . . until one day it wasn't. I don't know exactly when things changed, but at some point it was less about God and more about church.

"In some ways, church was like high school. Life was easier for people who were part of the 'in crowd.' I learned to like the music they liked, and to avoid expressing opinions that they wouldn't share. I learned that everything I did or said would be discussed and dissected, and my social stock would rise or fall depending on the reaction of the most influential people in the group. It was all so joyless, so fatiguing. Instead of pursuing God, I was negotiating the politics of church. Somewhere along the way, I lost God in the middle of all of that."

She probably thinks I'm nuts. Get to the end, get it over with, and say good-bye. "My biggest problem as a kid was being bullied in school. Church was no help with that, so I solved the problem on my own with fight training. Church was feeling less practical, less relevant all the time. The final straw for me was last year, when Loudmouth started yelling insults at my friend Roz. She was the fat lady I told you about. We were just leaving choir practice when it happened. Loudmouth attacked me when I stood up for her. You know I'm not a pacifist, but I belonged to a pacifist church. They had no idea I could fight, and they didn't approve." Eddie continued with the story, telling her all the things she didn't know; how he'd left under a cloud of condemnation and been cut off from his friends; how he'd let anger and loneliness drive him to violate his conscience; how he'd made excuses for every wrong action. "Whatever its faults, I can't blame the church for that. The church didn't make me stop reading my Bible and praying. They didn't make me go to The Wolf's Den or to TNT. That's all on me."

He paused, and still Melissa said nothing. Was she rolling her eyes? Holding the phone away from her ear? He wished he could see her face. He knew he was not likely to see it again. Still, the explanation he'd started needed to be finished. So he confessed to the rest: driving for the escort service, visiting the AMPs in lieu of visiting the clubs, and becoming aware of human trafficking only when he encountered Nicole.

"When I realized Loudmouth was a trafficker, I thought I finally would see him busted. You know how well that worked out," he said. "News of the shooting killed my father. I came home from the hospital and you were gone. I've never been in so much pain. That's when God reached out to me again, just like when I was thirteen. I found *myself* again when I found God again. But my dad is still dead, my old church still hates me, and I can't undo anything I've done. All I can do is live right from now on—and I intend to do that."

What else was there to say? Just one last thing: "Melissa, you were the only other good thing that happened to me over this whole last year. I've loved every minute I've spent with you. We never should have met, but I'm glad we did. I wish we'd met somewhere else, some other time. If we had, who knows?"

Eddie wished she would say something. Screaming at him, even laughing at him would be better than this tortuous silence. But she didn't speak.

"Well, I'd better let you go now. Take care, Mel. Goodbye."

The last thing he heard was her breath as she released a long sigh.

He hung up the phone and stared into space. It occurred to him that he didn't even have a photo to remember her by.

Five minutes later, the phone rang again. He looked at the caller ID and was surprised. "Mel?"

"Now wait just a minute, Bub." Eddie had heard that tone of voice before. He flinched, as if she could reach across the airwaves from wherever she was and jab him in the ribs. "Did you think you could get rid of me so easily? Make your grand confession, say goodbye and good luck, and drive off into the sunset?" Now it was Eddie's turn to be silent. He had no idea what to say.

"I called you because I needed answers," she continued, almost shouting. "We were so close, but in some ways you were still a stranger to me." She paused and lowered her voice to a more conversational level. "And I didn't like being in love with a stranger."

Eddie's jaw dropped. "Did you say—"

"That I want to talk face to face as soon as possible? Yes. Yes I did."

It was six o'clock the next evening, and Eddie raced home from a long meeting at Mike's place. It had been productive and Eddie was happy with the results, but he had a date to get ready for and only an hour to do it. He spent the last part of the drive stuck behind a slow-moving Jaguar which he only escaped when he turned into his own driveway.

Fortunately, he didn't have anywhere else to go. Melissa was meeting him here, at his dad's house. He'd spent most of the day cleaning and straightening and making the place feel like a fit abode for the living instead of a memorial to the deceased. Steaks were grilling on the patio, and a bevy of side dishes purchased from Boston Market lined the dining room table. When he stepped onto the front porch for a little fresh air, her car pulled into the driveway. She managed to stall it coming up the slight incline, and tried unsuccessfully to restart it. Apparently, she still hadn't replaced that bad fuel pump. He'd have to give her a hard time about that. As she continued to crank the starter, he waved and yelled.

"Hang on a minute. I'll run downstairs for some tools and be right back to get you all fixed up." She waved her acknowledgment.

Eddie's regular tools were in the garage, but the basement was closer, and he knew that somewhere on his father's workbench was a rubber mallet like the one he needed to resuscitate Melissa's moribund fuel pump. He heard her tinny horn bleat. *Have patience, pretty lady.* He rummaged around and found the mallet, and raced back up the steps. There was so much to say, so much catching up to do.

He got to the front porch and saw her driver's door hanging open. She was no longer in the car. He glanced around, but didn't see her anywhere. Would she have come into the house while he was in the basement? That didn't seem likely, but he had to check. During a quick walk-through of all the ground floor rooms, he called, "Mel? Mel, are you here?" No answer. He looked out on the back deck and was greeted by nothing but the aroma of charcoal and the sizzle of steak. This was weird. Where was she?

Eddie ran back out front, past her car to the road. He looked in both directions, unable to see very far in the fading light, but no one was about. Feeling more apprehensive with every breath, he went back to her car and peered in. The keys were still in the ignition. This was bad. *Call the cops.*

The phone shook in his unsteady hands. Just as he started to dial, it rang. It was her. "Mel, are you alright?" He realized he was shouting.

"I'm sorry Eddie. I'm in trouble here—"

She never finished the thought. "What the nice lady means," said a gravelly male voice, "is that you better listen up. If you wanna see her alive again, you'll do exactly what I tell you."

Something was familiar about that voice, that whiskey rasp. *Raspy!*

"Drop what you're doing and go to the Dunkin' Donuts on Concord Street downtown. You got ten minutes to get there. I'll call back with more instructions. No cops, or your pretty friend will get a lot less pretty." Eddie heard the click of the call ending. He sprinted toward his car. It wouldn't be easy to get there in ten minutes. They weren't giving him enough time. And why there? *They want a place with no cops and they choose Dunkin Donuts two minutes from a police station?*

Eddie skidded to a stop just in front of the garage, turned, and ran back to the house. Inside, he raced to his bedroom, praying and unbuckling his belt as he went. Removing the two spare magazines from their carriers, he tossed them on the bed and dropped the high-capacity magazine from his sidearm. He cycled the slide to eject the round in the chamber and replaced the old magazine with a fresh one from his nightstand before turning and running back to the car. Just before getting in, he grabbed his phone and banged out an eight-word text message while whispering a two-word prayer: *Please, Jesus.*

He had to drive up on the lawn to get around Melissa's car. He stopped and spent another few precious seconds grabbing her keys and closing the door of her car before driving off, tires spraying grass and gravel.

He drove as fast as the light traffic would allow. Sorely tempted to blow off the stop signs, he managed to hold himself in check. Getting pulled over now would be disastrous. Eddie pounded on his steering wheel and talked to the driver of the Volvo wagon who pulled out in front of him only to drive at three miles under the speed limit. "C'mon, c'mon, come *on!*"

The Volvo went straight. Eddie turned right onto Main Street and floored it. He immediately backed off the throttle, fearing the note from his aftermarket sport exhaust might attract the wrong kind of attention. "No cops, please, no cops." He was sweating and breathing hard, worrying and driving fast and trying to think, all at once.

He turned onto Concord Street. Dunk's was just ahead on the left. Rather than pull into the lot, he parked across the street and walked over. How long had the drive taken? He'd made good time, but wasn't sure how good. Why hadn't he looked at the clock when Raspy hung up? He couldn't afford any more mistakes.

Inside the coffee shop, he saw no police officers. Nor did he see Raspy or anyone who seemed likely to be in his employ. A coterie of teenage girls, hair died in primary colors, sat giggling in one corner. A couple of white-haired old women were seated at another table. At the counter, a clean-cut young man was placing an order.

Eddie approached the counter while the staffer was pouring the coffee. "Can I just have the key to the restroom, please?" The plump woman turned and looked him up and down.

"The restrooms are for customers only," she said louder than was necessary.

"Fine." Eddie pulled out his wallet and slapped down a five-dollar bill. I'll take a large regular or something. Keep the change. Just give me the key to the restroom *now*, please."

The woman behind the counter sniffed in apparent disapproval, but took the key off a hook and tossed it to him. Eddie rushed into the men's room and locked the door behind him.

He held the phone in his hand, willing it to ring. It didn't. Three minutes. Five. Seven. He was getting frantic. Finally, the display lit up with Mel's number. "Yes?"

"Why aren't you at Dunkin Donuts?"

"I *am* at Dunkin Donuts."

"My lookout says otherwise. You really wanna play games with me?"

"I'm here. I'm in the bathroom."

"Then come out. Show yourself."

"I need a couple of minutes."

"You don't have a couple of minutes. Come out now."

Eddie backed into a stall and pounded on the partition with his free hand. "Hear that? I'm in a *stall*. Do I have to spell it out for you? Give me a minute or two, and I'll walk out the door!"

Raspy paused briefly before answering. "Fine. Come outside, turn right, and walk to the parking garage. Stand outside the stairwell, the one closest to Lincoln Street. Be there in three minutes or I'll take my disappointment out on your friend." He hung up.

Eddie sent two short texts, identical messages to two different numbers. He deleted the record of both conversations and shoved the phone back in his pocket. Leaving the restroom, he tossed the key on the counter and headed for the door. "You're forgetting your coffee," he heard the woman behind the counter say. With no time to respond, Eddie didn't even turn to look.

He hit the door and started running. A car in the lot had its high beams on, illuminating the entrance. As Eddie sprinted the half block to Lincoln Street, the car left the lot and headed the same way. It barely registered in Eddie's mind until it turned right at the corner, a powder blue Jaguar XJ6 with deep tinted windows. It looked just like the car that had driven past his house earlier. It was the Jag in the Dominator's forum sig pic. *I should have made the connection.*

Two blocks up Lincoln, Eddie reached the parking garage. The stairwell door faced the cross street. The Jaguar was parked across from the entrance. When Eddie pushed on the door to the stairwell, it swung open a foot and hit an obstruction. A face appeared in the gap—Ronnie Big Hair. Ronnie pulled the door open wider, pushing aside a cinderblock that had been set in the way.

"Come in, Eddie. You're expected."

Eddie edged through the doorway and sidled toward the stairway on his right. He was standing at the bottom of a squarish three-story stairwell, open in the center. The stairs wound around the inside walls. Raspy's voice echoed down to him from a landing somewhere higher up. "Stop where you are. My associate's going to check you for weapons and take your phone. After that, we'll talk."

Eddie opened his coat to reveal the weapon on his hip, fighting the temptation to seethe as Ronnie took his gun. Murderous scumbags should never get to hold a weapon.

Ronnie spoke quietly to Eddie. "You kill Paulie with this? Maybe I'll return the favor." To Raspy, he yelled "Clear!"

"Check his phone. He make any calls?" Raspy was taking no chances.

Ronnie held his hand out, and Eddie deposited his phone into it.

After a few seconds of poking at the screen, Ronnie said, "Nope. Only calls are inbound from you."

"Good job, Eddie," Raspy replied. "You follow instructions well. Come up the stairs exactly four steps."

Eddie walked up four steps to the first landing. From this vantage point he could look down at Ronnie, as well as see Raspy leaning out over the railing of a landing between the second and third floors. He was holding Melissa by her belt and collar, pushing her up against the railing. Her wrists and ankles were bound with what looked like clothesline.

"Tell me she's not hurt," Eddie demanded. He saw the fear written on her face, but no obvious signs of injury. She looked at him, but didn't speak.

"She's not hurt. I wanted you to see how things are," Raspy said. "She'll stay unhurt as long as you do what you're told. There's a car parked across the street. Walk out to it. My associate is gonna open the trunk, and you're gonna climb in."

"So you can take me somewhere remote and kill me? Not interested."

"If you don't, I'm gonna dump your little friend on her head. We're not that high up, but I still think she'll make quite a mess on the concrete."

He's gonna kill her either way. She can identify him. Eddie needed to stall for time. "Why are you doing this?"

"Oh, I don't know; maybe because you stuck your nose in my business and killed my nephew? How's that for starters? Now get to the car."

"I only shot your nephew because he tried to kill me first. Come now, Dominic—may I call you Dominic? I can call you Mr. Capola if you'd prefer not to be on a first-name basis."

"How do you know my name? Explain."

"I know more than just your name. I know where you live. I know people who will give your name and address to the cops if something happens to me. What I *don't* know is whether Gabriella realizes her old man traffics in sex slaves. Does she think you're a decent guy, or is the whole family in on this?"

"That was stupid, showing off like that. You shoulda just answered my question. I'll find out what you know and how you learned it and who you told. And then you'll wish that you had just told me straight up. You'll be sorry you wasted my time."

"I promise I won't waste much more of it." Eddie took a long step forward.

"Stay right there! I'll drop her before you can reach me." He held Melissa up so that her feet dangled in the air. She let out a small whimper and squeezed her eyes shut.

Eddie was standing with his left foot two treads higher than his right on the staircase. He grabbed his left pant leg at the knee and hiked it up. In one quick motion, he drew a subcompact Glock G29 from an ankle holster and pointed it up at Dominic. "Harm her, and you'll regret it for the rest of a very short life."

"Ronnie! You stupid halfwit—you said he was all clear!"

Two is one and one is none.

Capola yanked Melissa back and held her vertically in front of him like a makeshift shield. He might as well have been an elephant trying to hide behind a sapling.

A few yards away from Eddie, Ronnie stood with his mouth gaping. He was still holding the confiscated gun. As Eddie started toward the second landing, things happened in rapid succession.

Ronnie raised Eddie's gun, pointed it at him, and pulled the trigger. A loud *click* reverberated in the stairwell as the gun's striker fell on an empty chamber. Eddie heard Ronnie rack the slide to load a fresh round from the magazine. Because the magazine was empty, the slide locked back. With a roar, Ronnie dropped the pistol and launched himself toward the steps.

Eddie turned and leveled his gun at Ronnie, who stopped in his tracks. "This one's loaded. If you want to live, take off."

Ronnie turned and bolted back down the stairs.

The door to the street swung open, and a huge man filled the door frame.

A level above Raspy, the third floor door banged open.

Dmitri! Andrei! They got my texts! Eddie was exultant.

"Outta my way!" screamed Ronnie as he raced toward the street exit.

Dmitri stepped to one side and cold-cocked Ronnie as he tried to run past.

Eddie turned and looked back up. Dominic was still holding Melissa, but backing up slowly as Dmitri's twin came down the steps toward him. Andrei must have come in from the garage's other stairwell. "Think about it, Dom!" Eddie hoped the man would see reason. "You're already guilty of human trafficking. Now add kidnapping. That's the FBI's jurisdiction, isn't it? Do you really want to dig yourself a deeper hole? Let her go. Do the right thing."

Dominic looked at the angry-looking monolith coming down the stairs toward him. He looked back at Eddie's drawn gun and the splayed body of his associate on the ground floor. "You won't shoot me in the back, choir boy." He turned to face Andrei. As he did, he tossed Melissa over the railing.

As long as he lived, Eddie would never forget the sound of her scream. He lunged, leaning out over the railing to grab at her as she fell. He briefly caught her shirt, but it ripped. He saw the terror in her eyes as she fell—right into the waiting arms of Dmitri standing in the bottom of the stairwell. He caught her with a grunt and a slight flex of his knees.

"It's all right!" Dmitri grinned up at Eddie, hoisting a breathless Melissa as evidence. "She's okay!"

Eddie turned again just in time to see Dominic slide uncon-scious to the floor with Andrei standing over him, rubbing the knuckles of his big right hand.

The three friends fussed over Melissa as they untied the ropes knotted around her wrists and ankles. Eddie gave her his jacket to put on over her torn shirt. A few feet away, Ronnie was starting to come to. Dmitri yanked him upright and admonished him. "I take you upstairs, put you beside fat guy. You struggle, you make noise, I hit you again. Hard this time." Ronnie didn't struggle.

Eddie picked up his fallen sidearm and holstered it. He was thankful he had taken the time to unload it, and equally thankful that Ronnie hadn't searched him thoroughly. He fished in his wallet, pulled out a business card, and called the number on it. "Detective McGlaughlin, this is Eddie Caruthers. We met in Plymouth that night three guys tried to lighten your load. I'm in Framingham, at the scene of an attempted murder, and I need some uniformed officers at the Lincoln Street garage . . ."

The police arrived quickly. After they had marched Ronnie and Dominic out, Detective McGlaughlin took statements from Melissa, Eddie, and their two new best friends. As they all got ready to leave, Melissa turned to Eddie and deadpanned, "Well, that was exciting. You think we might manage to have a date with a little less drama?"

Eddie grinned. "Next time, I promise you an utterly dull evening. You'll love it."

He braced himself for the inevitable poke in the ribs. It never came. Instead, she threw her arms around his neck and wouldn't let go. She was crying softly, and Eddie remembered her saying she hadn't cried about anything since the day her father had handed her fifty dollars through the front door and dismissed her from his life eight years ago. Well, she had earned a good cry tonight. Embracing her gently, he resolved to stand there and hold her until Christmas, if need be.

It didn't take that long. That night, Eddie put Melissa up in the apartment over the garage. The next morning, he drove her to Fast Track Automotive, purchased a new fuel pump for her car, showed her around the place, and even introduced her to Jason. Returning to the house, he led her to the patio, observing a moment of silence for the charred remains of yesterday's steaks, which were still on the grill. "Fear not," he said, winking. "I have a Plan B."

Plan B involved dragging a patio table out to the driveway and putting out a spread of Chinese food leftovers and ginger ale. While Melissa ate, Eddie began replacing her fuel pump. The pump was under the rear seat on the passenger side, so he was able to lean in from the driver's side rear and look across at her while they talked. As he laid out his tools and got to work, they spoke of many things.

"I think I figured out how those guys found my apartment," Melissa said. "They probably saw me at the first place and thought nothing of it. But then they saw me somewhere else and realized I was tailing them. They stayed so long at that spa in Waltham because they were calling in somebody to tail me. They left when he arrived, and that person followed me home, gave them my address."

"No doubt you're right. It's the only logical answer," Eddie replied. "I'm just glad all that's over now."

"I hope it is. I hope those guys don't have more associates that might take an interest in us."

Eddie pulled out the bottom seat cushion. "Don't worry about what-ifs. I'm praying there will be no more troubles. But if there are, I'm betting on us to come out on top."

She hoisted her plastic cup. "I'll drink to that. And speaking of praying—remember when you called me the morning after you got back from the hospital? It didn't seem like the right time to tell you then, but something happened to me the night before. I had this vivid dream. I can't say I heard voices or anything, but somehow I just knew that God or the Universe—I wasn't sure which at first—was telling me I needed to change. It was so intense it woke me up from a sound sleep. I stayed up the rest of the night just thinking about things."

Eddie knew she was talking about the same night God had dealt with him, leading him to repentance. *This is amazing.* "Go on," was all he said.

Her tone turned thoughtful. "I was working behind the stick in that awful joint every night and not getting any younger." Eddie intuited that "behind the stick" was some kind of reference to tending bar. Maybe it was because beer taps look like sticks of sorts? He didn't want to interrupt her to ask for clarification. He smiled encouragement at her, took off the pump cover and started prying the fuel lines off.

Melissa continued, "I was part of a business that degrades women. I was getting no closer to my dream of doing something noble. I had to get out of there, had to quit working a job I was ashamed to admit having. I made up my mind to put that part of my life behind me. The only problem was that *you* were from that part of my life. How would I explain you to decent people without bringing up a past I wanted to forget about?"

People were funny. For some reason, they took for granted that they could change, grow, and better themselves but acted as if others couldn't do likewise. They assumed that self-improvement meant leaving people behind. Come to think of it, Eddie had thought like that himself over the past year. He couldn't fault her for it.

"I understand," Eddie said. "So how *will* you explain me to decent people, assuming that's what you want to do?"

"I'll just tell the truth. We met someplace I used to tend bar, back when that was how I made my living. If people ask where, so be it. I'll never leave the past behind if I give it the power to haunt me."

Eddie dropped what he was doing and moved to sit beside her. No more multitasking; this conversation required his full attention. "That's a relief. You know, I never thought I'd hear from you again. Losing Dad and then losing you on the same day was pretty hard."

"I guess my timing stunk," Melissa said. "I'm sorry about that." She leaned her head on his shoulder. "I should have saved all that talk for later and just been there for you that day."

"No worries, Mel. I'm tougher than I look. I'm just happy you changed your mind about staying away from me."

Melissa looked down and toyed with her food. "Funny how that happened. I had figured out it was God talking to me in that dream, because I'm sure the universe can't talk, and if it could, it wouldn't much care about my career choices. But I didn't know God, and I wanted to. I wanted to talk to someone who could help me with that." She shrugged and took another bite before continuing. "I visited a couple of churches near me, just to check them out. But I didn't feel whatever it was I had felt after that dream. The churches seemed like places to do religious stuff without encountering . . . anything.

"Anyway, when I called you, it wasn't to talk about God. I just wanted to say thanks for the money, and to find out how you really learned about those massage places. I don't know why I started by asking you about the choir boy thing. It wasn't planned. But when you talked about finding God as a kid, I felt that same sensation again, that connection to God, like in the dream. It was even stronger this time. I was speechless."

Eddie grinned. "This is wonderful to hear. I imagined all sorts of horrible reasons why you weren't responding to anything I said on the phone. I thought you must despise me."

"Well, you know better now. It seems like we're travelling the same road. Only you're returning to someplace you once were, and I'm trying to find someplace I've never been. Maybe it's the same place. You still want to walk beside me like you said?"

"I sure do. I even know the way. We have a lot to talk about. Only tell me about that other thing first."

"What other thing?"

"You know, that thing you said . . . about being in love."

CHAPTER 17
MATTERS OF THE HEART

Eddie hit the parking lot at seven and parked close to where he had the first time he'd gone to Ace Massage. He'd never seen the inside of the place, since his previous visit had been interrupted by the arrival of Loudmouth and Ronnie, but he had a pretty good idea of what to expect.

He slammed the driver's door of the vehicle just as Andrei exited the passenger side. They headed for the front entrance. "Hey, hand me that flier, will you?" His companion passed him a sheet of paper he'd been holding, printed on one side with logograms that neither man could read. Eddie folded it into his pocket.

Once inside the establishment, they approached the front desk. The golden cat waved its greeting as a sharply dressed woman in her late forties or early fifties came around the corner. "May I help you?"

Eddie spoke up. "Can we see what girls are available?"

"One moment please. You want one hour each?"

"Let's start with a foot massage. Maybe we'll want more after that."

She nodded and asked them for $35 each. After they had paid, she disappeared around the corner. The men could hear what sounded like orders being given in Mandarin, and within thirty seconds, three young girls trooped out and stood in a line. Eddie and Andrei chose the two who seemed to be the least comfortable and most shy.

The women led them to a room with a row of plush chairs. They bade them sit down and remove their shoes and socks. After excusing themselves for a moment, they returned with tubs of warm water for soaking and set to work with brushes and various implements before beginning the foot massage.

The one positioned in front of Eddie seemed to be in her early twenties. A bit of small talk revealed a functional but limited command of English. Eddie handed her the sheet of paper from his pocket, saying, "Somebody gave this to me. It's Chinese writing, yes?"

He was fully aware that it was, since he had commissioned its creation. He'd located the pastor of a local Chinese Christian church and given the man an English script to be printed in hanzi, the Chinese writing characters. After the man had completed the task, Eddie had scanned and emailed it to a Mandarin instructor he found on the website of the Boston Language Institute. Once she verified the contents, Eddie ran off a dozen copies of the flier.

It read:

*Need help? Help is here! We know that many spa workers are forced
to work against their will. Maybe somebody is holding your passport.
Maybe someone has threatened you or your family. It doesn't matter.
Today is your day, and now is your time. We are an organization that
helps set captive workers free. Your rescuers are here. You will know
them by the way they are dressed. If you or someone else where you
work wants to be free of this place, just follow your rescuers out. Take
your wallet and ID if you can, and whatever clothes you can grab. Even
if you can't take anything, don't worry. Documents can be replaced. Do
not fear your boss or his/her enforcers. We won't let them hurt you. If
you wish to stay where you are, just do nothing.*

Eddie watched the girl's eyes scan the text. As she did, he
peeled off his sweatshirt, revealing a black T-shirt with gold
writing on it. In the center was the familiar heart symbol, like a
valentine's heart but without an arrow through it. Over the heart,
five English words were arranged in an arc: Hostage Extraction
and Rescue Team. Under the heart, in a straight line, the same
words were written in hanzi.

The girl finished the note, looked up at Eddie, and gasped
when she saw his shirt. He smiled at her and pointed to his
friend. Andrei had taken off his own shirt, revealing a T-shirt
identical to Eddie's underneath. The girls spoke rapidly and
quietly to each other in their native tongue.

Eddie nodded at them and gestured at the water tubs. "Please continue," he said.

After ten minutes of foot massage and quiet conversation between themselves, the girls left the room and returned with hot towels to dry the men's feet. "We'll do this," Eddie said. "And then we'll be leaving." He smiled again and reached for the towel.

The girls shuffled back into the hall. A few seconds later, Eddie heard raised voices as people yammered to one another through closed doors. The manager entered from the lobby and raised her voice authoritatively. Eddie could not understand the words, but he knew the sound of someone demanding answers.

Shoes back on, he and Andrei walked slowly toward the lobby. Four girls, including the two who had massaged their feet, came toward them from the other end of the hall, carrying large purses, duffle bags, and even one suitcase. The manager shrieked, "Emergency!"

From a back room came an angry-looking white male of middle years. He was wiry, with a pockmarked face and a hard expression that had "enforcer" written all over it. Andrei turned, grinned at him and spread his huge hands in what might have been an invitation. *Shall we dance?* The man took one look at Andrei's muscled bulk and decided he was not in the mood. He stopped abruptly, turned on his heel, and went back into the room he had come from, closing the door behind him.

Andrei shrugged and gave Eddie a disappointed look. "Wallflower, that is the word, yes?" Eddie almost laughed out loud. Andrei and Dmitri both spoke impeccable English, but sometimes trotted out the heavy accents and broken English when they were having fun. Eddie was feeling the stress of the day's high stakes, and marveled that his friend was apparently enjoying himself.

Eddie led the little group of escapees out the door and down the stairs, while Andrei brought up the rear. They crossed the lot at a brisk walk and scrambled into the white nine-passenger van as soon as Eddie had unlocked it.

The same scenario was playing out in Milford, Westborough, Randolph, Weymouth, Cambridge, Somerville, Plymouth and Quincy. Eddie had rented nine identical white vans and staffed each one with a pair of fighters recruited from Real Life Defensive Systems. Each van would visit a targeted AMP. Each nine-passenger van could rescue up to seven people.

Eddie exited the lot, headed to the Mass Pike, and took it to Route 128 north. Getting off the highway at the Lexington rest stop, he pulled up near a large charter bus idling there. He pointed at the bus and told the girls, "Your ride is here. It's a nice bus to Boston."

He led the four girls and their gear onto the bus. The driver smiled at them. In the front row of seats sat Reverend David Wang, the pastor who had helped Eddie with the flier. He stood and introduced himself, assured the women that they were safe, and told them he would provide translation services as needed. Beside him sat Reverend Byron Bullard. His role was to pray for the mission; to pray that many people would be rescued, and that violence would not be necessary. Just behind Bullard sat a woman from The Way Out, a Boston charitable organization founded to aid the victims of human trafficking.

One by one, the other vans pulled up with their cargo of liberated slaves. The total number of rescued women mounted: seven, twelve, fifteen. Eddie wasn't worried—it was a thirty-six-passenger bus. If they got more passengers than that, they'd just form a convoy with the vans.

The last van arrived. Eddie was standing by the front door of the bus talking to Byron Bullard, who had joined him, when someone grabbed his hand. "Nicole!" He wanted to give her a hug, but she preempted him by bowing deeply in front of him. After an awkward two seconds, he grasped her shoulders and gently encouraged her to straighten up. "I am glad we were able to help you." The van she'd been in had come from a spa in Westborough. "I came back for you, but you were gone. I didn't know where to look."

"Thank you very much," she said gravely. Then she smiled a shy smile and added, "I would like to tell you something. My name is Wenxiu. I will never again be Nicole."

Now it was Eddie's turn to be grave. He offered his hand and she shook it. "It is very nice to meet you, When Shoe." He couldn't match her inflections, but hoped his pronunciation of her name was acceptable. "I hope you'll get your education now. I wish you the best of luck."

Bullard shook Eddie's hand before following Wenxiu aboard. "Congratulations. This is why I wouldn't give you advice earlier.

Doing this required taking some risks. Since the risks were going to be yours, the decisions had to be yours too. For better or worse, you needed to do this on your own, and you did very well. You weren't overcome with evil. Today you overcame evil with good."

"Thank you sir," Eddie said.

The bus departed for Boston with twenty-four rescued women aboard. Soon the professionals at The Way Out would take over, providing counseling, temporary housing, and helping the young women replace personal documents and explore their options for either returning to China or starting afresh here in the United States. Pastors Wang and Bullard would facilitate the handoff to the nonprofit.

Eddie stood by his rented van and turned to his compatriot. "I'd call this a pretty good day."

Andrei rubbed his meaty hands together. "We should do it again. That was, how you say? Fun."

A few months later

Eddie sat in his car looking out at the Oxbow National Wildlife Refuge from the scenic overlook in Harvard. He'd driven there after hosting the first house church service at his own place. Sitting in silence, he mulled over the events of the past few months.

He had moved out of Dad's house so Lorna and her family could move in, using his cut of the sale proceeds to buy a condo in Wayland. It had garage parking for two cars, fifteen hundred square feet of living space, and was close to everyone he cared about. Better still, it was located just off a long twisty road, so he got a little asphalt therapy every time he came home.

Mike Manzanetti had completely recovered and resumed teaching duties at RWDS. Eddie liked teaching so much that he opened his own school in a rented barn in Framingham's Nobscot neighborhood. With a growing roster of students, he found increasing satisfaction in teaching people how not to be helpless.

Four months after the shootings, and just in time for Christmas, the Bristol County DA decided not to file charges against Eddie in connection with the deaths of Paul Cimino and his minor accomplice Zeke. It never should have been an issue. Eddie knew it, the police knew it, and the DA probably knew it all along. The time spent in limbo had been stressful, but that was over now.

The Feds took over the case against Dominic Capola and Ronald Woodson. Charged with racketeering, kidnapping, attempted murder, and trafficking people across state lines to commit prostitution, they were each held on high bail. Because they potentially faced decades in prison, each offered to testify against the other about various assaults, arsons, and other crimes. The information they shared as cooperating witnesses led to the arrest and charging of the three "baseball players" who killed Big Eddie Freeman.

There had been no sign of either Jenny or Alice on the rescue bus. Eddie didn't know whether they had been moved elsewhere or had been present and simply declined to leave when the opportunity came. He hoped they were all right. Perhaps as Andrei suggested, the H.E.A.R.T. would one day run more rescue operations.

Ace Massage Therapy and Orange Blossom Spa were both shut down by their respective towns' police departments. Within a month, both had relocated and reopened "under new management."

Eddie disengaged from his musings and concentrated on the scenery. Bright sun and blue skies gave the illusion of warmth, but the air spoke more of the lingering winter than of the coming spring. The wind blew, and the bare tree branches rattled against each other like chattering teeth, as if the forest itself was shivering. A few birds, swallows maybe, flitted about. Eddie gazed through the windshield and took it all in with his—friend, girlfriend, wife to be? Well, if a friend was someone who knew everything about you and liked you anyway, then the occupant of his passenger seat fit the bill. No question about girlfriend status either. She was affectionate, brave, compassionate, and determined. Eddie knew he'd run out of words before she ran out of virtues. Life was good in the girlfriend department. As for wife to be, only time would tell. Whatever the lovely Melissa Devereaux would someday be to him, he enjoyed her company immensely and found her nearness made the whole world seem a little warmer.

He reached toward her, and just as she took his hand, his pocket vibrated.

"Don't answer it," she implored.

"Won't take a minute."

She shook her head like one trying and failing to teach a simple concept to a slow child.

It was Jason. "Yo, bro," Eddie answered. "Yep, we'll be there. Call it an hour. Bye."

Jason and Lorna had decided to resurrect the monthly tradition of dinner at Dad's. Both had called Eddie to let him know he was invited. And they didn't even mind him bringing a guest. The children of Donald Caruthers would always be very different from one another. But it was beginning to look as if their father's final request would be honored.

"Hungry?" Eddie smiled at Melissa just for the pleasure of seeing her smile back.

"You bet." He forced himself to release her hand so he could operate his car's stick shift. That was the one drawback of a manual transmission. It was almost enough to make him consider getting an automatic. Almost.

Eddie pulled out of the overlook with a final glance over his shoulder. He motored down the road, plotting the most circuitous route he could think of to Lorna's house. After a few minutes of relaxed silence, he said, "I've been dreaming up an adventure for us."

Melissa's face lit up. "Tell me about it," she said. "I'm all ears."

ABOUT THE AUTHOR

John F. Harrison has been a minister, a musician, a business owner, and an author. He's still happily involved in three out of those four vocations, and greatly misses his music. John's greatest ambition is to get up eight times after falling down seven. He chronicles the tribulations and triumphs of deeply flawed people, because he knows no other kind. John lives with his wife in the Boston area.